S R

PRAISE FOR CAROLE NELSON DOUGLAS

"The indefatigable Midnight Louie series never seems to run out of steam." —*Booklist* on *Cat in a Hot Pink Pursuit*

"A lighthearted, original, and very enjoyable story . . . fans will not be disappointed by this delightful continuation of the series." —*Romantic Times BookClub Magazine* on *Cat in an Orange Twist*

"Midnight Louie defies critical comment. To some cat fanciers, he is as tasty as a fresh bowl of Fancy Feast." —*Booklist* on *Cat in a Neon Nightmare*

"Douglas just keeps getting better at juggling mystery, humor, and romance. . . . Established fans will welcome another intriguing piece of the puzzle." —*Publishers Weekly* (starred review) on *Cat in a Midnight Choir*

"Never a dull moment." —*Library Journal* on *Cat in a Leopard Spot*

Cat in a Hot Pink Pursuit

A MIDNIGHT LOUIE MYSTERY

Carole Nelson Douglas

FORGE®

A TOM DOHERTY ASSOCIATES BOOK
NEW YORK

This is a work of fiction. All the characters and events portrayed in this book are either products of the author's imagination or are used fictitiously.

CAT IN A HOT PINK PURSUIT: A MIDNIGHT LOUIE MYSTERY

Copyright © 2005 by Carole Nelson Douglas

A Forge Book
Published by Tom Doherty Associates, LLC
175 Fifth Avenue
New York, NY 10010

www.tor.com

Forge® is a registered trademark of Tom Doherty Associates, LLC.

ISBN 0-765-35268-0
EAN 978-0-765-35268-2

First edition: May 2005
First mass market edition: June 2006

Printed in the United States of America

0   9   8   7   6   5   4   3   2   1

For my oldest friend, Camille Greicar,
inheritor of my Nancy Drew collection
(I thought I'd outgrown them but apparently not),
with fond memories of our childhood summers
in Pisek, North Dakota

Contents

viii • CONTENTS

CONTENTS • ix

Cat in a Hot Pink Pursuit

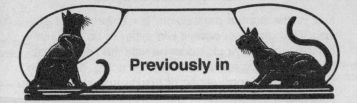

Previously in

Midnight Louie's
Lives and Times . . .

How sad that my singing voice is more scat than lyrics, for my personal theme song would have to be "There Is Nothing Like a Dame."

I admit it. I am a shameless admirer of the female of the species. Any species. Of course not all females are dames. Some are little dolls, like my petite roommate, Miss Temple Barr.

The difference between dames and little dolls? Dames can take care of themselves, period. Little dolls can take care of themselves also, but they are not averse to letting the male of the species think that they have an occasional role in the Master Plan too.

That is why my Miss Temple and I are perfect roomies. She tolerates my wandering ways. I make myself useful, looking after her without letting her know about it. Call me Muscle in Midnight Black. In our time, we have co-cracked a few cases too tough for the local fuzz of the human persuasion, law enforcement division. That does not always win either of us popularity contests, but we would rather be right than on the sidelines when something crooked is going down. We share a well-honed sense of justice and long, sharp fingernails.

So when I hear that a reality TV show is coming to Las Vegas to film, I figure that one way or another my lively little roommate, the petite and toothsome, will be spike-heel high in the planning and execution. She is, after all, a freelance public relations specialist, and Las Vegas is full of public relations of all stripes and legalities. In this case, though, I did not figure just how deeply she would be involved in murder most media.

I should introduce myself: Midnight Louie, PI. I am not your usual gumshoe in that my feet do not wear shoes of any stripe, but shivs. I have certain attributes, such as being short, dark, and handsome . . . really short. That gets me overlooked and underestimated, which is what the savvy operative wants anyway. I am your perfect undercover guy. I also like to hunker down under the covers with my little doll. My adventures would fill a book, and in fact I have several out. My life is just one long TV miniseries in which I as hero extract my hapless human friends from fixes of their own making and literally nail crooks. After experiencing the dramatic turn of events recently, most of my human associates are pretty shell-shocked. Not even an ace feline PI may be able to solve their various predicaments in the areas of crime and punishment . . . and PR, as in Personal Relationships.

As a serial killer–finder in a multivolume mystery series (not to mention a primo mouthpiece), it behooves me to update my readers old and new on past crimes and present tensions.

None can deny that the Las Vegas crime scene is a

pretty busy place, and I have been treading these mean neon streets for seventeen books now. When I call myself an "alphacat," some think I am merely asserting my natural male dominance, but no. I merely reference the fact that after debuting in *Catnap* and *Pussyfoot*, I commenced to a title sequence that is as sweet and simple as *B* to *Z*.

That is where I began my alphabet, with the *B* in *Cat on a Blue Monday*. From then on, the color word in the title is in alphabetical order up to the current volume, *Cat in a Hot Pink Pursuit*. (*Yeow!* Pink is not my usual macho color.)

Since I associate with a multifarious and nefarious crew of human beings, and since Las Vegas is littered with guidebooks as well as bodies, I wish to provide a rundown of the local landmarks on my particular map of the world. A cast of characters, so to speak:

To wit, my lovely roommate and high-heel devotee, Miss Nancy Drew on killer spikes, freelance PR ace MISS TEMPLE BARR, who has reunited with her only love . . .

. . . the once missing-in-action magician MR. MAX KINSELLA, who has good reason for invisibility. After his cousin SEAN died in a bomb attack during a post-high-school jaunt to Ireland, he went into undercover counterterrorism work with his mentor, GANDOLPH THE GREAT, whose unsolved murder last Halloween while unmasking phony psychics at a séance is still on the books. . . .

Meanwhile, Mr. Max is sought by another dame, Las Vegas homicide LIEUTENANT C. R. MOLINA, mother of preteen MARIAH . . .

. . . and the good friend of Miss Temple's recent good friend MR. MATT DEVINE, a radio talk-show shrink and former Roman Catholic priest who came to Las Vegas to track down his abusive stepfather, now dead and buried. By whose hand, no one is quite sure.

Speaking of unhappy pasts, Lieutenant Carmen Regina Molina is not thrilled that her former flame MR. RAFI NADIR, the unsuspecting father of Mariah, is in Las Vegas taking on shady muscle jobs after blowing his career with the LAPD . . .

. . . or that Mr. Max Kinsella is aware of Rafi and his past relationship to hers truly. She had hoped to nail one man or the other as the Stripper Killer, but Miss Temple prevented that by attracting the attention of the real perp.

In the meantime, Mr. Matt drew a stalker, the local girl that young Max and his cousin Sean boyishly competed for in that long-ago Ireland . . .

. . . one MISS KATHLEEN O'CONNOR, deservedly christened by Miss Temple as Kitty the Cutter. Finding Mr. Max impossible to trace, she settled for harassing with tooth and claw the nearest innocent bystander, Mr. Matt Devine . . .

. . . who is still trying to recover from the crush he developed on Miss Temple, his neighbor at the Circle Ritz condominiums, while Mr. Max was missing in action. He did that by not very boldly seeking new women, all of whom were in danger from said Kitty the Cutter.

In fact, on the advice of counsel, i.e., AMBROSIA, Mr. Matt's talk-show producer, and none other than the aforesaid Lieutenant Molina, he tried to disarm Miss Kitty's pathological interest in his sexual state by losing his virginity with a call girl least likely to be the object of K. the Cutter's retaliation. Except that hours after their assignation at the Goliath Hotel, said call girl turned up deader than an ice-cold deck of Bicycle playing cards. But there are thirty-some million potential victims in this old town, if you include the constant come and go of tourists, and everything is up for grabs in Las Vegas

24/7: guilt, innocence, money, power, love, loss, death, and significant others.

All this human sex and violence makes me glad I have a simpler social life, my prime goal being reunion with . . .

. . . THE DIVINE YVETTE, the stunning shaded silver Persian belonging to fading B-film star Miss Savannah Ashleigh and once my partner in some cat food commercials, and such a simple hope as trying to get along with my self-appointed daughter . . .

. . . MISS MIDNIGHT LOUISE, who insinuated herself into my cases until I was forced to set up shop with her as Midnight Inc. Investigations, and who has also nosed herself into my long-running duel with . . .

. . . the evil Siamese assassin HYACINTH, first met as the onstage assistant to the mysterious lady magician . . .

. . . SHANGRI-LA, who made off with Miss Temple's semiengagement ring from Mr. Max during an onstage trick and has not been seen since, except in sinister glimpses . . .

. . . just like THE SYNTH, an ancient cabal of magicians that may deserve contemporary credit for the ambiguous death of Mr. Max's mentor in magic, Gandolph the Great.

Well, there you have it, the usual human stew, all mixed up and at odds with one another and within themselves. Obviously, it is up to me to solve all their mysteries and nail a few crooks along the way. Like Las Vegas, the City That Never Sleeps, Midnight Louie, private eye, also has a sobriquet: the Kitty That Never Sleeps.

With this crew, who could?

Chapter 1

Hello Kitty

Homicide Lieutenant C. R. Molina's desk hosted two very different images.

One was a glossy 11-by-17-inch poster of a Barbie-doll-cute teen girl tricked out in industrial-strength amounts of hot pink.

The other was the same image, cut into jagged pieces that had been grafted onto photographed body parts of an actual Barbie doll.

The phrase "Teen Idol" on the first poster had morphed into "Twisted Sister," with a welter of blood-red spatters, on the second one.

"Sick," Molina said, unnecessarily.

They all stood gazing down on the twisted twin posters, neither of which was exactly wholesome. One was merely Extreme Fashion. The other had been refashioned into something freakishly violent.

"Being the mother of a newly teenaged daughter, finding this stuff strewn around a shopping mall parking lot makes me shudder," Molina said. "The slashed poster reminds me that some things are scarier than adolescent hormones."

"Mariah's thirteen already?" Detective Morrie Alch asked, surprised. He was comfortably into his mid-fifties and his lone daughter was grown, gone, and a mother herself.

How Molina envied him.

"Just turned," she said. "A month ago. I'm already considering a barbed-wire perimeter around the house. This is so sick."

"The Teen Idol concept," Detective Merry Su asked, "or the threatening poster?"

"Both." Molina shook her head. "So tell me about this Teen Idol thing."

"Reality TV hits Las Vegas," Su said. A petite, twenty-something, second-generation Asian American, Su looked ready to compete for a teen title herself.

"Can't prove it by me," Molina answered. "We've been hosting reality TV since the New Millennium Hotel went up five years ago."

"It's a quest to name a 'Tween and Teen Queen," Alch said.

"Two age groups, thirteen to fifteen and sixteen to nineteen," Su said.

"Got it. Teens-in-training and the full-media deal. Is this a singing competition?"

Being a closet vocalist herself, Molina had actually caught a few episodes of *American Idol*. She found the concept exploitive of the pathetic wannabes every art form attracts and a mockery of true talent by letting the public select winners for emotional reasons. Look who they felt most sorry for.

"More than that: talent of any kind, made-over looks and improved attitude." Su was always eager to overexplain. "This is the triathlon of reality shows."

Alch nodded at the unadulterated poster. "Yup. This girl here looks real athletic, all right. I bet it challenges her biceps to load on that amount of mascara and lip-liner every day."

"'Lip-liner?'" Molina called him on it. "Still keeping up with the girly stuff, Morrie, even with the daughter long gone?"

"You haven't hit the bustier stage in your house, I bet. Hold on to your Kevlar vest."

Molina chuckled, imagining some busty contestant wearing a bulletproof vest in a glamour roll call on TV. *Whoa.* Maybe that would have a perverse attraction.

She tapped her forefinger on the oversize plastic bag encasing the altered poster, protecting it for forensic examination.

"We've got . . . what? Dozens of teenage girl competitors from around the country pouring into a Las Vegas shopping mall in their Hello Kitty finery for auditions—and one sick puppy already announcing that he's out there waiting?"

"That's about it," Alch said. "No fingerprints. No way to trace the color copier to a local Kinko's."

"Kinko's are us," Su said.

"No kidding." Molina frowned. "You know the routine. Keep it quiet, keep an eye on the audition event. If we're lucky, the uniforms will find him before this ridiculous show launches. When?"

"This week's local auditions finish the selection process," Su said. "Then they narrow the field down to twenty-eight finalists in the two age groups and seclude them all in a foreclosed mansion on the West Side. For two weeks."

"Two weeks?" Molina didn't like the wide window of

opportunity that much time afforded a pervert with a publicity addiction. "This could be the work of a kook as harmless as Aunt Agatha's elderberry wine. Or not. Keep on it."

Molina was still at her desk, with a different wallpaper of paperwork covering it, at seven thirty that evening when someone knocked on her ajar door.

No one knocked in a crimes-against-persons unit. She looked up— glared—from her paperwork. As the only woman supervisor, she never let down her guard.

A man entered as if he owned the joint.

Brown/brown. Five ten or eleven. A stranger who acted way too at home on this turf. On her turf. In her hard-won private office.

"Yes?"

"Working late?"

"Always." She waited. His clothes were casual but hip: blue jeans, black silk-blend tee, khaki linen jacket, big diver's watch face full of specialty minidials, and a sleek gold bracelet with a subtle air of South American drug lord. Couldn't see his shoes. Too bad. A man's shoes told as much about him as a woman's.

"You don't recognize me." He sat in the single hard shelled chair in front of her desk, meant to discourage loiterers.

Recognize? No. He was way too hip for what usually showed up in police facilities, except for a five o'clock shadow too faint to be anything but a trendy shaving technique.

"You'll have to excuse me—" she began sardonically, still searching her memory banks.

"I consider that high praise."

"That you'll have to excuse me?"

"That you don't recognize me in civvies."

Okay. She ran a mental roster of uniforms, and came up blank. This was beginning to get annoying.

"I'm heading out," she informed him, slamming her desk drawers shut, picking up the black leather hobo bag she toted to and from work and nowhere out on the job.

"How about a drink en route?"

"How about an ID? And . . . no."

He laughed then. "You're usually onto this stuff. Tough case on your desk?"

"They're all tough. What's your name?"

"You really don't recognize me?"

He cocked his head, and then she had him.

"Dirty Larry?"

"All cleaned up."

"Gone Chamber of Commerce! To what do I owe—?"

"How about a drink on the way home? Some noncop bar."

"Why?"

"Personal police business."

She didn't like the way he drawled that out but checked her watch. Mariah had stayed after school tonight. Sock-hop committee at another student's house. Her baby daughter! Thinking about dancing with wolves. All harmless teenybopper stuff, hopefully. Staying at the Ruizes' for dinner until eight or so.

Dirty Larry, the Mr. Clean edition, waited. He watched her with an amusement that hinted he knew the pushes and pulls of her private life.

Bastard! Her vehemence, unjust, pulled her back from the brink. This was a colleague, after all. An undercover narc. Maybe he had something for her. He'd be used to private rendezvous in public places.

"Okay. Five minutes?"

He nodded, got up, and ebbed into the hall. She speed-dialed the Ruizes and got a commitment that they'd keep Mariah until ten, just in case.

Chapter 2

Spooks

In a city built on urban fantasy hotels with sprawls that rivaled the King Ranch, the Palms bucked the hotel-casino trend and lived up to its name. It was an off-Strip cylinder of gilded construction, like a tower of giant golden coins.

"I am not dressed for this," Molina said, meeting Dirty Larry at the Palms's side entrance, as agreed, their separate vehicles parked in whatever spot could be found.

"What *are* you dressed for?" He had an annoying knack for taking her simplest remark as a springboard for some deeper meaning. Dirty Larry the Existentialist?

"A crime scene," she said. "You going to deliver?"

"Not here. Not now. I'm off undercover." He looked around. "It's kinda nice to be escorted by an obvious cop. Like having a bodyguard."

"I'm that obvious?"

"Like you say, you're not dressed for the Palms."

"A psychologist could speculate that you want to get me off my own turf, at a disadvantage."

"Off your turf, right. Is that really a disadvantage?"

She shrugged and turned for the door, moving into a stream of tourists in tropical print shorts and shirts.

She knew what she was and she knew what she wore: low-heeled oxfords. Espresso-brown pantsuit. Oxford shirt, faintest baby blue, open at the collar. Semiautomatic in a paddle holster at the small of her back, steel blue. Talk about fashion coordination. Supermodels had nothing on a modern female cop.

They entered the usual jam-packed, ultra-air-conditioned smokehouse of a Vegas casino, an atmosphere lit by blinking slot machines that broadcast bling-bling bluster and the clatter of coins spilling into metal troughs.

In the craps area, Larry stopped to schmooze a pit boss who passed him some VIP comps. Comps papered the town, if you knew who to ask. The passes sent them to the head of a line that had formed even though the Ghost Bar had just opened, then onto an express elevator. Eerily, once aboard, all sound suddenly stopped, the casino's endless clatter replaced by the customary silence of half-pickled strangers packed together like kippered herrings in a tin.

The Ghost Bar perched fifty-five stories above all the hustle, a tourist attraction of the first water. Three of the four walls were glass and the view was jaw-dropping. Inside, the place was a *2001: A Space Odyssey* sixties wet dream of blue neon, streamlined silver seating pieces, and lime green accents. Icy in color and exclusive in attitude.

Molina took it all in with the same cool distance she used at crime scenes. She checked out the VIP clientele already seated as well as the ambiance and spotted sev-

eral vaguely familiar faces. It took a moment to realize
that they were stars, actors and singers, not escapees from
Most Wanted lists. Odd, the jolt of false familiarity you
could get from a household face.

"What do you think of the place?" he asked.

"*Playboy, Penthouse,* circa nineteen sixty-five."

"You talking the magazines or improper pronouns?"

"Both."

Posh or Mosh the Spice Girl wannabe did the waitress
dip to lay two cocktail napkins on their sleek tabletop.
Bowing to the power of the chichi, Molina surprised
Dirty Larry, and herself, by ordering a pepper vodka
martini. Larry ordered something called a Burning Bush.

Molina let her lifted eyebrows do the talking.

"Black Bush whiskey with peach, lime, crème de cas-
sis, and a dash of cranberry juice for health."

"Gack," she said.

"It lives up to its name on the tastebuds. You can try a
sip."

He nodded at the twelve-foot-high glass walls.

"On the balcony, you can stand on a Plexiglas rectangle and look down fifty-five stories, if heights don't make
you nervous."

Molina stood, uncoiling her own impressive height, almost six feet. "Shall we dance?"

Seconds later they balanced on the ghostly plastic platform over nothing. A rectangle of aquamarine sparkled
four thousand feet below, almost a mile, overrun by what
looked like small brown bugs.

"The Skin Pool Lounge," he said.

"Not a glamorous name but a literal one?"

"Skinny dipping is only on Tuesday nights."

Tuesday was the weakest night for customers, hence
flashing the flesh. "Only in Las Vegas."

They savored the glittering swath of the Strip's massive hotels, laid out like jewels on black velvet or, more apropos to their profession, a glitter-dusted body on an autopsy table.

Take that, T. S. Eliot, Molina thought. *You and your "night anaesthetized like a patient on a table."*

"Shamelessly hokey but a must-see," Larry said.

"Hokey should be shameless. I like it. That surprise you?"

"Yes and no. I've been to the Blue Dahlia. That's shamelessly hokey too."

She drew a breath, ready to retort, defend, deny. Instead she shrugged. "So?"

"So let's sit down and talk shop."

"Strange place for that."

Their cocktails were waiting in glassware as kooky as the retro-modern furniture. The classic triangular bowl of Molina's martini glass was supported by an off-center curve of crystal. His drink was served in a rectilinear tower of modernist glass.

He lifted it, not for a toast, but to offer a taste.

This was a way-too-early intimacy but Molina took him up on it. Dirty Larry had a challenging edge but she could match it. The bizarre ingredients produced a sizzling effect that explained the cheeky name that referenced both the religious and the obscene.

"So what was the Blue Dahlia crack for?" Molina asked after rinsing her palette with a swallow of clean, sharp vodka martini.

"Odd you should use that expression. Dirty Larry did a cocaine deal there once."

Molina frowned. He tended to refer to his undercover persona in the third person. Weird.

"A one-off," he went on. "Nothing habitual. The client had a thing for you."

"Oh, great."

"People get their kicks where they can."

"And here I think I'm singing for dedicated vintage music lovers. Listen—"

"It's okay. My lips are sealed. Your pseudonymous singing habit is safe. Everything I do undercover is off the record unless it involves criminal charges."

"You're not undercover now."

"I take . . . vacations. R and R. It messes your mind to play an undercover role too long. I'm doing accident investigations for a while."

"From drug traffic to traffic? Isn't that a bit tame?"

He nodded. "That's the idea. Nice quiet beat. After the fact. Fascinating, really. The evidence of a crash and burn but nobody there to threaten you or haunt you. Only evidence. Nice inert, cool evidence."

"People die on the streets from vehicular accidents too."

"But I'm not down in that pit with them. Biggest risk to undercover agents? Not gettin' fingered or found out. Not getting killed. Getting hooked."

"So why am I the receptacle of all this useful information from the opium den?"

"Just explaining where I'm coming from and going to."

"Going to. Which is?"

"One more big score. There's a funny ring operating. Dirty Larry can't get near it. I'm going to have to come back as someone else and try again. Meanwhile, I detox on Traffic Accident detail. But the instincts don't turn off."

"And . . . ?"

"And I never bought your act the other night with the report on that Nadir guy. I can read upside down and backward in my game too, Lieutenant. That address pan out?"

"Yeah. Thanks."

"Why would you think you could con an undercover guy?"

"Because I had to."

He nodded. "Good reason. Why did you ever think you could keep Carmen a secret?"

"Because I want to."

"Better reason."

They each sipped from their drinks, gazing at the spectacular 180-degree view, then back at each other.

"If you don't want something," she said finally, "and everybody does, why did you get me away from the office?"

"What's the worst I could do with what I know?"

"Blackmail? But I don't think so."

"No. Just exposure."

"I deny. I stop. Carmen gets paid in cash. She has no Social Security number. You could mess up my friends at the Blue Dahlia a little, but I could mess you up a whole lot more. And Carmen could fall off the planet. Officialdom would never notice."

"I would. Notice. I'd never do that, burn Carmen. She's a class act. I oughta know. Acts, that is."

"Then . . . what do you want?"

"Nothing. Everything. Just to get the cards on the table."

Molina stared at the tiny circle of plastic cocktail table holding their Art Moderne drink glasses. "What cards? What table?"

"This one. Here. Now. Call it a social occasion with overtones of business."

She finally got it. "You think this is a *date*?"

"Yeah. I thought you knew."

Her jaw would have dropped for the second time that night, figuratively anyway, if she'd allowed it to. She looked away and found an irritatingly famous face in every direction. Holographic portraits imbued the place's few interior walls, both hung on and burned into the wall. The Ghost Bar was a highly desirable destination in Las Vegas, and Dirty Larry had gotten them first-row seats.

A frivolous woman would have been impressed.

"You've got a lot of nerve," she told him, not happy.

"Oh, yeah."

He grinned and knocked back a big swallow of Burning Bush. Maybe the name was also a political statement.

The line for the elevator when they left a few minutes later was even longer, snaking through the casino. Lustful eyes followed them, envying their leaving a place most of them would never get into this night or even by four A.M. the next morning when the Ghost Bar closed.

Dirty Larry had just shrugged when she beat him to the credit card draw and slapped her Visa down on the tiny table. Thirty bucks plus a high-rise tip for a view through *Go Ask Alice*'s rabbit hole and a little atmosphere. That was the New Vegas, converted from cheap everything to entice gamblers to overpriced everything to entice tourists.

The parking lot was jammed but well lit.

"So you have pull with the pit bosses," Molina noted. "In which persona?"

"Just as me."

"Who is?"

"Just plain Larry Paddock."

"I like Dirty Larry better."

"Figured you might."

He followed her to her car. "Where are you parked?" she asked finally.

He waved in a vaguely distant direction.

"I'll drop you at your car," she offered. Insisted.

"You don't have to."

"You're sure it's safe out here with you bare-faced?"

"Should be. People look but they don't really see. That's always been my edge."

"You sound like a magician."

"Not a bad comparison, but you sound like you don't much care for magicians."

She leaned against the still tepid side of her Toyota. It took a load off her feet but also made their heights equal for a moment. She topped him by an inch or more.

"So what do we have here—?"

"Sergeant Paddock."

"Sergeant Paddock."

"We have a homicide lieutenant with a secret undercover role and a not very healthy interest in a drug-bust suspect, and we have a narc with a yen to play Joe Citizen for a while."

"Why play that role with me?"

"Because I like your style."

"I don't have one. Just a job."

"Right. That's the style I like."

"And you want?"

"Maybe I can help you with that Nadir guy. He was clean on this Maylords bust but something's wrong with him."

"I don't need help."

He grinned again. "That's my girl."

"Do you know how long it's been since anybody's had the nerve to call me that?"

"Too long?"

She jingled her key ring and let out a disgusted sigh. "I don't 'date' inside the department."

"No. You don't date, period."

"It's mandatory?"

"No, but it might be fun."

"I outrank you."

"I'm a free agent. I make daily life and death decisions commanders don't face. Rank doesn't intimidate me."

She straightened. "I'm taller than you are."

"Rock climbing's my hobby when I want to relax."

"I'm older than you are."

"Now how did you know that, Lieutenant?"

"I checked your record. I routinely do that on any

members of the force I have dealings with for the first time."

"Ditto. Except I checked you out after that deal went down at the Dahlia. You shouldn't have tried to rip off my file on Nadir. It got me interested again."

"Why?"

"I think you've got more secrets than going *Blue Velvet* every now and again at a local club. I find homicide lieutenants with secrets irresistible."

"Dangerous too, I bet."

"Hope so."

"And this is how you ask for a date?"

"Hope so."

Molina eyed the PG-model of Dirty Larry. He still had the sloppy posture of a *guy* guy, but his hair was almost buzz cut and his angular, currently genial features went down smooth with a cocky charm that probably stood him well in undercover work. He looked like an ex-pilot, civilized but a little bit warped in some wild-blue-yonder way. Not her type at all. But then it'd been so long, she didn't know what her type was anymore.

"You want to drag me out to some trendy hot spot again?" she asked.

"You're a dynamite singer but you're an even tougher audience. Not drag. Accompany. And not so trendy. Dinner."

She opened the unlocked driver's door and nodded for him to go around to the passenger side. A concession, but a small one.

"We don't have a thing in common," she warned him as he got in the aging car over the grumble of its engine.

"Except police work."

"A negative."

"We both have to play roles every day to survive."

She didn't comment on that because she was too busy backing out without being crushed by one of the many

Hummers scattered through the lot. Or because she was too uneasy about answering that assumption.

"West side of the lot. Black Wrangler." He push-buttoned down the window and braced an elbow on it, showing none of the unease most men did when they weren't driving, and a woman was.

One positive point to Dirty Larry.

"I've got two kids," he told the open air. "Shared custody with the ex-wife in—of all places, divorce central—Reno."

"Divorced ex-cop. Just the worst."

"You are too."

"I never married, but you know that."

He didn't deny it. "Smart." Nodding, looking out the window. "Saved yourself a lot of grief. Was it a cop?"

She declined to comment, instead slowing the car. "Here we are."

"All right." He got out, then leaned his angular yet boyish face through the window. "Thursday night dinner, say seven. Civvies. My treat. No ghosts. I'll pick you up at home."

"You're nosy as well as nervy, you know that?"

"Yeah. My best qualities. What can you lose?"

She didn't answer that but pulled away as he hit the remote open for his car.

Molina did a quick postmortem. Nancy Reagan had been right. She should have just said no.

Why hadn't she? Because she needed to figure his angle, and because he did indeed know too much about her. And because some of damned Max Kinsella's taunts when they were tussling in the strip club parking lot had gotten under her skin and were still festering there, like a splinter you can only get out through some deep digging with a sharp needle.

Finding out Dirty Larry's game might refute the magician's nasty insinuations that night. Like how she was too uptight for a real life, for a real man. A sense of shame still lingered from that flat-out physical encounter, a confrontation she'd lost for winning. Even though she'd finally won, had him down and cuffed, she had to wonder if he'd let her. Never arm wrestle a snake.

And he'd escaped the cuffs later in her car, anyway, when events announced over the police radio made his arrest clearly unnecessary. Thanks to his slippery magician tricks, he'd left her cuffed to her own steering wheel. Molina's mind winced away from recalling her struggle to reach the handcuff key he had left by the passenger door. Good thing she had long arms. She was still hoping the long arm of the law would reel in Kinsella one day. Hers, God willing.

But she enjoyed impudence if it was genial, like Larry's. He was refreshingly upfront, unlike most of the people—men—she'd dealt with lately. So far.

Chapter 3

Swinging for It

Max stared down through the glass window into the lightning lit pit eighty feet below. It resembled a medieval vision of hell but it was just the mosh-pit madness at the nightclub.

In the name of a good night's work, Max leaped down into that mélange of writhing bodies and flashing lights and pounding music almost every day now.

When you're a double agent with two physical personas, you're in constant danger of meeting yourself coming and going. Rather like having two portrayers of James Bond in the same movie.

As the cloaked and masked Phantom Mage, Max walked on air and juggled fireworks at the dark apex of the nightclub called Neon Nightmare.

As himself—the Mystifying Max, stage magician on hiatus—he'd crashed the hidden offices, spy galleries, and rooms beyond the noise and the neon of the club's public spaces. Private rooms were strung along hidden tunnels through the pyramid-shaped building for the use of Neon Nightmare's secret owners, a consortium of magicians.

Max as himself—bare-faced, clad in matte black civvies—was due to make another in-person appearance before the claque, the cabal, the clique of disgruntled old-school magicians called the Synth.

From the outside, Neon Nightmare was a dark mountain of architectural pyramid topped by the pyrotechnical display of a neon horse at the apex. Inside, it was designed like its ancient Egyptian role models. Once you were past the central open core where the bar and dance floor dominated, hidden paths led to unexpected chambers. If dead pharaohs didn't await, career-dead magicians did, brooding over the wrongs of a world that now favored the naked revelation of magical illusions over the ancient tradition that cloaked stage magic in the mystic.

Max found his way to the center of the Synth's secret world, an eternally stuffy Colonial club room, where the stout and storied sat and smoked and sipped and relived old triumphs.

He pushed the pressure point that turned black, unrelieved wall into a featureless door, then moved into a room that glowed the deep claret of a full wineglass. Crimson carpet, black leather, and ruby-stemmed glassware . . . it was like an Edward Gorey illustration, elegantly Edwardian and etched in black, white, and gray, except for the telling blood-red accents.

"Max! We were just talking about you."

That would do for the opening salvo in a war of words. Having been "just talked about" made one the outsider in an instant. The inconstant lover. The philandering husband. The betrayer.

"Where have you been?" the dramatic-looking woman

he had nicknamed Carmen demanded before he could answer.

"Certainly not onstage," said the mentalist named Czarina Catharina. She wore the caftan and turban that hid an aging woman's thinning hair and thickening waist. "No professional demands keeping you away. No excuses," she added coyly.

He shrugged and slipped into an oxblood-red leather chair, happy to fold his telltale six-foot-four height into lounging level. "I have matters to attend to anyway," he said.

"Matters?" Carmen's question was sharp.

"Financial."

"Ah." The portly old gentleman by the bar cart who'd performed as Cosimo Sparks smiled tightly. "He now performs illusions with numbers, in private."

"You must have made an obscene amount of money," Carmen speculated, her husky voice softening with lust, whether for love or money it was hard to tell, but Max's dough would be on the filthy lucre.

"Money isn't everything. And the stock market." Max sighed, spreading his fingers so eloquently that the assembled magicians stared at them as if seeing money melting away.

It had melted away too when he'd poured it into global counterterrorism actions after 9/11. Not into any specific government's efforts, but into the same shadowy, idealistic nonpartisan group that he and his mentor Gandolph had supported for years.

"You know what we are," Sparks said.

"I think I do. Does anyone ever fully know another?"

"Exactly. But we need to really know you."

"Aren't I enough of an open book for my fellow, and sister, magicians? You all know that I got caught in 'a situation' the night my performing contract closed at the

Goliath. I was unfortunately seen too close to a couple of thugs attempting to rob the casino, who inexplicably shot each other. It was flee or face charges. And so my career came to a dramatic end."

The bitter twist to his mouth on the last sentence was particularly effective, and truly felt. Honesty was always the best disguise among enemies.

"Your career was ruined," Czarina agreed. "But new ones beckon."

"Oh?"

"Join us."

"I thought I had."

Sparks answered for Czarina this time. "You've been tolerated, man, but remain unproven."

"We require a trifling . . . initiation ritual," the older woman put in.

"I found you in this rats' maze, didn't I?"

Sparks shook his head. Not enough. "We require more than fine discernment. We require risk."

"You're talking to me about risk?"

"Granted. But perhaps you've grown complacent behind your anonymity."

"Perhaps. I wouldn't bet on it."

"We're not. We're betting on you living up to, and surpassing, our highest expectations. Once you complete your assignment."

Max chuckled. It wasn't a reassuring sound. "I haven't had an 'assignment' since high school."

"We are Ph.D. level," Carmen noted languidly from her corner. Her working name was Serendipity and he supposed he'd better get used to it. She went by Serena among friends. "We require absolute loyalty, dazzling ability, and, oddly enough for magicians, transcendent honesty. To the Synth, anyway."

"What do you want?"

"The Czar Alexander Scepter." The slightly British accent of Cosimo Sparks slapped the words onto the table like a gauntlet.

Max snorted, delicately. "The centerpiece of the forthcoming White Russian exhibit at the New Millennium? You're joking."

"No," Czarina said. "We want you to get it for us."

"I'm not a thief."

"But you could be, an exquisite one," she coaxed him. "We don't care about the value of the piece. We care about the value of the act of taking it. You can return it, if you like."

"Or keep it."

"Or sell it and share the wealth with us, which would be a nice gesture."

Max fanned his fingers to produce a feathered bird of paradise, a faux one. No awkward droppings. "Magicians appreciate the nice gesture." He presented the bird to the Czarina.

"Then you'll do it?" she asked.

"I'll do it if I study the situation and decide it's doable."

"We should warn you," Sparks said in his fuddy-duddy way. "None of us has come up with a foolproof method."

"I'm your court of last resort?"

"You're our pledge, Mr. Kinsella. If you can't cut our initiation rite, you'll have to take our hazing."

The threat was unmistakable.

"I don't take anything," he warned back, "except what I want to. So I'll leave now and examine the situation at the New Millennium that has stymied you all." He stood to go.

"Just a minute."

He paused, looking impatient. "Do you want this trinket, or not?"

"We want your undivided attention."

"Have you seen the new act here at Neon Nightmare?" Serena, lying back on the room's sole sofa in a gown out of a Sarah Bernhardt portrait, practically purred the question.

"Besides yours?" Max asked back, sardonically.

"Tut-tut." Czarina intervened. "No need to get testy. You're an untried factor. We must be sure you're reliable."

"So." Sparks was looking excited and a bit nasty. "Have you seen the Phantom Mage perform here?"

"No, and with that impossibly hokey name, I don't want to. I'll be going."

"I hope not." Serena uncoiled herself to rise and take his arm, a seductive gesture that was also custodial. "Why in such a rush to leave us?" she purred. And her voice did indeed rumble deep in her . . . ah, chest.

"You want me to steal the most prized object in Las Vegas or not?"

"Stay just a while," she coaxed. "You might find this new fellow interesting."

"I find little that is common interesting. I must be off."

"No." The tone and the glance was commanding.

Max removed Serena's arm from its entwined position on his.

"Yes."

"It's imperative you stay." Sparks stood as well.

"Come to the window," Serena cajoled, entwining him again, like a velvet boa constrictor. Max was very glad he'd decided to drop the nickname Carmen for her. She was acting completely out of character for the Carmen he knew.

He made her work to draw him toward the tinted rectangle on one-way glass that framed the dark upper pyramid of Neon Nightmare.

"I really have better things to do. . . ." But he let the sentence trail off.

Everyone was watching him, like rats at a cheese tray.

He stared out over the empty darkness, glancing at his watch without seeming to. The Phantom Mage was scheduled to start a set just about now. . . .

Everyone behind him had tensed, as had Serena, so close and yet so far.

Max kept his own tension bottled, his limbs as loose as linguini. He could see Serena frown as she detected this.

Don't worry, lady, he thought, *I can produce the requisite tension when needed. . . .* Which was not now, when everyone expected one and only one outcome for this charade: Max would fail because the Phantom Mage would fail to appear.

He knew they suspected that Max and the Phantom might be one and the same person. The Phantom's performing gear, mask, and cloak certainly made his identity doubtful.

Beyond the glass, music was ratcheting up to introduce the night's featured act: the Phantom Mage, aka Max.

Inside the glass, someone smiled pleasantly at the Czarina.

Max.

Breaths were held. Not his.

The space beyond the window remained mere space.

Then! A caped form swooped past the window, caroming off the dark sides of the narrowing apex of the pyramid-shaped building, strewing light wands and iridescent glitter.

He came plunging directly toward the one-way glass window. He saw it as only another of the Lucite mirrors positioned to reflect the neon fireworks. He touched toe to the surface and rappelled off like a mountaineer in Batman guise.

For a moment, the vision was face-to-face with Max. Or mask-to-face, rather.

Breaths released audibly behind him.

"The bastard!" Max exploded, tense now, so tense that Serena released him and reflexively jumped back. His muscles were knots of indignation. "He's ripped off my old act's finale. No wonder you wanted me to see this so-called act. The bloody bastard. Punchinello on a stick! This is a travesty."

"Exactly so, lad," Sparks said. "This is why the Synth exists. The true artists remain, uncorrupted. This is why we have to make a statement."

"Damn right." He turned to regard them with burning eyes. "Consider the Czar's scepter your joystick."

They stood as one, and applauded.

"But I expect fifty percent of the proceeds for setting up my comeback act."

The applause never died.

Max bowed and melted into the black and featureless passage.

He wiped the infinitesimal mustache of sweat from his upper lip and headed up into the pyramid's apex, by ways even the Synth hadn't found yet.

Gandolph awaited him up top, sweating as he retracted the flexible dummy in Phantom Mage guise.

"Did we reel in our fish?" he asked.

"The entire school."

Gandolph collapsed against the wall, so close in these close quarters. "I'm too old for such shenanigans. This thing weighs a ton."

Max pulled the dummy onto the narrow catwalk and peeled off the costume.

"They were suspicious. It was crucial to give this fellow a chance to swing."

"I've been called a 'puppet master' in my counterterrorism years, but never so literally, my boy. So you're in like Flynn."

"No, I'm in like Max Kinsella, cat burglar."

"Cat burglary is always an elegant sideline for a magician. I'm pleased to see you expanding your repertoire."

Max quickly donned the dummy's costume: the half-mask, the tool belt, the swirling cape.

"Can you do what they want?" Gandolph asked, stuffing the dummy into a large dark garbage bag like a dead body.

"Without getting caught?" Max, accoutered as the Phantom Mage, poised on the brink of plunging into the darkness below on a bungee cord. "Not easily. Why else set up the challenge? I'll have to do it, though, if we want to embed me deeper in the real heart of the Synth."

He swung out over the abyss, half Batman, half Spider-Man, all magician.

Gandolph would leave by the secret tunnels honey-combing the building, which he'd found even before Max had first come here, sniffing around.

For Max, there was no way out of the Synth's challenge but to mount a one-man raid on a major casino museum. Get caught and he'd satisfy Molina's deepest wet dreams, for sure.

Get caught and he'd betray and wound Temple past any patience and passion she still held for him. No matter what he did to lay his undercover past to rest for good, he only augered in deeper. And Temple paid as much in the present as he had. He was neglecting her, dangerously, risking their relationship in the hope of breaking free to enjoy it forever. Again.

If he didn't get caught he'd be an actual thief on a global scale, but he'd have won the trust of the darkest levels of the Synth. He'd be well on the way to finding out who really backed this cadre of disgruntled magicians, and what they hoped to achieve.

He'd worry about the difficulties of the museum job later. Right now he had more important worries: how to "disappear" for the time required to set up the job without seeming to abandon Temple. Playing relationship Russian roulette with the woman he loved. Again. How many times could he risk that, and not lose?

His booted feet hit the opposite wall and he caromed off it like a cue ball cleaning up the table. He was flying, like Peter Pan, and it was fun. Thrilling actually. A Never-Never Land of adrenaline and adventure.

But he sure didn't want to leave Wendy behind, alone in the family bedroom.

Chapter 4

Male Call

Temple stood on her tiny triangular balcony, one of the perks of living in a round building and having what passed for a "corner" unit.

She was marking a sure sign of spring: her upstairs neighbor, Matt Devine, doing laps in the pool.

She watched him cut a swath through the becalmed aquamarine water. She was also regarding a crime scene through the foggy lenses of time. Electra, their landlady, had only recently told Temple of witnessing Matt's first encounter with their joint bête-noir-to-be, Kathleen O'Connor, at that very poolside months ago.

Temple could picture that scene right now. Kathleen O'Connor made a very vivid, deceptively attractive ghost: maybe five-foot-five, in pumps, wearing an Irish-green silk pantsuit, and looking like a girl from a ballad. The fall sunlight would have glistened off her black,

black hair, her ruby lips, her skin as white as snow. Snow Black.

As Temple retro-daydreamed, Matt finished whatever number of laps he'd set himself, and pulled himself onto the wooden decking that surrounded the pool.

Now only Matt remained of the word picture Electra had recently painted, and he was the same: lightly tanned, muscled enough to be fit without making a fetish of it, white swim trunks and teeth, blond hair glinting pure platinum in the sunlight.

Okay . . . yum. Good enough to eat alive. Kitty O'Connor had thought so too. Only literally. Luckily, she'd left. Permanently.

Temple watched him snatch a towel from a lounge chair. White. Both the towel and the vinyl straps of the lounge chair. Temple, single, female, and thirty, ducked out of sight.

This lurking was pathetic! You'd think she didn't have a perfectly good beau of her own, also out of sight, unfortunately.

A long *merow* drew her back to the living room sofa and was interrupted by an even longer yawn. Midnight Louie was stretching until his toes reached the armrest, where he riffed off a few earnest rips with his front claws.

"Louie, no!"

He looked up with a lazy blink of green eyes but his toes stopped doing the Watusi over her upholstery, which was tough but not impervious. That might describe Louie himself, or even Temple as she liked to think of herself. Small but sturdy. Petite but persistent. Spoken for but not blind.

Meanwhile, Louie was yowling from the couch for more personal attention. She went over and attended to him, rewarded by a hoarse meow of contentment and a purr loud enough to mimic a light plane engine passing overhead.

"That's a good boy," she told him, scratching his tummy while he twisted and flipped from side to contented side. "You should stay at home for a while and get some first-class petting instead of roaming all over the city and getting into trouble."

Only belatedly did Temple realize she could have been advising her often-AWOL significant other, the Mystifying Max Kinsella.

Like Louie, Max always managed to be there when she really needed him, but the times in between were stretching longer and longer . . . like Louie on the sofa right now.

Her doorbell rang. Actually, being a fifties' vintage doorbell, it didn't just ring. It chimed. It yodeled. It caroled a multinote phrase.

She opened the door before it had rung through its sonorous sequence.

"Oh. Hi."

Matt was on her doorstep, towel like a flyboy's white scarf hung around his neck, no longer dripping as far as she was able to discreetly see, but still all tan and bare. Bare. Oh, my.

"Electra corralled me for errand duty in the lobby. Seems you forgot to get your mail yesterday."

"Wonder why?" Temple murmured, taking the four or five envelopes he held out. "Something bad in the neighborhood? Like a meltdown at Maylords Fine Furniture? Glad that's a done deal. Come in."

"I might drip."

"It's okay. Area rug. Right by the door. See?"

"I never noticed that before." He was smiling at her, the implication being why would he look down any farther than her face.

Well . . .

Temple decided to flip casually through her mail, such as it was. "Speak of the devil. Oriental rug cleaning service advertiser. Political flyer. The usual suspects for shredding to keep my address safe and secret."

He quirked a smile at her tepid witticisms. "I have to go out of town next week."

"Speaking engagement?"

"*Amanda Show,* in Chicago."

"What day? I can record it for you."

He shook his head. "Not necessary. I long ago overdosed on my own image on TV. Just wanted you to know I'd be away. And—"

"Yes?"

"I'd like for us to have dinner when I get back."

"Dinner?"

"Someplace nice. Maybe the Bellagio."

"Someplace expensive! *Every* restaurant at the Bellagio is."

"Money's no object." He was smiling now. "The company is."

"Oh. Any special . . . reason?"

"Only that we don't get a chance to just sit down and talk."

"About what?"

"Just . . . anything."

"Un-huh. Well, sounds fine. Just let me know when."

"I'll be back in several days. Any special time you're free?"

"Pretty much all the time now," she heard herself saying, wanting to retract the brittle tone as soon as it passed her lips.

"Fine," he said after a pause. "I'll let you know as soon as I get back. I might even stay over a few days more."

"This trip is more than a quick TV gig, isn't it?"

"Yeah. I'm finally doing what my mother wanted. I don't know if unlocking the past is a good idea, but I've got an appointment in Chicago that might lead to my father. My real father."

"So you could have news when you get back?"

"Maybe. But that's not why I want to have dinner."

She was not going to ask the obvious question. "So, good luck."

"I'm hoping for that." His unexpectedly brown eyes, unusual in a natural blond, crinkled a bit. At her. "Thanks."

She was swinging the door shut even while wishing it was going the other way. From the living room, Louie let loose a long, abandoned howl.

She started toward him, still flipping through envelopes over and over. Dinner? Bellagio? Just to "talk"? Were they talking "date"? Oh, my.

Temple stopped dead, between her entry hall and living room. Louie yowled unanswered. A bold return address had caught her attention completely.

This was it. A response on the "LV PR Job of the Year." She ripped open the envelope to scan its contents. And rescan them. Again. Stamped her size five feet in their Via Spiga slides to wake the dead, i.e., the unfortunate tenants in the room below her, who were probably off at work anyway.

Temple stared at the form letter in her hand.

She couldn't believe it.

"We thank you for your interest but—"

She'd lost the hottest PR account in town to . . . Crawford Buchanan, fellow freelance flack and part-time gossip guru for KREP-AM radio! Pronounced *KREEP* in her book, as anything relating to Buchanan was.

Nattering Nabobs of Negativity! This was so unfair. She had the background—former TV news reporter, former PR director for the prestigious Guthrie Repertory Theater in Minneapolis, current PR rep for the classiest hotel in Vegas, the Crystal Phoenix. What was there not to prefer over Awful Crawford? Plus she was a *girl,* and you'd think that would be an advantage on an account like this for once!

Temple stared at the hot pink headline over the bad black-and-white news.

CALLING ALL TEEN QUEENS! The letters were an inch high and as curly as her natural red hair. TV'S HOTTEST NEW REALITY SHOW HITS VEGAS! FROM 'TWEEN IDOL TO LEGALLY LIVE BAIT! THEY COMPETE FOR THE GUY, THE GOLD, AND THE GOOD LOOKS!

And the sleaziest PR hack in Vegas, not to mention the biggest lecher on Las Vegas Boulevard, would be handling all the publicity, not to mention the contestants if he could.

Temple shook her head. She hadn't been entirely at ease with being head flack for a reality TV show anyway. Especially one that would turn the twenty-four-hour spy cameras on vulnerable young women of tender years. If you could find any of that breed around these days.

She deposited the letter in the wicker wastebasket near her living room sofa.

The position paid spectacularly well, and she certainly could have done a better job with it than Crawford, even with one manicured hand tied behind her back, but *que sera, sera*. She was probably better off out of it. The potential PR headaches were as big as the payoff.

The possibilities unscrolled in her mind.

Number one, permissions. You don't put underage kids on TV without parental permissions up the wazoo. Then, too, how do you run a peep show involving minors without getting hit with child endangerment or abuse charges? More parental permissions.

Then there was the financial tangle of who would benefit from any resulting prizes or payments. Kids, or parents?

Not to mention the ugly matter of stage parents who push their kids into this kind of media exposure for their own needs, otherwise known as JonBenet syndrome. One thing that ugly unresolved investigation had never made clear was where that offbeat name came from. That answer might explain a lot.

Kids tote a heavy load of parental expectations, Temple mused. Cats too. Maybe Louie hadn't really wanted to be a TV commercial spokescat.

Nah. Louie had been born to attract attention, unless he was sneaking around, up to feline mischief, and then he was Mr. Invisible.

Chapter 5

Mail Call

Lieutenant C. R. Molina was doing a surprise inspection of her clothes closet and not liking what she saw. Not that any of her wearable troops were out of uniform and disorderly. Quite the contrary.

A row of black, navy, and brown pantsuits in serviceable twill for winter alternated with a row of taupe, navy, and charcoal gray pantsuits in sturdy cotton for summer.

They weren't cheap, but they all came from conservative career clothing for women catalogs, where she could find styles long enough for her five-foot-eleven-inch frame.

At the other end of the closet hung the limp folds of a few choice silk-velvet evening gowns culled from vintage stores in Los Angeles and Las Vegas over the past fifteen years.

She looked from one end of the closet to the other.

"Lieutenant Jekyll and Ms. Hyde," she muttered. She moved down to flip through the vintage gowns representing her years as Carmen the chanteuse. The rich velvets seemed to echo the tones of her bluesy contralto voice: dark mossy forest green; shimmering black, ruby-burgundy, deep magenta, blue velvet.

Her hand paused in pulling out that last gown. Couldn't even remember buying it. Usually she knew the where and when of every costume . . . even, or especially, those found during her L.A./Rafi Nadir period. Her mind danced away from summoning those dread days beyond recall but her hand clung to the blue velvet. Was she losing it? She let the fabric fall away. No, just too much on her mind that was much more important nowadays, including Her Hormonal Highness, the periadolescent Mariah. Oh, for the pigtails and skinned knees and kiddish enthusiasms of yesterday!

But this inventory of her closet had nothing to do with Mariah. It had to do with one uppity narc. A date! Was he nuts? Was she nuts? Because here she was: single mother cop with teenage child, looking down the barrel of forty thinking she could go on a date. Just like that. When she didn't have a thing to wear. Neither Jekyll nor Hyde was cut out for a dinner date. What the heck had she been thinking?

For some reason the image of Matt's friend, Janice Flanders, popped into her mind's eye. Okay. Also a single mother and no kid herself. Tallish. One dignified lady. A wardrobe role model? No . . . those New Ageish artsy-drapey clothes with cryptic images weren't her, whoever "her" was.

She slid the closet doors shut and went to the living room. Caterina and Tabitha, the tiger-striped cats, were curled into yin-yang formation on the sofa, dreaming of electric mice. Mariah was off at another one of her extracurricular activities . . . band or chorus or just something way too girly for her tender thirteen years . . . at her new friend Melody's house.

Carmen heard the grinding gears of the mailman's mini-Jeep outside and moved into the hot morning sunshine, hoping for a catalog with some outfit labeled "middle-aged single mother dating ensemble."

She got three catalogs, with cover images that made some hitherto untapped fashionista in her soul go "yuck." And a letter. Addressed to Mariah.

Carmen frowned, staring at the unthinkable type in the sunlight. *What?* Now they were trying to push credit cards on middle-schoolers? Were there no limits? No. It must be a magazine solicitation, going by the fancy type in the return address, which looked vaguely familiar. Mariah had suddenly become a huge consumer of *Seventeen* magazine and a whole new slew of its ilk.

Shaking her head, Carmen went in, blinking in the dimness of her living room, automatically snatching the letter opener and slitting through the taped flyers for new air conditioning units et cetera, even through the flap on the envelope addressed to Mariah.

The pitch letter was two-color: pink and black. Carmen shook her head. What would her so very "now" daughter think if she knew that color combo was even older than her mother. "It Came From the Fifties" . . . Carmen chuckled.

And then she read the letter. And sat down. And read the letter again. She looked at the return address. The headlining "sell" graphics.

She took a very deep breath. She wondered who she could call.

No one.

She wondered what she would do.

Whatever it was, it would be disastrous.

Lose-lose.

Oh, hell.

Chapter 6

Undercover Chick

Temple was hammering out a new proposal on her computer, trying to forget about Awful Crawford and reality TV shows and all their satanic ilk, when her doorbell did its vintage doo-wap on her ears.

Matt? Something more to say before he left? *Hmmm.* Max wouldn't ring, and Matt usually knocked, so maybe Electra, the landlady. . . .

Optimistic, as usual, she swung the door wide open, and found a figure as high, wide, and unwelcome as she could remember filling the doorway.

"Lieutenant."

"Miss Barr. May I come in?"

"You have a warrant?"

"You have nothing to fear. This is a personal consultation."

Temple stepped aside to admit a woman who was almost a foot taller than she into her humble domain.

Thank goodness Temple had resident "muscle" on the premises.

Molina stopped cold in the archway to the living room. *"Him."*

"Louie lives here," Temple said. "No doubt he's thinking *'her'* at this very moment."

"Actually, I like cats." Molina crossed the invisible barrier between entry and living area to loom over Louie. "What a handsome fellow."

Louie was buying none of it. He fanned his long, curved nails and licked dismissively between his spread toes.

"What can I do for you?" Temple asked, making small talk.

Molina's laser-blue eyes fixed on her insincere face. "A great deal. Can we talk where you have seating units not claimed by alley cats?"

"My office?"

"Better than mine."

So Temple led her into the spare bedroom-cum-office, wondering madly what this was about. She heard Louie thump assertively down to the floor as he followed them.

Temple indicated the casual wicker chair opposite her computer desk and sank into the comfortable sling mesh of her teal Aereon size A chair.

Louie leaped up on the computer desk and sat there like a silent partner, switching his long black tail over the side.

"I didn't expect a familiar," Molina said.

"Think of Louie as Paul Drake, and of me as Perry Mason."

"Not possible." Molina's lips suddenly quirked.

"What?"

"I could buy Nora Charles and Asta."

"Oh. I could do *The Thin Man!* I do so love vintage clothes and vintage quips."

Louie growled.

"Louie, however," Temple added airily, "does not do dogs."

Molina spread her hands, dismissing the parallels. "Perhaps Bucky Beaver, then. I need to hire your services."

"A PR person could do a lot for your department."

"For me."

"For you?"

"And not PR."

"What for then?"

"You've shown some . . . zany aptitude for undercover work."

"Me?"

"Tess the Thong Girl ring a bell?"

"Well, that was just—"

"I know. You were just Little Red Riding Hood with a basketful of thongs trying to save the Big Bad Wolf from the Evil Huntsman."

"Max isn't a Big Bad Wolf! Although you're an excellent candidate for the Evil Huntsman. You probably went after Snow White for the Evil Queen too."

"Let's set personal issues aside, Miss Barr."

Temple saw those laser eyes shift, eyeing the room and conceding to Temple's domain for the first time.

"You really do want to hire me?"

"Yes."

"For what?"

"I want you to enter the Teen Queen reality TV show competition."

"What!" Temple leaped up from her chair. "I'm too old!"

"That leap says not. The upper age limit is nineteen. You can pass."

"But—"

"You can pass. You think I don't know who can go undercover and how well? You're a shoo-in."

"Get Su! She's small for her age."

"I would, but she's a homicide detective. She's not used to undercover. I've decided, abhorrent as the conclusion is, that only you . . . will do . . . for this job."

"Abhorrent to you or to me?"

"To us both. Equally. It's a Mexican standoff, Miss Barr. That should make it easier for you. You win, I lose. I lose, you win."

"Why?"

Molina looked down. "My daughter—"

"Mariah. Nice kid."

"She's entered the contest. She's a finalist."

"Mariah? A Teen Queen? I don't think so."

"You haven't been on the Teen Queen scene lately. But you will be now. With a vengeance." Molina bent down to her big black purse that was half briefcase, and pulled out a plum. A one-sheet familiar to any PR person around. A flyer. An advert sheet. A—

Temple felt her pulse spike even as her jaw dropped. "This is . . . sick."

"We have a stalker. A teen runaway has recently been found dead. That could be unrelated, but another adulterated poster like this was found in the general vicinity of her body. You realize what that means."

Temple reluctantly took the paper.

"It's a color copy," Molina said. "You can't hurt it. I wish you could."

Temple nodded. "You're asking me to risk my life."

"You did it for him."

"Because . . . I love him."

"I love Mariah."

"You can't ask this."

"I can ask. The deal is, I lay off Kinsella."

"Max for Mariah? You can't nail him for anything; you're not even close to him."

"But you are."

Temple shook her head. The paper trembled in her hands. Who would deface the image of a young girl like that? And would he do as much to her body? That was the question.

"You want me there as a chaperon for Mariah? Why not just tell her she can't do this?"

"I tried. Six hours of pleading and recriminations. Her whole soul is into this. She thinks she can sing. I'm afraid she actually can. I could at her age. Then, it wasn't worth much. I could say she can't aspire because I couldn't. But I'm afraid she actually could win her division."

"You could shut this down right now. Just say no."

"Obviously you haven't a clue about parenthood. Sure, I can say no and win this battle but lose the war and my daughter, forever. I suppose when you grew up in Wisconsin—"

"Minnesota."

"—where it was old-fashioned, mid-American, and too darn cold for teenage girls to get much more from necking than frostbite, parents didn't have to worry about their kids growing up way too fast too soon."

Temple couldn't help smiling. "We weren't totally frozen out when it came to being rebellious teens. There was always punk ice-skating."

"Not funny. I am hanging onto this kid's future by the nape of her neck. She's got a new bad-girl girlfriend. She's under all the commercial pressures girls her age face: buy-buy-buy, be sexy, be hip, show it all, get guys. Never think of what you might lose by it. She could bolt if I said no. Better she try it and work out her energy and aggressions in a controlled arena. And—"

Molina looked away, to the tack board bearing the news articles on Temple's accounts.

"Mariah has a passion to achieve girls my age, from my place in the world, were denied. Weren't you? Twenty years ago. Weren't we all denied? I can't stop her. I won't stop her. But I can protect her."

"With me?"

Molina nodded. Her expression tightened. "You're all I've got. My agent on the scene."

"You don't like me."

"No. But I've . . . come to respect your . . . pluck and dumb luck." She sounded like she was swallowing a pickle.

Temple sat back, feeling slightly smug. "I've only fought for what . . . *who* I believe in."

"I can't buy that. I wouldn't under any other circumstances in the world. But I can arrange things. I'll have people outside the Teen Queen Castle. You can't . . . won't tell anyone. I don't want the great Max Kinsella racing to your rescue and getting in the way. This is going to have to be a solo job for you. As it is for Mariah. And me. Maybe it'll be good for all of us."

"I can't guarantee I'll make the finals. You know what teens are like nowadays. I don't know if I can cut it. Mariah might not either."

Molina stood up. "I know you both. Unfortunately. I don't doubt that either you or my daughter can make the final cut if you set your minds to it. You're two of a kind."

"Me and Mariah?"

"Thorns in a mother's side."

"My mother would beat you to death with a fast-food chicken limb if she knew what you were asking her baby daughter to do."

"She can do it with my blessing if both our baby daughters don't come through this. I wouldn't let either one of you even try out if I weren't pretty sure that this . . . pageant threat is a long shot. All the finalists will be confined to the same quarters for two weeks. Very hard for a bad actor to get in."

"Or easy. Film crews are gypsies, hard to do background checks on them."

"We'll know them from the birthmarks out."

"And you'll really give Max a free pass from now on?"

Molina raised her right hand. "Absolutely. Unless he stands there with a smoking gun over a dead body right under my nose, I'll totally forget he hangs out somewhere in this toddling town, up to murky business and possibly larceny or even murder. If you can live with that uncertainty, I can."

"You have him so wrong."

"I don't have him. You do. That's *your* problem. It's a crime I have to compromise on this, but I'm off his case."

"If I do this. Wow. How long do I have to get into character? I'll need . . . cool clothes. Um, a couple body piercings, ears at least. A quick rundown on the latest slang and hot boy bands."

Molina was reaching into that bottomless briefcase again. "You'll have to try out locally but you'll need to bring a tape. Here's Mariah's winning little number. Can we check it out?"

"Other room."

Temple was feeling pretty numb as she followed Molina there, but then the bipolar reactions set in. Shocked/challenged. Scared/excited. Worried/confident.

Molina shot the video tape into its slot and Temple manned the remote.

In a minute they were both hunkered down on the sofa, watching with fascination as Mariah spoke, sang a clever pitch, and cavorted for the camera.

"This is Mariah?" Temple marveled. "I haven't seen her for a while. She's really grown."

"Teened out," Molina said grimly.

"Who filmed this?"

"New friend from a tough school. I'm lucky the only

thing that girl talked Mariah into doing behind my back was this nonsense."

"Didn't she need your permission to do this?"

"One would hope, but nope. It was only an 'open preliminary audition.' The permissions come later, when or if the girls are actually accepted for the reality show cast, and there are a ton of them. As there should be. And . . . the show selected her.

"We've already got the preshooting packet. Mariah will be put on a diet. Sensible, they claim. She'll have acting and singing classes. She'll get clothes and a cosmetic Extreme Teen makeover and will generally hang out with her peers while competing ferociously."

"So what's so different between this and junior high?"

"Catholic school. Mariah hasn't been exposed to the dark side of adolescence. She'll be a chick in a yard full of foxes."

"Maybe you've protected her too much."

"Maybe." Molina grabbed the remote and stopped the film.

"You're expecting me to get selected? The competition for my so-called age group—Senior Teen Queen—must be killer."

"I hope not. I'm counting on you being just as able and clever as Mariah in getting attention, even if it's the wrong kind."

"Then there's that dumb luck thing of mine."

"Exactly." Molina stood. "The tape's a copy. You can study it. I gotta admit the kid has chutzpah. Sophistication won't cut it. You'll have to find your inner teen queen. Your shoe collection should help."

"And you'll really, really, forget about Max?"

"Who?"

Temple nodded. "And if I don't make the cut and the show doesn't want me?"

"Then I still want Kinsella, and this time I'll get him. For something, even if I have to make it up. But I won't. He makes it too easy."

"Okay. I guess I'll let you know when I hit"—Temple consulted the fat, glossy, and expensive press kit—"the Teen Queen Castle. Oh, boy."

"Oh, girl," Molina corrected. She wasn't Molina if she wasn't correcting somebody.

Temple showed her out, then gazed down at Louie, who'd accompanied them to the exit like a major domo in a cat suit.

"Think I can pass as a teen queen, Louie?"

He rubbed against her ankles, nodding his head up and down as he left his scent on her shin bones. Now that was a vote of confidence!

Temple returned to the living room and ran Mariah's tape again.

Couldn't tell Max, couldn't tell Matt. Wouldn't have told Louie if he hadn't been here.

She frowned, remembering the dismembered Barbie doll parts in the color Xerox image. If she got to the Teen Queen Castle, she'd really rather have some undercover backup that she knew about.

Not Max. Not Matt. Surely not Louie. Then who?

Chapter 7

Bait Boy

Not once during her pitch did Miss Lieutenant C. R. Molina specifically forbid Midnight Louie his own self to go undercover.

Wise of her. I am always undercover, anyway.

I have watched the video with both eyes wide open, thinking how I would feel if Miss Midnight Louise put herself on the chopping block in such a fashion. I guess it is not a chopping block unless the purveyor of the mutilated flyer makes it so. It is more like an auction block.

I cannot approve of these little dolls parading for the entertainment of the masses. I cannot approve of anyone parading for the entertainment of the masses.

Unless, of course, they held a midlife-macho-dude competition. That would be right up my alley.

Everything I have overheard today convinces me of one thing: I must be present in the Teen Queen Castle for both the gore and the glamour of the competition, the guts and the glory. Miss Temple needs some undercover muscle she can count on, i.e., something more than human.

Speaking of which, I could use some spiritual guidance. Or at least a hint of what is to come. Or at least a good laugh at the gullible.

So, once Miss Temple is in her bedroom throwing clothes and shoes around, I bounce open one of the French doors to the balcony. I know this is her usual ritual for gearing up, quite literally, for action.

Me, I hop aboard the old palm tree leaning so conveniently over our balcony and ratchet up the shaggy trunk to the penthouse floor, just below the spreading vanes of leaves.

This entails an agile leap over the wrought-iron railing and a three-point landing on the plastic pad of the lounge chair. (Three-point because one of my shiv-holders slips off the cushion.)

But I am good to go as soon as I sit up and shake my coat into dapper order.

I have another rank of French doors to break through. These have not been trained by me to open at the jiggle of a mitt under the bottom. So my entrance is not the usual blend of speed, skill, and silence.

I find myself expected.

Karma is not hiding under the furniture, as is her wont. (These psychic types loathe daylight.) No, this time she is sitting there bold as a bronze statue of Bast. The gaze she casts upon me, though as gloriously blue as Miss Lieutenant Molina's, is pure steel and just as caustic.

She is a leggy rangy lady, her coat a longish soft cream shade and her mitts all gloved in pristine white. Yet she wears the brown facial mask of the formidable Siamese martial arts expert, which only emphasizes her blue-heaven eye color. While she is lovely to look at, one does not wish to annoy her. The breed is deemed sacred for defending a dalai lama against assassins ages ago. They have never forgotten it, nor should they. Nor do I. Hence their mystical gifts, if you believe in that sort of thing. I sort of do, despite my street sense. But at the moment she is crooning a not entirely welcoming song at me.

"By the prickling of my pads, this way comes the king of cads."

"Oh, I say, Karma! That is harsh. If you are miffed that we have not had discourse lately, I have been mondo busy with various and sundry cases all across Las Vegas, from desert to downtown."

She emits a sound that wavers between a growl and a purr. No wonder we dudes do not stick around the females of my species. They are one tough house to please.

I decide to play the mum dude-about-town and simply polish my nails on my shiny black sleeve.

"Oh, very well. Come in." She rises and leads the way into the dim room where vintage pieces of upholstery graze like bison of yore . . . huge, dark, shaggy, and humped. They are mostly mohair or covered in large jungle prints.

No wonder a dude does not feel welcome in this dark, vaguely hostile homescape.

"Miss Electra Lark?" I inquire politely.

"Is absent." Karma turns to give me another piercing look. "It is just we two."

"Somehow it is never 'just we two' when I consult you."

"Oh, so you have elevated me to a consultant. I thought you had dismissed me as a flake."

I raise a defensive mitt. "Now do not get your dander up. I have had more than one brush with the mantic arts."

"Your current case is hardly in that direction."

"No. It is a silly-sounding affair. These human kits are quite playful, you know, and the females are overpampered. In fact, our kind has become the mascot of their blooming femininity. Have you heard of the Hello Kitty and Pinkie's Palace phenomenon? Everything pink and frothy and marabou and glittery for girls from three-to-thirteen is decorated with the more beauteous of the feline species."

"Crass commercialization. We are the superior species. We are not clowns."

I do not know about that. I have encountered some pretty big clowns in every species.

We are in the room where the green globe on top of the fifties television cabinet shines like a cat's eye at midnight.

Karma sits down again, tucks her fluffy train around her feet like a thirties torch singer, closes her eyes, and begins to croon.

"Very bad, Louie. I sense danger for all of the 'little dolls' under your protection, and now they are legion. Well, at least thirty or so. I see blood. I see many evil intentions. I see boiling oil. And that is just the normal course of events when so many competitive females are assembled together.

"I see . . . oh, my! You will be subjected to much of the health food that you so unwisely deplore. I see weight loss."

"No! I need my fighting strength."

"Not yours, alas. I see . . . hidden ways and motives and means."

"Like what?"

The blue eyes slit open. "That is for me to know and you to find out."

So, fine. I do not like the sound of blood and boiling oil, but at least they are forthright, unlike Karma.

"You are warned," she intones in her most inscrutable whine. "You will encounter three divine emissaries of Bast herself and an old ghost. You will find the way of the dog your most useful weapon. Your efforts will get no credit."

So what is new? I offer Karma a polite bow in farewell, taking care not to back into anything damaging to my undercarriage as I make my retreat.

As with all seeresses, Karma is best understood in retrospect.

Still, I have a few things to bear in mind. Particularly the boiling oil and the dog part.

Chapter 8

Separate Lies: The Sequel

Little Red Riding Hood put on her visiting duds, picked up a basket, and walked through the woods to grandmother's house, only a big bad wolf was waiting for her.

That night, after failing to sleep, Temple put on her best red Dorothy shoes, low-heeled slides with rhinestoned vamps across the toes, packed a basket full of adult goodies like a French loaf of jalapeño-cheese bread, a bottle of Chianti, and cinnamon-scented massage oil, among other delicacies. She then got into her red Miata to drive to Max's house, where a recently distracted wolf was *not* expecting her.

She couldn't explain her post-midnight raid on Max's place, except that she wasn't happy with their recent interactions, or lack of same. It was time to face the music and dance, like the song said. Or not. Either way, she'd know what the future held.

The horse knew the way, although that was from another fairy tale, the one where grandmothers' houses still lurked down rural lanes.

The Miata's hundred-some horses took her to Max's neighborhood, all the houses decently dark. It was just past eleven P.M.

She parked three doors away and watched her back as she approached the familiar front door.

What she would do if he wasn't home, she didn't know. She also wasn't sure he would be home. Max was up to something he wasn't telling her about. She hoped it was something she could live with if she found out what.

No huntsmen seemed to be lurking in the vicinity, a good sign.

She rang the bell. Boldly. How else can you ring a doorbell at eleven P.M.?

When the door swung open, Granny was nowhere in sight. Just Max in his usual black, looking surprised, then pleased, then . . . worried.

"Temple." He immediately grasped the purpose of the basket. "On a mission of mercy. To me. I could use it. Come in."

"I'm not disturbing you—?"

"Oh, you are, but in the nicest of ways."

He led her into the living room where a talk show she seldom stayed up long enough to see dominated a wide plasma TV screen.

"That's new." She pointed to the screen.

"This is newer." He dredged the blue velvet one-shouldered maillot swimming suit from her basket. It was 50 percent spandex and looked just big enough for a Barbie doll. "You want to hit the spa?"

"Sort of the idea."

"I could use it myself but . . . there are reasons. Why

don't I just open the wine. You can get warmed up in all that hot water?"

Actually, she was getting pretty warmed up without the aid of a hot tub.

She changed into her suit in the guest bathroom, then brought the basket out to the deck where an underwater Blue Hawaii light lit the bubbling hot water from below.

Heavenly!

Temple hadn't realized how worried she'd been about her impromptu expedition to Max's turf until she slipped under the hot water. *Aaaah.* Who would have thought the young woman had so much tension in her?

Two bubbles of glassware appeared on the drink indentations built into the spa's side. Red wine, gleaming like Burmese rubies. Max sat on the hot tub lip.

He tugged at her one blue velvet shoulder strap. "Can velvet get wet?"

"Modern miracle, spandex for water babies."

He chuckled and offered her a cracker with cheese from her CARE basket.

"I wasn't sure you'd still be up," she said.

He gave that remark the long pause any inadvertent double entendre deserved.

She laughed and sipped room-temperature wine, which felt cool compared to the hot tub.

"I'm glad you came," he replied soberly, in kind.

"We seem to have been passing like ships in the night lately."

"Agreed." Max sipped from his wineglass, then spoke. Soberly. "I'm working up a new act. It's secret. That's why I've been so distracted. So absent."

"Ummm." She put her wet arms up to clasp his still-clothed ones, cables of steel. "No wonder you feel like Superman. That's wonderful! Why didn't you tell me?"

"I don't know when I'll be ready to make it public. Maybe not for . . . months. It takes—"

"Discipline. Zen mania. Max! This is great news. I thought—"

"What?"

"That you'd lost interest in . . . things."

"In magic, or you? Never you. Am I now breaking my thirty-five-year-old back to make waves in the magic game? Yes. Guilty. I can't say when my new apprenticeship will end. I have to make a spectacular comeback."

"Of course. I'm so glad. I thought you'd given up on magic."

"No."

"Well then." Temple snuggled down into the churning water. The aquatic blue light reminded her of something? The Blue Light special at Kmart? "I have to tell you. I may be AWOL myself for, oh, a couple weeks or so."

"So long? Really?"

She nodded, her chin dipping into a froth of bubbles.

"I have to . . . go home. Minnesota. My dad. A minor cardiac thing. A stent? Anyway, they want me there."

"Of course." He kissed the top of her head. "I hope your father is all right. I'll miss you," he said.

What a liar she was! She didn't deserve sympathy! At least Max wouldn't worry about her.

"I'm sorry, Temple." His voice vibrated somewhere above her head but she felt it in her heart. "Things will be better later, won't they?"

"Absolutely. And now . . . they're just perfect."

"Just perfect." He pulled away to lift his wineglass as her fingers curled around the stem of hers. They drank ruby velvet.

"Get in," she said. "You don't need a suit."

"Can't. I've got a midnight appointment."

"With whom?" She hadn't meant to sound sharp, she was just surprised.

Max trailed a hand in the warm, bubbling water. It ran up her arm. "I'm working out in secret. Using the Caped

Conjuror's home setup while he's dazzling the second-show set at the New Millennium. I can't stay."

"But—"

"But there's no reason you can't stay here and enjoy the spa. The door will lock automatically on your way out."

"I didn't come here just to enjoy the bubbles."

"I know. And do you think I'll enjoy several hours of working out twenty-five feet above a terrazzo floor on bungee cords?"

"Max! It sounds—"

"Dangerous? Yes, what I'm doing is dangerous, Temple." His blue eyes looked opaque, black against the night's own darkness.

"But spectacular."

Max laughed. "If you mean I could make a spectacle of myself. . . . Comebacks are hell, Temple. You have to give up a lot, including your dignity. And a private life." He bent down to kiss her. Her fingerprints made darker blots on his black sleeves.

"Rain check? Ciao."

It almost never rained in Vegas but when it did, it was a gully washer.

Temple floated in the spa's programmed turmoil, feeling her internal boiling point mounting.

Odd. The blue lagoon waters now reminded her of something less pleasant than tropical nights: Lieutenant C. R. Molina's sharp, ever-watchful laser-blue eyes.

But no one they knew was here. Now. Temple let the water roll her over as she turned to watch Max's back disappear into his house on his way out.

Magicians did that. Disappeared. For a living.

Sometimes lovers did that too.

Bitter disappointment made Temple rain two teardrops into the sizzling spa water. They instantly eddied away, lost in the sea of foaming warmth. Temple knew better than to feel rejected, but she did, dammit.

Selfish Temple! She knew how hard Max worked at both of his professions. Now, at last, he was reclaiming the public persona of magician instead of being consumed by the invisible cloak of spy. Times were more perilous worldwide than they'd ever been and Max had been out there, was still out there, trying to prevent disaster.

A game little woman would stand behind her man, even when he wasn't there. Especially when he wasn't there.

Still . . . Her hand slapped the water. This time droplets jumped up at her eyes, stinging them into blinking.

Blink. And Max had been gone without explanation. Blink. Lieutenant Molina had come asking brutal questions, painting the missing Max as a likely murderer. Blink. Enter Matt Devine, ex-priest, new neighbor, always there to help or tempt through no fault of his own.

Love and fidelity were great . . . when a couple actually spent time together now and then. But Temple was no longer feeling loved, even if she was, and Matt—God, Max! Wake up and smell the latte!—was finally outgrowing all those years of celibacy and coming on to her with Intent to Commit Relationship.

Temple laid her chin on her hands on the spa's hard-shelled rim and let the swirling eddies float her body up, up, and away.

Men! They were maddening. Eve must have wanted to strangle Adam when he'd blamed the Apple Incident on her! Temple bet Eve had missed becoming humankind's first killer by . . . this much! Justifiable homicide, in her opinion.

Like the song says: a total eclipse of the heart.

Chapter 9

Bling-Bling Babies

Molina sat, sober as a judge, on her comfy old living room sofa, reading for the fourth time the entry form that Mariah had filled out.

She'd reached the fiction part now, Mama Molina's own creation: Julio Sanchez, heroic off-duty cop killed helping a citizen change a flat tire on the side of the notorious Los Angeles freeway system.

Would the TV-show staff research the contestants' family histories? Or take them at face value?

"You're still not mad at me," Mariah said hopefully from the armchair, where she lounged on her tailbone, petting Caterina.

"Not mad. Disappointed."

Silence. Mariah was still new enough to teenhood to cringe a little at that word. Disappointment.

Molina tossed the entry form aside, making a mental note to fax a copy to Temple Barr. Had to give the kid credit; she'd beat out a lot of candidates to get a chance at the reality show slot.

Molina sighed and checked her watch. Mariah surreptitiously checked her mother's face.

Standing up, Molina stuffed her bare feet into moccasins. "Come on. The mall's open until six. A Teen Queen wannabe will need some new duds for her stay at the Teen Queen Castle. In fact—" Inspiration hit. It was a galling inspiration, but then the whole situation was galling from the get-go.

She drew her cell phone and hit a preprogrammed number. To this she had sunk.

Mariah watched, blinking.

"Yeah," Molina told the phone when the ringing stopped. "Mariah and I are hitting the mall for some drop-dead Teen Queen garb. Maybe you'd better come along. Yes, it's 'kinda an order.' Half an hour. Right. We'll meet you at—?" Molina lifted interrogative eyebrows at her daughter.

"Junior department at Dillard's."

"Junior department at Dillard's." Molina flipped the phone shut and grabbed her buckskin hobo bag.

"Who was that?"

"Image consultant," she said.

"Who'd you know that I'd want having anything to say about my clothes?"

"You'd be surprised." Molina shot a smile Mariah's way as she snatched the car keys from the kitchen countertop. "You go to all the trouble of being on a national TV show, no matter how tawdry, you ought to get a little help."

Molina felt naked as she followed Mariah into the dark garage. She wasn't carrying tonight, for the first time in a long time. It would have been too awkward. Mama needed a new pair of shoes, and then some too. She just hoped to heck that tonight was not the one some gang member decided to go postal in the mall's Hallmark Card Shop.

Temple Barr appeared to know the junior department as well as Mariah.

In fact, Mariah had about three inches on the woman. Molina hoped she'd stop growing soon. But maybe too tall was no longer a female liability.

Molina stood uneasily in the main aisle, eyeing rows of skirts the width of cummerbunds and see-through mesh tops skimpier than sports bras. The color and glitter were showgirl seductive, but there were so many clothes, and so little of them.

For the first time she felt like her own mother.

Red head and espresso-brown head bowed together over the racks, pulling out selections and tossing them over arms or thrusting them back onto the chrome poles, rather like blasé strippers.

"Cool color." "Oh, too rad." "To die for."

The murmurs were both vapid and excited. Molina smiled, maternally, as she observed Temple and her daughter together. Temple acted like an older sister, caught up in the same girly ritual but far more sophisticated than Mariah with her cherubic halo of baby fat still intact, thank God.

Good pick, Molina told herself. Temple Barr was exactly what she herself always had lamented not ever being—petite and pretty enough to pass as a teenager.

Temple looked up as if Molina's speculation about her was tangible and she'd felt it. Good instincts for an amateur. "Mama have a budget for this extended prom party?"

"Whatever you think she needs."

Temple's eyebrows raised, borrowing that tic from

Molina. She consulted the two stapled sheets advising "contenders" on "what to bring."

"We are in plastic heaven, kiddo," she told Mariah. "Let's rock."

Two hours later they emerged from the dressing room, giggling like classmates on a spree. Temple's arm held almost as many draped items as Mariah's. That's what Molina had hoped for: Mariah's taste would clue in Temple on current hot teen items, and Temple's PR influence would guide Mariah to what worked on TV.

If Molina had cherished any reason but bodily safety to encourage a relationship between the two, she might even have found their bonding . . . sweet.

If they made the show, Mariah would have to know that Temple was there as a stooge before the charade began. No way would she be fooled. Hey, the kid would probably get off on being part of an "undercover" team.

How had a smart homicide dick like her ended up in such a mess? Daughter dearest and her mad, hopeful, predictable, determined desire to be somebody five years older than herself.

Molina played her prime parental role: she laid plastic on a checkout counter and watched the LED numbers hit the mid four figures. Yikes.

Temple Barr, she was pleased to note, had done as well. Molina supposed she should reimburse Temple but let that be a surprise after the ball at the Teen Queen Castle was over. If there was one for her.

Molina checked her watch.

"Done with still an hour's time," Temple chimed in, shooting a conspiratory glance at her pal Mariah. "Shoes, maybe?"

"Actually, I need to make a stop," Molina said.

"Ladies' room?" Temple asked.

How heedlessly insulting. Temple Barr would make a

fab teen queen. "No. Family members appear in the audience on the final show. I need something . . . less casual."

Temple eyed Molina's jeans, moccasins, gauze cotton top, and suede bag. "I guess! Your cop shop pantsuits won't cut it either. And I don't suppose you want to trot out Carmen"—she cut off as Molina glared from Mariah to her—"a Carmen Miranda ensemble."

"Who's Carmen Miranda?" Mariah wanted to know.

Trust kids to sense when adults were getting their lies and deceptions in a wad.

Temple vamped expertly into a diversionary path. "Oh, an old-time performer. Wore these tall, tall headdresses of tropical fruits. Sang, danced. One hot Hispanic cha-cha chick. The movies in the forties were big on Latin music and performers."

"The forties?"

"During World War II."

"Latin was in?"

"*Olé!* There were some great, fun movies, all black and white. You should rent a couple."

"Sounds coolio."

"As coolio as Julio Iglesias."

Mariah frowned. "Don't you mean Enrique?" she said, mentioning Julio's cleft-chinned singer-son in the sexy chip commercial. "To die for!" Nauseating sigh.

"Right," Temple backpeddled. "Enrique."

Molina feared that Temple's love of vintage anything was giving away her age. This was definitely not an Iglesias, Sr. crowd. Molina would have to warn her about that.

Temple turned a sharply focused eye on her. "Now. What does Mama Bear need? Something not too casual, not too formal but just right. For what reuse once the show is over?"

"I don't know." Molina did know but she wouldn't say that. "Something suitable for dinner at one of the big hotels. Maybe."

Temple reared back, obviously daunted by the challenge. "Let's hit Ladies' Dresses."

"I'm not much for dresses," Molina objected. "They're always too short."

"Not with long skirts so hot right now." Temple did the teen eyeroll like an expert. "If I don't buy petite sizes I have to roll up the waistbands until I look like I'm pregnant."

Mariah giggled hard at this notion that her mother had hoped would never cross her mind under any circumstances, except when saying no to boys, until she was in college.

What have I done!

The stroll through Better Dresses was agonizing. Molina understood for the first time her Jekyll/Hyde clothing philosophy: slacks and jackets, jeans and tops for on- and off-duty. Vintage velvet for Carmen, a distant star who was seldom coming out at nights to sing these days. And in between these two extremes lurked a jungle of fussy, expensive clothing that did not scream "date" with a maybe man.

Temple Barr, however, obviously relished the extreme challenge of making over Molina. Temple Barr thrived in the messy middle ground. She and Mariah ravaged the racks, then pushed Molina into the dressing room with armloads of improbable clothing.

She ended up with an outfit chosen by their mutual consent.

"Car-wash skirt, definitely," Temple told Mariah.

"Very cool," Mariah concurred.

"It looks like Jack the Ripper's been at my hem from the knees down," Molina grumbled.

"Dangerous," Temple said. "Ideal for a law-enforcement type. And not black. Deep, dark plum. Good contrast for your eyes."

"My eyes don't need contrast."

"Absolutely right," Temple said. "Just a little mascara—you do use mascara? No! Makeup counter's on the way out, Mariah. Take that down. Lash Out, just the thing."

Mariah meekly wrote that at the bottom of her clothes sheet.

"An eyebrow waxing would be a gift from heaven," Temple mused.

"I'm *not* going to go through that sort of ridiculous assault in the name of female exploitation."

"Too timid for a little pain in the name of self-improvement, Mariah. So like a guy! Add a Tweezerman to the cosmetic counter list. You might be able to sneak up on her when she's asleep and pluck."

"Scratch that!" Molina ordered. "Or I cancel the credit card charges."

Mariah did as told.

But Molina had been conned into the skirt with the shredded hem, $128.00. A black sleeveless top shaped from bands of ribbons. And a net shawl of purple, black, and turquoise iridescent beads.

"That is so cool, Mom," said Mariah, who was sold on the outfit. Mariah had never seen Carmen.

"This may be a little dressy," Molina said with a frown, eyeing herself grudgingly in the mirror. Short, tiny Temple had a feel for supermodel togs.

"You'll need heels," Temple decreed.

"No. You do heels. I don't do heels."

What, Temple had been about to say, *about those vintage forties platform heels Carmen wears?*

Molina could read the entire sentence as it formed in her mind and her eyes. But Carmen did not exist here, and besides she stood solo on stage and sang. She didn't have to worry about dwarfing some insecure man from the stage.

Not that she had an insecure man in mind when she rejected heels. She just had an insecure woman in mind, who had minded these things since the eighth grade.

"Shoe department," Temple said in a threatening tone.

Actually, it had been an anticipating tone but Molina found that threatening.

There, Molina held her ground. She would not wear so much as an inch-and-a-half-high heel.

Mariah, trying on every tarty spike she could find, pled with her. It was sad to see how much a teen girl wanted a glamorous mother. Molina almost caved.

Except that Temple, of all people, gently praised and prodded Mariah into demure slides with small, low heels.

"She's too heavy for those spikes," Temple commented as Mariah pranced before the mirrors in her petite princess shoes, feminine to the max. "Maybe later, when the baby fat goes."

"You don't want me to wear them?"

"Carmen's vintage platform forties heels, with all those industrial-strength straps, scream sturdy as much as sexy. They're fine on someone of your height. But these stilettos aren't. You'd wobble. And I bet you'd hate to wobble. High heels should look able to support their wearer."

"I'm amazed. You make shoe selection sound like an art form."

"It is." Temple frowned at Molina's size nine feet. "I'd like to see a tiny heel, but since you won't have it. . . ."

She darted away like a dragonfly with no credit card limit.

Moments later she returned with an utterly flat shoe, a thong sandal with a beaded triangle over the instep that perfectly matched the shawl.

Like a dragonfly, the improbable sandal reflected the light.

"Oh, Mom, that's perfect," Mariah pleaded.

Mariah wanted her to sparkle because then that meant she could too. Like mother, like daughter.

Molina bought the dragonfly sandals, not sure whom they would remind her of more—Mariah the would-be Cinderella, or Temple Barr, the reluctant fairy godmother.

Later, she and her daughter celebrated their first mutual girly occasion (for Molina, it was her very first girly occasion): they whisked out their purchases in the living room, while Caterina and Tabitha gamboled on fallen pieces of colorful tissue.

"This is so cool, Mom. Thank you! I know I can win."

"It doesn't matter if you win. It matters if you have fun, keep your head, and . . . stay safe."

"Temple is so cool." Mariah, head bent, held up some ridiculous glitzy top to her underdeveloped breasts. "She hardly acts like an old person at all."

"I really hope so, honey."

Mariah looked up, catching her change in tone.

"Because we three have a secret, and it'll be up to you to help carry it off."

And then she told Mariah that Temple was working undercover to trap a potential perp, and Mariah would have to help her carry off the masquerade.

Mariah the cop's kid looked even more amazed and happy than Mariah the potential 'Tween Queen.

Chapter 10

Louie Goes Ape

What has happened to my dear little roomie, Miss
Temple?

She was always a spirited, happy little human.

She always got a kick out of life and having a humongous high-heel collection. She was perky but not
sappy. Full of mischief but not slaphappy. Upbeat but
not nauseating. Cute as a ladybug but not too girly to
rock and roll.

Now she has done a complete turnaround.

I watch her upend about a zillion shopping bags on
the bed I have honored with my reclining presence.

I am adrift in a blizzard of mall-style plastic . . . the
Gap, Victoria's Secret, The Icing, et cetera. She has
been on a shopping spree wild enough to smother me
had I not beaten off a rain of plastic bags with the
Ginsu knife shivs so conveniently attached to my ex-
tremities.

"Oh, sorry, Louie," she remarks offhandedly, trying on a faux-leather bustier over her faux-front gel cups in the full-length mirror on the wall.

I am used to seeing my Miss Temple in a state of undress, due to our intimate relationship in the bedroom, i.e., we share my king-size bed.

I am not used to seeing assorted tattoos and rings on her upper arms, ankle, neck, and the . . . gasp, small of her back, which is pretty small, her being a Lilliputian human.

When did she go berserk at a piercing parlor without consulting me, I would like to know! Obviously, I have been derelict in my duty of shepherding her through life as we know it in Las Vegas.

When she pulls out the Cher wig and tugs it on over her own tortie-red curls, I know I have to take action.

She turns from the mirror, looking like something from the back of a squad car on *Cops,* the first and most-forgotten reality TV show.

I am aghast to see that her eyes are as vibrantly green as mine . . . then I realize that she has borrowed Mr. Max's performing trick: green contact lenses for that mesmerizing gaze. Trouble is, it works on cats and magicians but I am not sure it works for my Miss Temple.

"Well, Louie, do I look like a reconstruction project?"

She looks like an escapee from the city pound, especially with that rhinestone dog collar around her neck.

"Am I ready to take on the world of reality TV?"

Hmmm, I already observed that she looked like an escapee from *Cops.*

"Am I post-'Tween Queen in the making?"

'Tween tweezings, I think to myself. Not to mention a ripe candidate for brain implants.

"Do I look sweet, swingin' nineteen going on Goth thirty?"

Goth? As in I "goth" to get outa here?

I take my own advice and retreat to the outer room but resolve to keep a very close eye on her from this moment on.

Chapter 11

Good Golly, Miss Goth Girl

The mall was mobbed with 'tween girls from just-thirteen to a tarty fifteen. And a few good legally blonde bimbos from sixteen to nineteen. The decibel level in the vaulted central atrium suggested a jungle of screeching parrots.

Temple had never seen so much metallic and iridescent nail polish, so many spandex capris, thong flipflops, and belly buttons in one place since a Britney Spears concert. And she'd never seen a Britney Spears concert except in TV commercials.

Temple glimpsed a shadow of herself in a Gap display window. It took her a moment to pick herself out from the crowd. She couldn't believe she was doing this: standing in line, hiding her hair, and showing her belly button.

This was the screwiest self-marketing job she'd ever done. She'd decided that the subject of a TV makeover show should require some major makeover, plus. And she needed to disguise herself enough to fool any possible acquaintances, so . . .

She craned her neck to see if her little buddy—or was that "budette" in this case?—was anywhere around. But Mariah was not here. No. The Molina kid had made the smart move. Applied early. Before the humiliating cattle call. Mariah was less than half Temple's age, and she was already a finalist, a contender. Temple was a raw recruit.

Temple, aka Xoe Chloe—"pronounced just 'Zoey Chloey,' or 'Chloey Zoey' if you like that better," she'd told the babe with the clipboard collecting their application forms—stared down the endless line forward, and then back along the endless line backward.

It felt creepily like instant aging in a horror movie to be bracketed by so many *genuine* tender young things. Skin creamy as a South Beach diet ricotta cheese dessert. Zits, yes, but young, plump, cherry-colored zits, almost beauty marks, not the occasional pale pink spot staking a pallid postdated claim on the shoulder blade of thirty years' duration.

Well, she had the right shoes. A girl could do anything with the right shoes: go to the ball, leave Oz, shave a decade or so off her age. Temple stared at her Heavy Metal Hot Pink Funk–painted toenails in their red rhinestone slides. Excellent color clash. The toe rings added a nice trashy touch. Her feet alone demanded a serious redo.

Then there was the black, straight-haired Cher wig from the singer's Cleopatra period. Las Vegas had wig shops galore filled with celebrity dos. Even Temple was amazed by how totally a redhead with short curly hair could vanish behind glossy dark eyebrow-length bangs and shoulder blade–brushing strands of thick black. A Maybelline black eyebrow pencil covered the last of Temple's natural coloring. Any freckles disappeared under pale foundation and dead-white face powder accoutered with assorted magnetic studs and rings at eyebrow, nose, and lip, adding a modern touch to the Queen of the Nile. And she hadn't forgotten the belly button ring, clip-on. She was a fraud from sole to poll.

Except for her long painted fingernails, each one a color of the rainbow. They were real under that lacquer.

When she'd given her remade self a once-over in the bedroom mirror, for a surreal moment she was struck by the fact that she almost resembled the black-haired, rice-powdered persona of the evil she-magician, Shangri-La, who had kidnapped Temple and Midnight Louie months before. Now Shangri-La was missing in action and Temple was, *ta-dah*, suddenly a black-haired teen bad girl. Think the twisted slayer Faith on *Buffy, the Vampire Slayer.*

But that was then, and this was now. Temple shuffled forward in the line. Her feet were killing her. Normally wimpy little inch-and-a-half heels wouldn't bother her. But she was used to flying around, on the job. Standing, shuffling, on these aggregate-stone mall floors. Killer!

She clutched the sheet she'd filled out in tilted block letters with the *i*'s carefully topped by circles as fat as a cartoon dialogue balloon. Favorite hunk. Favorite punk band. Favorite junk food. Favorite class to skip. Favorite cosmetic. Favorite fast food.

She peered around the snaking line of bare shoulders and barely covered rears. Oh, at last! She glimpsed a long table at which people actually sat. They must be the interviewers, the *American Idol*–style judges who would say yea or neigh.

Nay! This was not a horse race. *This was an empowering opportunity for today's savvy young women.* Was she quoting the TV show propaganda, or what?

Stand. Shuffle. Shuffle, shuffle, shuffle. Stand.

Behind her, someone snapped her gum. A nauseous odor of banana-strawberry almost put Temple down for the count. A woman of thirty ought never have to smell that again!

Suddenly . . . open air ahead of her. A table clothed in linen to the floor. Four adult humans sitting behind it. All looking at her.

Four maybe-human adults . . .

Because one of them was (gasp!) Savannah Ashleigh, fading film starlet and an acquaintance.

Another was (gasp!) a very ripe Elvis impersonator, big and bellied, complete with tinted aviator sunglasses, long, dark caterpillar-fuzzy sideburns, neck scarf, glitzy white jumpsuit and more knuckle-buster diamond rings than Liberace. Well, she supposed Elvis had been an expert on teenage girls, including his almost-child bride, Priscilla.

Another was (double gasp)—once you're thinking in terms of cartoon bubbles you're lost—her very own maternal aunt, Kit Carlson, aka the romance novelist Sulah Savage!!! What was she doing here, all the way from New York City?

And the last (thank whatever gods may be!) was a Strange Man who looked like Simon Cruel, i.e., Cowell, on *American Idol.*

Two of the four judges knew Temple Barr, for better or worse. Was this going to be a cakewalk or a shambles or what?

More like, or what.

Temple, ex-TV newswoman . . . ex-community theater thespian . . . former repertory theater PR woman . . . decided to regard this debacle as an opportunity to stretch her dramatic muscles, i.e., her I.Q. Insincerity Quotient.

"Zoo-ee," Savannah Ashleigh was reading from her cheat sheet with her usual skill at the cold read, rhyming *Zoh-ee* with gooey.

"*Zoh-ee,*" Aunt Kit corrected. Smartly.

"A zoo, all right," the Simon clone bellowed loud

enough to reach the back of the line. His diction was Aussie, not British, but just as scalding as Simon's. "Child. Give those capris back to the zebras, there's a good sheila. 'Twould be a mercy."

"Mercy," Elvis repeated, frowning down at his sheet. He probably needed reading glasses. (The real Elvis would be—my gosh!—seventyish by now.) Maybe this guy's vision would lose focus going from the sheet to her.

"So why are you here, my dear?" a woman with a wireless mike popped out of nowhere to ask. She was almost as astounding as Xoe Chloe. A woman past early middle age was a rarity on TV and this one was fighting age all the way: phony black-dyed hair, all Shirley Temple ringlets where Temple's was all long, razor-cut bob. Her papery complexion emphasized baby bright blue eyes and an attitude of relentless good cheer.

Temple shrugged. It directed attention to her shoulder with the temporary tattoo: a tail-lashing crocodile.

"If you don't know, lady, I don't know. Somebody said I should. I'm blowing this gig. It's been unreal."

"Now wait a minute." Savannah was squinting at Temple, sans the glasses she obviously needed. "You look—"

Temple cringed, expecting the dreaded word, "familiar."

The Ann Landers with the mike seized her arm. "This girl is not all brash insouciance. She's got goose bumps."

So would anyone with those vanilla-ice-painted talons running crosswise on her forearm!

"You can see she's trying to make a statement," Savannah said. "Girls these days think they have to be so hard. You can be a lady and succeed."

"Why?" Temple answered. "You obviously didn't."

"What d-d-do you mean?" Savannah was stuttering. "Succeed or be a lady?"

"Both. I'm outa here. I got a grunge band to run."

"Really?" Elvis had finally exchanged his shades for a pair of half-glasses to read her entry blank. He regarded her over their rainbow titanium rims. "I think you're all bluster and sass, young lady. I think you're a fake."

Coming from him . . . now Temple was considering stuttering.

"But a sublime fake, mate," the Australian Simon was saying. "This girl has cheek. Love that bicep croc. And the underlying sentiment: 'Green Machine.'"

"You would," Aunt Kit noted. "You're nearly breaking your neck to see what those hip-huggers are embracing from behind."

Temple, recognizing her advantage, shook her Cher locks and her booty at one and the same time. "Dream on, old dude."

At that moment, the middle-aged angel with the mike—she really did remind Temple of the good witch Glinda from *The Wizard of Oz* movie, all that chirpy upbeat optimism—thrust herself into Temple's field of vision. Cameras were rolling from the sidelines.

"I'm Beth Marble, creator of this show. And I sense, dear girl, that despite your bold front, you're really desperate to make the cast. Isn't that true?"

Temple eyed the Simon-clone. "I think he's the one into bold fronts." Then she stared into the emcee's impossibly sincere eyes, heard that impossibly syrupy voice, and managed to nod, gruffly. If one can nod gruffly, Xoe Chloe was the girl for the job.

The four judges' vastly incompatible heads were nodding together as annotated pages passed back and forth.

Scratch "annotated." Not a Xoe Chloe word. How about . . . pages scribbled with cool graffiti.

"Do you do anything entertaining?" Elvis looked up over his granny rims to ask.

"The lambada," she said, "while clipping my toenails."

"At least she confesses to clipping them," Savannah ventured. "That's a start. We could really fix her look, but—"

They all frowned at Xoe Chloe. Temple sensed she was

losing her audience, particularly Simon Pieman, whose real name was Dexter Manship, and who was sitting back with his arms crossed over his designer T-shirted chest, one bicep bearing a Crocodile Hunter tattoo. No sell, the body language screamed.

Temple thought she knew the type and what pulled his Hell's Angel's chain. She boogied around in a tight little circle, all the better to show off the back of her waist-high thong panties almost fully revealed by the plunging low-rise capris. Rise? Heck, they'd never heard the word.

Temple'd seen this classless getup on a teen mall salesgirl at Frederick's of Hollywood last week, her attention drawn to the outfit by a pair of clucking old ladies. She had proudly and promptly appropriated it for bad girl Xoe.

Dexter was moved to chuckle. "I said she was cheeky. Let her in. We could use a juvenile delinquent."

Aunt Kit was frowning at Xoe's sheet, looking like someone about to cast a dissenting vote. Temple nailed her with a quick, pleading look the instant Kit looked up, her mouth already open and the no verdict on the tip of her tongue.

Temple watched long enough to see the surprised expression forming, then looked away, defiantly sullen. Actresses ran on empathy and prided themselves on seeing beneath the surface. Aunt Kit should be a shoo-in now, and Simon Pieman was all Xoe's—muscles, tattoo, and libido. But the Elvis impersonator . . . what was he doing here, except maybe as a tribute to the Elvis-loving man who'd built the house and was now long gone. And maybe because Elvis, dead or alive, real or false, always drew a crowd.

Temple did a series of three quick-on-her-feet cramp rolls and assumed a *West Side Story* stance. "Hey, Officer Elvis, you ever do any break dancing during your film career?"

"Break dancing? I invented it in my 'Jailhouse Rock' routine." He seemed surprised she had appealed to him as a dancer. No, shocked. His persona was mired in the seventies. His Vegas audiences were determinedly middle-middle-middle. Middle-aged, middle-class, middle-of-the-road.

"I do the mosh pit thing," she said. "You'd go over big today if you had one."

He laughed at the idea of a bunch of moshing middle-middle-middles, then glanced at the others. "I might be able to teach this one something, if she'll listen."

"Why, Mr. Presley, I would always listen to you . . . sing."

"You talk tough, Xoe Chloe," he answered sternly, "but you haven't worked until you've worn your tail and toes off on a rockabilly dance floor. Are you game?"

"Sure. I got rhythm."

"Thank you. Thank you verra much."

On that surreal closing note, the judges conferred again, checked their watches, eyed the long line behind Temple, and the anxious face of the woman named Beth Marble who held the portable mike. And was possibly the real power here.

"In," Dexter Manship declared for them all.

Temple got in a mock curtsy before she allowed herself to be hustled off to the sidelines by another gofer with clipboard. She was in. In! She'd made it, purely on her hidden punk power. Her Inner Bad Girl.

The gofer, one of the twenty-something girls in hot pink who ran errands, sat Xoe Chloe down with another sheaf of papers to sign.

Xoe could have cared less, but Temple read every last word, appalled at giving blanket permission to be recorded in every media known to man and woman but mostly audio-video, in all forms, now and in the future. In the universe.

She'd be ceding all rights to her own self . . . except that own self was purely fictitious at the moment. Luckily, the phony driver's license Molina somehow got for her attested that "Sharon Carlson"—*please!* No wonder "Zoe Chloe" had been born—was nineteen and therefore free to sign away her own rights to privacy.

She finally signed the thing with an *X* for Xoe and dated it.

Miss Pretty in Pink came back and asked for a real name.

"It is a real name. Mine."

"We need a normal name."

"I'm as normal as you are," Temple said. Being a teenager again was more fun than the first time! You could act out and act up and everyone thought it was the norm.

"I need a real last name," the hot pink chick repeated.

Temple rolled her eyes, sighed, grabbed the clipboard and wrote "Ozone" after the *X*.

"X Ozone? I don't think so."

"Have you ever heard of the Artist Formerly Known As Prince?"

"Maybe."

"He used an alien scribble for years. In purple ink yet. I think it was algebra. Surely you've heard of algebra? Why can't I be X Ozone? It's better than X Chromosome."

Miss Pink frowned. "Chromosome. I've heard of that name. Somewhere. Maybe it's Greek."

"See! I'm famous."

"Is there an apostrophe between the *O* and the *Z*?"

That gave Temple pause. "Yes, two," she said. "Just chill."

The woman put the equivalent of quote marks after the *O* and darted away on her pert pink patent-leather slides.

She was back in about two minutes after conferring with the angel lady with the mike.

"I'm sorry. We need a real last name. Like legal."

She hadn't asked for Temple's *real* last name.

"Carlson," Temple said, appropriating her mother's maiden name, and her aunt's, which Molina had somehow come up with. She added the name to the X with a flourish.

"Carlson. Isn't that a cavern somewhere?"

"In the brain," Temple said soberly. "You're right. A cavern in the brain. We all have a Carlson cavern in the brain."

"I knew I learned something in science class." Beaming, the young woman bore away all the rights to Temple's brand-new persona.

Shoot.

Chapter 12

Turnabout Foul Play

"Stabbed through the neck," Officer Dunhill said. He was young and looked a trifle green. "The entry point is ragged. Really vicious."

Molina stood there in the lukewarm early morning dark of another 24/7 Las Vegas eternity. She'd asked to be called on any teen deaths.

The girl lay in the middle of one row, halfway between the fat painted line that delineated parking places on either side. Probably attacked just as she was leaving, or about to return to a car.

All the cars were gone now, and the girl remained. Sprawled within an invisible chalk outline. (Police departments seldom outlined body positions nowadays; recording methods, especially video, were far too sophisticated to require the romance of old-time techniques.) The blood from the neck wound was a discreet rivulet mostly hidden by shadow. A lurid pool of pink puddled near one hand that still touched a crushed ice cream cone. Walking to the mall with a strawberry cone in her hand.

"Where'd that come from?"

Dunhill eyed the sickly pink splotch vaguely shaped like Australia. "Parking lot mobile vendor. My partner did the interview. She bought the cone at seven fifty."

"So she could have been headed for the Teen Queen auditions at eight o'clock."

"With a fistful of calories?" He sounded doubtful.

"Hot night. Slim girl. I'll have the reality show people check if any candidates didn't show up. I assume there was ID."

He nodded, flipped back a couple of pages. "Tiffany Cummings." He shook his head. "Sixteen. Wasn't sexually molested, from the state of her clothes. That's a blessing."

Molina eyed the clothes in question—the teenage uniform that drove a mother like Molina nuts for a couple of reasons: tight low-rise jeans, skimpy thin top. Too revealing, too predictable.

Dunhill shook his head again. Obviously he hadn't been called out on many homicides. "First response couldn't do anything for her. Except get the names and addresses of all the owners who'd parked in the vicinity."

"Any hot prospects?"

"Mostly women or women with children. All shocked to death themselves."

"That many women? Alone? Shopping this late, in the dark?" Molina asked.

Dunhill shrugged. "Multitasking. The wife complains all the time that there aren't enough hours in the day. All we've got here as onsite evidence is a short rubber burn and an air-conditioning puddle over there. Looks like a car stopped fast and stayed long enough to leave traces."

"Or to startle and then kill our vic." Molina glanced up at the brilliant lighting. This poor girl had been "shined" like a deer in the headlights by the very technology meant to protect her.

"They held the Teen Queen auditions here today," she observed. "This could be another message."

"That's right! I heard about the mutilated Barbie doll images. You think this is related?"

"I think this is going to be pretty hard to explain to the press, much less the parents. I'll ask the captain in the morning for more personnel to put on the so-called Teen Queen Castle that reality TV show is using for the next two weeks. Can you imagine a more captive population for a killer like this?"

"For this nut? Likes offbeat weapons. Nervy enough to attack in a major public place. No, Lieutenant, I can't. Hey!" Dunhill was looking beyond her. "Get outa here! Scat!"

By the time she whipped around, all she spotted was a lean dark shape vanishing under a Nissan Sentra.

"Damn cat." Dunhill was not happy. "Sniffing at the evidence. That pinkish gunk."

"Probably licking at it. Lots of scavenger cats and birds around a shopping mall. Forensics will have already bagged a sample; don't worry, officer."

"This is my first murder call. Then to have it be a kid like this—"

"Kids 'like this' you never get used to, thank God. What did you say her name was?"

"Tiffany—" He again checked his notebook. "Cummings."

"That contest inside. Find out if she was a contender."

"She sure isn't now." He slapped his notebook shut.

Mariah was still safe at home in her messy bedroom, thank goodness, Molina thought, but tomorrow night she wouldn't be. Her kid had made the final cut. Tomorrow she'd be in the Teen Queen Castle, hopefully safe behind a moat of cameras and the foolishness that passed for network TV these days.

Molina returned to her Toyota, parked far enough from the crime scene to preserve evidence. Something about the crime scene bothered her but she couldn't say just what.

Someone caught up with her.

"What's going on?" A voice behind her.

She turned. "Larry. What're you doing here?"

"Heard the buzz. Now that I'm off undercover, I can't sleep nights. Did too much action then. So I listen to what's going down on the police channels. Looks like a tragedy." He nodded back toward the fallen girl.

"Sixteen? Yeah, a tragedy."

He scanned the mall's hulking profile, haloed by the city's constant aurora of artificial light. "The most innocent public places are where the dirtiest deals go down. Malls. Hotel parking lots. No safe place anymore."

"Not news."

"You've got a kid. Is she too young for malls by herself?"

"Young," she conceded, recalling the recent madcap shopping expedition with the trace of a smile. "And not 'young' enough for my taste."

"That's why you care. That's why you came out personally."

Molina shook her head, leaned against her car's front fender. "No. That wouldn't keep me up nights. It's a case, that's all."

"Are you sure it isn't personal?"

"Anyone killed on my watch is personal."

"That's a lot of responsibility, Lieutenant."

"Goes with the job title."

He leaned against the car beside her. He'd be sorry.

She recalled that it was dusty. Who had time to visit a car wash? Multitasking.

"I, ah, lost that sense of being personally responsible," he said. "I miss it. I was responsible for living up to my false identity. Period. It took all my energy and all my cunning."

"Cunning. I think of that as a criminal attribute."

"Right. I needed criminal attributes."

"Must be hard to drop."

"The hours are. Let me follow you home, make sure you get there."

"Are you kidding? I can't drive this town at night alone, why have a firearm or a shield?"

"I'm trying to be a regular guy here."

"Why?"

"Maybe because I think you might have a regular girl in there somewhere."

"Regular equals helpless?"

"Regular equals liking company."

"Not now. I'm not a babysitter for insomniac narcs. I've got my own baby to sit."

He backed off, literally. "Sorry. You're right. I shouldn't have come out. I'm just not used to being out of the loop, that's all. Guess I just wanted to bullshit about the crime scene, whatever. Talk the talk. See a . . . friendly face."

She could've sworn he was about to have said "pretty."

Unbelievable! But maybe she was doing him an injustice.

Sensing her irritation, he shifted topics. "That guy you tried to con me out of. You know, the address the other night. I'm betting that *he's* personal."

"If he is, then it's really none of your business."

He ignored her warning. "Ex-cop. L.A. I see that's where you came here from."

"I see that you've been digging deeper into personnel records."

"You did it first. Karlinski in Records mentioned it to me."

Molina felt her face heat up, whether from annoyance or being caught, she couldn't tell.

"Listen." He came closer and lowered his voice. "Undercover cops know better than most that the lines between professional and personal can get blurred in police work. You wanted to take something from me without my knowing it. Think what a lot more you could get if you were up front about it. That Nadir guy is trouble, I can smell it, and he worries you. Accidents isn't putting me to work 24/7, the way I used to work. I got a lotta free hours. I could help."

"You're volunteering? For what?"

"Whatever you need."

"Why?"

"I'm bored."

"Not what I need."

"And I think you could use more of a social life."

She pushed off her car. "What would give you that idea? That's the last thing I want, need, have time for."

"Case closed."

"I don't even like you."

"Not a problem." He grinned. "I'm still losing my street persona. I'll get cuddlier."

"Give it up. You are not my type."

"Oh, you think you have a 'type.' That's progress. Let me guess: tall, lean, and mean. Early Clint Eastwood, right?"

Molina felt herself flush for real. "You're pursuing this, not me."

"That's the way it's supposed to be, have you forgotten?"

"Maybe. And I like it that way." She opened her car door, paused, considered, and said "Good-night."

He backed away to let her drive out of the parking slot,

hands in the pockets of his nylon shell jacket, watching her with head lowered, a bit boyishly.

She headed into the maze of access roads that circled the mall.

Not her type.

But better than Rafi Nadir.

Although, who wasn't?

At home, sweet home Dolores napped on the couch while early-morning TV blared. Molina hated to awaken her, but she knew Dolores would want to be home with her own kids and husband. So she saw her out and watched her cross the street to her own door and safely enter.

In the distance, low-riders grumbled like very disgruntled thunder. That was a negative of living in a Latino neighborhood, but in Anglo neighborhoods it would be costly car stereo systems cranked up loud enough to keep the canals on Mars awake. One way or another, the young bucks in the neighborhood have to make their presence known.

Mariah was sleeping hard in her room, face buried in a tangle of covers.

Molina went to her bedroom and deposited her weapons in the closet gun safe. She could never open the large metal cabinet without brushing against Carmen's array of vintage velvet gowns. Velvet and steel. It sounded like the title of a supermarket romance novel.

Carmen hadn't come out to sing and play at the Blue Dahlia lately. Maybe the on-premises body a few months back had accomplished that. Maybe Molina had just been too busy.

She started taking off her clothes . . . shoes kicked off first. She slipped out of her jacket and blouse, slacks, then sat on the bed to pull off the dark socks she wore with her working "uniform."

Something slid into her back as her weight created a sinkhole for whatever was on the bed.

What *was* on the bed? Shouldn't be anything. She kept a military-neat room, unlike her darling daughter, the mistress of mess. . . .

A box lay there on her grandmother's patchwork quilt. A gaudy gilt-paper box. Had Mariah performed one of her random acts of preteen sweetness?

Molina opened it, not surprised by the array of fancy chocolates but by the unfamiliar handwriting on the tiny envelope inside.

She pulled the flap loose to withdraw the stiff note card. The same handwriting that had written "For you" on the envelope had written "Sweets to the sour" on the card inside.

She stood there staring at the black-ink block lettering in the dim light of the overhead ceiling fixture.

Was this some clumsy attempt at humor, or a threat?

Mariah, veering wildly in the bipolar state that was 'tweendom, might be apologizing and complaining at one and the same time. Or . . .

This might be from someone else. Like Dirty Larry. Was he a colleague, a would-be boyfriend . . . or a stalker? He was the only new man in her life . . . or was this a calling card from a former man in her life?

Rafi Nadir. Now that they'd finally run into each other, he knew that she lived and worked here in Las Vegas. He had a lot of reasons to resent her. *Sweets to the sour.* The line reeked of bitter anger; was it for leaving him without notice? Like you'd mention to a strike-poised rattlesnake that you'd decided to back off.

Had he found her address after she'd visited him the other night without warning to give *him* a warning? Turnabout foul play?

Molina spun on her bare heels and padded through the hall and living room into the kitchen. There she ransacked drawers looking for something she ought to remember right where it was.

Damn! Whoever had left that candy was no friend and maybe a lot worse. She marched back to her compromised bedroom, plastic sandwich baggies in hand. The note went in one baggie via the offices of the new tweezer from her adjoining bathroom. The box went into the quart-size bag, for analysis by forensics. She'd think of some reason in the morning.

For now . . . she went through the house from garage to seldom-used front door, checking closets and locks.

All secure, doors dead bolted, sashes nailed shut yet easy to open in case of fire. The place was a freaking monument to advocated domestic security measures, courtesy of your local police department.

So. Someone had gotten in, and gone. And left the poison. Maybe not literal poison but mental poison. *Who's been creeping into my bed with Ethel M candies?*

She didn't even want to finish undressing to don her Land's End sleep-size T-shirt.

But she did.

Then she unlocked the gun safe, set the semiautomatic on her nightstand, and shot the bolt on her bedroom door so Mariah couldn't wander in.

The illuminated nightstand clock said four-twenty A.M.

Molina was thinking now that she might actually welcome having Mariah out of the house and under the constant surveillance of reality TV show cameras for the next couple weeks.

What's a mother to do?

If she's a homicide lieutenant, maybe a lot more than some cowardly stalker might imagine.

Chapter 13

Macho Nachos

"Dinner? At your place?"

Matt knew he had sounded unflatteringly shocked, but it was too late to backpedal. That was another disadvantage to years spent in the priesthood: an inability to shift rapidly into glib social lies.

"Just casual," Molina said quickly. "I've got some issues I want to bounce off you."

These must be *some issues* to merit a social occasion at Casa Molina, Matt thought.

"Yeah, fine. I'm always available for dinner."

"Usually, I'm not. But, what say, six thirty tomorrow?"

Very pressing issues. "Sure. That's perfect. Saturday night supper. I'm leaving town for a few days early next week."

"Glad I caught you before you left. We'll have something, oh . . . something. See you then."

Matt stared at the phone receiver for a moment before

replacing it. Molina was always busy when she was at work, and she was almost always at work.

He immediately dialed Temple's number, but after five rings her slightly raspy voice informed him she'd had to leave town on a family matter and would be back in two weeks or so.

This time he stared at the receiver as if it were an alien artifact.

Curiouser and curiouser. Guess he'd have to go take two hours' worth of lonely hearts phone calls at WCOO-AM, which is what paid his bills, and find out what was going on with the hearts and minds he thought he knew later.

The morning paper had a splashy front-page story about the young woman found dead outside the shopping mall.

Matt skimmed the report, which was all too similar to other senseless killings in every city and town across the country: savage attack, senseless slaughter, and another family torn apart by another demented killer.

So . . . surely Molina would cancel their casual dinner. She must be on this case 24/7.

The cancellation call never came. Matt changed his knit golf shirt to a long-sleeved shirt that matched his khakis, rolled up the sleeves to the elbow, and headed over to Our Lady of Guadalupe convent at about five thirty.

He found the nuns preparing dinner. They let him kibbutz while they bustled around the communal kitchen. Convent life had been characterized as "communistic" in the big, bad fifties when a Red was seen under every bed, but Matt would call it "democratic."

Each nun had her duty and went about washing salad greens or stirring soup as if that were the most important task on earth. Next week the duty roster would change and today's washer would become that week's stirrer. Just as today's mother superior would defer to another leader when the time came.

Peter and Paul, the stray cats that had unofficially joined the community when they'd wandered into the convent yard as kittens, had arranged themselves in supervisory positions. Peter, a chubby yellow striped cat, was tolerated on one chair seat, while the darker striped Paul was lying on the wide windowsill above the sink, absently patting at the intermittent faucet drips.

There was a placid joy in the way the nuns moved, with long familiarity and an efficient grace that brought to mind the floor-length, flowing habits they'd once all worn, still welcoming a visitor to their modest domestic ritual as if he were a king, or a wandering saint.

"How's that darling redheaded girl?" Sister Seraphina, Matt's former grade school teacher at St. Stanislaus in Chicago, asked right up front. That was "Sister Superfine," dynamic and blunt. "I never see her at mass with you anymore."

"She's Unitarian," Matt explained, or didn't really.

But the nun just nodded and invited him to dinner. He was tempted, but. . . .

"Not this time. I've got a dinner appointment in the parish, though."

"A date?" Elderly Sister St. Rose of Lima beamed the way nuns who like to play matchmaker do.

It touched Matt that his past in the priesthood was taken as a given here. He'd been officially laicized, leaving with permission, unlike most ex-priests. But like all newly ex-priests, he was still sensitive about his new noncelibate status. He found it endearing how these elderly "sisters"—the last, almost, of their uniquely devoted kind—gave him a free pass on their own turf.

"Not a 'date.'" I'm heading over to Lieutenant Molina's."

Eyebrows raised.

"Those aren't exclusive subjects," outspoken Sister Seraphina said. "Carmen Molina has achieved commendable responsibility in her job but she's not a lieutenant all the time."

"I couldn't swear by that. I think she wants to find out something that relates to her job."

"How do you know that?"

"Molina? Entertain for dinner?"

Sister Seraphina stopped bustling and folded her arms. "Too much work and no play is bad for everybody. Carmen too. Maybe you can get her to forget about her job for a few hours."

"That would be an act of charity," Sister Mary Monica said slyly.

Matt laughed and headed for the door. "Gossip is a sin, sisters. Don't get any ideas."

Their chorus of good-byes drifted out the screen door behind him like a breeze.

Trying to second-guess Molina was futile.

Matt pulled his new silver Crossfire to the curb in front of her house, got out, and heard a low wolf whistle.

She was standing on the threshold of her seldom-used front door.

"Not you. The car," she said. "When did you develop ambitions to race in the Grand Prix?"

"It just looks fast. And I finally didn't need an undercover car," he added, referring to his former stalker, as he came up the walk.

"Better stay at the speed limit. That's a real ticket-magnet. At least it isn't red."

This was a Molina he'd never seen. She was wearing a gauzy white puffed-sleeve blouse and paprika-and-turquoise-pattern gauze skirt. Mexican casual. And she was barefoot. She looked fifteen years younger and about twenty-five years more relaxed.

Still no jewelry, though, and no makeup except for a faint color on her lips.

Matt thought he'd never seen her looking better.

"Maybe we can go for a spin in the Crossfire after dinner," he suggested.

She laughed, and looked beyond him to the fancy car a bit ruefully. Maybe Sister Seraphina was right.

"This is a no-diet zone tonight," she warned as she led him into the modest one-story house.

"You diet?" He was surprised. She was a strong five-ten, at least. Neither heavy nor thin. Sculptural, like a pillar, especially in those long, lean vintage velvet gowns from the forties she wore when singing at the Blue Dahlia.

Few knew that Carmen the occasional chanteuse was C. R. Molina, the 24/7 Vegas homicide cop. Those who did found the contrast perplexing.

"I thought you'd call this off," he commented as they entered the homey living room, complete with two cats. What was it about cats and the Our Lady of Guadalupe neighborhood?

She turned to fix him with a Lieutenant Molina interrogatory stare. Her vivid blue eyes were her best feature, and against this Ole Mexico getup they made her electrically exotic.

"Why?" she asked. "Oh. The murder. There are always murders in Las Vegas, my friend."

"I just thought you'd need to be on the job."

"What makes you think I'm not?" she asked with some irritation.

"I don't see myself as part of your job."

"No. No, you're not. Sorry. Sit down, get some cat hair on those khakis. I'm glad you could come."

She clattered and rustled in the kitchen until the microwave tinged and then she brought out several small vivid pottery dishes of various salsas and a big platter of nacho chips wearing a mantle of cheese and sliced fresh jalapeños.

Matt grabbed a big blue linen napkin and dug in. "This is better than Friday's," he said.

"Yeah. A lotta Velveeta, a little Rotel, some fresh peppers to tart the whole thing up. Sorta like tonight."

Matt stopped scarfing and got wary. "Oh?"

"I got you out here on false pretenses," she admitted.

"Fast food?"

"Fast talking. I need your advice."

"Oh. Well, that comes with the territory. 'Will advise for food.'"

"I'm not good at plying my . . . acquaintances for free advice."

"Well, then break out the Dos Equis. That'll get me talking. You do have some?"

"Oh, my God! I forgot the beer."

Matt smiled as her bare feet slapped kitchen tile and the refrigerator door shot a sliver of light into the dim living room.

The cats yawned and stretched, as if used to slapdash improvisation in feeding at Casa Molina.

Matt hated to admit it, but the nachos with bottled salsa sauce were superb: hot, greasy, and crispy.

A condensation-dewed long neck of Dos Equis landed on a cork coaster on the coffee table in front of him. By now the jalapeños had hit pay dirt on his tongue and he downed several swallows.

"Milk would be better," she observed.

"Not manly," Matt said, still choking a little. "Okay. What's it all about, Alfie?" he looked around, suddenly aware. "Is Mariah off with her friends?"

"Yes, and no. And, yes, we are alone here. I arranged it that way."

"Really? Is this entrapment? This is very low-alcohol-content beer."

"Only entrapment for your professional opinion."

"You didn't have to ply me with dinner for that."

She sat back on her tailbone in her chair, balancing her beer bottle on her stomach. This was no Molina he'd ever imagined.

"Mariah is away from home for a couple of weeks."

"What does that mean?"

"It means that my naive, gutsy daughter got herself accepted by some stupid, exploitative reality TV show, and Mama couldn't say no without being cursed for life. So . . ."

"Wait a minute! Is that the Teen Queen thing?"

"And 'Tween Queen," she corrected with loathing. "Mariah thinks she wants to be a singing star and win a date with the latest Boy Toy nonsinger around. What's a mother to do? I could take any casino boss in town in for questioning, but I can't put a leash on my only daughter."

Matt chewed some nachos while he thought about it. "No, you're right. You can't. She got accepted? On her own?"

"Yeah. Every kid has access to a video recorder nowadays."

"Mariah? She's just a baby."

"Are you out of it! This is not what I want your advice on. Here. Watch her homemade video. The one that got her on the show."

Molina got up, skirts swaying, to pop in the offending video.

Matt began to understand her mixture of panic and pride. Mariah had shot up. Those chubby baby features and limbs were starting to look coltish and graceful. Her eyes were as dark as her mother's were light, making Matt wonder about the father again. Likely Hispanic.

Molina was half and half, although what the other half was he couldn't guess.

Mariah's voice was a contralto that blared like a boom box on occasion. She was a belter, unlike her crooner mother, and suited the pop music mode of her own day. But she had a voice. Too.

Molina got up to eject the tape and dropped it atop the TV.

Matt decided it was time to gently probe at the maternal wounds. "So the problem is . . . Mariah is unrealistic about a performing career?"

"Who isn't unrealistic about a performing career? Everybody dreams. Maybe a tenth of one percent lives the dream. No, the kid can try it. She might break the odds. I think this freaking show is foolishness, but that's not the problem. It's possible that a killer is stalking the contestants."

"My God."

"I've got people on the stalker thing. That's not the big problem."

"What on earth could be, then?"

Molina leaned back, drained a bottle of Dos Equis, eyed the pathetic level in his own bottle, and got up.

"We're out of beer, and the chili on the stove is about to desiccate. Come, sit down and eat."

Chapter 14

Bad Daddy

The chili was red, full of beans and beef, and hot enough to fry the soles off a pair of Dr. Scholl's sandals.

Matt tucked in.

He and Molina sat at a small round table in a tiny bay window off the kitchen. He sensed this nook was hardly ever used for dining. Instead, quick bites were taken at the elbow-height eating bar between the kitchen and the living room.

Molina had poured their beers into thick glass mugs chilled in the refrigerator. Correction: Carmen had done that.

"So the problem—" Matt began when the first edge of his hunger had been soothed.

She had only picked at her chili—the plump bean here, the chunk of ground beef there. An occasional ring of soft-cooked jalapeño. She leaned back in her chair, suddenly Madame Interrogator again.

"You know what it's like to be a bastard."

Professional interrogator. Always went for shock value.

"Yeah. It means your mother is called names for the sin of being trusting and honest. Is there a woman in the world who gets caught in such a situation who anticipated it, or wanted it?"

"Maybe only the Virgin Mary."

"She got a warning from an angel."

"So. I know you resented, even hated, your stepfather. Have you also resented your real father?"

"This business of 'real' parents is interesting. There are genetic parents, and spiritual parents, and stepparents. Any and all of them can be horrible, or great."

"I don't need generalizations."

"That's mostly what's out there, like it or not."

"I like it not." She took a swallow from the beer mug. "Mariah's father is in town."

"The guy . . . from Los Angeles? Your—?"

"Yeah. My 'question mark.' I tried to divert him by setting Kinsella on his trail but then I ended up with two snakes on mine."

"How does Max come into this?"

"*Max!* Even that's a damn anagram, not a given name. *Michael Aloysius Xavier* Kinsella. The man's a puzzle from the most elementary fact."

"All good Irish-Catholic given names," Matt said, savoring the effect.

"Like Matthias," she lashed back.

"Not particularly Irish Catholic. Look, I know this is serious, but I also think you're seriously hung up on Max Kinsella. He's not the father of your child, and that's who's really got you riled."

She huffed out a sigh, part anger, and part exasperation. "You're right about that. Screw Max Kinsella. He's off my most-wanted list. It's this other guy."

"You mentioned him to me a long while back. The one you were living with in L.A. who got you into that ethical corner of unwanted pregnancy. To abort or not to abort. Didn't you think he'd pushed a pin through your diaphragm?"

"I can't believe I'm sitting here discussing this in depth with a priest."

"What do you think I did all those years of being a priest? Discussed the unthinkable with the unwilling. I've heard it all."

"But you haven't lived it all."

"No. That's my weakness."

"What's mine?"

"You think you've lived it all. So this guy is here in town now."

"Worse. He's finally put two and two together. He realizes I live and work here. Next thing, he'll find out about Mariah. Your little friend is pretty helpful in that quarter."

"Temple? How so?"

"She's hooked up with him somehow. She fairly reveled in having him pretend to nab a perp in my last case. I admit I was on her about Kinsella but that's no reason to sell a thirteen-year-old down the river."

"Wait a minute. Temple wouldn't do that. She doesn't know this guy is Mariah's father."

"You didn't tell her?"

"No. The time you mentioned it to me, he didn't have a name, much less a local mailing address. I'd have never told Temple anything about it. That was . . . confidential."

"Confessionally secret?"

"Not technically, but as far as I was concerned. I'd virtually forgotten about it. Believe me, Carmen. No one knows but you and me, and I'm not talking. Ever. Not even to you if you want it that way."

She took a deep breath, leaned back in her chair,

rubbed a hand over her forehead, disarranging her Dutch-cut bangs

"Never ever?"

"Never ever."

"Then do you think I have to tell Mariah about her so-called father, or vice versa? Can't he just go away?"

"What do you think?"

She paused to do just that. "There's unfinished business. He won't go away, now that he's found me, because I went away from him all those years ago."

"I can't believe Temple would champion him."

"I rode her about Kinsella for over a year. I imagine it's sweet revenge."

"Temple isn't vengeful."

"What you know about women I could put in a thimble."

"Do you sew? Not very useful then. So what are you asking me?"

"Do I need to let Mariah know about him before he finds out about her and tells her himself?"

Matt didn't hesitate a moment. "If there's the danger of the latter, yes."

"That is not what I wanted to hear."

"Yes, it is. You wanted to hear the truth from an uninvolved person. And you did."

"You're uninvolved?"

"Pretty much."

"What does that make you, then?"

"In worse shape than you are. Oughta be some comfort."

She smiled and scratched her neck. "Actually, it is."

Matt insisted on helping with the cleanup, which mostly involved soaking the dishes in one side of the sink while Tabitha patted the bubbles.

"You remember seeing me wear a blue velvet dress at the Blue Dahlia," Carmen asked out of the . . . well, blue.

"No. I remember a ruby-purple one. And black. But not blue."

"I've got one in my closet and can't ever remember wearing it, much less buying it."

"You don't wear them that often, do you? Especially lately."

"That a hint that I oughta climb back onto that stool and sing?"

"It must be hard to keep your voice up if you don't exercise it regularly."

"True."

The doorbell rang, catching them both with hands in soapy water.

Carmen tossed Matt a towel after she'd blotted her palms, and headed for the front door with raised eyebrows, obviously not expecting company.

Matt heard voices from the living room. The other one was male so he ambled out there, just in case, although Molina was a match for most men on the planet.

A guy about his size in a black jeans jacket was just inside the door, talking faster than a Fuller Brush man.

Seeing Matt stopped him dead. "You've got company, sorry. I thought you wanted these documents right away."

"Tomorrow at work would have done," Carmen was saying coolly, but her manner was edgy.

The guy was one of those dirty blonds whose face was all angles sharp enough to cut you. You could see him as the scrappy kind of kid who always got into playground fights. Tough in an oddly admirable way. He seemed too lean and hungry to be a beat cop; those guys tended to have sloppy beer bellies and neat mustaches, and the deceptively laid-back attitudes of those who know they're in authority.

In the ensuing silence, Carmen did introduction duties, clearly loathing every word.

"Larry Paddock, Matt Devine." She emphatically avoided saying what either of them was.

Paddock nodded, Matt nodded back.

Matt was the guy with chili powder on his breath, so Paddock had to leave.

He ducked his head and backed out, looking none too pleased.

Carmen put the small manila envelope, unopened, on the TV cabinet. "This job never leaves you alone." Larry Paddock's drive-by visit had broken the off-hours mood.

Matt fished for the car keys in his pocket, making leaving noises himself.

"Don't rush off," she said, "right after I've drafted you for manual labor."

Did she think Paddock might be waiting for him to go?

So he settled on the living room sofa and accepted a tiny glass of Tia Maria liqueur and commented on the cats until her unexpected visitor was long gone enough so he could go too.

The night outside was as warm as a sauna. Larry, he thought later. New one. Matt got in the Crossfire, sitting for a moment to lower the window for some breeze—now they had a convertible version out—and to savor the newness of everything, the new-car leather scent, the dramatically night-lit dashboard, before starting the engine. New Car Whine.

Carmen came running out of the house, her bare feet slapping concrete, and reached him before he could shift into reverse.

"Matt! Can you come back in for a moment?"

"What for?" Trust an ex-priest, on seeing a woman run after him, to know it was for some reason quite impersonal.

"To find out if I'm going freaking crazy or not."

Chapter 15

Sweet Tooth

Matt followed Carmen back into her house.

By the time he caught up with her, she was pacing back and forth in the tiny fifties foyer like a tiger in a rabbit cage.

"I can't believe it. While we were here talking! It had to be."

"What?"

"You have to see it. Come on."

He followed her through the living room and down the long narrow hall. Most of Las Vegas's older homes were one-story and built like rat mazes. What kept the sun out also kept the interiors dark and cramped. Matt had never been more appreciative of the Circle Ritz's round construction style. There, every unit had an outside wall of windows.

Matt was in her bedroom before he had time to think what a leap in intimacy that involved. He'd never been in any woman's bedroom before, except a guest room in a convent, which hardly counted. And Temple's. But only in passing.

This room wasn't such an exotic locale, after all. It was furnished with the usual suspects, in this case serviceable furniture store–style bed, dresser, and nightstand.

Molina was at her closet door, holding up a curtain of velvet for his inspection.

"First this." She shook it like Exhibit A in a courtroom.

He went over to see it better, recognizing one of the dark velvet vintage gowns she wore to sing at the Blue Dahlia.

"These old evening gowns are beautiful. What's wrong with it?"

"What's wrong with it is that I don't remember buying it. I have a deep forest-green one, a wine one, a scarlet one, and several black ones." She pulled the skirts of the gowns in question out into the light to illustrate her point. "I've never had a blue one."

"I don't see why not. It complements your eyes."

"You don't get it. This isn't a wardrobe crisis. I wasn't sure at first, but I never bought this thing. It just . . . appeared in my closet."

"You're busy. Super busy. You must have forgotten."

"That's what I thought. Until this arrived."

She threw the blue velvet gown across her bedspread and bent to pull a box from the lowest drawer in her nightstand.

Matt eyed the box. Not a simple square or rectangular box, but curvy. Candy-box shaped. He was beginning to get it. "How did it arrive?"

"Showed up on my bed. With a card."

Matt frowned at the handwritten note through the plastic baggie that encased it, displayed like a fresh scalp in Carmen's uplifted hand.

"'Sweets to the sour,'" she quoted the message inside. "The first really wrong note."

"'Note' indeed. Sour note. You baggied it."

"Yes, of course."

"Like you bagged Temple's waylaid ring from Max," he couldn't resist adding. She winced at the comparison. "So someone's been snooping in your closet."

"And now this. The latest. Just now!" She handed him a small plastic device, now bagged. It took him a moment to recognize the late-model Game Boy. Except someone had stuck a Post-it note on it reading "Game Girl."

"I found this in Mariah's bedroom. Thank God she's away from it for a while."

"You've got a stalker," Matt said quietly, remembering his recent and violent liberation from one. "Why, do you think?"

Carmen wrapped her hands around her elbows and began her Big Cat–pacing again. "I don't know, but whoever it may be is circling closer and closer. Classic pattern. Cowardly psychotic creep—!"

"I know. They're good at that. Sure can't be mine transferring affections to you."

"No. Nothing to do with you, except you were here when that piece of slime snuck this last little token into the house."

"Mariah's away, you said. How long ago could it have been left?"

"Six hours, maybe? I checked her room for anything she might have needed at the . . . at the place where she's staying. That little bomb wasn't there then."

"Where was it?"

"On her pillow."

"You're right to be upset. Can't you, of all people, arrange for surveillance?"

She stopped to hug her elbows to her rangy frame. "No. No, I of all people can't do that. Not openly. Not officially. This . . . stuff could be from her father."

Chapter 16

Monday Morning Coming Down

Xoe, aka Temple, arrived at Hell House, aka the Teen Queen Castle, first.

Cameras were rolling, and so was she.

In fact, she wore Rollerblades. And skin-tight capris, a sweatband reading *Go Gurrrl,* and a hot pink sports bra liberally assisted by various boob-building devices.

Xoe! *Zowie!*

The cameras followed her as she did a wheelie at the mansion's front door.

What an entrance. The doorway, not hers. Double doors, of course, of embossed copper with pewter hardware. The effect was more like the entrance to a bank vault than a residence.

She noted the security camera leering down from above and blew a huge bubble of well-chewed pink bubble gum right at it before she entered. On Rollerbladed feet.

Beth Marble, the show's guardian angel, was waiting for her in the marble-tiled foyer.

"No edged instruments allowed inside the house. That includes Rollerblades."

"That also include fingernails?" Temple fanned her impressive ten.

"Fingernails are feminine. Allowed."

"That's what you think." Temple bent to detach the Rollerblades.

"You're an interesting case."

"I thought a case had an alcohol content."

"You're not as tough as you act."

Duh!

Temple sneered. Being a *bad,* ballsy little broad, as Rafi Nadir had named her once, not mentioning the *bad,* was fun.

"Here, honey." She handed over the heavy, bulky blade set. "Hang this on your hope chest." She stared pointedly at the angel's decidedly flat version of same. "You need one."

No hope there.

"Listen, kiddo," the woman said, dropping her voice into a soft, warning tone. "I came up with the Teen Queen concept. Consider me the show shrink. Part of your makeover involves an improvement in attitude. If you want to have a chance at the Teen Queen slot, you'll use your time here, with me, to get that beehive-size chip off your shoulder."

"We gotta see each other?"

"Every day for an hour. Be prepared to open up your baggage or drop to the bottom of the first wave of wannabes on Day Three."

Xoe made a face but kept further comment to herself.

Beth thrust a shiny hot-pink folder toward her. "Here are the house rules and your daily schedule of self-improvement appointments. Remember, we work on body, mind, heart, and soul, so be prepared to bare all four."

"You sure this is legal? A lot of these girls are underage."

Beth's patient smile hinted at perennial martyrdom. "We're well aware of that. We're assigning rooms on a Big Sister/Little Sister basis, so roommates won't be competing at the same level. The name of your Little Sister is in the folder."

"A mini-me! How hip. Who *is* the little devilette?"

Temple let her long fingernails do the walking through the half-inch wad of loose papers inside the folder.

Mariah Molina. Her roomie. The gods, or at least the Great Goddess Cop, had smiled on her so she could ride shotgun with poor little Mariah.

Why any right-thinking kid would want to coop herself up in a phony media circus like this was beyond Temple, but then Temple was too far beyond the Teen Dream stage to remember.

Beth Marble glanced around all sides of Temple and then nodded her satisfaction.

"Glad you're not dragging any more than your one bag and your bad attitude in here. The 'Tween Queen branded sweat suits and other workout wear you'll be using during your makeover are in your room, in the proper size. Your personal stylist will confer with your personal trainer on your new wardrobe, when it's time for your 'reinvention.'"

"Meanwhile," Temple observed, "it's in the army now."

"That's right." Beth's *Stepford Wives* smile never faltered. "You are a private and we are the commanders. We're here to help you but only if you're willing to commit to helping yourself. You may go to your room until our Cheering Session at five P.M. tonight."

"It sounds more like PMS," Temple muttered as she shuffled off in her stocking feet.

"What?" Beth asked, a trifle uneasy.

"Nothing you're not too old for."

Two faint frown lines on Beth's forehead indicated she might have sensed an insult.

Awesome! The woman seemed made of the same impervious veneer as the remade toothy smiles on the women from the makeover shows.

The house was huge. It was a perfect pick for a castle because of the copper-topped towers that surrounded the huge copper dome at the place's center. These mysterious copper roofs glittered enough to be seen from the Strip. They'd been treated to keep their bright copper-bottom-pan gleam and not age into a verdigris color with wear and weather.

That new-penny look always bothered Temple when she glimpsed the place. It was rather like Burt Reynolds during his cosmetic face-peel stage: so shiny and smooth that it gave you the creeps.

It especially gave Temple the creeps. Las Vegas was the kind of high-profile place where new scandals and sensations constantly made yesterday's atrocity fade into prehistory. Yet she'd learned the horrific history of this house when she'd first come to town two years ago. And a good PR person never forgets.

Over the past twenty or so years, the house had been a white elephant, huge and impossible to reinvent. It had been a Halloween spook-show place for a while. A theme restaurant. (Middle-Eastern, with the Disneyesque Neuschwanstein castle towers appropriately repainted as minarets.) A funeral home. That was the weirdest and last incarnation. And lately, it had stood perilously empty, inviting vandals, until it had been turned into the set for a presumably hot reality TV show.

The first time it had made media news, it had just been another sprawling tribute to big money and minuscule taste.

Temple was one up on the other contestants.

As a media person, she'd heard of the bizarre tragedy that had made this place the house that no one wanted to own. The builder had been Arthur Dickson, a reclusive techno-geek who'd wired it for every media known to man at the time and filled it with high-tech toys and Elvis trivia. He'd gotten married here to a former showgirl and mother of a young daughter, who reportedly topped him by six inches. . . . Of course, the marriage disintegrated in a haze of vindictive heat over sex and money. During the trial separation, the wife and stepdaughter got the house.

It ended with a big shoot-out one night. When it was over, the stepdaughter was seriously maimed, caught in the crossfire; the showgirl-wife had been shot in the shoulder, her male friend had been killed, and the husband had vanished.

Since then, no one had seen Arthur Dickson, the man who'd bought and rebuilt this mansion in tribute to Elvis. He was presumed dead. A second cousin had later brought suit charging that his body had been spirited away, because after seven years his estate had reverted to the wife and he had been declared dead.

So Temple approached this house with the notion that it had best served its history when it had been a funeral parlor, not the set for a frivolous TV program.

The doorbell pealed out "You Ain't Nothin' But a Hound Dog."

It reminded Temple that Dickson had been an Elvis nut. The place boasted a grotto outside the pool fit for a mass burial. But Graceland it was not. This house had a purely Las Vegas mystique, from the copper-domed four-story towers along the sprawling façade to the rumored wine cellar vault in the bowels of an unusual Las Vegas real estate feature, a basement.

Temple edged into the entry hall, not knowing what to expect but ready for anything.

At least Xoe Chloe was.

Chapter 17

Mr. Chaperon

Imagine the Taj Mahal with a copper roof and a six-car garage and you have a pretty good idea of what the Arthur Dickson house looks like.

As my Miss Temple in her new outré garb vanishes inside, its white stucco walls shimmer in the midday Las Vegas sunlight like a whited sepulcher. Wait! I have a more topical simile. It shimmers like those Da Vinci dental veneers you see on the queen of TV makeover shows, *The Swan.* I bet old Leonardo himself is rolling over in his sarcophagus in Italy to hear how his name is being bandied about in everybody's upscale mouth these days. Fame is one thing; foolishness is another.

Speaking of foolishness a wee bit closer to home, it is more than somewhat clear to me that if my Miss Temple is not acting her age, I need to be on the scene from the get-go to keep her little masquerade from turning dangerous.

So I enter the place with the film crew, who are obligingly loaded with so many long aluminum equipment boxes that a crocodile could slink in at their ankles and they'd never notice.

Make that one svelte black puddytat, and not even Tweety Bird would notice little moi.

I cannot imagine how my expedition has escaped the notice of my nosy partner in crime solving, Miss Midnight Louise, my wannabe daughter, but so far I am solo on this case and relishing the peace and quiet. This joint is so grandiose that it is easy for me to slip around wherever I feel like it. The floors are all marble or wood but my tootsies come stocking shod when I want them to. I skate over the shiny surfaces like a shadow glimpsed out of the corner of someone's eye.

I overhear one of the tech guys joking that the place is supposed to be haunted by an Elvis imitator's ghost.

Better and better. Elvis and I have a noncompetition agreement when it comes to haunting. And any untoward noise I might make is likely to be taken for an unearthly phenomenon.

I check out the kitchen first, because . . . oh, just because. Without Miss Louise on my tail demanding explanations for my every move, I am free to do as I please.

Wow. This place is huge. You could hold basketball games in the kitchen, which has three huge stainless-steel Sub-Zero fridges big enough to stash a limousine's worth of bodies. Basketball-player-size bodies.

With the black granite countertops and black marble floors, this is not the kind of kitchen that tolerates the errant crumb. I see that I will have to do some creative cadging to provide my own meals during my stay here.

I eyeball the back yard, which has all the comforts of your average five-star health club . . . pools, spas, air-conditioned exercise pavilions, distant athletic courts, none of them the sort of facility I would care to spend a minute in. Amazing how humans have to force themselves to physical action when my kind knows that sleeping twenty hours a day is the key to a healthy lifestyle.

In fact, I stretch out in the sun for a few minutes and someone coos and the next thing I know a camera is framing my lissome figure in its single eye.

"He must come with the property," a camerawoman says. "This place is so big and bland, it'll be nice to have a little animal interest to focus on."

"When we are not close up and personal on all these teen sluts," a guy answers.

"They are not sluts. This is a very life-affirming program," she says indignantly.

Like most indignation, it is lost on her hearer, a cameraman with a world-weary attitude.

"These reality shows are just a new network twist on T and A. You do remember T and A programming? And I do not mean Transit Authority. Back in the eighties. Jiggle shows. About the only life-affirming activity around here will be all those Ts and As getting exercised to within an inch of their lives and being uplifted into prime shape. Looks like your new pal the cat could use a little time on the treadmill, and maybe a shave and a haircut."

I honor the crass slob with a hiss and a glare.

"See. He heard you! Animals are amazingly sensitive to human emotions."

"That was not a human emotion. That was a professional opinion."

A reeking boot swings at my mug. The smell almost knocks me over, though the boot never even grazed a whisker. Humans have no idea how overwhelming ground-level odors are.

"Watch your sneaky step, kitty. If you try to steal a

scene and get in the way of my camera, you will be shredded cabbage."

I do not deign to tell him I have kung fu moves that would make Jackie Chan look like he was standing still and whistling Dixie.

Let them underestimate you.

The woman coos at me and stands guard, arms folded, until the creep takes his hand-held camera and leaves.

"Poor fellah," she says, bending down to pat my head. "Dick really lives up to his name. He's a good cameraman but pretty pathetic in the public relations department."

I hate to say it but during her solicitous gesture I get a really good view of T and A. Luckily, they do not attract in my case unless fully furred.

I give her a short appreciative purr, rise, and go back inside while the sliding kitchen door is still ajar, exhaling morgue-cold air-conditioning on a desert world. At least there is no icky orange scent here to banish the odor of decay. Yet.

There are four ways upstairs: the front stairs, which resemble those at the Paris Opera House for marble-paved elegance, and the back stairs, which are plain unvarnished wood, steep and twisty, and intended for servants, or at least mothers-in-law. Then there is the elevator, which is way too small for me to easily blend in with the human passengers, and the silent butler in the kitchen, a capacious box open on one side, which operates at the push of a button and has shadowy recesses. Think of it as a large litter box set sideways and in upward and downward motion. Or a mini-elevator for domestics. Or domestic cats. I do.

I press the button with my strong right mitt and hop

aboard. Soon, it wafts upward. I press toward the back of the box, like a lizard in a mailbox (a common phenomenon in this climate). When the mechanism stops, I peek out, find the upper hall empty, and thump down to the floor.

More wood.

In an hour, I have made a quick tour of about thirty-five bedroom-with-bath suites. This place is built like a bed-and-breakfast for Attila the Hun and accompanying Mongol horde.

Only once during my tour did anything untoward happen.

It was in bedroom number fourteen, I think. I was nosing around the perimeter when I noticed some unopened high-end luggage in the room, all in pink high-denier and all bearing the cursive initials S. A.

Of course, I naturally think of South America and wonder if Charo is in residence, speaking of T and A, or about to be. But then, as I backed away to the wall when I realized the room could be occupied at any time, I rear-ended my way into an impediment.

A somewhat wishy-washy impediment but an impediment nevertheless.

I whirl to face it and find myself confronting another pervasive pink canvas bag, except this one has a familiar look. And there is a familiar name emblazoned on it. Yvette.

My heart stops and does a double-axel somewhere two feet above the floor.

I inhale the rich, perfumed scent of the Divine Yvette. She is not here at the moment but she has been, and will be again.

What a lucky break! I can protect my Miss Temple from fire, flood, and overexposure on national television and still pursue my courtship of Miss Savannah

Ashleigh's pampered Persian siren at one and the same time.

I tiptoe out of the divine chamber, branding its location on my brain. Now to lay low until all the players are in place and I can be about my quiet and stealthy work . . . and, as it happens, play.

Chapter 18

Pretty Putrid in Pink

Despite the bravado of Temple's Rollerblading arrival at the Teen Queen Castle, she had hit the moment that made her quail: orientation.

This was like joining a sorority in public. Not only was Xoe Chloe not sorority material in any reality, but Temple herself was known by several of the show's officials. Was her pre-makeover makeover good enough to fool them?

Max had always said brazen was the best disguise. She was about to find out.

The contestants assembled in the large and impressive library, good enough to serve as a set for the mystery board game Clue.

There, the organizers informed them that they were twenty-eight of the most promising young ladies ever assembled and would be working with the celebrity judges and coaches to bring out their true potential.

Temple wasn't sure if this was an all-girl version of *The People's Court* or an NFL draft. In addition, Hollywood's most hailed hair and makeup artists, personal trainers and wardrobe consultants would oversee their transformation into fully gorgeous, empowered young women.

There was Ken Adair, the Hair Guy, and Kathy Farrell, the mousy makeup specialist in army green knit stirrup pants and a shapeless nightshirt top. Avis Campion, the physical trainer was an awesomely buff black woman with the take-no-prisoners air of a drill sergeant. Marjory Klein, the dietitian, was the oldest advisor, a spare, unadorned woman in her fifties dressed in the cheerful animal-figured loose pants and top favored by nurses nowadays.

And, finally, Beth Marble announced, the winner, besides snaring a small role on *CSI: Crime Scene Investigation,* Las Vegas—Temple figured it would be a closeup as a corpse—would also win a date with one of two male singing heartthrobs: Aiden Rourke of Day-Glo for the sixteen- to nineteen-year-old Teen Queen winner, and Zach French of Boys Ahoy for the thirteen- to fifteen-year-old 'Tween Queen winner.

Thirteen unlucky girls in both categories would go away losers, Temple thought, but no one mentioned that except to say that every girl would leave with a brand-new self. The assumption being that any old self was pretty expendable. And that even a brand-new self wasn't enough sometimes.

Temple tapped her foot with impatience, one glitzy little mule sliding off her toe.

Instantly, she sensed a camera zooming in on the gesture. Sure enough, one of the camera crew had his lens pointed at her foot.

Good grief! Talk about being under a microscope. Two weeks of this would drive everyone batty.

Not that they didn't have a running start at it.

As Beth Marble, the cooing cheerleader, formally introduced the coaching judges, Temple eyed Mariah, who was searching the fourteen over-fifteens for Temple. Temple was cheered considerably that Mariah was completely confused for now. Once everyone stood up, though, Temple would be the only over-fifteen whose stature belonged in the under-sixteen group.

Beth introduced herself as a pop psychologist and self-help author who had designed the program. Aunt Kit Carlson was introduced by her pen name, Sulah Savage, as a writer of "chick lit fantasy." Huh? Temple had thought the genre was historical romance. Spin was everywhere.

Ken Adair, the Hair Guy, was a hip metrosexual who probably had done Matt's quick highlighting job a couple weeks ago when Matt had impersonated a dead man for a few very weird hours. Dexter Manship was introduced last, a lanky, outspoken, and egocentric Aussie in a tartan vest who glowered at the assembled girls as if he were thinking of beheading them.

"This won't be a cakewalk, ladies," he warned. "This is not some girly pajama party where you play with makeup. This is a makeover! We're going to tear you down and build you up right. You don't sweat, you don't starve, you don't bare your pathetic little souls, you don't fight hard to leave all the other girls in the dust, and you'll be a bigger failure than you were before. Two weeks, ladies, to become kick-ass winners. Or nothing."

A pained look crossed Beth's determinedly pleasant features. Watching people humiliated on national TV had become a countrywide diversion lately. Beth must know that the shows needed brutal drill-sergeant types like Manship. Simon Cowell had proved that on *American Idol*. Brits appeared to do scathing better than Americans. Witness Ann Robinson's schoolmarmish dominatrix and her terse tagline, "You are the weakest link. G'bye."

That was the unsaid mantra for every reality TV show.

Temple eyed the under-fifteens huddled in an excited, scared girly mess on their side of the massive room. Mama Molina worried about some nutcase killing their bodies. But what about the process scarring their minds? Did the parents who signed the fistful of papers realize what a risk they were taking with their kids' self-esteem?

On the other hand, the girls who'd volunteered for this all overflowed with oodles of that bounce-back crazy-kid optimism Temple remembered from her own youth. She smiled, recalling her secret application to San Diego's Old Globe Shakespearian theater right out of high school. She'd gotten a very nice letter—encouraging her to apply again when older—that she still had. And now look at her, starring as Xoe Chloe on TV! From Shakespeare to reality TV. Her mother, if she knew about it, would have had a cat fit either way, then or now.

Beth had taken over the wireless microphone. "You'll find your program kits on the library table against the wall, alphabetically by name. Your roommate's name is also affixed, so you can meet and go to your rooms to get a great night's sleep for the program launch tomorrow. Remember, young women, you are likely to be caught on camera at any time, so be on your best behavior at all times. We have our own public relations representative. Crawford, will you step up to the mike?"

Temple found her fingernails driving into her palms as a small dapper man with delusions of hipsterdom headed toward the mike.

Like many radio personalities, he'd cultivated a deep, mellow voice that was reassuring only if you liked buying swampland in Florida. He wore a lime green jogging suit and resembled a rather unripe banana. His graying hair was slicked back and dyed black for the visual media, with a fringe of curls at the nape of his neck, rather like an unwanted "ring around the collar" in laundry detergent ads.

"Thank you, Beth Marble. Now, girls, if you have any questions be sure to ask me. My name is Crawford Buchanan of KREP-AM, and I've logged a lot of live time on mike and many on-camera miles. I can advise you on how to look and sound good, even though I'm not an official coach. So come to me any time."

Temple shuddered at the very idea and was distressed to see many earnestly naive faces watching him with gullible intensity.

While she was seething about the stupidity of letting Awful Crawford loose in a harem of impressionable young girls, the introduction ended and would-be 'Tween and Teen Queens proceeded to mingle.

Temple shook her head to see Dexter Manship and Crawford Buchanan immediately surrounded by eager questioners.

"Cool tattoo," a voice said softly in her ear. "I bet they'll make you cover it with makeup."

She turned to the svelte and sensuously packaged champagne blonde behind her, who was ogling the drawn-on image of a motorcycle on Temple's left bicep—had that been a chore!—and spoke her doom again.

"Bad Girl isn't gonna make it in this crowd."

"Maybe I don't wanna make it."

"That's a new one. Anyway, name's Blondina."

Temple nearly swallowed her bubble gum. Since the wad was as large as a ping-pong ball, that would have been a life-threatening event. Was there any way out of here but blonde?

"Xoe," Temple said. "With an *X*."

"As in X-rated? All right! See you around. And watch your backside. Everyone else will be."

Actually, that was Temple's fervent hope. Her selection of provocative piercings and drawn-on tattoos was aimed at distracting people from her face and false hair. Not to mention her lying green eyes.

She didn't want there to be any chance that Xoe Chloe Ozone would be a finalist, much less a serious contender. This was not a *Survivor*-style kick-you-off show. Everyone stayed until the bitter end when the final talent show and announcement of the winners took place. If she was written off as a sure loser early, she'd be free to observe and protect.

Temple toddled to the built-in bar, which was stocked with nonalcoholic mixed beverages bearing cute names.

She ordered a My Tai Chi—green tea and lime juice—and turned to study the room.

"Pity." The voice behind Temple set her spine on edge.

She whirled. Dexter Manship himself had been eyeing her unawares. A shoulder-hoisted camera was eavesdropping and recording over his shoulder. The man holding the camera was half-hidden behind the mask of his equipment. Temple guessed they'd all come to take this constant surveillance so much for granted, they'd soon hardly notice it.

"You've got quite a creative look, in your own trashy way, but it'll all have to go, from the tattoos on out. We want little American beauties here, not five-dollar hookers."

"You let me in."

"For a bit of amusement and contrast to the real contenders. This is reality TV, sweets. Freaks sell."

"You're living proof of that. Maybe I'll surprise you and get the votes of the real judges."

He laughed, turning to play directly to the camera. "Guttersnipe but cheeky. It takes all kinds in America. Or, rather, America takes in all kinds." He turned to pinch Temple's overheating cheek before ambling off.

Temple turned to the camera herself. "Somebody

should tattoo the words 'male chauvinist pig' on his condescending hide."

Barely had the cameraman cruised away in Manship's wake than a voice near her said, "Tut, tut, tut."

Beth was hovering nearby, oddly nervous. "You don't want to take on Dexter Manship, my dear. He can be vicious."

"How do you know?"

"Oh, well. His reputation. He's not afraid to say the most outrageous things in front of, and about, everybody. I'd stay away from him, if I were you."

"He can't seem to stay away from me."

"That's another warning sign, isn't it? Perhaps if you dressed less provocatively?"

"Tell it to Britney Spears. If you can get past her bodyguards."

"We're looking for a more wholesome female role model."

Temple eyed the room. Every candidate was dressed to kill. Even nervous thirteen-year-olds like Mariah wore clothes designed to show off, if not outright incite. It must drive their parents bananas.

The word "bananas" brought her gaze back to Crawford, surrounded by his gaggle of naive young things who'd heard the word "media" and rushed like lemmings to any sleazeball therewith associated.

It was really hard to be a sedate thirty pretending to be today's exhibitionist nineteen. Temple had the same mixed feelings toward the Teen Queen contest as she did toward strippers.

These young women and girls were desperately upwardly mobile. The tangible rewards they fought for were superficial, and in her heart of hearts she felt they were selling themselves short.

"Don't be glum, dear." Beth squeezed Temple's upper left arm, motorcycle tattoo, ladder of little chains on her knit top, and all. "I know your edge is just an act. You'll learn here that you can be yourself and still succeed."

Not really, Temple thought. The only way I can succeed here is to *not* be myself and keep Mariah safe.

Only what was she saving Mariah from? A lurking killer, or the corruption of becoming a Material Girl?

Chapter 19

Chicklets

"Wow. You look cool-io. No wonder you didn't buy a thing at the mall without metal on it."

Mariah stood in the middle of the room they shared, staring at Temple. Admiringly. Especially at the skimpy hot-pink stretch top with the short silver chains that were all that held the slit sleeves together.

Temple caught Mariah in a quick embrace, even though the thirteen-year-old was already taller than her five-feet-nothing and probably hated to be hugged.

"Careful," she whispered in Mariah's ear. "I bet we're all on *Candid Camera* here 24/7. Supposedly we don't know each other."

Temple drew back. "You're a pretty cool chick yourself, kid. I was thinkin' I'd draw Suzy Square for a roomie. You look like a with-it kitten."

"Thanks, but I've got a lot to work on."

"Like what?"

"Like my weight." Mariah opened her pink glossy folder. "Look at this slop they have me eating."

"It's called vegetables and fruit."

"You sound like my mother."

"Gad!" Temple mimicked a heart attack and fell back on the huge king-size-plus bed they'd share. "Heaven forbid! I'm just trying to help Bugs Bunny sell his line of veggie delights."

Mariah giggled and sat on her side of the bed, a full body-length away. "You look like you've been living on radishes."

"Yeah, I got a great metabolism but no boobs. You, kiddo, could have a J-Lo figure if you don't let adolescence pack on the pounds."

"Really?"

"Really. That's why the diet and exercise program for you. What you do now sets your babe appeal-o-meter for life. Capische? Suffer now or pay later."

"You're not entirely flat."

"Thanks," Temple whispered to Mariah, "but I'm implementing things for my role as the Bad Girl candidate."

"No, really." Mariah, a quick study, whispered back. "You look cool. What's with the wig, though?"

"I know some of the folks around here, and don't want to be recognized. 'Cuz they know me too."

"Oooh, too bad. I keep forgetting you're here to finger a bad person."

"Thanks for the compliment, kid." Temple lifted her voice to a normal tone. Time to play to the concealed mikes.

"I like to go by 'Mari.'"

"Why, girl?! You've got a great name. Look at Mariah Carey. She's cool."

"And she's just changed her name to 'Mimi.' My mother liked that name, but even Mariah Carey thought it was lame."

"Listen, if I knew why my mother named me what she did, I'd have a Ph.D. in parental psychology."

"So you hate Xoe?"

"No, it gets attention and distracts them from who I might really be. Oops." Whispering again. "Neglected Basic Step One in Spy-Girl 101."

Temple then proceeded to check the large room and adjoining bathroom for all the usual suspect places for hidden cameras and bugs. Mariah watched with round eyes, then joined in the hunt.

"What a posh joint," Temple exclaimed for the unseen recording devices. "Wonder why the dude who built this place went bankrupt? It's on sale for four-point-six million. I bet somebody will pounce on this white elephant once it's become famous on national TV."

"Like us?" Mariah asked.

"Well, I hope somebody doesn't pounce on us . . . unless we want him to. How about that win-a-date thing? You like the boy band guy, Zach French?"

Mariah shrugged. "He's okay. For a kid. I like the guy your age group gets, Aiden Rourke, way better. He's such a stud."

"Now, how do you know that? He could be a dud. You young chicks always go for the older guy. It's a stage."

"The whole world is a stage," Mariah retorted, spreading her arms and shamelessly playing to the presumed cameras.

Temple wished she had spotted something but maybe it was too early. Or maybe there was some law against secretly filming underage kids like Mariah. There oughta be.

Though the place seemed clean, so far, Temple advised her roomie via whisper that they'd better discuss "real stuff" only in the bathroom from now on.

"Gotcha, girlfriend." Mariah high-fived her. "You really like my name?"

"I love it. Your mom, who's way off base on soooo much, was dead-on about that one."

"She *is* kinda square."

"Not square, hon. Wrapped tight. Probably because she worries so much about you, which mothers do. I had one of those myself once. Still do."

"What would she say about your being here?"

"She wouldn't say a thing, Mariah, because she'd be passed out cold in a faint on the entry hall floor."

Mariah giggled again. "You are so funny. This is gonna be a riot."

Temple devoutly hoped not.

That night they found that the Pink Fairy had visited their closets. Each had a pink Teen Queen sleep T-shirt and terrycloth robe and matching jogging suit and workout wear, all with their names embroidered in silver on the shoulder.

Once clothed like Stepford-wife wannabes, each contestant was singled out from the herd after breakfast on the patio and marched off to either exercise regimes or consultations with the coach/judges and various gurus.

Savannah Ashleigh told Temple her Goth look was "dead," never getting the humor of the pronouncement. She also said it was "aging," as was her Cher hair, and had to go.

Dexter Manship, told her she had control and authority issues. Surprise. He did too.

Her Aunt Kit Carlson said Temple needed to find a more positive cultural role model and expressed dismay that her talent selection would be a rap number she would write herself.

Beth Marble told Temple her persona hid a sensitive soul that needed to fight free and fly.

She was given a schedule of meals, exercises, and appointments with all of them, and signed up for a shopping expedition with a wardrobe consultant on the second-to-last day.

In the mansion's sprawling den, Temple found several of the contestants sprawling on the off-white upholstered furniture.

They eyed Temple as warily as sheep would a wolf when she entered the room. Mariah was still undergoing interviews, but some girls her age sat on the floor trying to get the Xbox to work.

Like the other media equipment in this room, it seemed to have been disabled.

"No distractions," a lanky blond girl commented, watching Temple take in the scene. "Come on in. I'm Norma Jean. All we can do here is exercise our butts off, consult, train, primp for the ever-present cameras, or hang and get on each other's nerves. You don't look like any competition to worry about."

"Thanks."

"Too short," another girl said, her long legs stretched out on the floor and her hair color so blond it touched dead white on the color scale. "I'm Blanca."

"Too dark," said yet another blonde, this one even yellower. "Call me Honey."

"Too flat," pronounced an ash blonde with platinum streaks who filled out her spandex top like helium does a balloon. "I'm Silver."

"Too freckled," complained a dishwater blonde who'd bothered to come close enough to ogle Temple almost nose-to-nose. "I'm Ashlee."

So much for sisterhood.

Every girl in the place except Temple hailed from the merry old land of Clairol.

At least no one said "too old," which would have really given the game away.

Temple took a seat on a giant ottoman, not sure how one began talking with piranhas. The last time she'd been in a female competition had been high school softball, although some might say females were always in competition.

As the aura of all that blondness grew familiar, Temple saw that none of these girls were as picture-perfect as the magazine ads. Yet they all had terrific facial bone structure, like the radical makeover candidates on *The Swan*. These reality show producers were savvy enough to start with a good foundation before they worked their "magic" transformation.

"Hi. I'm Amber. Don't listen to them." A lanky strawberry blonde with thunder thighs joined Temple on the ottoman, which could probably seat forty. Temple didn't envy her. That body type was hard to change. "We're all hyper-nervous about our own evaluations. Have you done your interviews yet?"

Temple nodded. Suddenly, she was the center of everyone's interest.

"Are they too beastly mean to stand, like Simon on *American Idol*?" Silver asked.

"They're pretty blunt," Temple said. "It wouldn't be good TV otherwise. You can see the cameras and you know they want to make you sweat."

"Who could see you sweat with that mop of dyed black hair?"

"You sound just like Mr. Adair, the Hair Guy. At least I stand out in a crowd," Temple added pointedly. "Why did you all want to be in such a pressure-cooker, anyway?"

"Same reasons you did," Ashlee said.

"I don't think so."

Temple doubted anyone else in the crew was a plant. Or a mole . . . oh. There actually *could* be a fake mole, as opposed to the real mole part Temple was playing. Reality shows loved to use fake contestants as insiders who could stir up trouble, keep everyone on edge, and rat to the producers on them all.

"What are your reasons?" Honey asked as if beeswax wouldn't melt in her mouth.

"Needed to get away from the family, such as they are." Temple snapped her gum for emphasis. "My brothers' bike club was keeping me up nights."

"You're brother's a biker?" Blanca asked with a curdled expression.

"Brothers. Plural. I have . . . six, I think. Yeah. You ever heard of the Demon Dozen?"

"No."

"Why'd they let you in here?" Ashlee made no secret of the fact that this was a comment on the bad taste of the producers, not merely a question.

"That's a no-brainer. I'm the only one here who isn't a Paris Hilton clone. Thin and dumb is getting old."

"Would you please stop chewing that tacky gum!" Blanca said.

"If it weren't tacky, it wouldn't be gum, sis. Can't stop. It's my weight-control secret."

"Gum?"

"Yeah." Temple blew another big pink bubble, then reeled it back into her mouth. "Burns calories. The longer you chew it, the more you lose." Now that she had their rapt attention, it was time for a kicker, the more ridiculous the better. "And if it's green tea gum—very rare, that stuff—you'll lose a pound a day."

"Really?" Amber edged near, her lips almost quivering to acquire a wad of green tea bubble gum.

Temple was seriously wondering how she could "manufacture" such a thing.

"All right, girls. Ready to rock-and-roll on the exercise mats?"

They all turned to regard the Barbie doll in bright pink spandex yoga pants and top. "I'm Brandy, y'alls personal trainer, and an hour a day keeps the cellulite away. We'll be working out by the heart-shaped pool. Won't that be inspiring? Follow me."

Silver was both preening and frowning. "Didn't Jayne Mansfield have a heart-shaped pool? She was the best blonde bimbo since Marilyn."

"She had a heart," Temple said, "but not a head."

Only ex-newsies would remember the car accident that had decapitated the actress in nineteen-something ancient. The newspapers and TV stations always like to recall the date of anything grisly once a decade or so and call it an anniversary mention. That was one reason Temple had left the news biz for the PR biz. Grisly did not go over big in PR. Except, somehow, it seemed, on accounts she handled. . . .

The crew of identically clad contestants, joined by the Little Sisters from the breakfast room, marched behind Brandy out to the welcome sunlight of the house's expansive grounds.

What a sight to behold.

Twenty-eight hot pink yoga mats surrounded the heart-shaped swimming pool, its gunite walls painted pink for the occasion.

The only thing that marred the pink perfection of the scene was the whipped cream letters lying like fluffy clouds across every mat, spelling out . . .

Everyone else stopped cold in the hot Las Vegas sun, frowning into their hot pink sweat bands, but Temple/Xoe just had to step forward and count:

Die, you damn heartless bitches!

Twenty-eight letters exactly, counting the punctuation marks. Twenty-eight little candidates all in a row.

Someone was a perfectionist.

Chapter 20

Whipped Scream

You have not lived until you have seen the Las Vegas crime scene investigation folks (now famed on TV) photographing twenty-eight hot-pink yoga mats with whipped cream pooling on them in the sun.

By the time that they, and I, have been alerted and are on the scene, the colorful language, laid out one letter and/or punctuation mark to a mat, has melted enough that the *b* in "bitches" looks more like a sideways *w*. The authorities have to take the witnesses' word for it as to the original intention.

I, however, have to take no one's word, and never do. That is why I am such an ace detective. I am incorruptible. I must admit, though, that the whipped cream was a temptation too yummy to leave untasted. I was alone on the scene then. My Miss Temple, aka Xoe Chloe for the nonce, had been shepherded indoors to await the police, along with everybody else. Human, that is. Or what passes for it on reality TV. The show security staff, i.e., bronzed gods in loin cloths, were arrayed along the doors to the pool area, facing inside to keep twenty-eight agitated candidates and assorted staff members from messing up the scene of the culinary crime.

So I was free to explore on my own.

The first thing my shameless taste test discovered was that the whipped cream was not even beaten. It was, in fact, a particularly soapy shaving cream, one that offered a full-bodied texture and a risqué and amusing hint of mint.

Not my vintage, thank you. And I thank Bast that I am not required to shave. It would be a full-time job.

My unstunted white whiskers—vibrissae to the cognoscenti at the vet's office—were double-dipped in fluffy white after my explorations, so I paused under a bush to wash off the evidence.

Yuck! No wonder people wash out the mouths of their sassy kits with soap. I would not even refer to a female dog by the proper term after a close encounter with this stuff.

I am clean-shaven as far as my kind is concerned but fighting residual nausea when I notice that a couple of curious cats have whiskered in on my action.

Before I can throw my weight around and order them away, I realize that both are of Persian extraction, and one is of the sublime shade of platinum blonde known as "shaded silver."

I drop my laundry mitt and stand at attention with every muscle in my body.

Although the sight of her personalized carrier told me the Divine Yvette would be on the premises, her personal presence is still a potent form of shock and awe. Not to mention also encountering her kittykin, for the fulsome blonde of blended apricot, gold, and cream shades is her shaded golden sister, the Sweet Solange.

No one told me the Shaded Sisters were part of the deal.

I leap out from my place of concealment but naturally must play the brusque (though noble) crime scene guardian.

"You there!" I cry as they are about to dip their dark little tootsies in the *c* of the word formerly known as "bitches." "Desist."

Aqua-green and moss-green eyes circled in black mascara regard me with calm surprise and no hint of obedience.

Seeing the pair of them side by side is the human parallel of viewing a Jaguar XKE next to a Lamborghini. Where is a guy to look first?

I should mention one of the most unusual and charming aspects of the shaded Persian breed. Pale as their silver and golden coats may be, the leather on their persons—nose, eye surrounds, pads—is black, as are the hairs on the bottoms of their feet, which is why I call them "soot foots." Purely to myself, you can imagine. No Persian worth her pedigree would answer to such a lowly description.

I trot over to enforce my order, for the females of my kind are not the docile and downtrodden type. *Au contraire.*

Hmmm. I see the Divine Yvette's presence is the usual bad influence already. I am starting to think in French.

"*Bon jour,* girls," I say.

"*Hssss, les flics,*" the Divine One says, which is the French equivalent of "Cheese it, the cops!"

(I should also make clear that the Divine Yvette is not the slightest bit French, unless rubbing shoulders with teacup poodles on Rodeo Drive makes her so. But she likes to think that others think so. And they both bear French names. Why people attempt to social climb via their animal companions' names, I cannot tell you.)

Me, I was born nameless, and the street people gave me my moniker, Midnight Louie. Fine with me. I think every male on the planet is secretly a Louie, only they just do not know it. Yet.

"Ladies, ladies." I have arrived, panting slightly, whether from haste or another, less conscious cause I will not say.

"Louie! I did not expect to see you here." The Divine Yvette blinks her aquamarine orbs as if doubting the message they are sending her.

Miss Solange regards me with her usual expression, which is calm but devastating.

"I can understand that," I say, "but you can see crime has called me like a plate of lasagna calls Garfield."

"Please," Yvette sniffs, "do not mention that common yellow striper. He is not in our league."

"No, of course not. He is a joke. But I must ask you ladies to keep your delicate nails out of this fluffy white stuff. It is evidence that the Las Vegas Metropolitan Police crime techs will soon be"—*hmm,* "sifting" does not quite do it—"nosing around."

"What an unfortunate lime odor." Yvette shakes a dainty foot in demonstration.

"The brand is Razor's Edge," Solange adds.

I gaze into those mysterious and soulful eyes. Too bad I am previously and seriously attached to her sister Yvette, because this is one great big beautiful doll in her own right. "How did you detect the brand?"

She sighs, which our kind does by looking sideways.

"One of our mistress's . . . mates used it. Detestable stuff! So declassé."

"I do not think lime scent is 'the classy' either. So your mistress, Miss Savannah Ashleigh, is present here? In what capacity?"

"Our mistress," Yvette explains patiently, "does not have any capacity whatsoever. You must have noticed that in our previous mutual encounters."

Unfortunately, "our previous mutual encounters" were way too mutual. I am not one for three-ways, despite my roguish reputation. So most of my close encounters with the Divine Yvette have meant her air-head mistress was also present.

"What has brought out Miss Solange on this occasion?" I ask, for I only met her formally once during our separate but mutual jaunt to New York City and ad agency shenanigans, back when Yvette and I were cat food commercial performers.

Ah, the lights. The cameras. The action.

"Our mistress has been promoted," Solange explains. "She is a judge now."

"Miss Savannah Ashleigh, the low-amp of Savannah, is a judge? What are federal appointments coming to?"

"A judge of the 'Tween and Teen Queen competitions," Yvette corrects me.

If one must be corrected, the Divine Yvette is the one to do it.

"It is like *American Idol*," Solange adds, "with a panel of celebrity judges."

"More like *American Idle*," I mutter. It is no secret that Miss Savannah Ashleigh has been living off the TV commercial residuals of her feline companions rather than her own efforts.

"Our mistress is doing very well now," Solange says in her defense. "Her old movies are now considered 'camp' and she is having a career revival. So she has semiretired us and we both travel with her now."

I bring up a sensitive subject with Yvette. "And what about the, ah, you know . . . the patter of little paws?"

(I had been falsely accused of felonious littering during our last commercial assignment when the Divine Yvette ended up expecting. However, my Miss Temple fought that charge tooth and fingernail in *The People's Court* and proved me innocent. Well, innocent of that particular outcome. The Divine Yvette proved to be the victim of attack when all her kits were born wearing the stripes of my rival spokescat, the yellow-bellied Maurice.)

"Oh, them." Yvette yawns. "They were forced upon me and after birth were quickly allocated to other homes."

I glance at Solange. Apparently the maternal instinct can be a fleeting thing.

"Poor Yvette," she answers indignantly. "Attacked and left in an unwanted condition. Good homes were found."

"They all came out yellow-striped," Yvette adds with a shudder that sends all her fine silver hairs rippling.

I quite understand how an unwed mother might resent the resemblance of offspring to a foul attacker but . . .

"Is there not a strain of Stripe in the Shaded line?" I ask. "Were not common tabbies responsible for the Shaded's sublime black leather and faint tracery of markings amid the fur that lends such a rich sheen to the divine silver and gold?"

Yvette shrugs again. "Stripe is common. Black and brown are the weediest variety of cat colors. If we have any Stripe in us, it goes back countless generations and therefore does not count."

I did not mean to impugn the Shaded pedigree but

must take exception to her characterization of black and brown, being of the very common House of Black myself.

Solange addresses this before I can. "I am actually the older type of Shaded Persian. There was a time when kits of my ilk were tossed aside as unvalued throwbacks. Fortunately, we are coming into new favor and our more robust coloration is prized now, in the show ring and out of it."

"Hear, hear!" I say, eyeing Solange with new appreciation.

There is a little bit of tabby in every cat, and particularly in every alley cat.

Yvette has wandered away during my mutual admiration society musings with Solange.

She is patting at something under a bush.

I cannot have her disturbing my crime scene, so I rush over.

Well, well, well. I will have to see that the Las Vegas CSI, the real-life ones, find this prime piece of evidence pronto. It is a can of Razor's Edge shaving cream, lime scented.

"Good job, girls," I say. "Now huff your ruffs back inside. I will be sure to direct my associate's attention to this useful clue."

"You must visit us and tell us what happened, Louie," Solange manages to say as I hustle them toward the glass sliding doors where they can paw pitifully until admitted.

"Where will I find you?"

"Lavender Wing, with the judges and Team Queen members."

With that I return to the deserted pool area and the too-obviously abandoned shaving cream can. This job must have taken several cans. Where are they?

I sit and regard the empty can. I wonder what the

CSI will make of the pad prints amid whatever human traces remain. Which is likely nothing. This can is a message, not a clue.

I picture the cops "fingerprinting" the Divine Yvette and Solange when their presence at this overall crime scene is detected.

Then they will be "soot foots" indeed!

I am very glad that I will not be wielding the inkpads on that occasion.

Ouch!

Chapter 21

Hanky Panky

Temple and Mariah huddled in their room that night, comparing notes on hastily scrawled pages they tore up and packed away.

As befitted a 'Tween 'n' Teen Queen competition, half of their shared notes concerned the rules of the contest, the rituals of competition, psyching out the judges, and a keen awareness that their every word and gesture could be recorded.

The other half concerned the skullduggery.

Skullduggery. Temple liked that word but Mariah adored it.

She was her mother's daughter, though the very expression would have made Mariah howl. She was so into being "not Mother" at the moment.

For a final consultation, they huddled in the bathroom for a fast five minutes, shower running full blast and steaming up the mirrors, the air, and possibly parboiling any electronic bugs and cameras. Such devices weren't allowed in the bathrooms anyway.

Still, that was the underlying paranoia of reality TV. One could never be sure.

So their conversation was as veiled as the air.

"What if that shaving cream had been acid?" Mariah theorized, "and all of us had been lying there exercising and trying to get tans and burning our skins off?"

"You have a morbid imagination."

"Thanks. Whatcha think?"

"Thanks for asking. I think it was a stunt to get attention, which worked. And I don't know if we really have a stalker among us, or if it's the producers trying to throw the contestants off-balance, or—"

"Or a crazy killer?"

"Right. Like there are a lot of sane ones." Temple leaned her arm past the shower curtain to crank the water force up the last notch. "Hand me that razor, please."

Mariah did, looking a little jealous that Temple was so proficient at shaving her armpits. Hey, this was Feminine Hygiene 101. She should be a pro.

"I don't think my mother shaves," Mariah said glumly.

"Are you sure?"

"No, but it doesn't seem like something she would do. You're really good at it."

"Thanks." Temple tore off a hunk of toilet paper and put it on the nicked shin that had happened when Mariah had opined that she didn't think her mother shaved. Only her mustache!

"Those drawn-on tattoos are cool."

"Tattoos are cool when they're temporary. When they're permanent, they're a problem waiting to happen."

"Why?"

"Well, we always reinvent ourselves as we toddle through life. We should aim to be a blackboard, not a pincushion with no expiration date."

"Huh? Oh, I get it. You're funny."

"I hope so, because this situation is getting less so every day."

"It's like boot camp." Mariah picked at the dead skin around her big toenail. She sounded 'tweenage sullen again. Temple found herself suddenly sympathetic toward Carmen Molina. "Everybody tells you what to do. 'Exercise.' 'Suck in your stomach.' 'Eat your vegetables.' 'Smile.'"

Temple smiled. "Imagine making smiling an order? How many of those rules does your mother harp on?"

"The vegetables."

"That's not too bad."

"No. But being a girl is harder than that."

"Being a *girly* girl is harder. We don't all have to be pretty in pink."

Mariah squinted up at Temple. "I can't see the real you in pink. But it does go with that Elvira wig in a weird sort of way."

Temple pushed the hot, damp hairdo back on her forehead. It felt like a heavy wet turban.

"This thing makes one admire Cher in concert. Pink doesn't go with my natural hair color, so it's kinda fun to wear it now. I feel like a 1958 Cadillac convertible."

Mariah giggled. 'You're not big enough to be a huger-rific car like that."

"No, but I can think I am. You see anything suspicious around the camp today?"

"I snooped, like you said, and I found six cans of Razor's Edge in the contestants' lockers."

"Good work! Empty? You didn't touch them?"

"No! Only picked 'em up with a towel. All of them were pretty light. You know what I'm thinking?"

"That whoever sprayed those yoga mats used what was on hand?"

"Yeah. How'd you know?"

"With this vast cast of competitive characters, it's so easy to spread the blame. I bet our perp used latex gloves though."

Mariah nodded. "My mom has a whole box at the house. She never leaves home without 'em."

Temple giggled this time. "She sounds like a gynecologist."

"Ah, I have my first appointment after this is over."

"The pits!"

"Is it scary?"

"Oh, yeah, but you get used to it. I mean, we all have to do it. Consider it a badge of courage."

Mariah considered while Temple watched, remembering her own first gynecological exam. No matter how prepared you were, it was always a bit of a psychic violation.

"We heard about that in school," Mariah was saying. "The badge of courage story. It was about war."

The red badge of courage for women was a different kind of war, Temple thought. The onset of menstruation. Of being different from men. Of being capable of being hurt just for your gender, physically and psychologically.

Temple was a modern girl. She bought her own "sanitary protection" with careless regularity, somewhere between the way she bought breath mints and condoms. The euphemistic phrase "sanitary protection" still made the process seem dirty and secret, even today. What did you tell a girl on the brink? Relax and enjoy the anxiety, the shame of doing something guys don't and sometimes mock?

Where was Carmen Molina when you needed her?

Adolescence was murder.

For guys too, remember.

Temple pointed to the bloody nick on her shin. "Nothing is smooth, Mariah. Everything hurts a little. That's how we know we're alive. And we want to stay that way.

I'm afraid someone around this competition doesn't feel the same way."

"Yeah." Mariah ran the disposable pink razor up her still fuzzy lower leg. "That's obvious. We gotta find out who. That's why my mother sent you here."

"You think so?"

"No, she wanted you here as my babysitter but I'm not a baby anymore, so you might as well do something more useful."

Temple gave her a high five. "Baby, you are so right!"

They were all on a schedule. Boot camp for beauty. That made them predictable targets.

Temple didn't like being separated from Mariah for most of the day but they were on opposite ends of the age meridian.

The moment when Temple realized that she was old enough to be Mariah's mother, she got cold chills. And then she heard her own biological clock ticking. What did she want? To be a pal or a parent?

But this wasn't about her.

And then there were more one-on-ones with the judges in their advisor capacity.

First up was her very own maternal aunt, Kit Carlson.

Temple went to that one chewing a wad of gum big enough to choke a camel (and therefore disguise her voice).

She slumped on her tailbone on the single rattan chair before the Consultant Room One desk, and snapped gum.

Aunt Kit remained admirably cool to the whole act as she flipped through Xoe's file.

"You wouldn't be here at all if Manship hadn't liked your cheeks," Kit finally noted, slapping the file shut to gain Xoe's attention, and staring at her over the rims of her half-glasses.

"Men are easy."

"Men are only fifty percent of the vote."

"Yeah, what's that Elvis guy here for anyway?"

"Apparently local color. I think he's like Jai on *Queer Eye for the Straight Guy*. A cultural consultant, always a vague and unrewarding position."

Temple shrugged. "Who cares what any of you do or think? I don't want to win anyway."

"I bet not. Losing can become a way of life. You get to sneer at the winners, whine, be cynical."

"Cynical. Like it's a *sin*? Sins are cool."

"You try not to show it but you're obviously a very bright girl."

Temple sat up, indignant. "What makes you say that?"

Kit smiled, making Temple feel like a rat for the masquerade.

"You worked that guy like a pro," Kit said, woman to woman.

"Pro what?"

"Pro girly girl. No prob. That's what this exercise in media exposure is about. Question is, is there a real person under that persona?"

"Persona? Lady, what big words you use. I'm more real than all those bottle blondes out there put together."

"Granted. But what wins? The obvious. I almost voted against admitting you to the contest but I had to admire the crass way you played on Manship's crassest inclinations. I have a weakness for chutzpah."

"Is he really the deciding vote?"

"He's the audience favorite. Everyone has a mean little devil inside aching to bust out. He feeds that need. That makes him a man of power. The temptation for women everywhere is to play the man of power. That's the way women lose it. Lose it for winning."

"So what are you doing here if the game's so crooked?"

"Restoring balance? Plus, I've never done anything like this. I thought it'd be interesting. And it'll help my career."

"You're just in it for the fame and fortune."

"Anything wrong with that?"

"Just don't go pretending you actually care about any of us."

"But I do."

When Temple snorted and looked away, Kit went on.

"If we women leave it up to men to judge women, we'll end up with the Taliban."

Temple was speechless at the conviction in her aunt's tone but Xoe squirmed in her chair. "This is way heavy stuff, lady."

"She ain't heavy, she's my sister."

Temple blinked. Maybe she had to banish tears. "That's *brother,* lady, that quote. 'He ain't heavy, he's my brother.'"

"It can't work both ways?"

"Not in my world."

"Get a different world, then. Make one."

"I'm trying." For an awful, role-playing moment, Temple *was* Xoe Chloe Ozone, teen girl rebel. Her Aunt Kit was good. Very good.

Kit smiled crookedly, at her. "Try a little less hard, and try being a little more soft, huh? Being interesting isn't the kiss of death in the real world. It just looks like it sometimes."

"Yeah. Thanks." Temple stood and slouched away.

She was such a fraud.

Who else around here wasn't?

Including a stalker/killer.

Before she reached the door, Kit leaped up to intercept her.

"Oh, fashion faux pas! You've got mascara smudges

under both eyes. You surely don't think raccoon eyes are punk?"

Before Temple could defend her waterproof brand of mascara, Kit leaned close and whispered, "We need to talk somewhere. Privately." Kit nodded to a small door at the left and whispered again. "Adjoining privy. They had it right in the old days, didn't they?"

Temple recognized the word for "private" as applied to old-time bathrooms. But Xoe Chloe just looked puzzled, then nodded and followed Kit past the coffered wooden door into a bathroom equipped for a Victorian household, wood-paneled, with matching enclosed tub and toilet.

Once there Kit turned the faucets on full, retrieved a pair of thong panties that were drying over the edge of the tub, thought better of it, grabbed a tea-rose-embroidered hand towel instead, and tossed it over some sort of sprinkler spigot in the ceiling.

Thong panties? Temple thought. "I don't think they can have cameras in the bathroom," Xoe Chloe whispered.

"Just to be safe, sweetie." Kit sat on the broad tub surround and kicked off her shoes, a pair of svelte but sensible pumps. Pink. She was an ex-actress after all, and tended to dress for real life as if it were a play.

"Not in the bathrooms," Temple said. "Invasion of privacy. Even for reality TV. Cross my heart. But it never hurts to be safe."

"Exactly," Kit said. "What's up, niece?"

"Oh, darn! I was afraid you'd make me."

"The big, black hair and big bad attitude did the job until I spent a bit more time with you. It's not nice to fool Mother Nature, and it's even worse to play your old Aunt Kit. What happened to your dear curly red head, which I first glimpsed when you lay in your mother's arms spitting up on my fifty-dollar infant jumpsuit christening gift, which was a lot of money when you were born, dear, although now it wouldn't make a decent tip at Lutèce."

"Wigs are us here in Las Vegas. So I was an ingrate from the first, huh?"

"An expressive child, I would say. Not one afraid to make her opinions known, of the infant menu or the world at large."

"How did you end up here—?" they began in unison.

Kit took the next line. "Money, dear heart. My feeble celebrity as a romance author doesn't get me many freebies but this was one of them. I bet the producers thought my theatrical background would make me more exciting on camera. Poor things. The stage was my métier."

"You're plenty lively. And just who are the producers? We keep hearing about them but never see them."

"Money men. It's the same everywhere. They keep out of sight so no one can dun them for funds or tell them what to do. I call this particular set Toddman and Goodson, an old-fashioned pair of late-middle-aged men living vicariously through the stuff that dreams and network profits are made on. All the hip young producers are making *CSI* imitations. I imagine you haven't seen them, my dear, because they look like accountants and you'd never recognize them as the powers that be. So, why the wild child persona?"

Temple took a deep breath and explained, and then she swore her aunt to silence.

Temple was scheduled to see sweet-faced Beth but couldn't stomach that after her confession to Kit. Beth was a super-sweet lady who seemed to live in a dream world, and Temple didn't feel like deceiving another nice middle-aged lady who deserved a better menopause than an appointment with Xoe Chloe. She decided Xoe didn't abide by schedules.

She headed for Consultant Room Three, Dexter Manship's. It would be fun to play off someone she despised, a Crawford Buchanan substitute, so to speak.

Xoe didn't knock, natch. Just swaggered in, swinging her hips and her belly button ring.

The high-backed leather chair behind the desk was turned away from her. (Wouldn't you know sweet and savvy Aunt Kit had been assigned a room that looked like a porch but Dexter Manship had a Lord of the Manor study to commandeer?)

"Hey, man. I'm here." Temple waited for an answer but got none. "A little early, like a couple hours, but what's the point of being a go-getter if you can't wake up the troops."

No answer, not even a creak of leather.

Xoe leaned over the desk (all the better to create some cleavage) and shoved one wing forward with all her might.

The chair whirled around faster than Norman Bates's mother in *Psycho*.

No wonder. It was empty.

Xoe put a hand on her bare hip and pouted for the cameras. She looked around. "Dude! Dude?" A glint of mirrored glass caught her eye. She swaggered over and helped herself to a swig of scotch on the rocks.

"What a setup," she told the room, and the cameras. It was wonderful not wanting, needing, to win this thing. She could be her not-self. Very liberating. "Bet that's a casting couch in the corner. The whole thing's a setup. Right?" She toasted her glass to the room's four corners. "It's been fixed."

She walked to the windows behind the desk, which overlooked the pool area. Two groups of seven girls were working out on the new hot pink mats or swimming in the heart-shaped pool while the other two groups were making the rounds of the diet/beauty/wardrobe consultants or "counseling" with the judges-cum-advisors and gadflies.

And she was indoors, in this shadowed room, with no one to shadow box. She set her glass down dead center on the desk, and ambled to the door. No coaster to buffer the expensive wood.

She didn't know what she'd expected to find in here. Maybe a scorpion to tease, a statement to make. For a moment, she'd thought she might find a body waiting to be discovered.

But the room was empty, and the cameras had recorded a solo performance.

There was only one thing to do: go to her actual appointment with, sigh, Savannah Ashleigh. Late.

Chapter 22

A Meeting of Minds

Temple sidled into Consulting Room Four twenty minutes late, prepared to make surly obeisance.

Not to worry.

Savannah Ashleigh was striding away on the elliptical walker in the office, the TV tuned to the soap operas and a *Cosmopolitan* magazine splayed open on the machine's control panel. Apparently, each judge had been allowed to import whatever they wanted to their offices.

Well! Temple was dying to see at what level, speed, and calorie-burning rate the woman was operating. However, the *Cosmo* issue effectively hid everything but its own provocative contents.

Savannah Ashleigh's shiny spandex workout attire hid nothing. She had a Hollywood body, that was for sure, narrow but rounded. Her Dolly Parton hair bounced in one platinum blonde wave as she glided along at a rapid pace, her face delicately sheened with sweat.

Xoe leaned against the door and applauded, slowly.

That threw Savannah out of her rat race. She shook her head, batted her eyelashes, and observed her observer.

"Are you my ten fifteen?"

It was now 10:35, but Temple nodded. (Xoe was a shrugger, not a nodder, so Temple had to step in for her from time to time.)

Reluctantly flipping the magazine shut, Savannah pressed her forefinger to the control panel and the green level control vanished . . . not before Temple noticed it was solid all the way to the top. Savannah was a serious strutter.

She eyed Xoe for the first time. "My, you're a grim little thing. Pastels and brights, hon, are what you need. And, of course, someone will talk to you about that hair."

Temple was willing to bet Savannah's hair was about as natural as her own.

"Now sit down in that cute little chair, and I'll sit at the desk and we'll go over your program."

"I have a program?" Xoe slouched into the seat indicated. "That makes me sound like a computer."

"Don't we wish. Program out the calories and carbs, program in the veggie shakes and distilled water."

"That'd give me the shakes, all right."

"Now." Savannah was paging through the contents of the standard hot pink folder. "Hmmm. Could lose ten pounds. Definitely a hair and face makeover. I've been through your wardrobe—"

"When?"

"When you were out of your room, dear. Such trash. If it doesn't chime, clatter, cling, or clash with every other color in your wardrobe, except for black, it isn't there. We'll be looking for something light, floral, and airy for you."

"Are you recommending a scent or a wardrobe? 'Cuz your recommendations stink."

"A very good point, uh, Ex-oh-ee. A signature fragrance would be a fine addition to your wardrobe. I don't think any other girl has mentioned a stinking problem, so you would be ahead of the competition. On that matter."

"It's Xoe-ee."

"Oh. As in 'Zoo.' Well, you might consider a name change while you're at it. Perhaps . . . Daisy." She looked up to register Temple's expression. "Or perhaps . . . not. Anyway, I've ordered some darling things for you, which should fit whether you work off those biggy, piggy ten pounds. Or not."

Savannah rose, dabbed at her forehead with a floral hand towel, and escorted Temple to the door.

That was when some poor 'Tween or Teen Queen candidate who had actually been left alone for a moment began to scream to wake the dead.

Savannah stood paralyzed in her tracks, hands over her waves of hair-sprayed curls.

Temple sprinted out into the hall, not only beginning work on the biggy, piggy extra ten pounds but to find out whether a contestant had killed or been killed, or had just broken a fingernail.

Chapter 23

Exercised to Death

The screams continued, leaving no doubt that most of the contestants possessed well-developed pairs of lungs, not to mention any superstructure above them.

Mariah was three steps behind Temple, and Temple never thought for a moment of telling her to stay back for her own good.

They were both committed to serving time in what was quickly becoming a House of Horrors and deserved to know what was going on firsthand.

Temple and Mariah were apparently closest, for they burst through the double doors to the indoor workout room and found Silver standing hunched just inside the doors, screaming her heart out.

What riveted her gaze was instantly obvious.

A blood-spattered figure in a hot pink leotard lay slumped over an elliptical walker machine . . . the very kind of machine that Savannah had been putting through its paces, or vice versa, just moments before in her private office.

Mariah gasped, and Silver screamed until her hair should have turned white had she not bleached it that shade long ago.

Temple gradually realized that the figure on the walker had *pointed* hands and feet. And then she saw that its bubble-gum-pink flesh, spattered with a measles of blood drops, was rather . . . rubbery.

Footsteps were pounding into the room behind them and stopping.

"She looks like a Barbie doll," Mariah's clear young voice said.

Temple nodded. She'd heard of defaced and mutilated Barbie doll images showing up around town from Mariah's mother.

But this was worse. This figure was life-size.

"It's not a real person, it's a blow-up doll," Temple murmured.

"What's that?" Mariah's dark eyes demanded an honest answer.

"Later," Temple hissed under her breath. "Cameras."

By now the kitschy security forces were pushing their way into the room . . . and coming up mortified at the scene they confronted.

No way bronzed Greek god he-men were going to deal with butchered sex toys.

Beth Marble had finally arrived. Her voice could be heard urging the girls to leave immediately.

Temple went over to take Silver's arm. "Easy. It's just a doll. You can't kill Barbie. She's forever. Come on."

Silver moved in tiny baby steps like an old, old woman. Amazing how shocking unreality could be.

Yet Temple couldn't underestimate the sick mentality at work, or how bold it was. Someone knew the setup and was exploiting it.

Someone? Anyone. The crew was an assemblage of workers from here and anywhere. The contestants were selected from anyone who chose to enter. Temple knew for a fact that being a finalist could be manipulated. This could be about more than a single demented prankster-cum-killer. It could be a conspiracy.

The producers could have arranged it. Maybe this had always been more horror show than beauty/makeover pageant. *American Idol*-cum-*Fear Factor.*

"I'm calling the police," Beth announced from the hall when the room had been cleared and the double doors firmly shut on the bloodied doll.

The bloodied life-size actual doll. The faux victims were getting bigger, and the "attacks" closer together and bolder. More personal.

Temple was interested to see three nervous men she'd never spotted before, overdressed for members of the camera crew. Must be the "suits" from the producers' office. They had to be lurking around here somewhere, clean-shaven bland-looking men whose ages were in the indeterminate twilight zone of forty to sixty. Two of them immediately nixed calling the police.

Beth shook off their opposing voices. "Everyone go to your rooms and stay there until further notice."

Everyone but the suits was forced to drift away, whispering to one another despite the ever-eavesdropping cameras and mikes.

"Scream Queen," someone whispered before they all dispersed to their separate cells . . . rooms. "Silver should get a lot of screen time for this."

"So what got everyone unglued about that doll, besides the blood?" Mariah asked in the shower-steamed bathroom, while water pattered into the tub and down the drain. Xoe and Mariah watched from the center of the room. They would shortly be regarded as the cleanest candidates in the competition. "Sure it was gross, Xoe Chloe, but it was just a dead balloon. I mean, talk about airheads—"

And what, Temple wondered, would Mama Molina think of Xoe Chloe (Mariah obviously loved the comic book name) enlightening her sheltered daughter about sleazy ads in the back of men's magazines?

But she explained, as delicately as she could. She'd always heard that parents should be honest about sex education. Even dragooned *in loco parentis* types like herself.

Mariah reared back. "Gross! Guys are so pathetic. And now gruesome too. Whoever is doing this is major sick."

"Some guys. And the red may not have been real blood. And the perp may be sick, or just pretending to be."

"What do you mean?"

Temple mopped at her sweat-dewed brow. The wig was looking very natural thanks to all these steam baths. It was relaxing, growing just like real hair. Maybe someday soon she would become a real Xoe Chloe, like Pinocchio became a real boy.

"These are flashy incidents," Temple said, "designed to upset people and just begging to bring in the authorities. Maybe someone has it in for the show's producers. There's a point when too much freaky publicity hurts rather than helps a project. I'm Miss Public Relations. Trust me on this."

"So someone's trying to ruin the show." Mariah nodded. "Could be."

"Or it's an elaborate setup."

"Or it's a real sicko."

"Those are the options."

"Do you think my mom will get involved in this?"

"Like a Kevlar vest on a SWAT team."

"Oh . . . shoot. She'll ruin everything. Can't she ever just let me do anything by myself?"

"Hey! She okayed this whole deal, despite your never telling her in advance, but it's going way beyond any of us being Teen or 'Tween Queens. It's starting to look like Junior Miss *Fear Factor.*"

"If we solve this thing, we can get this show back on the road."

"To me, that is not a good thing, Mariah."

"Oh, no. You're cool. You've got a real shot at this."

"You think so?"

"Absolutely. Nobody here needs a do-over more than you."

"Thanks."

"I mean, it's brilliant. You are just awesomely wrong. I wish *I* coulda had that much to start with."

Chapter 24

Great Big
Beautiful Doll

It seems the Divine Yvette has taken it into her pretty little head that since the little doll named Silver found the big doll named Balloon, a shaded *silver* Persian is likely to be the next victim of random spattering.

"She is very superstitious," sister Solange explains to me in the hall when I am denied access to the suite accorded to Miss Savannah Ashleigh and dependents. "She will not leave her carrier or take food. Other than caviar and sirloin tips, of course, which our mistress must hand-feed to her."

I would like to see Miss Savannah down on her knees doling out the tidbits to the pink canvas carrier, for the Divine Yvette when in a mood is as likely to snap as to snarf.

However, I am out in the hall with her shaded golden sister, and Midnight Louie is not one to overlook an opportunity of any color or stripe.

"Since we are clearly not needed during the present crisis, we can take a stroll on the grounds and perhaps figure something out."

"The grounds?"

"Yeah. Out by the pool. All the freak show people are huddling in the den trying to think up security ploys. It seems the producers threw a hissy fit at the idea of bringing the police in. Might close the show down. Luckily, my Miss Temple is already in place."

"She is? Where?"

I feel a rush of pride for my little doll and her success at the undercover arts. The stunning Solange did meet her when we were all in the Big Apple last Christmas auditioning for the big come-on of an À La Cat contract. Unfortunately, murder-most-Noel put the whole commercial deal on the back burner.

Also, an unwanted delicate condition sidelined the Divine Yvette's performing career for a few months, causing the sponsor to invoke the morals clause in her contract. Miss Savannah Ashleigh in turn leveled a wrongful paternity suit at moi. It is no wonder the Divine One is a bit high-strung. We all came out of that incident worse for wear but at least Miss Temple went to *The People's Court* to prove me innocent as a lamb. Still, I do my best to avoid the instep-arching spikes of Miss Savannah's footwear, as she would still like to nail me for daring to befriend Yvette.

"Where?" Solange interrupts my reverie, reminding me that past embarrassments should not upstage the presence of a lovely and unescorted lady with jade-green eyes.

"I am not at liberty to say but am glad to know that she is safely disguised. This looks to be a rough crowd."

"Oh, it is." Solange amiably follows me down the hall to the back areas of the mansion. "These girls all have such long claws, and they chitter and coo every time they see Yvette or me and try to pick us up and pet us. All that nasty hand and cuticle cream lotion on our freshly powdered coats." She shudders delicately. "Our mistress can be distressingly dense at times, but she always wears cotton gloves when handling us."

This strikes me as more than somewhat fastidious. "My Miss Temple does like to run her nails and fingers through my hair, but she is always gentle and I believe that her natural oils add sheen and polish to my coat."

We have by now eeled through the kitchen door, aided by our collaborative doorwoman, the cook, who has taken quite a fancy to Solange.

"My mistress has no natural oils but she has rows and rows of unnatural ones she applies to various portions," Solange reveals as we step into the shadow of the portico, then into the unfiltered sunlight. "My! Your coat is indeed as sleek as black satin. You could go to the Oscars and be a star on the red carpet."

"Alas, our commercial endeavors are over, and I doubt they would have garnered us a nomination. The members of the Academy have certain prejudices, you know."

We settle in the shade of a rattan lounge chair by the pool. It is like retiring to an airy pergola. Small slivers of sunlight pierce our retreat, oroating entrancing patterns on Solange's golden back.

"First the pool area," I muse. "Then the exercise room. Does that suggest a pattern?"

"The prankster is striking at various areas of the house where pageant activities are scheduled."

"Scheduled. That is exactly it. Each day here is laid out from hour to hour on schedules all the entrants and participants are following. Pretty easy to get one jump ahead of them."

"Yet the shaving cream used in the pool area was

'borrowed' from the freebies in the girls' lockers. That sounds like an impulsive move."

I regard Solange's sweet, contented Persian face with surprise. I had always thought of her as Yvette's larger darker plumper sister but maybe she is to her sister Yvette as Mycroft Holmes is to Sherlock, bigger and brighter. She shows some talent in the problem-solving department I have never spotted in my Divine One's makeup.

"And," she adds, licking a fluffy mitt and applying it to an airy eyebrow hair, "the bad-boy toy in the exercise room would need to have been imported, which implies premeditation."

"Say, you are no slacker in the logic department."

"I owe it to my mistress's elevated TV-viewing tastes. She is hooked on *CSI*."

I spit. It is all I can do not to hiss in the presence of a lady. "That bogus show elevates the humble evidence technician, when it is us detectives who really do the fancy footwork and ferret out the answers."

"Ferret! Do not mention that miserable creature. I had an unfortunate encounter with one of that kind."

"I am not fond of ferrets either. They are sly and sneaky."

"Exactly. If one were on the premises, I would know whom to suspect."

"Wait a minute! One *is* on the premises. A human ferret. And we must not overlook the possibility that a human male on the show personally imported the overblown lady . . . and someone else appropriated it as an object of fear and disgust."

Solange slaps her mitt back to the pavement. "I do not like crime solving. It requires thinking and rethinking, and I really should be in my room having my beauty rest. Except that Yvette is getting all the attention with her usual spoiled behavior."

This small temper tantrum on Solange's part reminds me of the intense competition between the Teen Queen candidates. All the hoopla and dirty tricks might only be Mean Girls in action.

One can never underestimate the human propensity for malice, spite, and mayhem.

I escort Solange back to her quarters but we are forced to duck into a doorway when we spot a man's big black boot emerging through Miss Savannah Ashleigh's door.

I am sorry to say that I recognize the rest of the man when I am able to see as high as his face, and give a low thrum of recognition.

"Ay, carumba!'"

"What is it, Louie?"

"Well put. Not so much a 'who' but a 'what.' We are regarding Miss Lieutenant C. R. Molina's worst nightmare and a serious fly in the ointment my Miss Temple will be none too pleased to see here either."

"He is tall, dark, and grim looking but what other kind of monster can this man be, and why is he leaving my mistress's quarters? Are she and Yvette all right?"

"I cannot reveal matters that I am confidentially informed about but that are hidden from the rest of the world. Let us just say that Mr. Rafi Nadir is bad news to everyone I know."

Chapter 25

Close Encounters of the Weird Kind

Temple decided that Xoe Chloe would not be one to cower in her room at the sight of a dead life-size blowup doll. Even if it was bigger than she was.

So she began a tour of the strangely deserted mansion. Apparently, the other candidates were the sort to cower in their rooms at the sight of a dead blowup doll, even if they were all bigger than it was.

It had taken all her persuasive PR powers to convince Mariah to remain safely in their room. Unauthorized explorations through the pageant house could very well get the younger girl disqualified. She didn't want to risk that, did she?

"What if you get thrown out?" Mariah asked passionately. (Girls her age were always passionate.) They spoke, as usual, under the cover of the thundering shower water.

Both she and Temple were getting Irish-soft skin from all this steaming, and were winning spontaneous compliments from Team Teen Queen for their "glowing" complexions. Subterfuge does have its pluses.

"They won't throw me out," Temple said. "This show needs a Bad Girl like Buffy the Vampire Slayer needed evil slayer Faith."

"You watched *Buffy: The Vampire Slayer?*" Mariah's voice broadcast new respect.

"Still watching reruns. So. If you recall, sometimes little sister Dawn couldn't come along. This is one of those times. And think how mad your mother would be if I got you tossed off the show, after all the trouble she went to seeing you had a partner in crime here on-site."

"I can't believe she let me come, with those creepy show posters turning up."

"I can't believe she *made me* come."

Mariah gaped at her for a moment, her soft features looking absurdly fifth-grade for a second. "My mother tells you what to do too?"

"Sometimes. She's da cops, you know."

"I know." Said with discouragement.

"That's okay. We've got an inside track on what's really going on."

"Why are you doing this?" Mariah's face suddenly showed an adult expression, half worry, and half hope.

"Your mom offered me my heart's desire."

"She can do that?"

"In my case. And . . . after I saw that defaced poster, I agreed that you needed a partner inside."

"Yeah. That was creepy. I can't believe she showed that to me."

"I think she wanted you to see that she could treat you like an adult."

"Really?" The word had ended on an adolescent squeal.

"Sometimes. If it's important. But you've got a ways to go before you earn the right to be treated that way full time."

Mariah grinned and leaned back against the sweating bathroom tile. Niagara Falls roared away into the bathtub, making it into a hot tub. "A long way. Like lying around here under the hidden cameras in the bedroom reading my pink Teen Queen folder while you pussyfoot around and have all the fun."

"Yeah. Like that."

"Okay."

Temple smiled as she fronted down the hall, always aware of the cameras. Some maturity was creeping into Mariah, making her a heartbreaking blend of reliability and impossible imaginings. Teenagers had hot flashes too, Temple decided. Easy for her to say, caught as she was in the great long slog between maturation and menopause.

Meanwhile, she could play thirteen-going-on-twenty again and act out.

What struck her first was how tortuously this house was designed. It was an assemblage of separate wings joined by modern breezeways, with Mondrian-like windows inset here and there.

What struck her second was how difficult it would be to do mischief here, given all the hidden cameras. That meant the perp was either part of the production crew or had access to the camera installations.

Like a major hotel casino, the house would need some sort of central spy chamber where the images from all the cameras unreeled. Where someone watched and recorded. Several someones. Most likely the technicians and producers but perhaps also someone with a more sinister purpose.

Temple was thinking about who this Sinister Someone could be so hard she turned the corner into the den area of the house and ran right into someone coming the other way: face-to-face and, ick, belly-to-belly, as in the oldie "Zombie Jamboree" song.

Double ick!! Rocketing Rollerblades! Where were Lexan bullet-proof shields when a girl needed them?

She had ended up cheek by jowl with the diminutive Crawford Buchanan!

Temple disengaged as fast as Xoe Chloe's size fives could manage it.

"Hey, little lady!" He reached out to steady her from the impact.

He should be so lucky.

"Chill, dude."

Temple skated away from him on the smooth marble floor despite having no Rollerblades beneath her feet at the moment. She could still move like a street skater. (In fact, her four older brothers had taught her to waltz on Minnesota concrete years ago. Without knee or elbow pads. You never knew what you would be grateful for, thanks to obnoxious older brothers, years later.)

"You're quite the spunky little dark horse," he said.

"Just send me a ticket to the Belmont Stakes," she rejoined.

"All this ugly hullabaloo and here you are, out and about like a Dead End Kid."

"A dead what?"

"Guess you're way too young to remember that old film stuff. I'd like to do an interview with you. Crawford Buchanan, media personality. I'm embedded here for KREP-AM radio."

"Embedded? Dude, that sounds sooo sleazy."

What a ferrety little weasel! Or was that piling on animal comparisons? No doubt, Temple knew she'd like ferrets and weasels a lot better than Awful Crawford. What a phony, with his cultivated basso that rumbled like gang warfare and his salon-styled hair that reflected every trendy fashion. She couldn't believe the new gold highlights in its already dramatic black-and-silver tones, courtesy of Mother Nature.

The highlights reminded her of Matt Devine, who was so much more worthy of bumping into than Crawford Buchanan. She wondered what he was doing in Chicago on his vacation. Would he ever believe . . . ? No, and he'd certainly never approve of doing such a wild and crazy thing, this dangerous masquerade, all for the sake of Max Kinsella.

Or was it?

"So, kiddo." Crawford was waxing oily again. "The old place is pretty spooky now that someone's leaving funny valentines all over it."

He'd immediately snapped her attention back to the here and now.

"What did you call it?" she asked, struck by his phrase. "This harassment?"

"Funny valentines. You know, the fluffy cream on the hot pink yoga mats. The . . . strawberry syrup spray on the, uh, balloon lady in the workout room. It's all a joke."

"And if it isn't?"

"Don't worry, babe. I'll be here to rescue you and record it all for KREP."

Hmmm. Another hanger-on, another motive. Maybe Crawford needed to bolster poor drive-time numbers. These flashy incidents could do it.

"I don't listen to those middle-of-the-road stations, man," Xoe sneered in answer.

"I'm not middle-of-the-road—" he replied, frowning.

"No, just road kill. Scram, old geek, or I'll run my spikes right through you."

Temple fanned out her claws and pushed past him into the empty den. She breathed out her relief when he didn't follow her in. How odd to think of everyone hunkered down in their rooms for safety's sake . . . when they were all being spied upon and recorded 24/7.

This whole setup was a voyeur's dream, she realized. Not the vague, general voyeuristic public instinct that supported reality TV but an honest-to-God, freaky, perverted voyeur of the old school.

The den was eerily deserted. Three large plasma TVs were blank gray screens on the wood-paneled walls, looking like modern art frames someone had forgotten to put the pictures in.

The many oversize white leather ottomans that the candidates had lolled upon in teen preening positions were empty now, and resembled giant poisonous mushrooms sprouting from the exotic wood-inlay floor.

The vast room was so dim and deserted that Temple braced herself for spotting another doll-like corpse, however ersatz.

But she was the only girl in residence.

Though not quite the only resident.

A figure stood, rising from one of the huge paired wing chairs near the see-through fireplace that served both the den and dining room.

It was tall, dark, and . . . familiar.

It leaned over to turn on a nearby torchère, casting light upward that defused before it reached the twenty-foot ceiling.

Cheese it, the cops! Cop, singular. Very singular.

And not Molina.

In fact, the anti-Molina.

Rafi Nadir, attired in casual black, like Max, but much less expensively than Max, came toward her.

She stood paralyzed. He'd already seen through one half-hearted disguise of hers. Would he detect this much more thorough one just as fast?

He looked leaner and meaner than his usual bloated, discontented self. He looked serious.

"What are you doing roaming around this place?" he asked.

Fight or flight? Rafi wasn't going to go away. Might as well find out now whether she could fool him or not. If not, maybe she'd have an ally inside. But, for now, undercover was her best option.

Temple/Xoe snapped her gum, then mumbled around it, "I'm a contestant. This is supposed to be . . . home."

Luckily, his eyes were scanning the overall scene, only half on her. "It's a TV set. And somebody is altering the script. You belong in your room, little girl. Better get back there."

"I suppose you can make me," Xoe challenged.

That girl never could keep her mouth shut when it mattered.

"Yes." He was two feet away now. He looked away again. "But that's not my job. That's just some advice from someone who knows when a situation is escalating into the weird and dangerous."

"I like the weird and dangerous."

He looked her up and down. "You think you do. I'm private security. I can't tell you what to do. I just say you oughta get back to your room. Lock the door. Do your nails. Wait for the producers to say the show must go on."

"Private? Like a PI?"

"God, no."

She knew that'd get his goat. Like all ex-cops, even disgraced ex-cops, Rafi hated private detectives.

"I was thinking of hiring you, is all."

"Yeah, right." He actually chuckled. "You Teen Queens think you're Britney Spears when you're really Nancy Drew. I'm already spoken for."

"Oh?" Temple tried to sound indifferent but Xoe sounded interested. "By whom?"

"By Savannah Ashleigh, the judge, is whom."

"She's no judge. She's just an actress, and a bad one."

"I don't judge clients. But I think she's right in being worried. So why a punk little chick like you is boogying around Hell House after all these unsettling incidents beats me. Given all the black you're wearing, must be a death wish."

"I don't like being penned up."

"You might consider that's exactly what might happen if there's another nasty prank and you're wandering around unaccounted for. I'd skedaddle back to my safe little room if I were you."

"It's not little."

He suddenly lunged forward, his booted foot smacking the floor.

She jerked back, retreating. It had worked. Xoe Chloe had made him too mad to see past her cheesy, mouthy exterior.

"Listen, *little* lady." He caught her arms and pulled her close and spoke low. "My job is to guard the Ashleigh broad but I'll give you some free expert advice. Somebody around here is this close to the edge. You don't want to end up spattered on the exercise machines, stay in your room. Don't wander around alone; do as you're told."

"And you're protecting Savannah Ashleigh by lounging around in the den?"

His grip tightened. A fist came up.

Temple dodged but she couldn't break free. Her "pal" Rafi wouldn't do this to her, but it was instructive to see what he'd do to some unknown young girl. How had she ever thought he might be a smidge better than the sleazeball Molina had made him out to be?

She winced, expecting a blow.

Instead he waved a cat-whisker-thin black wire at her.

"This place is bugged. Surveilled. All for the camera crews. But someone, maybe anyone, must be using this setup to watch and hear whatever he wants to, anytime. I'm going to track his ass through the same wires he uses to terrorize you people. Get it? Now shut up, get back to your room, and save your own pierced little skin."

When he let her go, she almost lost her balance. "Surveilled" was not a word but Temple decided this was not the time to mention that. He stalked off without waiting to see if she was taking his advice.

He was right, though. They were all experimental rats in a maze. Technology was their reason for being here, and their Achilles' heel.

Could Rafi himself be the creep who was stalking the show, relishing being called in to track himself?

What a mess. The cast and crew were too large, the pool of victims too numerous, and the potential evil-doer too easily hidden.

It was just a matter of time, she knew—and Rafi had indicated that he knew too—before someone really got hurt.

And not even Lieutenant Molina could do a thing about it.

Rafi was right about one thing: she belonged upstairs keeping an eye on Mariah, 24/7.

Chapter 26

Midnight Attack

"So what'd you find out?"

Mariah was sitting cross-legged on one side of the giant bed, painting her toenails atop the pink silk bedspread.

"Whoops!" Temple grabbed her notebook, opened it flat, and poised Mariah's chubby little toes on top of it. "You might drip."

"I won't drip," she said, looking up.

Temple looked down just in time to watch a red glob of nail enamel hit the notebook and pool there like a gobbet of designer-shade blood.

"So spake Dracula," Temple said. "Everybody drips painting their toenails. It's a girly rule since the Garden of Eden. Eve did it. Evita did it. Even the Dixie Chicks do it. We don't want to trash the room. That'll give us black marks in the competition."

Mariah said nothing but bit her lower lip in concentration as she painted her last big toenail.

"You're acting like one big drip," Mariah finally said. "You're like my mother. I can't do anything right."

"You're doing everything fine, just not over the pink silk bedspread with the scarlet nail polish, all right?"

Temple sat on the bed's end. "Is something wrong?"

"Just that this whole place is stupid, and everybody in it."

Temple pasted a cautionary finger to her lips.

"I don't care," Mariah said, even louder. "This place is creepy, even without the shaving cream threats and the just too gross rubber . . . thing on the exercise machine. I can't believe I'm saying this but I want to go home."

"What's wrong?"

Mariah starting picked at her cuticles where the polish had smeared, peeling off tiny flecks of dried enamel.

"I'm the only girl in my category who has to do two hours of workouts a day and live on Bugs Bunny leavings."

Temple paused, not knowing what to say. Then Mariah said it for her.

"I'm the only girl here who has to lose weight to win. It's not fair! I've only got a week left, and now all I can see when I do the treadmill is that stupid, bloody balloon girl. Maybe she got spattered because she was too fat too."

"You're not fat."

"You sound like my mom, and I don't believe her either."

"It's baby pudge. You haven't hit your full height is all. You'll be willowy like your mom in no time."

"Her? Willowy?"

"Well . . . maybe maple-y. She's a little solid for a willow; cops need to be. But she's not overweight."

"Oh, yeah? She's a member of Weight Watchers and she's always on me to join too."

"Weight Watchers." Temple felt numbed by surprise. She'd never pegged the terrible Lieutenant Molina as out of control in any area.

"She only has to go once in a while 'cuz she's a life member," Mariah added. "I'd have to get weighed every week and sit around with a bunch of fat old ladies."

Molina a lifer in Weight Watchers. Okay, that did fit with what Temple knew of the woman. Disciplined. Did it once and it was over. The kind of person who could quit smoking in one day. But once upon a time . . . Molina had been pudgy too? Hard to imagine but very pleasant to contemplate nonetheless. Even though Temple was noticing her own weight creeping up since hitting year thirty.

"Listen," Temple told Mariah. "If you've got a few pounds to lose, start now while it's easier. You already look pinchier in the cheeks and waist, so that rabbit food and extreme exercise must be working. A lot of it's probably only water weight."

"That's another thing. I hate that! It's so gross. It hurts and it makes me look fatter."

"Listen, kiddo. Everything women do makes us look fatter, including appearing on camera. Maybe it isn't us looking fatter but the world deciding how we should look. You made the finals, just the way you are. They must really, really like you."

Mariah frowned. "That last phrase sounded familiar."

"Sally Field on winning an Oscar. Everyone thought she was too kiddish and 'lightweight' to do that. But she did. Twice."

"Is that the little old lady who plays somebody's mother on some sitcom? She did? She won two Oscars?"

"Against all odds, and with the usual monthly bloat."

Mariah set her nail polish bottle—the label read "Hot Hibiscus"—atop the nightstand beside her.

"I'll think about it," she allowed.

"Good. Can I turn the light out now?"

"I guess."

Temple took that as the teenage equivalent of a yes.

She slipped out of her wig and into her nightshirt once the light was off, and then into the *aaahhh*-cool, four hundred-count sheets right after that.

Molina a Weight Watcher? Nothing wrong about that. Admirable, really. Except Temple couldn't stop grinning. Molina with her shoes off, weighing in like a lamb? Counting calories instead of counts on a rap sheet? Worried about that universal female bugaboo, weight.

Ummm, sweet dreams are made of these.

Temple awoke in the dark, suddenly disoriented. Strange room, strange bed, very strange sense of unease.

Had she just heard something? She listened. The hidden cameras didn't click, rattle, and roll, so the constant surveillance wasn't making her antsy.

Something was.

What?

A restless, hungry feeling. The menus at this place were low-carb, low-sugar, and low-fat. That could get on one's nerves.

Temple pushed herself up on an elbow and turned her bedside light onto the lowest wattage.

Not too low to show her a bed that was way too flat on the other side.

"Mariah?"

She pushed out of the bed and went to the bathroom door. It was shut. Was the poor kid having her period now? No wonder she had been so down.

Temple let her knuckles rap gently on the door.

No answer. She pushed, gently. The door wasn't locked but opened into utter darkness.

A flick of the light switch produced a fluorescent flood of light that left Temple blinking.

In the bright-white glare, something red stood out.

After about thirty seconds, Temple could tell what it was.

Red letters. Red letters written on the mirror above the sink. Studying them made her eyes water but she spied the bottle of Hot Hibiscus on the countertop.

YOU'RE A BUNCH OF BLOODY BITCHES the nail polish block letters declared. Well, sometimes. Yes. Mother Nature was like that.

Had Mariah done this? Not likely. Had Xoe Chloe sleepwalked and scrawled this angry comment on her competitors? Not likely.

Someone had been in here, though, appropriated Mariah's nail polish, and gone to work behind the closed bathroom door with neither of them the wiser.

Or maybe not. Because Mariah was gone. The bed was flat, the bathroom was empty. The closet—Temple swooped the sliding doors open on a plethora of nauseous pink—was turned into a Stepford Wives zone and was empty of human habitation. Under the bed the cupboard was bare.

Mariah was gone.

Oh, bifurcated Barbie dolls! Temple's prime assignment was missing in action.

She shoved her feet into a pair of low-heeled mules, pink, of course, but her own bunny variety from home, and headed for the door.

Ooops. First she doused the lights and felt her way back to her bedside, whisking her Cher hair off the lampshade and onto her head.

Outrageous is the best disguise.

She grabbed the key-chain pepper spray from her purse and burst out into the hall. It was as black as the bathroom had been before she'd turned on the light.

Someone was having fun with the mansion's light board. And not a hidden cameraman. They craved light.

She felt her way along the wall, with no idea of where she was going, only that she'd trace the power outage to its origin.

The producers had been diligent in soft lighting every inch of the place so that their cameras could record every twitch of a contestant. Only the bedrooms provided absolute dark.

Mariah. Temple felt cold sweat break out all under the irritatingly hot wig. Her charge. The reason she was here. Gone.

And someone painting bloody threats on their bathroom mirror while they slept.

While Temple slept.

She began to appreciate the constant needle of maternal anxiety. It was a drug, being responsible for someone else, for a young, helpless, naive someone else. Mariah. A picture in Temple's mind's eye, teenage whining, painting her toenails fluorescent red.

If anything had happened to her . . . forget Molina! Remember Temple's own panic.

Something brushed her legs.

She screeched and hugged the wall.

It brushed again.

Furry.

An eighteen-inch-high tarantula? She wouldn't doubt it in this Hell House.

Some sound between the first low buzz of an alarm clock and a purr pushed against her bare legs.

High furry boots, or . . . Puss-in-Boots, Las Vegas style.

"Louie?" she rasped. Whispered. Ground out.

The feathery presence drifted away but a step caught up with it.

Okay. She was either tailgating an ostrich or following a fine-feathered friend who just happened to have a cat tail.

In the dark, all things being equal, it was probably a cat. Her cat. Hers not to question why. Hers but to do or die. Into the Valley of Doubt marched Temple and her phantom feline.

A slice of light beckoned in the distance.

Was this a trap laid by a sneak-thief psycho nail-polish correspondent? Or . . . enlightenment?

Temple felt another plumy brush against her bare calves and decided she need to be very Zen right now, right here.

She pushed toward the light, into the light . . . and through a swinging door into the mansion's brightly lit and darkly designed kitchen, all stainless steel and black marble and granite.

And all . . . Mariah. Sitting on a black granite countertop in her pink Teen Queen nightshirt, sucking on a raspberry Popsicle.

"You total idiot!" Temple accused, knowing this was not the proper esteem-building tone but she had lost that concern. Funny that relief could be so enraging. "I was worried to death."

"Around this place that's serious," Mariah said. "How'd you find me?"

"You'll look terrific on spy TV."

"One Popsicle. Sugarless. That's the best they have in those three giant refrigerators. It's not a federal case."

Temple eyed the Popsicle stump. "Sugar free, really? Where are they?"

"Bottom freezer drawer, fridge on the left."

Temple eyed the black marble floor between here and there. Not a creature was stirring, not even the proverbial mouse. Or tarantula. Or cat.

"How'd you know where to look, really?" Mariah asked. She wanted an answer.

"Oh, maybe I was ready for a taste of faux sugar myself."

"It's fructose. Real fruit sugar. That's better than added sugars or even artificial ones."

Temple boosted herself up on the kitchen island beside Mariah. The black granite's chill seeped through her thin cotton T-shirt.

"I'm sorry I was crabby," Mariah said.

"That's all right, kid. I get crabby too." She leaned into Mariah's ear. "You'll be even crabbier when you know that someone used up your whole bottle of nail polish writing nasty notes on our bathroom mirror."

"No!" Mariah looked around, her soft young features squinching into suspicion, and annoyance. "This place is getting off the wall. The show's gonna be ruined."

"Unless the Teen Queen slant was a front from the first, and the show was always intended to be an updated game of Clue."

"What's Clue?"

"Let's shuffle off down the hall again. I think that's safer than talking here. And we sure don't want to steam up our bathroom mirror again."

"Why not?" Mariah jumped down and actually held a hand out to help old Temple make the same leap.

"Evidence," Temple whispered against her ear again.

She had a feeling the location of this last prank would merit some serious, and open, police involvement. And probably the presence of the one person that the two of them least wanted to see here: Mama Molina.

They sat up the rest of the night, leaning against the foot of the giant bed while Temple explained the game of Clue to Mariah, and Mariah explained current teen hotties to Temple.

All of their dialogue was suitable for public replay.

Breakfast was served at seven, just like at camp. So

once Mariah had been escorted to the 'tween dining area, which was ashriek with excited girls having so little to chew on that they were chewing on each other, Temple headed for the Teen Team offices.

"Oh, Beth, thank God you're here."

The bustling, plump woman paused in pawing through an open file drawer.

No wonder. That had definitely not been a Xoe Chloe opening line.

"Why, Zoo-ey, what are you doing here, dear? You're supposed to be at breakfast right now."

"I kinda lost my appetite. Got a stomach full of red nail polish last night."

"You . . . you drank some red nail polish! Oh, I knew you looked like a paint sniffer. This means expulsion."

"Hold on to your granny panties, lady. The nail polish was the writing on the mirror in Mariah's and my bathroom. Like the hot foam jobs on the yo-yo yoga mats in the patio area the other day."

"Writing? Like—?"

"Like handwriting? Like graffiti. You know, nasty messages in public places. Only our bathroom is private. I thought."

"I must see it . . . we must see it. At once."

"Then you'll call the cops."

"The police? Oh, no." Beth Marble paled, if that were possible for one so wan. "The producers don't want them here."

"Gonna be hard to keep them away. Better if you play Sally Citizen and call them before they call on you. Cops get agitated about the littlest things."

"How do you know?"

"Well, I'm a little thing, right?" Xoe Chloe spun to indicate her punk but petite form.

"The police." Beth Marble imitated her last name and

plunked down into her chair as if the weight of Michelangelo's David had suddenly descended on her from above. "Dexter will be so disagreeable about that."

"What's new? Besides, he doesn't run the show. You do. Don't you?"

"Yes. I'm head coach. The show was my idea. But Dexter's the star."

"I thought all of us mini-teen wonders were the stars in the making."

"You're not the draw. No one knows you. As the show unfolds, yes, they'll get to know the candidates and like or"—she glanced significantly at Xoe Chloe—"dislike them. And then they'll vote for the winner. But Dexter has the right to discount an audience winner at the last moment. The final decision is his. He's the star maker. Thus, he's the star."

"Thus. You learn that in Latin class forty years ago, lady? So. Dexter has audience veto power. I wonder what an enterprising girl has to do to get ole Dexter's vote. Sleep with him?"

"No!" Aghast. "You're almost all minors. That's unthinkable. Such a thing would never happen."

"Happens all the time in the halls of junior and senior high schools. Read the paper."

Beth frowned sternly. "Not here. We have cameras all over the place. Any hanky-panky would be recorded."

"All the better to titillate the viewers, eh? Then you must have our bathroom action on tape. Whoever wrote the hate note would have been sneaky, and pretty good at it. But no one could write in the dark, especially with something as thick and quick to run out as nail polish. It took a whole bottle, which means it took some time."

"We aren't allowed to record in the bathrooms, young lady."

"What about alerting the police?"

"Oh, I don't think we need to involve them in these malicious little pranks."

"Do you mean that 'these malicious little pranks' are part of the show script?"

"We are unscripted!" Indignantly said.

"No. No, you're not. Somebody's pretty good at writing in a lot of 'unauthorized' scenes. If you figure out how my roomie and I are going to get a decent night's sleep after this, send us a memo. Just don't leave it unsigned on our pillowcases. We need our beauty rest, you know."

Chapter 27

Midnight Assignation

It was during the Night of the Living Lipstick (okay, it was nail polish but that does not sound as good) that I decided I must take what they call "a proactive role" in the proceedings.

I, of course, had remained cleverly concealed, listening in with my awesome radial antennae (i.e., pointed little ears) when my Miss Temple and little Miss Mariah discussed the defacement of their bathroom mirror.

Now, I am not much for mirrors, though I long ago figured out that the suave gentleman in black I glimpsed in them was merely my own self. Many of my kind are convinced they are viewing twin littermates. These benighted sorts are not candidates for more sophisticated roles in human society, such as shamus.

As an ace gumshoe, I immediately decided I needed more inside operatives and must call on the Ashleigh girls.

I did say "girls," did I not? I have already discovered that they are well acquainted with mirrors but are among the deluded type who mistake their own image for a rival (although a bewitchingly attractive rival) for their mistress's affections. It is bad enough that there are the two of them. Luckily, both are inverse images of each other, so they will never mistake a sister for a twin. If that makes any sense.

I paw their bedroom door, shivs politely retracted. That subtle sound, rather like a steel brush hissing across a snare drum skin, instantly perks up the ears of my kind. It has the advantage of sounding like some leaf blowing along a sidewalk, a phenomenon universally ignored by *Homo sapiens*.

And speaking of *Homo sapiens,* surely Miss Savannah Ashleigh must be the sappiest around.

So, in a moment, a curled soot foot is pushed under the door frame and then come tempting little jiggles of the door, abetted by my leaping to apply my weight near the doorknob until the catch springs . . . and out through a narrow opening push the pretty-in-pink noses of the Persian sisters.

When I compliment them on their pink proboscises, they feign ignorance of the word "proboscis" and state that the breed standard for their kind's noses is the color rose.

So a rose nose is a rose nose is a rose nose, but plain old pink in my book.

Once in the hall and over our terminology debates, I explain that what I need is not noses, of whatever shade you want to call them, but eyes and ears.

"Quite right, Louie," Yvette says with a shaded silver brush along my side. "Noses are a canine sense: loud, snuffly, and vulgar. We can see and hear without being seen and heard, in perfect silence."

"I agree," say I, "especially about the perfect part."

Behind us, Solange makes discreet retching noises. It may be the common malady of a hair ball, or it may be an editorial comment.

I know better than to be caught between them. That would be like being the Jack of Spades sandwiched between the Queen of Hearts and the Queen of Diamonds. Lunch meat.

I tell my new staff about the latest Zorro attack: evil words on a bathroom mirror.

"Our mistress writes in the steam on the bathroom mirror all the time," Solange offers.

"Indeed. You would say she is a skilled graffiti artist then?"

"I would say," Yvette puts in, with a corrosive glance at her sister, "that family secrets are family secrets. She writes down the phone numbers of her various gentleman friends so she does not forget them."

"Why would she not use a little black book, or a computer?" I wonder.

"Blackmail," Solange purrs thrillingly. "Too easy to access. The tabloids are always stalking her."

I do not point out that they do so because Miss Savannah Ashleigh always provides them with useful opportunities, such as sunbathing in the nude with Yvette and her litter of unwanted kittens. The tabloids got a lascivious closeup of Yvette nursing with Miss Savannah Ashleigh's bare anklebone in the background that time.

"We could use some tabloid photographers on these crime scenes," I point out. "The only cameras here are indentured to the producers. They will either be suppressed so the show can go on, or . . . even more devious, the show planned these disruptions and this is a *Fear Factor* pattern rather than a makeover pattern."

"What is a makeover?" Yvette asks with touching curiosity.

"Humans," I explain, "do not all come with luxurious

coats of fur, airy whiskers, dainty limbs, kaleidoscope eyes, and expressive tails. Many of them are handicapped from birth. Hence their need to remake themselves in a better image."

"Poor things!" Solange cries.

"But our own," I point out. "I am sure you wish to serve Miss Savannah Ashleigh as much as I do my Miss Temple."

"But, Louie." The Divine Yvette's voice rises to an imperious tone. "Your Miss Temple is not here."

Ooops.

"That is correct, Yvette. As usual, your perceptions are formidable. However"—I am thinking, thinking, thinking—"however, little Miss Mariah is here, and she is not only an acquaintance of my Miss Temple, but in my own view, she and her mother, a noted law enforcement personality in this town, are to be commended for adopting a pair of"—here I gaze soulfully at Yvette—"striped homeless kittens last fall. In my own view."

A silence holds. Yvette unwillingly bore a litter of yellow striped cats once erroneously purported to be mine. They were given up for adoption, naturally, once the tabloid interest had died down. I cannot believe that Yvette is indifferent to those who adopt striped nobodies.

She sniffs. I cannot tell if it is the usual French sniff, as is used to dismiss an inferior wine, or a snuffle, as is used to record a deep but unacknowledged emotion.

"I understand, Louie," she says finally. "Your devotion to the underdog does you credit."

Hmmm. This is an edged compliment at best but I let it pass.

"Yvette and I," Solange agrees in the flash of an eyelash, "will happily aid you in protecting the Mariah kitten."

Hallelujah! It is not easy to turn purebred Persians into legmen. Er, leg ladies. And I certainly expect a lot less back sass than I get from Midnight Louise. Having claimed to be my relative, she is therefore free to call me anything she likes.

Devoted is not on that list, along with a lot of other sterling qualities.

Chapter 28

Contingency Plan

"I'm glad Old Cold Marble isn't calling in the police," Mariah said. "My mom would be all over this place, and I'd be outed."

She was sitting on the bedroom carpet with Temple, leaning glumly against the end of the bed and facing the door.

They'd decided to do their own guard duty. Light from one of the bedside lamps cast a soft campfire glow on the lavish furnishings.

"Why does someone hate the contestants so much?" Mariah asked after awhile.

"Let's see. It could be one of us."

"No way! Why would anyone ruin her one chance at fame and fortune?"

"Fame and fortune, my latest Lash 'n' Flash eyeliner! Did you read the contest rules? All the contestants get is a non-invasive makeover and a few new clothes. That doesn't begin to offset the fortune your mom paid for your Teen Queen clothes. So the two division winners get a highly chaperoned date with some boy band has-been and a few more new clothes and a rhinestone crown you can get at a dozen outlets in Vegas. So what?"

"And a car!"

"And a car. A really sexy Dodge Neon, sure. Don't you have three years to go before you could drive it anyway? That's forever in Teen Time."

"Two and a half years. Then I get a learner's permit." Mariah's dark glance slid toward Temple. "You're one to sniff at a car. I've seen that red Miata you drive. You got yours. And you can diss boy band guys. I hear you have a real Bad Boy on the string."

"Really? Exactly how did you hear that?"

"It's a small house. I can't help overhearing things. I heard my mom and her friend Matt talking about him once. Max." Mariah slid her another glance. "He sounds cool."

And lately Max was being way too cool, Temple thought. "Your mom's mistaken about Max."

"She's not usually wrong about her job."

"She's wrong this time. Max is not a criminal. He's just a magician. Sometimes they act similar."

"All I know is my mom doesn't much think about men but he's sure got her paddle holster in a snarl."

"So. You see a lot of Matt at your place?"

"Some." Mariah picked at a fleck of nail polish on her thumb cuticle. "He's a little old to be in a boy band but he sure is cute. My mom says I can ask him to my father-daughter dance at school. The other girls would be so fried!"

This bit of news offered Temple two opportunities for choking on her next words: surprise that Matt was becoming a domestic fixture at Casa Carmen Molina, or horror that poor Mariah didn't know that the man actually entitled to escort her to the father-daughter dance was right here at the Teen Queen Castle right now, doing surveillance.

"Are you falling asleep yet?" Mariah asked.

Not after this discussion. No way. "No. But we do need to get some rest. Why don't you try to sleep and I'll watch? Then we can switch."

"By then it'll be morning," she said.

"Yeah. That's okay. Dark circles around my eyes just save me applying my Smudge Pot kohl eyeliner in the morning. Nothing like lost sleep and hollow eyes to make a modern girl look hip and interesting."

"Add enforced starvation." Mariah tilted her head to listen to her tummy growl.

"Now you got the program!"

Kids were amazing. Mariah was off to sleep sitting up before Temple could count to thirteen.

That left Temple on guard duty, and therefore free to brood.

Matt was taking Mariah to the school father-daughter dance? Max was a topic of Molina household discussion, and not in flattering terms?

Temple was feeling decidedly like the odd woman out with everyone she knew. Xoe Chloe, the rebellious loner, began to seem less like a role and more like a dose of reality.

Temple sighed deeply, wondering what was going on in her life, and if she would be the last to know.

Screeches two decibels lower than a klaxon in pitch and strength ripped down the hallway outside their bedroom door.

Mariah awoke, as punchy as a toddler having a nightmare.

Temple was on her feet. "Stay here! I mean it. Sit. Down. Freeze."

She sprinted out the door, paused to identify the direction of the god-awful noise, and raced left.

Their room was near the end of the wing housing a third of the contestants, so she wasn't surprised to hear vague buzzes and shuffles behind her.

The guttural cries and high-pitched shrieks ahead never faded.

Temple charged through the ajar door between her and the unceasing hullabaloo.

Lights were glaring but everybody in the room was still blinking, so Temple had to assume the lights had just been turned on an instant before her arrival.

She crossed the threshold and stopped, stupefied.

It wasn't what she saw. It was who.

Savannah Ashleigh. White-faced, straw-haired, and shaking, wearing a filmy mauve peignoir set off the cover of a 1970s paperback Gothic romance, the kind with the big house with a light in the window behind the fleeing figure of a nightgown-clad woman.

Rafi Nadir. Clad in durable black denim jeans and a heavy cotton turtleneck shirt alarmingly like a Kmart version of Max's garment of choice. Puzzled, angry, and uneasy.

Midnight Louie, his fur punked up into damp spikes and his tongue hanging sideways between his bared white fangs.

Savannah's purebred Persians, one silver, one gold, and both with their coats messed up as if by a whirlwind, still snarling and spitting, mostly to themselves.

"What on earth happened here?" Temple asked, raising her voice into Xoe Chloe's more hyper range. This would put the Xoe Chloe makeover to the acid test. Both Savannah and Rafi were acquainted with Temple though they'd never expect to see her here, in this guise.

"That's what I want to know," Nadir said, still staring accusingly at Savannah. "I turn on the light and get one hysterical female and three pretty raggedy cats, all ready to chew my ass."

"I glimpsed him," Savannah shrieked like a wind-up doll that, having been set for one mode, can't escape it. "He wore black."

"I'm your bodyguard," Rafi said. "I just got here. I came when I heard the caterwauling. Are you saying some guy in black came in here and attacked you?"

"In black like you, yes."

"Bodyguards wear black. Especially at night. It's useful if people don't notice us. I came as soon as I could. Did you maybe glimpse the cat? He's all in black."

That directed Temple's attention to Midnight Louie. Again. He was sure dogging her footsteps on this one.

Savannah's eyes dilated even more. "That cat!!! That devil! He's been the ruination of Yvette and now he's come to get me. That's Midnight Louie, I know it!"

Rafi's dark eyes narrowed as he assessed Savannah. "You superstitious about cats? Is that it? Ma'am?"

The address of respect had been added way too late.

"Just that one. I'm sure that's the one that ruined my darling Yvette and he's here to ruin me."

Temple actually felt a twinge of pity for the woman. Obviously something had occurred to frighten her, and she was all alone in this suite, unlike Temple and Mariah. Temple suspected that Louie had come running, just like her and Rafi. Temple had tried to ignore Louie's skulking presence around the place but now she understood it. He'd always been sweet on the luscious Yvette, who now sat shaking and licking her pretty little front paws by turns.

Time for Temple's new persona to sink or swim. This was Zoe's second run-in with Rafi. Brash Xoe Chloe's extreme looks and attitude would either fool these two close-up. Or not.

"Hey, lady!" Temple kept her naturally foggy voice

high and a bit nasal. "This is just a black stray cat. Chill. I don't know who this 'Louie' is. Your bookie? But this ole cat here is just some innocent stray. I mean, could those big green eyes lie?"

Here Xoe Chloe turned to eye Rafi Nadir up and down much more thoroughly than Temple would ever do. His eyes were in no way green.

"And this man can't have been here earlier," she decreed. "Look! Those cats have lost a lot of nail sheaths engaging someone in this room tonight." A few pearly scythes still glinted from the navy carpeting. "Some would have clung to that denim and cotton-knit and showed up like dandruff on all that black. Someone else walked out of here dripping nail sheaths. But not your bodyguard. Look again! There's another one by the door."

"Oh." Savannah looked from Rafi to the carpet to the door, but not at Xoe. She pressed a hand to her bony chest and sank into seated posture on the end of her bed. "Then I did see someone in black. Just not this man."

"Maybe." Nadir bent to the rug, glanced at Temple with no great favor, then followed the trail of nail sheaths to the door. Opening it, he encountered a herd of pink-shirt-clad contestants, looking like agitated sorority sisters.

He quickly shut the door. "What happened?" he asked Savannah, his voice brusque with urgency. "How exactly were you attacked?"

"It was dark. I heard the door open. When I got up, someone or something pushed me back onto the bed. Then there was this shrieking, like bats or banshees or something."

"Cats," Xoe said. "It sounded like a cat fight from forty feet down the hall."

"My cats were fighting *something big*," Savannah insisted, pushing herself upright on the bed. "I glimpsed a man's figure, just as the lights went on. And off again. And on again."

Rafi rubbed his forehead. "I came in and hit the lights."

"No. No, he must have been gone by then. You had to have passed him in the hall."

"I didn't. Nothing to run into, not even a current of disturbed air. Nobody went out of here."

Temple swaggered to the door in Xoe's motorcycle boot gait, which is hard to do in bunny slippers.

From Rafi Nadir's expression, he'd come to the same conclusion as Savannah.

"Hey." Xoe Chloe blew a kiss at her own bizarre reflection. Totally not-Temple. "You got a full-length mirror here. Next to the door. How'd you rate?"

"Yes." Savannah was pleased by her observation. "That's part of my contract wherever I appear. A full-length mirror installed next to the room door. So I can check myself just before I leave. So many women end up dragging toilet paper on their shoes or with hitched-up skirts or worse from not checking their full-length reflection in a mirror before they leave a hotel room."

"You're saying—?" Nadir pressed Temple/Xoe with the same weary skepticism his no-longer-significant other used.

"I'm saying the mirror by the door, in dim light, could confuse a witness. Or a victim."

"A victim?" Savannah's voice—never sweet, gentle, and low—rose to new hysterical heights. "I was to be a victim?"

Temple nodded, though she wasn't entirely sure about that. "The cats must have sensed a problem and attacked the man in black in the dark, before the lights went on. Their eyes don't require much light to see."

"The cats." Savannah glanced around. "My little darlings! Fighting for their mommy tooth and nail."

"Nails," Temple corrected, pointing out another lost sheath with the pink felt nose end of her bunny slipper.

Nadir frowned and dropped down to the carpet to mark

the spot with an X of tape he'd taken from a dispenser on the spindly-legged desk near the door.

Temple, meanwhile, advanced on the mirror. Midnight Louie was shadowing her ankle like it was his lost love. She hoped that wouldn't give her away. Savannah certainly wasn't praising him as her savior.

But then, unlike Rafi, he wasn't Savannah's bodyguard. He was Temple's.

She glanced down. In the now overlit room, Louie's dark pupils were the eye of the needle in his enigmatic green eyes. They were aimed like arrows toward the target of the mirror.

Once in front of it, Temple's fingernails tested the frame, looking for a mechanism.

Rafi came up behind her, his dark reflection encompassing her pageant-pink one for a moment, like an ugly storm cloud swallowing a remnant of the sunset. Would he recognize her now? Or had her gift for disguise fooled even a suspicious guy like him?

He eyed her for a long while. But it wasn't really her he was looking at, for he then lifted the mirror off its hook as if it were made of cardboard. As if to prove something.

And revealed . . .

A paneled wall. A wall paneled in picture frame panels, rather.

His black work boot pushed at the bottom. The inside of the panel clicked inward, revealing a dark and mysterious passage beyond.

He stepped into the patch of black. "Stay here."

"Wait a minute, dude. I found this."

"Drop the dead-end-kid act."

Temple's heart dropped instead. He'd made her! Then he went on.

"You think you're such a tough twerp. You're a kid. In your nightie. Stay here."

Temple rammed him from the side and forced her leg through, bunny slipper and all.

"This is nuts! The city is crawling with ballsy little broads. Stay here and pet the cats or something."

"I'll raise such a ruckus you'll be the last person on earth to see inside that passage."

Rafi, glowering like a World Wrestling Federation personality at intermission, reluctantly stood aside.

"Ladies first." He didn't, of course, mean either word of it.

That didn't matter. Neither one of them would be first into the dark.

Midnight Louie hefted his tail into the air at a ninety-degree angle and preceded them into the lightless secret passage beyond.

Temple followed and so did a thin beam of light. She turned back to see Rafi hoisting a cigar-size flashlight he'd pulled from his jeans pocket.

The passage was pretty dull. Instead of being dank and vermin ridden, it was dry and dusty. Nothing moved in it but them. Louie spotted a few snakes to pounce on but they turned out to be electric cables.

Rafi pointed his narrow light at the seam where ceiling and walls met. More cables, affixed to the support beams by huge staples.

"The man who built this place was a bit paranoid, like Elvis," Temple noted.

"Perfect setup for wiring and surveillance. That's why the producers picked this house. It was wired for everything already. Must be more of these access passages all though the place."

"Perfect system for sick pranksters to use," she noted.

Rafi laughed. "Yeah. I'd call the producers of all these

rigged reality shows sick pranksters. Amazing. People protest the increased surveillance touching their lives because of terrorists but love to watch their fellow citizens being eavesdropped on and filmed on the sly and tricked in these cheesy reality shows."

"Inhumane nature," Temple commented sagely.

The flashlight picked out the black shapes of hidden cameras strung along the corridor like suspended bats in a cave.

"The technicians must be running up and down these all the time," she noted. "What keeps a really nasty voyeur from being among them?"

"Not a thing, bunnie babe. Not one thing. I suppose there's no hope for it but to go back and guard that Ashleigh broad. Ain't it amazing how the most irritating one aboard is the most careful to protect herself?"

"Oh, Miss Ashleigh isn't the most irritating one here."

"You have a better candidate?"

He obviously had not considered the male contingent. Dexter Manship . . . Crawford Buchanan . . . Mr. Hair Guy. Male chauvinism can be blinding.

They re-emerged smelling of dust and, it turned out, covered in it. (Only Louie seemed to relish the fact. He shook himself dust free in a few seconds, then began licking his coat in the proper direction again.)

No one much noticed their less-than-triumphal return. The room thronged with cooing girls in pink pajama sets intent on both soothing Savannah and courting her vote.

Even the Persian girls were now ensconced on the bedspread beside their recumbent mistress, purring away in solace and solidarity.

"Frightening," Rafi noted.

Temple was sure that Midnight Louie concurred, and she was ready to join the both of them.

"I'm being stalked," Savannah insisted. "I suspected as

much but now that this demon, this evil black ninja, has shown up in my very room, I'm certain of it."

The accusation caused all eyes to turn toward the trio returned from their expedition through the looking glass, all black in some sinister way. There was Louie, black as a witch's familiar from toe to tail to tip of ear. Temple and her ebony Cher hair. Rafi Nadir and his Middle-Eastern looks in black denim. The lion, the witch, and the . . . Temple glanced at Rafi. No, he did not qualify as a wardrobe. Thank goodness.

"There's a hidden passage," he said, "behind the mirror. Anyone could have come in or out."

Savannah sat up, all disheveled blonde hair (her usual style anyway). "My babies were in danger!" She gathered Yvette and Solange close, their eyes slitting in an expression of utter feline distaste mixed with bored sufferance.

Come to think of it, that exactly matched the expression on Rafi Nadir's face.

"Nail it shut," she ordered.

"Can't," he said. "The mirror covers the entire door."

"Well, I can't possibly move. It would upset the girls. Cats are far more attached to places than to people."

Rafi visibly struggled not to say that in her case such a reaction would be justified. While he dawdled, Rome burned. Or at least Savannah's baser instincts.

"Then you'll just have to keep watch all night on *this* side of the mirror," she purred.

Yes, she *purred.* She had doubtlessly been called upon to purr a line or several in every one of her B and C movies, and probably a few Ds, Temple thought. Or were those cup sizes: before and after augmentation?

As Rafi looked around in horror at his frilly duty-station-to-be, Savannah took charge. "You can sleep—or catnap rather, for you certainly don't want to miss another intrusion—on the chaise lounge."

He regarded this bejeweled pillow-heaped upholstered torturous curl of feminine furniture as if it were a medieval iron rack.

"I'll do whatever it takes to prevent any further incursions," Rafi said, through his teeth, "but I'll sleep in the hall right outside the door. Just a scream away. Yours or theirs."

He nodded at the languid Persians.

Savannah pouted but didn't object. Temple supposed luring any man any nearer at all satisfied her vanity and reduced the fuss and muss of actual intimacy. But Rafi's resistance to the siren of soft porn surprised Temple.

Was he possibly tiring of the superfeminine stereotype? Then again, he'd hooked up with Molina years before, so he must have something of a soft spot for hard women.

Scratch a male chauvinist and find a . . . masochist secretly in search of a dominatrix? Interesting.

"Good." Savannah snuggled down in her many decorative bed pillows, dragging the Persian sisters with her. "You girls can leave now. I have a bodyguard."

The Teen Queen candidates pitter-pattered out, the young and the sleep deprived, a herd of blonde bunnies.

Temple regarded her bunny slippers, a Christmas gift from her mother. They belonged with the herd. The rest of Temple/Xoe did not.

"You want me to take the chaise lounge?" she asked Rafi in a *West Side Story* teen-gang accent, using Savannah's misnomer.

"No. I can handle both sides of the door, girly. Take yourself back to your bunk bed."

"My little sis is probably having hysterics," she conceded.

When she ankled out into the hall, Louie was making like Saran Wrap on her ankles again.

Everyone had accepted him as some stray mascot that

had adopted the house. Cameras lingered lovingly on his liquid feline progress through the rich environs and the gathered Teen Queens. He strutted like a sultan with a private harem.

Temple decided she could do worse than to adopt the attitude everyone else had.

Mariah was waiting at the door to their room, as ordered, but barely.

One foot and an elbow and an inquisitive nose were in the hall.

"What happened? Who screamed?"

"Savannah Ashleigh and her cats."

"Oh." Mariah instantly diagnosed a false alarm. "That airhead gives Clairol a bad name. Every time anything male crosses her path, including that black cat there, she swoons. I thought that went out with corsets."

"No one told Savannah. And corsets are back in, since Madonna. But Miss Ashleigh is a judge, so good little contestants don't want to be caught on camera dissing her." Temple looked up. "Although I'm betting all the cameras are trained on Savannah Ashleigh's bedroom after tonight's scare."

"I need a shower," Mariah declared. She looked in Temple's direction and sniffed. Pointedly. "Where have you been? Smells gross. Let's go."

This call for a private talk was about as subtle as Emeraude perfume, but Temple retreated into the bathroom with Mariah for a quick consultation. She actually relished the moisture falling hot water would pump back into her desiccated sinuses. That "secret" passage had been as deserty dry as a pharaoh's tomb.

"No!" Mariah, red faced and dewy from the makeshift sauna a few minutes later, was rapt. "A secret passage."

"Packed with recording equipment. Nothing Gothic about it. Just high-tech snooping."

"And with that bodyguard guy. He looks hot."

Temple wasn't ready to hear this from Mariah but allowed for teen exaggeration. "He's just a middle-aged private cop," she said carefully. "Nothing glamorous like a Day-Glo boy."

"My mom hates those guys."

"Day-Glo boys?" Temple asked, startled. From Max to boy bands? Where would Molina's prejudices end?

"No, private cops."

Maybe, but her mom hated this particular private cop even worse.

"He's right, though," Temple said. "All the pranks here smell like producers' tricks to up the ante on the competition."

"Cops have no imagination," Mariah said authoritatively.

Nor did cops' kids, thank goodness.

"Is that cat going to sleep with us?"

Temple considered Louie. And the fact that Mariah had seen him once, months ago, with Matt, and didn't know he was Temple's cat. Or, actually, he wasn't Temple's cat. She was Louie's person. As such, he would sleep with them.

"Probably," Temple said. "He's an outcast. Savannah would never let him bunk with her precious Persians."

Giggles were Mariah. "I'd love to see that! Her cats sure are pretty, though. Mine are kinda scrawny and stripey."

"They're delightful. I remember them as kittens. They were the cutest things."

"'Cute' doesn't cut it." Mariah had suddenly plunged into one of those teen dives on a bungee cord to self-esteem hell.

"Look. I've been 'cute' my whole life, and I survived it."

"Yeah . . . but."

"I am not a 'yeah . . . but.' I am a real girl. Remember, your police professional mom hired *me* to look after you."

"She did, didn't she? That was weird. My mom doesn't depend on anybody but herself."

"Maybe that's a problem."

Mariah reared back. She had bought into Supermom herself.

"She can't be everywhere," Temple pointed out. "And you gotta admit some strange things are happening here."

"But none of them are really real, are they? They're all threats but no action."

"You've got a point. This is a 'reality' show but the action is strangely unreal. You might even say surreal."

"What does that mean?"

"Surreal?" Temple smiled at Midnight Louie, now sprawled out in the vast wasteland between her and Mariah's sides of the gigantic bed. "Surreal is sort of like saying this big black cat here is our personal bodyguard."

"Who'd want a cat for a bodyguard? I'd want Enrique Iglesias. Who'd you want?"

Temple considered. "Not Kevin Costner."

"Who?"

Oops. Already over a decade out of date. "Ummm." Nobody Mariah might know came to mind. "The Pink Panther."

"The Pink Panther? Who's that?"

And that gave Temple an opening to tell a fairy story about a world long ago and far away and very funny. She took them both miles away from the Teen Queen Castle with its secrets and strangers and perplexing puzzles that seemed to lead nowhere.

Chapter 29

Home Sweet
Harassment

Molina couldn't believe it. Only five days at the Teen
Queen Castle and Temple Barr had phoned to report four
incidents of threats and harassment. All of it sounded
pretty amateur, but even one loose cannon in that hothouse situation was bad news.

She certainly had time to think this whole thing over
at home. The house felt incredibly empty without
Mariah in it, so empty that she hadn't been able to
sleep. This did not bode well for the coming teen dating
years.

The competition house was being watched around the
clock. It would have been hard enough to send Mariah off
on her first independent stay away from home under normal circumstances. To do it under the wacky auspices of
a reality TV show was way worse. To have edgy little acts
of violence surrounding the Teen Queen competition
made it a mother's nightmare.

She wandered into the kitchen and opened the refrigerator door. The ostensible reason was to feed the cats, Caterina and Tabitha, who were also up and hyper, looking lean, mean, and neglected. *Meee-ow.* Feed me. Their girly caretaker was gone.

Not to worry. Mama to the rescue.

The underlying reason to feed the cats was to search the fruit/vegetable drawer, then the freezer, for something sweet, fatty, and delicious.

No such animal in the Molina household.

Drat!

Wait!

What the heck is this?

A non–Weight Watchers frozen dessert.

Caramel. Chocolate. Six hundred calories. Thirty-three carbs. Eighteen grams of fat . . .

Mariah must have imported this anti-diet bomb to the family fridge.

No, she'd been fanatic about low-fat, low-carb foods the past month. Probably because she'd been hoping to get The Call from the Teen Queen people.

How could a detective-mother have missed that change of habit?

Been a little busy at work?

Molina balanced the frozen dessert package on one palm, weighing its presence here as well as its calories.

The frozen package chilled her hand. The icy chill drove deeper as she realized . . . this wasn't just some forgotten purchase. This was another "gift" from the anonymous stalker.

She slid the kitchen drawer open and pulled out a large plastic baggie, one-handed. The frozen container might not hold prints and there probably wouldn't be prints anyway, but she would check.

Meanwhile, her daughter was on her own in the Teen Queen Castle, which was also beset by stalker incidents.

Okay. Temple Barr was on the teen scene. Not bad for an amateur. A gifted snoop. But no professional.

What to do?

For one wild moment, Molina wanted to rip the dessert from the protective baggie, gobble it down, eat the evidence, take two aspirin, and think about it in the morning.

She picked up her cell phone.

Something bad in the neighborhood? Who you gonna call?

What was happening with Mariah, and how could a mother under siege deal with it? Not to mention Rafi Nadir stalking out of her past like a mummy brought to life.

Who you gonna call?

The latest number on her instant dial was Larry Paddock's. Paddock. Hip, available, suddenly there and suddenly interested.

Not . . . unattractive. Probably a damn good undercover cop.

Suddenly there.

Molina hit a pre-programmed number. It was answered despite the late hour, thank God, but she'd expected no less.

"Molina. No, not exactly. Got a minute? Or twenty. Good. Thanks, Morrie."

Chapter 30

The Extent of the Law

Matt still saw stars, not his fellow guests on today's live edition of *The Amanda Show,* but from the intense television studio lights.

The lights made everything beyond the hot, faux living-room set seem unreal. No matter how many times he appeared on the talk show, and this was his seventh or eighth visit, he never lost the sense that everything on camera happened in an overcivilized dreamtime, not unlike the Australian aborigines' mystical cycle.

Nothing mystical about leaving the studio for Chicago's hyperactive streets. Now he was in a cab on traffic-jammed Michigan Avenue near Water Tower Place.

New York City soared, a stone forest primeval with thin tall buildings. Chicago squatted. The city's broad, heavy-set edifices were also high and huge, but Chicago post–Carl Sandburg was more a sumo wrestler of a city. Manhattan was a wirewalker.

Now Matt was trading one thick tower for another, from the TV studio to an office building a few blocks farther up Michigan Avenue.

He carried a slim aluminum briefcase, accoutered more as a celebrity dilettante than a legal eagle. He'd bought it for this one occasion: broaching the law offices of Brandon, Oakes, and McCall. That decades-old name had been on the papers giving his mother title to the old, two-flat residence in the city's decaying Polish section almost thirty-five years ago.

By now, sitting on the hot seat of a television talk show set was old hat and Chicagoans he had contact with coming and going might recognize him. Might comment on the day's topic. Tell him about their brother/sister/kid who should be on *The Amanda Show*. He had become what Temple so aptly called a semicelebrity. A regular on a surviving talk show. Not quite *Oprah*. Not *Ellen*. Not *The View*. But comfortably second tier. When it came to being in the spotlight, Matt liked second tier fine. That was where the fitful public limelight didn't fry your private life for dinner.

Dignity was not necessarily a requirement for the job but he'd managed to keep his, so far, during his media ramble. Dignity would be the key to getting any kind of honest attention from Brandon, Oakes, and McCall.

And dignity was the reason he was visiting this old established law firm. His mother's. She wanted to know more about the man who had sired him. A boy, really, from what little she'd told Matt about the circumstances of his conception. A young man determined to volunteer for a foreign war his family had the means to keep him safely out of. Meeting a girl from the wrong side of the WASP tracks in a church on the eve of shipping out.

It was hard for Matt to imagine his timid, conservative

mother being young enough to fall into first sex with a stranger she'd met in a church, before the flickering candles at a saint's station.

But she had. And what came of it? Only him, a fatherless child in a working-class Catholic neighborhood that didn't forget sins of carnal knowledge.

Matt found himself shaking his head in the back of the cab, which smelled of chewing gum and smoke. Its lurching progress through the rush-hour traffic was making him sick. Or something else was.

His mother was fifty-four now, looking remarkably young yet leading a life circumscribed by her underachieving job and the Church. What good would it do her to know the name of her particular hit-and-run Joseph?

He had died, that privileged boy who'd rejected his get-out-of-war free card. Over there somewhere. The family lawyers bought amnesia from mother and son with the title of a two-flat that would keep them, with a spare unit to bring in steady rent. Matt's mother had never known more than his father's first name but he'd been somebody, whoever he was. Any seed he'd sown on the way to annihilation was . . . so much wildflower along the highway. Unnamed, unnoticed. Unacknowledged.

So much chaff in the wind. Then he thought of his stepfather, Cliff Effinger. Why had she married him when he'd been just a toddler? He'd asked that question at six and he still asked it of himself today, almost thirty years later. Effinger. Now dead, and Matt not sorry one bit. A mean, lesser man than the sainted boy Mira met at the saint's station in the church.

How could she? How could she have turned them both over to an abusive creature like Effinger? Unless she'd felt she deserved punishment? Unless she'd been so beaten down that she'd needed to marry a permanent punishment. Matt finally had grown old and big enough to banish punishment, but it hadn't been soon enough.

His mother wasn't to blame; it was the social milieu that said that pain was a fallen woman's only lot. It was her righteous, callous family and the Church he'd run to himself at the earliest opportunity for ultimate approval. *Holy Mother of God*. He too had deserted her for his own petty salvation.

Matt probed for the right bills as he paid off the cabby and got out to face a fifties building of pale stone and castlelike crenellations.

He didn't need this. Want this. His mother did. A bad idea. If he . . . she . . . learned nothing, it was another disappointment in a life replete with too many. If they learned something, it was . . . a slap in the face; they weren't wanted here, not even Matt with his seminational media profile.

Still. He had his national TV suit on, which was a lot better than Dr. Phil's, and his new seriously slick briefcase, and his smooth, photogenic media cool. None of it was bedrock real, but then neither were the high-priced lawyers from this firm who had bullied a naive young mother into settling for down-at-the-heels real estate as shabby security instead of real information about the most traumatic, and apparently transcendental, moment of her life.

How much you want to bet a Chicago lawyer even knew what transcendental meant?

Matt walked in, read the tiny white type on the big black plaque by the elevator, and was whooshed, ears quickly blocked, to the forty-fifth floor.

Brandon, Oakes, and McCall offered a reception suite paved in plush plum carpet and furniture upholstered in espresso-dark brown leather.

The receptionist reminded Matt of a high-priced Las Vegas call girl: tall, chic, managing to be both icy and sexy.

He ought to know, thanks to his latest unwanted adventure in the land of neon and sex for sale.

The woman's demeanor warmed as he neared the desk. She glanced down at the appointment ledger and frowned. "Mr. . . . Devine? You requested an appointment with a senior partner."

"Yes."

A few junior female clerks were dashing in and out of the smooth wooden door beyond the receptionist's arena that kept the uninvited out. They glanced at him, then looked again, then outright gawked.

Okay. He was getting used to these epiphanies among the female population. Maybe it was his blond Polish good looks. Maybe familiarity from his stints on *The Amanda Show.* Maybe it was the highlight job from his last bizarre undercover turn in Temple's Everlasting Carnival of Crime and Detection.

Ms. Fashionista Receptionist smiled intimately at him in recognition of his high profile in the waiting room.

"You may go right in. Miss—" She hesitated before bestowing the honor on just the right one of the paralyzed paralegals. "Miss Hendrix will escort you."

Miss Hendrix leaped forward, clutching a bouquet of legal-length manila folders to her pin-striped heart.

"Certainly, Mr.—?"

"Devine." He expected his name to generate references to his latest appearance on Chicago TV, but Miss Hendrix blinked as if confounded, then stuttered forward like a geisha on her four-inch spike heels toward the unmarked, exotic zebrawood door.

Puzzled, Matt followed. Certainly his yellow hair alone hadn't merited this reception. But if they didn't recognize his media ties, what else could account for this quick and cordial reception?

The office he was ushered into was the size of a racquetball court and about as welcoming.

Glass winked coldly from a ring of expensive modern prints. Leather and wood was slathered everywhere, enormous distances separating desk and chairs from facing walls of built-in bar and audio-video equipment. Beyond all this, looking like a gigantic print, was the sweep of distant gray skyscraper towers through a window-wall.

"Mr. Brandon will see you shortly," said Miss Fluttering Legal Briefs. "Please. Be seated."

He took one of the three tufted brown leather wing chairs placed before the desk, set the silver briefcase beside it, and commenced to wait.

"Mr. Devine!"

The voice from the doorway was both powerful and jocular.

"My wife loves your appearances on Amanda's show. What brings you to our offices?"

So that was it. Mr. Big himself had recognized his name.

The voice advanced on him from behind, its energy bouncing off the window-wall. Matt turned in the wing chair, started to rise.

"Charles Brandon."

His . . . host, it sounded like, came into view around the curl of the chair's obscuring wing.

A chubby hand accessorized with a three-carat star sapphire ring was extended.

Matt rose to take it, then watched shock rinse all the welcome from Charles Brandon's pink and fleshy face.

It was too late to stop the handshake. Matt kept his grip firm but not pushy. The hand he shook went limp with the surprise the face had registered first.

"Mr. Devine," the man repeated, as if impressing the name on his memory. "You are the visiting family counselor on *The Amanda Show*. Aren't you?"

"Among other things, yes." Matt studied the man, watching him juggle preconceptions.

"Well, sit down." Brandon bustled around the desk to

install himself on the gray leather behemoth of a chair behind it. His formerly flushed skin tones now matched the ashen hide. "Ah, as I was saying, my wife loves you. I mean, she loves your, ah, point of view, I guess. You know women, always into that relationship stuff. So. What can I do for you?"

While Matt reseated himself, reaching for the briefcase, Brandon kept talking in the way of a man who makes his living by it.

"You must forgive my surprise. You're not what I expected."

"In what way?"

"Oh, you know. Dr. Phil. Fat and fifty. I had no idea you were such a . . . handsome young fellow. No wonder my wife, eh?"

"I've been told I'm telegenic. That word always sounds like an exotic affliction to me."

Brandon chuckled, his face and manner resuming their earlier bonhomie. "Clever fellow too. How'd you get into the TV shrink game?"

"I'm not a shrink. I was a Catholic priest for most of my adult life."

"Now that surprises me. Also relieves me. Can't have the wife too enamored of sharp young men on TV. You left, then?"

"Officially, yes, the priesthood. One doesn't ever leave the Church, I'm told."

"I've heard that same sentiment from Chicago's most famous priest, Father Greeley. Wonderful man."

Matt felt he had now been firmly pinned to whatever part of the bulletin board Brandon reserved for such alien life forms as celibate priests, current or former.

"What can I do for you?" Brandon repeated.

"Not for me so much as for my mother."

"Your mother—"

"She lives here. In Chicago."

"And you?"

"I live in Las Vegas now."

"Las Vegas? Really? Quite the switch for you, I imagine."

"It's mostly a city that ordinary people live in. That's where my syndicated radio talk show originates."

"Syndicated. Indeed."

Matt hated to use his media connections but they appeared to work.

"Would you like my girl to get you a cup of coffee or tea? Something stronger?"

"No. Thank you. What I'd like is for you to take a look at this . . . document my mother signed thirty-five years ago. Your firm drew it up."

"An old document. Quite the mystery. Now you've got me curious. Let's see it."

Matt lifted the briefcase, unlatched it, and brought out the three-page agreement that bore his mother's signature.

Brandon lowered his silver-haired head to the pages, skimmed the first page. Flipped the paper back over the staple in the upper-left-hand corner.

"A deed transfer. Straightforward. Your mother was given title to a two-flat." He hit the third page, where she was required to seek no more "compensation" and to make no further "contact" with the unnamed party who had transferred ownership of the two-flat to her.

"Most . . . unusual."

Matt had watched Brandon's face fade again to gray. He'd heard people described as "going white" with shock but he'd never actually seen the phenomenon before. It was more a grim tightening of the features than actual paling, but there was no doubt that what Brandon saw in those papers disturbed him.

"An unusual deed transfer but quite binding, I'd think." Brandon held the papers out to Matt, who didn't take them.

"It was a compensation for my birth. Child support of a sort, if you will. My mother was very young, not even eighteen, and she signed it without legal advice."

"Still, she signed it."

"But I didn't. I'd like to know who the unnamed 'party of the first part' is."

"Impossible. The anonymity is as binding on this firm as your mother's agreement to seek no further information was, and is, on her."

"I'm not her. I want to know the name of the family that made arrangements for my domestic life. I want to know my family name."

"You have a perfectly good, and fairly famous, one now: Devine. I advise you to be happy with it."

"It's a phony name, Mr. Brandon. Do you know where my mother got it? From her favorite Christmas hymn, 'O Holy Night.' The line goes, 'O Holy Night, O Night Divine . . .'"

Brandon kept his eyes on his lizardskin desk set. "However it came to be, it's very . . . telephonic. Stick with it and forget delving into the dead past."

"'The dead past' involves how I came to be. I'm not going to leave it alone."

"I can't help you break the confidentiality of a document this firm constructed."

"Why not? 'The truth shall set you free.' My mother was a naive teenager in desperate circumstances when she signed that document. Encouraging her to do so might be construed as fraud. Who paid her off to keep her, and myself, ignorant of my father's identity?"

"I can't tell you."

"Why not?"

"I have to protect the party of the first part, our client."

"But it's my birth, my life, hidden behind these three sleazy little pages buying silence and selling souls."

Brandon waved the papers at Matt again. His face crinkled with appeal. "That was almost thirty-five years ago, young man! Take my advice. Forget about it. You have a successful life. I assume you can take quite good financial care of your mother."

"Someone felt guilty, or that paper would never have been drawn up. Guilt doesn't melt like hailstones. It sits and festers. Whoever wanted that secrecy enough to buy it doesn't really sleep well at night, thirty-five years down the drain or not. I'm doing him or them a favor. And I won't give up or go away. Quite frankly, I started this on my mother's behalf. I tried to advise her against it with the same platitudes you're now urging on me. But Shakespeare said it best: 'the past is prologue.' That's the story of all our lives, if you think about it, and we all deserve to know our own pasts."

Brandon jabbed the papers at him one last time.

"Keep that," Matt told him. "It's only a copy. I'm after the originals."

"You're quite eloquent, you know that? I'm glad you're not an attorney. But the law's on my side. I can't help you, or your mother. I'm sorry. I can't."

Matt stood up. "I want to know. I need to know. I intend to know. Maybe other attorneys in this city would like to know too. Maybe Amanda would like a personal story from an expert on her show. Maybe a lot of possibilities are out there somewhere. Like the truth. Thanks for your time. Give your wife my regards."

It was a long walk to the door. He took it as if he had won, not lost. Hearing Brandon make the same arguments to him that he had given his mother had turned Matt 180 degrees on this whole issue.

She had a right to know. He had a right to know. They had a right to know.

Opening the door, he almost bumped into the lurking paralegal.

"Oh. Mr. . . . Devine. May I show you out?"

He smiled. "Sure. Thanks. These offices are a rat maze."

"Don't we know it? So many junior partners."

She happily led him through carpeted hallways that turned and twisted, always passing by more paper-filled work cubicles.

"When do you find time to watch *The Amanda Show*?" he asked as they neared the central reception area.

"*Amanda Show?* Daytime TV. Oh, I don't. Ever find time, I mean. I know it's a Chicago institution. Why do you ask about it?"

"Because it's a Chicago institution, like *Oprah*," he said, shrugging as if he didn't care.

So her amazing interest in him didn't derive from his TV appearances. Surely his recent *Queer Eye for the Straight Guy* hair highlighting job wasn't solely responsible for these frequent dewy glances?

"Here we are. Reception, Mr. Win—" She glanced, mortified, at the appointment roster in her hand. "Oh, yes. Right. Mr. Devine."

"Thank you."

He'd never meant those two words more. Moving through the crowded reception area, barely seeing the blur of briefcase-carrying men and women, he mentally repeated the young woman's slip of the tongue over and over:

Mr. *Win* . . . *Win*throp? *Win*ston? *Win*ter? *Win*terhalter? *Win*scott. *Win*gate. The Chicago phonebook would be crammed with enough possibilities to make his vision blur at the tiny type repeating *W-i-n* into infinity.

So, suddenly, there were possibilities. He had been mistaken for someone. A client. Apparently there was a marked family resemblance. He looked like someone alive in this world besides his mother.

The feeling was weird, and frightening, and infuriating.

He would find out who, one way or another. *Win* is for *Win*ning.

Chapter 31

Kissing Cousins

Matt's mind was running in circles as he headed to his mother's apartment in a cab through rush-hour traffic. He'd happened on a hornets' nest at Brandon, Oakes, and McCall but exactly what variety of wasp had he stirred up? Legal shyster? Loyal attorney protecting a client?

Maybe he should have stayed. Watched the employees leave for the night. He had a hunch someone would be hearing about his visit. But . . . no one would be showing up until tomorrow. If ever. Let your fingers do the walking, use the phone or e-mail nowadays. Never show your face. Someone might notice your lying eyes.

"Here you are, bub."

Said pointedly. While Matt had been enacting various scenarios in his head, they'd arrived at his mother's apartment building. A bland block of windows. Horizontal glass windows, tall vertical exterior columns of stone. Plaid fifties-era urban high-rise.

Matt paid the driver, tipping him way too well. He couldn't be bothered calculating a few dollars when his whole life was suddenly a million-dollar question. He entered the echoing lobby, so much more pretentious than the Circle Ritz's music-box proportions. And therefore, so much less homey. And no Temple here to run into.

He was whistling by the time the elevator disgorged him on the twenty-second floor, thinking of Temple. The key his mother had given him on his last visit to Chicago turned in the plain apartment door with its lofty four-digit number. He was already relishing the peace and quiet of an empty apartment—Mom was at her job as a restaurant hostess, miles away. Wouldn't be back until eleven P.M.

By then he'd have relaxed, chilled out, gathered his wits so he wouldn't blurt out his discovery before he had any hard evidence. . . .

The door gave and opened before the key had finished its turns. A tallish young woman stood behind it.

"Matt! Come in."

"Krystyna! Krys. You're here."

"Yup. Live here, off and on. Didn't Mira tell you?"

"Uh, no."

"Don't *you* look as yummy as a caramel sundae! What's with the bleach, dude?"

Talk about the pot calling the kettle black. Blond in this instance. His cousin Krystyna's hair was a kaleidoscope of platinum-on-blonde-on-black.

He put a dismissive hand to his hair, remembering it looked different. "Photo shoot for the radio station. I'm told it'll wash out." Close enough. "You, on the other hand. . . ."

"Madonna, Evita-in-Krakow style. You like the indigo highlights?"

"Colorful. I'm surprised to see you."

"Have I got a Mae West line for you! Never mind. Not

suitable for ex-priests. I guess my job is to entertain you until Mira gets home."

"So . . . you live here. Off and on. I take it the punk boyfriend is around during the off?"

"Huh? Him? Oh, history. I was young and stupid then."

"Three months ago?"

"Yeah. Want a beer?"

She was poised on the carpet verge next to the linoleum that marked off the alley kitchen.

"Yeah." Matt realized he needed one.

Krys. She changed like a rainbow. Since he'd first met her when he'd connected to his Chicago relatives six months ago, she'd gone from breathless teenager to rebellious young adult, heavy on young to now . . . assertive single chick. Cousin. Assertive single cousin.

First cousin. Like it mattered to her.

She brought a Bohemian beer, the dark brown bottle sweating goose bumps of condensation. She didn't offer him a glass.

"So." Leaning against the eating bar that divided kitchen and living room. Five-foot-nine of fine Polish womanhood. Blue eyes both guarded and challenging. "How'll we kill some time until Mira gets home? Cousin dearest."

He suggested that they sit and talk. That was his profession, after all.

Or watch some TV. The remote was front and center on the small round fruitwood coffee table.

"I watched you on *The Amanda Show* today," she told him, settling beside him on the couch. Settling way too much beside him.

"Really? It's amazing how many people in Chicago miss my golden hour."

She sighed. "You're really good. I studied advertising

in class. TV is a 'cool' medium. The cooler and more laid back you are, the hotter you come across."

"Glad you're learning something in college. Is Uncle Stash letting you major in art?"

"No." She sat up from her couch-lounging position, took a long swig of beer. "He still treats me like a kid. A *woman*."

"I thought you wanted to be treated like a woman." Matt was surprised at himself for challenging this incendiary cousin with a crush on him.

She grinned. "Not that way. Like the kind of woman you write off and put down. Polish Catholic burqa anyone? Like a nobody with nothing about her that counts."

"He's old-fashioned. He can't help it."

"So I should suffer?"

"No."

She set down the beer. Moved closer on the couch. She wore a soft black sweater that ebbed off her shoulders like ebony surf. Cashmere maybe, or just a really good acrylic.

Wow. He was really absorbing a lot from Temple. Including enough savvy to regard his high-spirited young cousin as sheer poison.

"I'm mad at you." She sounded like an adolescent again, emotionally bipolar. Also like a Lolita.

"Why?" Might as well walk into it.

"It could have been you." When he continued to look blank, she added. "Last Christmas."

Matt sipped the beer, knowing he wouldn't like where this was going.

She mirrored his gesture, eyed him sideways. "Instead it was that loser Zeke."

"I met him. You brought him to the restaurant where my mother works. Apparently he wasn't such a loser then."

"If you remember him, you know I'm not lying."

"He . . . like most guys his age he's just self-involved, dead set on being too cool to care. Or too cool to appear to. He'll civilize in a few years."

"I wish you'd told me that before I lost my so-called innocence to him."

"You—Krys, I don't need to know this."

"Are you shocked?"

"I don't hand out moral judgments anymore. Gave that up for Lent, along with my Roman collar."

"You're shocked, I can tell."

"Not shocked. Just not comfortable discussing this with you."

"You discuss things like that all the time on TV and the radio, in front of thousands of people."

"I don't know them."

"I'm just being honest."

"You need to be honest with yourself. You don't have to share the news with other people."

"You're not other people. You could have been the one."

He shook his head. "Never would have happened. Face it; we're first cousins. Even civil law, not just ecclesiastical law, frowns on that. I know family dynamics. First cousins are often first crushes but I've been too messed up myself to do unto others the same. It's not that you're not bright and attractive, trust me."

"Are you still—?"

"It's none of your business."

"You are!" It was an accusation. "Why?"

When he didn't answer, she shook his arm. "Are you saving yourself for someone?"

Matt thought for a long moment. She had nailed it. The question was, should he be?

"Because if you are, maybe a little preliminary practice, a dry run, would be just the thing. Cousin."

Chapter 32

The Wig Is Up

"The show must go on" is an ancient theatrical maxim probably going back to the Greeks and the first ever chorus line on some hill in Thessaly.

It was all too evident that reality television shows still abided by the same philosophy.

Except that Temple and Mariah had been on Candid Camera much more frequently than the other candidates, so Big Brother and Sister had been watching Xoe Chloe's every far-rambling move.

Mariah returned to their room from her morning lifestyle counseling session feeling both nervous and rebellious.

Temple had slept in, in her wig, which was now looking matted as well as lank and dispirited. In fact, it looked like the road kill of some thankfully unrecognizable species.

She awoke grudgingly from dreams of Rafi Nadir and

Matt Devine escorting her and Mariah to the father-daughter dance, except that Temple got Nadir for a father!

"What a nightmare," she muttered as Mariah shook her awake. Although, the alternate possibility of Matt as her "father" escort was even worse. And far more Freudian.

Mariah was whispering in her ear. "They say I'm missing my beauty sleep and getting into trouble. I got a big lecture about bearing down on my diet and exercise program and staying away from you."

"Good idea." Temple struggled up and pulled the bedside clock closer to read it in B.C. time. Before Contacts were installed for the day.

"Yikes! My lifestyle session is in eighteen minutes. Gang way!"

In fifteen minutes, Xoe Chloe was fully assembled, bedhead and all.

"The great thing about punk," Mariah noted from her watching post on the bed, "is that you can be considered put together no matter how ragged you look."

"Thanks, kid." Temple dashed into the hall where she ran into the Golden Girls, advancing in a pack and sniggering at her approach. This was not a promising sendoff to her lifestyle consultation.

"Are you going to get it," Silver predicted.

Temple's faux-green morning eyes blinked in the glare generated by so much pink, shiny spandex in a group. Even if they were all as stick-thin as flamingos.

"What do you mean?" she asked.

"You haven't buckled down to the program," Honey said. "I hear the coaching team will be reading you the riot act."

"Shape up or flunk," Ashlee added.

This was not good. If Temple was totally out of the running, she'd be of less use to Mariah, and her mother.

"Outa my way, Blondies." Temple ploughed through

the permanent wave of sugar and spice and everything not nice.

Under the current regime, the house's den had the feeling of a headmaster's office. Temple paused at the closed double doors, then opened one and strolled in.

The whole Teen Queen team sat around the big oval wooden table. Only one chair was free, at one end of the oval.

Temple slid onto the huge leather chair, feeling like Little Orphan Annie called onto the carpet in Daddy Warbucks's office.

Four judges and the five consultants glanced up, away, and shuffled folders. Not promising. Their spandex-shiny hot pink folder covers looked ludicrous lying on the dignified walnut conference table. Arthur Dickson might have been a tad eccentric, but he would be spinning in his presumed grave to see this crew taking over.

"Normally," Beth Marble announced, "at this point in the competition we're starting to see real improvement in the candidates."

"I am too." Temple nodded sagely. "I met a bunch in the hall coming here. Their high-pitched giggle quotient is way lower and I think they're all developing larger calf muscles. Must be from the spike-heel footraces."

"You always have a sassy answer." Beth shook her head, putting her halo of curls in motion. "That hides nothing but your own anxiety."

"Hide my anxiety? Not my idea. Anxiety is the watchword of our modern age. I'm visibly neurotic and proud of it."

"I don't think so." Ken Adair, the Hair Guy, rose and walked toward Temple. "Everybody wants to be confident and secure, and you too are going to get that way if we have to browbeat you into it."

Temple rolled her eyes, trying to think up a suitably Xoe Chloe comeback. "Anybody recording this? Sounds like lab-rat abuse to me."

Adair reached her chair, spun it to face him, and scalped her.

"Yeow-ouch!" She gazed up at a foot of limp coal-black monofiber filaments dangling from the hairdresser's viselike grasp.

"You are a fake, Xoe Chloe." Beth Marble came to stand behind him.

"A freaking fraud," Dexter Manship added to the chorus, while still balancing on his tailbone in his matching leather chair.

"A spirited but self-deluded girl," her own Aunt Kit threw in, trying to put a positive spin on this shocking revelation.

"A . . . a has-been," Savannah added after a long and visible search for words that hadn't been used yet. Apparently, she could only come up with phrases that applied to herself.

"So I wear a wig." Temple/Xoe sat up boarding school straight. "So does Cher. And Dolly. And a lot of performers. You going to tell me that's not true?"

"Why a black wig?" her aunt asked, playing the defense attorney role.

"Sim-ple. I've got red hair."

"So?"

"So who wants that? It's unlucky. And mine's curly too. Who wants to be Shirley Temple in a world where the Good Ship Lollipop is dropping anchor a day away from Guantanamo Bay?"

"No politics!" Beth commanded. "We are an issue-neutral show."

"Yeah, right. So anyway, curly red hair's a drag. It belongs in a comic strip. Like I'd want to be mistaken for that loser comedian, Carrot Top? Black is the new red."

"My dear child," Beth said, "wigs are not allowed. We're going for natural beauty here."

Temple snorted. "Tell that to the Golden Girls. When they sit in the bleachers, it's at their hairdresser's. Right, Mr. Adair?"

"Nothing wrong with subtle colorations, Miss Xoe. Subtle," he repeated in a voice like a drill bit.

"Subtle sucks," Temple said airily. "It's the refuge of uncertain minds."

"Well, we're certain about one thing." Manship had risen and was staring her down. "That rats' nest of fake hair has got to go. What's under there can't be any more pathetic. Color and restyle, Adair. Right now."

Temple would have opened her mouth to protest, except Adair had her by the shoulders. He was dredging her out of the chair and marching her down the hall before she could say "Garnier Fructose." In one minute flat, she was shoved into a room where the reek of hairspray was sickly sweet enough to choke a skunk.

This was a part of undercover work Molina had never prepared her for: beauty boot camp.

For the next ninety minutes, Temple was buckled into a rotating chair where she was washed, styled, spun, dried, spindled, and mutilated.

She felt like a duck in the weeds whose shelter is ripped away one reed at a time. Huddled under a pink plastic cape, she watched tiny feathered remnants of her past haircut fall like residue from a tarring and feathering. Too many people inside the Teen Queen Castle knew Temple Barr, redhead and PR whirlwind. Her cover was being stripped away and blown dry even as she sat strapped to the chair.

"I don't know why you hate your red hair," Adair said. "So many girls do. Guess they feel like Raggedy Ann dolls. A shame. Red rocks for me, but change what irritates you. Take a look, pussycat."

He handed her a mirror.

Temple glanced sideways at her reflection through squinty eyes. How would she face Molina when she admitted to having lost her cover to a pair of barber's shears, leaving the policewoman's daughter alone in a house crawling with secret tunnels, cameras, and sick stalkers?

Temple, shrinking in the chair, straightened.

So had her hair. Straightened somehow.

It had been bleached into a medley of warm and cool blonde shades! And straightened and razor-cut into shoulder-brushing length. She looked like . . . nobody she knew. A stranger. The Power of Blonde: hide behind your hair color.

Her cover was not blown! It was . . . better than ever. *Hallelujah!*

Of course, imagining what the grow-out would be like was a nightmare, but for the moment . . .

"Pretty foxy." Her Aunt Kit was standing there, beaming down on her niece. "This girl has a chance at the prize if her attitude improves."

Thanks be to savvy aunts! What an actress! Still, Kit might be onto something. Temple was still studying herself in the mirror. Dang if the blonde hair didn't make her green contact lenses even more dominant. An eye of another color was a slim sliver of a disguise but it had worked for Max. Temple guessed that her new pale honey hair would even make her real eye color, a wishy-washy blue-gray in her own opinion, resemble the dangerous, deep steel blue of a Fontana Brother's Beretta.

"Pink is not her color," Kit told Adair, "too sweety-sweet with her pale complexion. If she were on one of my book covers, she'd be wearing Nile green or peach velvet."

Vanetta, the show's wardrobe witch had appeared as well. "We'll go with the icy Easter tones . . . peach, aqua, and pale lilac for her. This will be one of the more dynamic makeovers. From jet black to liquid blonde."

Vanetta, a brunette and therefore one who might be expected to have issues with blonde, instead grinned from ear to ear. "I love it. I have to put everybody else but that Molina girl in pasty pastels. This honey-warm blonde at least gives me a mid-tone palette to play with."

Temple was startled to realize that she and Mariah were the only not-blondes in the finals. And also the reason why: in states with a large Hispanic labor force, Anglo women, even natural-born brunettes, didn't want to be mistaken for "the hired help."

On the other hand, not being blonde made the two of them stand out in a crowd. For a wild, wonderful moment, Temple pictured Mariah winning her category, in her glory, going—oh, all right, no dog in a manger, Temple—going to her school father-daughter dance with Matt Devine, a "dad" to die for.

Oops. Another prominent brunet haunted the premises: Rafi Nadir, Mariah's real father. Temple didn't see him playing a role in any fairy tale ending except one of the darkest tales by the Brothers Grimm, maybe Iron John.

Meanwhile, the moment was all about her, Xoe Chloe, debunked brunette and closet redhead now transformed into a mainstream blonde bombshell. If only Max could see her now. Not Matt. He didn't have Max's theatrical instincts and would probably just be shocked.

"Okay, pumpkin." Adair the Hair Guy was suddenly her best friend. "What d'ya think?"

Xoe Chloe had only one thing to say to the mirror. "It rocks, dude!" She slapped palms all around and stood up. Her sigh blew snips of hair into a small whirlwind around her.

Still in the game, Temple thought. Who knew a new hairdresser was the best disguise? Probably the eighty million women who patronized them regularly, which had not included her. Until now.

By that afternoon, the ravishing, newly conventional Xoe Chloe had instantly blossomed into the lead in the make-over sweepstakes.

Matte-black Xoe Chloe'd had so far to come that the transformation was breathtaking. Blondes of all description—tall, taller; thin, thinner—darted stiletto glances her way as Temple put in her forty minutes on the elliptical machine and her twenty-minute jog around the Hearst Castle–size pool, slathered in the sun screen recommended for her pale complexion, sweating into her extravagant dye job, which seemed up to the abuse.

It occurred to her that, having proven herself the most dramatic makeover so far, she might also be the freshest candidate for harassment.

Every cloud had its silver lining.

She was ready.

First she had to put up with reactions.

"Hey, toots! Love the paint job. Looking good. How about an interview for KREP?" Awful Crawf suggested, slinking alongside her at the pool.

She cringed. Without the wig she felt naked. Worse, recognizable. Was blonde really the best disguise? Maybe for Marilyn. But her? She easily outtrotted him, avoiding the moment of truth.

"Wow. Oh, wow." Mariah. "Wonder what they'll make me look like? I should be really spectacular. Well, I'm younger. Way younger. Although you look pretty teen-y for a . . . you know." She glanced about for cameras and mikes. "For an older woman. Will they dye my hair too? My mother will kill me."

Rafi Nadir was a study in skepticism when she passed him in the hall. Quickly. But he didn't seem to recognize the "ballsy little broad" he knew now that she was a blonde. He recognized something about her though.

"You don't look like a chick who'd go down a dark hidden passage anymore."

Temple was annoyed to discover herself insulted.

Chapter 33

Upping the Auntie

Temple knocked on the door of room number two with her knuckles, almost hoping no one was home.

"Come in."

Drat. Watch out for what you claim you want; you might get it.

Kit Carlson sat at a French desk, clickety-clacking away on a large-screen laptop computer, lips moving silently and eyes fixed on the text in front of her.

After a minute, Temple said in a little girl voice quite unlike her natural husky rasp, "I hope I'm not interrupting anything?"

Kit's head finally turned, slowly, from the screen to recognize her presence.

"Just the climax of my latest book."

"I thought you wrote romances."

Kit's eyes looked over the plastic rims of her glasses. "Exactly."

"Oh, that kind of climax. It's happening . . . right here?"

"You don't suppose I compose in the bathtub?"

"I wouldn't doubt it. I don't know if my jet-black mascara goes with my blindingly blonde hair. You have a lighter kind of mascara?"

Kit pushed her glasses up on her nose. She was a small woman with chin-length hair that insisted on assuming large loose strawberry-gray curls. She seemed better cast as some well-aged French chanteuse in a small nightclub, gargling throaty world-weary songs sans mike, a glass of poison-green absinthe sitting on the piano beside her.

"Of course. Dead-black mascara on me makes me look like Elvira, Mistress of the Dark. I have a nice warm brown shade that should compliment your new Goldilocks locks. Come into my parlor for a moment."

Once they'd hied into the privy, Temple asked her most burning question.

"Do I still pass as undercover agent after being forcibly stripped of my wig?"

"A dreadful thing for a double agent, to lose the cover of darkness. But I must say Ken Adair did a terrific job of making the real you look utterly unlike yourself."

"So my new look isn't a dead giveaway?"

"Oh, no, dear. It's a spectacular success."

"So you're saying I look too good to be mistaken for myself?"

"Except by a relative. Or an intimate. Any more of those here?"

"Only an enemy or two."

"Oh, you'd fool an enemy. They tend to fixate on specifics. As long as your trademark hair is history and your eyes are an astonishing shade of green, your secret is safe."

"So what do you think of all the scary things that have been happening?"

"Scripted," Kit said promptly. "The producers are bent on stirring things up. Stripping the contestants to their barest emotions."

"With this crew of exhibitionist blondes, that's not hard."

"Now, dear, don't be brutal to blondes. They have so much to overcome nowadays, like Jessica Simpson and Paris Hilton."

"So you think we're all lab rats being teased by the producers? No lurking evil-doer in sight?"

"Oh, evil-doers are always lurking. I often use them in my books. Is that why you're here, pretending to be young and difficult? Who would be so dreadful as to force you back into revisiting your teen years? That dishy boyfriend I met in New York? Max . . . something . . . yum-yum?"

"Max isn't aware of this. I'm here on unofficial police business. Well, unofficial official police business."

"Surely no one is taking this circus of hokey threats seriously?"

Temple didn't feel she could mention the mutilated poster and Molina's concern for her daughter's safety. For once she agreed with her enemy. Something nasty was going on here. But what?

"Maybe not." Temple rose from her seat upon the commode, reassured. "I hope you didn't lose any major inspiration."

"No. Guido was about to do something interesting with a box of Lady Godiva chocolates. Deep dark bitter chocolates, do you think, dear, or perhaps white ones?"

"Never touch 'em," Temple said, retreating toward the main room. "I'd better get back on observation. For some reason, the Teen Queen team gets nervous if they don't know where I am every minute."

"You're a perfect little delinquent, Xoe Chloe Ozone! That's why. My straitlaced sister would be . . . appalled."

"You won't ever tell Mom?"

"Not if you don't tell her about my quandary with Guido and the gourmet candies. Karen was always so . . . Midwest."

"If you stay in town long enough after this is over, Aunt, remind me to introduce you to the Fontana brothers."

"Mobsters? I can always do research."

"Yum-yum young mobsters. Definitely the white chocolate type."

"Really?" Kit rose from her seat upon the tub surround to show Temple out, like Lady Macbeth rising from trying out the throne of Scotland. "Plural, you say. Very intriguing."

"Thanks for the use of the biffy," Temple/Xoe said once they were within mike and camera range again in the main office room. "I've got eighty million little tiny hairs to rinse off from that salon job they gave me. You'd think that Adair guy was a mini–Bucky Beaver."

"You look smashing. A death of a thousand hair snips is worth the agony for the result. Take lots of long showers to rinse off the little pricklers, and keep your self-esteem up. You show great potential, Xoe, if you don't get stubborn and blow it."

"Thank you, ma'am," Temple returned, emphasizing the "ma'am" as Kit grimaced in distaste. "I'll do my best to be a candidate you all can be proud of."

Then she left, without gagging, miraculously.

Chapter 34

Two-Faced

While my Miss Temple is doing the beauty bit, I spend my time prowling from boudoir to kitchen. My two favorite chambers, it is true, but at least Miss Midnight Louise is not around this time to point out my failings.

I have been accepted as a walking mascot, always good for the occasional camera shot. So have the Persian girls. I hear the camera operators slavering over our natural grace and good looks. We have no bad angles, they say. Unlike other objects of their lenses, apparently.

Of course, a full head . . . and shoulders . . . and legs . . . and tail of hair does wonders to hide any conformation flaws. And our eyes are naturally green without benefit of artificial enhancement. And the Ashleigh girls are the reigning hair color, silver and golden blonde. I must admit that my Miss Temple looks alarmingly unlike herself even with the dead-skunk hairdo now history.

Things are proceeding apace here at the Teen Queen Castle, and I am getting more nervous by the moment.

Perhaps this atmosphere of female pheromones has lulled the male factor into a stupor. Even Rafi Nadir, a man meant to notice danger if not bring it into play himself, is strangely mellow. He is demonstrating a certain gallantry to these mostly underage ladies, especially the younger set.

Of course, being employed by Miss Savannah Ashleigh would immediately encourage any nearby male to elude her obvious toils and focus on the more refreshing and Innocent of her gender.

I cannot help thinking, though, that they all have been lulled into the calm before the storm. That the juvenile dirty tricks going on are camouflaging some serious mischief that is brewing.

So I prowl the perimeter, looking for signs of anything amiss. I suffer camera close-ups, and attempted molestations by the herd of blondes. I poke my nose into odd nooks and crannies, and follow any more of those sinister hidden passages I can find.

I begin to find secrets to follow, such as Crawford Buchanan's odd special entrée to ringmistress Beth Marble's office.

I whisk right in with him, knowing that the ladies always have a welcome mat out for a suave and continental guy like me. They are suckers for a kiss on the hand and I am a past master at that art, having spent years studying Tantric grooming, so I am as versatile with my tongue as Mr. Mick Jagger or Mr. Gene Simmons of KISS. And you know what those dudes are. International rock stars.

Life is so unfair! I could have given them both a run for their groupies and their millions if only I had been born a lot taller, with access to a semi-thorough body-wax job.

But I ankle over to Miss Beth Marble and make with the ankle rub, which soon has her purring.

"What a disgusting alley cat," my pal Crawford comments.

A mistake. When push comes to shove, many a lady would take a cat over a mere man anytime. And why not? We are genteel but sheer steel under our satin topcoats. We are discreet. We can keep a secret, or dozens of them. Mum's the word. We will never grow mustaches suddenly. We have all the attributes of a fur coat without the angst of politically incorrectly offing other creatures, plus a nice baritone purr much like certain sensual aids advertised for big money in the back of *Cosmopolitan* magazine. Our company and affection are free. We keep their feet warm. We do not ask for custody of the children, or the car. We are invariably neat. We never miss the toilet unless we have a serious point to make. We are always willing to eat out.

What is not to love?

I feel the tendons in Miss Marble's heels tighten at Buchanan's slur.

"He is harmless," she says.

Erroneously. That is what I love about little dolls. They are so sure they know what is what. So what would they do without me knowing better?

"Anyway," the Crawf goes on, sitting so carelessly in the chair opposite her desk that even I hear something on his person scratch leather.

I cringe in tune with Miss Marble's entire frame. It is not her leather chair, merely a loaner for the length of the show, but she takes responsibility for all that occurs at the Teen Queen Castle. Boy, is she in trouble!

I murmur sympathy under her desk and resume massaging her ankles. Let the Crawf do his worst (and he has plenty of that). No one does ankles better than Midnight Louie!

"Anyway, what?" she asks.

I stiffen. She is starting to rebel. Any fool or feline could see that. Not the Crawf.

"I have kept the unsettling events here off the air," he whines on. "That gives me access to the tape recordings, as we agreed."

"We agreed that you would not release them before the end of the show."

"Right. But . . . things have changed. I need something lively to keep my exclusive coverage syndicated. Gossip. Cat fights. Dirty tricks. I want the last batch."

"Mr. Buchanan." She makes the title and name sound even more despicable than I could manage with my most dismissive spit and hiss. "I cannot say I understand your influence with the producers, but ultimately I am responsible for the ethical operation of this program. We are halfway through, only a week to go. I submit that you can wait."

She stands, forcing me to jump aside to preserve my second most valuable appendage. If she has forgotten my presence she is one miffed little doll!

I leap upon her desk, fangs bared, backing her up.

She strokes my back and, um, upright member, which is fluffed out like a radiator brush, should anyone alive still remember that useful tool.

"You are upsetting the cat," she tells Pukecannon, "Whatever hold you have on the producers, the show is almost done now and I no longer need to kowtow to your demands. You already have extorted far more scoops than any of the legitimate media. You will just have to get your new information on your own. That should be interesting, as I doubt you have ever got anything in this world solely on your own."

His already pasty complexion (the curse of a life on the airwaves; luckily Mr. Matt leads an outdoor life that prevents such disabilities), pales. I love the way people can change their skin color at the drop of a four-letter word or even a two-letter word like no.

"You will be sorry," he says, using the ancient playground threat heard around the world.

"Not today," Miss Marble says. She pauses to run a hand along my spine all the way to the tip of my quivering tail. "And not any other."

It is a great closing line, and I give her a two-tail salute at ninety degrees upright in recognition of same.

Too bad it is ruined by this long, sustained piercing shriek somewhere on the premises.

I beat Crawford Buchanan to the office door by sixteen lengths of my you-know-what versus his you-know-what.

Chapter 35

Diet of Worms

Temple was resting in her room, trying to figure things out, when she heard the scream, probably along with everybody in the house, and what's worse, she recognized the screamer. She'd always had an ear for various vocal tones.

She took off at a dead run, the cute little flapping Xoe Chloe mules keeping her from running quite fast enough. So she let them fly off in the hall and pounded on barefoot.

Knowing the tone of the scream . . . alto vibrato . . . told her who but not where it was coming from. Her bare arms had broken out into so many goose bumps of unhappy premonition you'd think she'd been having a wet dream about Spike the Vampire.

Holy shiitake mushrooms! she thought. *Let me be wrong!*

Her heart was pounding way past the safety zone, her

bare soles hitting hard on the concrete beneath the carpeting.

Turn here? Maybe. Or there?

Or . . . maybe just follow the dark flowing contrail that was Midnight Louie, ears back, tail straight back, body low as a jet-black Maserati?

Where did he come from? No matter. Go with the flow, as long as it was feline.

She zigged and zagged and bumped into blondes fleeing in the opposite direction. Where was Paris Hilton when you needed her? Overbooked, that's where!

She was entering the portion of the house allotted to the Teen Queen coaches, running her memory of the day's schedule sheet through her mind like a white shirt through a mangle.

Friday, Xoe Chloe interview with Beth Marble, office number three at two P.M. And at three P.M. . . . in office number four. Oh, my goddess! Oh, no! Let it not be—

Louie's low-flying tail vanished through a doorjamb just ahead. Temple almost turned an ankle making a right-angle dodge to follow him.

Office. Very . . . plain. Almost stripped. A scale in the corner. A chart on a wall.

A body in a leather desk chair, throat tilted back. Face . . . darkened. Red black. Unrecognizable.

And oh, holy moley, wholly Molina! Mariah standing in front of the desk, chair and all. Screaming. Screaming for all of her just-teen worth. A real little belter.

Something bad in the neighborhood. Someone *dead* in the neighborhood. The dietitian. The mousy, by-the-book, plain-Jell-O dietitian. Marjory Klein.

Found dead in her office chair. By Mariah.

Temple raced up to put her hands on Mariah's shaking shoulders, pressed down hard.

"It's okay. I'm here. Hel-lo! Look. Even the silly cat that's been prowling around the place is here too. He wouldn't risk his skin if it weren't safe. Have you ever known a cat that wasn't totally cool?"

Those last two words finally jerked Mariah's focus off the dead body.

"Cat?" she asked. "Cool?"

If a cat could look at a queen, or even a dead body, maybe she could too.

Louie used the opportunity to twine around Mariah's ankles, over and over again. It was fine feline therapy but it wasn't enough. Mariah suddenly spun into Temple's embrace. Grabbed on to her like a leech. A growing girl big enough to rock Temple off her bare heels.

But Temple recovered and held on back. They were roomies, after all, and that went way beyond silly reality shows and even Mother Superiors in common.

"I'm sorry," Temple told her. "So, so sorry. I was afraid it would come to this. Hoped not."

Mariah just sobbed. Temple remembered sobbing that hard. Long ago, when she was so young that every setback, real or imagined, was a total tragedy.

This was all too real though. This *was* a tragedy, period. The dead woman was such an unlikely object of another person's venom. Of murderous hatred.

Just yesterday she'd been earnestly urging legumes and cruciferous vegetables on that hopeless Xoe Chloe creature.

Temple found herself crying along with Mariah.

Still, another part of her brain sounded warning. *This will bring Molina herself into the equation.*

Not a good thing for either Mariah or Temple. Or Xoe Chloe, for that matter.

Later, Temple was very glad she and Louie had been the first to arrive on the murder scene. That meant that she and Mariah were partners in interrogation. She could fulfill her undercover role and stick up for the poor kid if necessary.

Temple was relieved that Molina hadn't shown up, yet wasn't surprised to see Detectives Alch and Su arrive shortly after the uniformed officers had come, dismissed the EMTs, and sent for the coroner and the crime scene team.

Molina would want her favorite investigative team on scene in her stead. While patting Mariah's back and being otherwise the wise, stable big sister, Temple was madly speculating whether Alch and Su would see through her colored contact lenses and blonde blow-dry job to the annoying amateur sleuth they knew and could do with a lot less of.

She and Mariah huddled together on one of the giant leather ottomans that dotted the house's domestic landscape, in a corner of the murder room where everything else was thankfully obscured.

Morrie Alch squatted down before them, as you would with children, leaving his petite Asian-American-princess partner, Merry Su, to do the looming.

A man in his comfy fifties, he was graying a little, gaining even a little more around the middle, and putting a heck of a strain on his aging knees at the moment.

"You're the young lady who made the sad discovery," he told Mariah. "Mind if I sit down here and ask you some questions?"

Her earlier sobs had quieted into the occasional hiccup. She knew Detective Alch but she wasn't supposed to show it. Her color grew high and feverish, and her dark eyes burned with anguish.

"I guess."

"Okay, sweetheart. What's your name?"

Like he didn't know! Temple thought.

He got up, knees creaking, and sat beside Mariah,

pencil poised over a narrow-lined newspaper reporter's notebook.

His pencil needed sharpening. It didn't need his gesture in licking it first but the whole act made him into Uncle Morrie, a man to be trusted.

Temple know no homicide detective was a man to be trusted, including Mariah's own mother.

"Who are you?" Su asked Temple in a far less gentle tone.

"One of the other contestants."

"So which of you got first dibs on the corpse?"

Morrie cleared his throat to signal Su to go easier. He might as well have waved at the moon.

"Well?" Su insisted.

"I was here first," Mariah said. "Alone. I found . . . her."

"She had an appointment," Temple pointed out quickly. "That's why, when I heard the scream and recognized her voice, I knew where to go. I must have reached the scene only seconds after she came in and found Mrs. Klein dead."

"I'll thank you not to put testimony in the girl's mouth, Miss—?"

"Ah, Ozone."

"Ozone?"

"It's a stage name. Like Axl Rose. Or Sting."

"Why don't you step this way, Ms. Ozone Sting?" Su suggested.

Temple hated to leave Mariah to the mercies of kindly Detective Alch. The kindly part was true, and he was certainly well aware he was interviewing his boss's kid, but all of that only went so far in the homicide biz. Temple, meanwhile, was totally undercover and totally suspicious.

"Now." Su sat Temple down on a most uncomfortable modern sofa in the room's opposite corner. "You tell your story."

"It's not a story. Mariah and I are roomies. Roommates. She's a 'Tween Queen candidate and I'm a Teen Queen one. They pair us up, little and big sisters."

"So you feel a responsibility for the girl?"

"Yeah, right. Of course." And why wasn't Mariah's mother here now?

"You've never met her before?"

Maybe that was why. Conflict of interest. Not wanting to finger her own kid. Or her own kid's secret babysitter. Temple was on her own here. Thank heavens for Xoe Chloe.

Su's almond Asian eyes were bent to her notebook. Temple danced around the truth as if it were a Maypole. "Nope. We're all strangers here."

"And you are?"

"Xoe with an *X*."

Su's ballpoint pen (unlike Alch, she was unlikely to change her mind or anything else) stopped dead in the middle of one line. "And how do you spell Zoe with an *X*?"

"Easy. X-o-e. *Zoe-ee*."

"And 'Ozone' is your last name? Do you spell it with an *X*?"

"No. And I actually go by Xoe *Chloe* Ozone."

"Where do you go by this?"

"Performance art. In the clubs. You know. And at the Rollerblade havens."

"You're a Rollerblading performance artist?"

"That's it. Body and soul. Synthesis. That's my thing."

"So, what did you find when you entered the crime scene?"

"Uh, you mean, the room?"

"Yes."

"Well, um, the scale."

"The scale?"

"Yeah, the weigh thing. I do not like scales. I don't suppose you much avoid them, being one skimpy girl, but we're all on television here and every ounce looks like a pound."

"That's why the dietitian was part of the package. You were all supposed to lose weight?"

"Yeah. Pretty much all of us. You can never be too rich or too thin."

"What does money have to do with it?"

Xoe Chloe (she was *baaaaack!*) shrugged. "Hey, we get named Teen or 'Tween Queen, we get money, fame, and a new car, not to mention a date with a sex symbol."

"What passes for a sex symbol on a reality TV show these days?"

"Nobody you'd recognize. Frankly, nobody I'd care to share a straw with. Much less . . . well, you know."

"No, I don't know, Miss Ozone. That's why I'm asking you questions."

"Here's the deal. I hear the scream, like everyone else I come running, except they're all going in the opposite direction. I find poor little Mariah shrieking her head off in the middle of the room, and poor Marjory looking all laid back in her desk chair. How on earth did she die? Heart attack? Her face was all dark. As a card-carrying Goth girl, that doesn't frighten me, unless it's done without makeup."

"Speaking of cards, let's see yours."

"My what?"

"Your driver's license."

"Uh, I don't have one." Actually, Temple had a fake one from Molina she could flash later but figured Z. C. would only produce a plain-Jane name under intense pressure.

"You don't? Why not?"

"I Rollerblade, silly. Don't need a license for that."

"What about when you go into bars?"

"Hey, I may be Goth but I'm not a lush. I don't go that much into bars."

"But when you do."

"Simple. I don't drink. Would you believe I'm a born-again Christian?"

"No."

"You'd be right but I still don't drink. I just rock and roll along and nobody bothers me."

"Well, they will now. We'll want your fingerprints and some legitimate ID."

"I was born illegitimate," Xoe Chloe said, "but you can have my fingerprints. Like everyone else's, they'll be in the room. We all had appointments with Marjory."

"And what did she recommend for you?"

Temple let her nose squinch up. "More fruits and legumes. Heck, there are enough fruits around here to form a conga line of Carmen Mirandas."

"Not funny. You are no longer on *Candid Camera*, Ms. Ozone. You are in the sights of the Las Vegas Metropolitan Police Department Crimes-Against-Persons Unit. You know what that means?"

"Of course. CAPers! I love it. Such a merry word for the murder unit. Bring 'em on."

"Oh, we will, Ms. Ozone." Su stood, all wiry four-feet-eleven of wily Asian-American brains and martial-arts-buff body.

Su glanced over to where Alch was bidding Mariah adieu with a friendly pat on the shoulder.

"Mariah's thirteen, you know," Temple said.

Su must already be aware of Mariah's age and maternal unit but didn't bat a black eyelash.

"Most of the suspects on this scene are under twenty," she noted. "That doesn't mean we won't investigate all you 'tween-teen types, from date of birth to date of last period. Get it?"

Temple did.

* * *

Temple "showered" solo that evening.

Mariah, pale and tired, slept the sort of long drugged sleep teenagers major in. No wonder Sleeping Beauty remained such a popular fairy tale.

Meanwhile, Temple sat on the commode, the shower pelting into the tub and steaming up the mirrors. She speed-dialed Mama Molina's private home-phone number.

"Hello?" came the usual brusque opening.

"Agent Ninety-nine reporting."

"Cut the quips. This has gotten serious. How the hell did you allow my daughter to blunder onto a crime scene?"

"She didn't blunder. She had an appointment. I've been thinking about it and find that significant, don't you?"

"Someone *wanted* Mariah to find the body?"

"Someone wanted a 'Tween Queen candidate to find the body."

"Why would anyone be after Mariah?"

"They know her family connections?"

"Who, besides you?"

"Awful Crawford is here. You know, Crawford Buchanan, the KREP-radio guy. He gets around enough to know who's who in Las Vegas. Wouldn't take a master's degree to figure out that Mariah Molina might have relatives in high police places. And . . ." Temple paused, really hating the other possibility that had occurred to her.

"And what?"

"Most of these 'tween and teen candidates are hardy veterans of the beauty wars. They're obsessed with their physical appearances."

"Mariah's not."

"No. No JonBenet Ramsey, she. You reared her right. But . . ."

"But what?"

"Weight's an issue with her. The dietitian had Mariah in her sights. As far as I could tell, she's the one with the biggest weight issue here."

"She's barely a teenager! So she could lose fifteen pounds. It's not a killing offense."

"Everything's a bigger deal here. Maybe better, maybe worse. Someone could say, testify, that the dietitian was particularly hard on her. Mariah complained to high heaven, publicly, about eating beans and rabbit food."

"That's not a murdering offense."

"We mature women wouldn't think so but these are all *girls,* and most of them drama queens. Mrs. Klein had a vote on the winners. If someone was getting enough of a hard time. . . ."

"Killing a coach or judge will stop the show cold. Not productive."

"Not to our incisively logical minds. But our hormones have settled down. I assume. I can't speak for you, of course. Have you forgotten how desperately important every little thing is at that age?"

During the long pause that resulted, Temple couldn't help thinking that she and Molina were conspiring on the phone like teenage girlfriends planning a parentally un-sanctioned outing.

Bizarro!

"I'd rather not remember," Molina said at last. "How's Mariah holding up?"

"Okay. It wasn't a pretty scene. What killed the poor woman?"

"The autopsy hasn't been done yet but Coroner Bahr tells me she was likely choked."

"No way could Mariah be a suspect then, that takes strong hands, right?"

"Right, but not that kind of choking. It was lima beans."

"Oh. She was a huge advocate of bean eating. And lima beans are dry. I can see how she might be wolfing them down for a quick lunch at her desk. She did have a small fridge and microwave in that office and—"

"Nice fairy tale, Barr. Now I see why you've hung in

there with Mr. Unreliable Max Kinsella for so long. You're an optimist to the point of pathology. They were stuffed down her throat, probably spiced with Jalisco peppers hot enough to set her choking in the first place. It wouldn't take long to disable her that way, especially if the attack was unexpected."

"She was stuffed to death?"

"It may be a little more complicated than that. An allergy or some lethal substance may be involved that caused her throat to swell up on contact."

"What would this have to do with the defaced Teen Queen contest posters?"

"Nothing we can see. By the way, Alch and Su find Xoe Chloe—where do you come up with these things?—a suspicious character, but they haven't made you yet. You must have put together some disguise."

"At least I've never been fingerprinted."

"Yet. I'm thinking about it."

"The illusion of Xoe Chloe won't hold much longer anyway. The makeover process is stripping away all my best points."

"The show is suspended for now. It suits us to keep you all bottled up in the house, and maybe even let them start filming and recording again. It's like *Candid Camera, Crime Watchers'* edition. We're going over everything they recorded so far."

"The producers must be frantic."

"Are you kidding? They love it. They're planning to pick up the pageant as soon as we clear the scene and spin the show into *Dying for Beauty* or some such title."

"Then we're all stuck here, like a sequestered jury?"

"Right."

"But there's a killer among us. I guess I can do some snooping."

"Please. You're a glorified babysitter. Don't get a notion of being a professional snoop."

That hurt. Temple found Xoe Chloe pouting into the **cell phone.** Good thing Molina couldn't see her. She **wiped her** brow of the sweat the steamy bathroom had deposited. Better to assume the producers lied and that cameras and mikes were still recording.

"So what do you want me to do?"

"Stay with Mariah as much as you can."

"What'll we all do?"

"Exercise, eat or don't eat, watch each other. Alch and Su will be there too. I'll make sure they look for a suspect a little farther afield than Chloe Zoe."

"Xoe Chloe."

But Molina had disconnected.

Temple sat there puzzling. The least likely person on the premises had been murdered. Why? And what about the lurid threats to the show and the mischief inside the house? That seemed to be from an entirely different script than Marjory Klein's quick, deviously planned death.

Script. Maybe a script for mock mayhem was part of the "reality" here. And someone had taken advantage of the distraction it provided to commit murder for a totally unrelated reason.

Xoe Chloe was going to have to snoop around plenty. Luckily, she had the personality for it. Temple stood up, still puzzling. She didn't dare leave Mariah alone now though. What to do? She couldn't be with her all day; they had separate exercise schedules. Mariah would actually appreciate the show's suspension; she could make more progress.

What to do about Mariah? But wait! Temple knew an "inside" man already on the premises, a pro for her to recruit. It was a fiendish idea, but Molina was giving her no rope so she'd just have to live with any lifeline Temple could come up with on such short notice.

Chapter 36

Diet Drinks

A soft knock on the bedroom door awoke Temple sometime between midnight and five A.M.

She glanced across the gigantic bed. Mariah was a completely concealed lump under the covers. When she was in this state, Temple had discovered, not even an earthquake-style shaking could wake her.

Temple crept to the door nevertheless and turned the interior key in the lock. The person in the hall was about her height, so she edged the door open.

Her aunt scuttled in.

"Are we alone?"

Temple nodded at the giant tortoise shape on the bed. "As good as. But come into my office."

Once they were ensconced in the bathroom, Temple turned on the small fluorescents surrounding the mirror. Kit Carlson wore her trademark big-frame eyeglasses, and an elegant vintage nylon peignoir set—red, studded with rhinestones which were somehow very attractive on a small, energetic woman. She also carried a Manhattan-big tote bag. From it, she pulled a bottle.

"I never travel without my dessert sherry."

"Oh, thank God." Temple pulled the toothbrushes out of the matching water glasses and rinsed them at the faucet. "I deserve a break today, even if it's tomorrow. What time is it anyway?"

"Three A.M.," Kit said in a spooky voice. "When ghosts walk."

"You spot Mrs. Klein in the hall on the way here?"

"No. But I had the oddest impression that someone saw me. Maybe it's just a hangover from this twenty-four-hour oversight we're getting."

"The spy machines are off for now. The homicide lieutenant on this case told me so herself. The show is 'suspended.' We're all stuck here until the police know whodunit."

"Oooh! *Ten Little Indians.* Agatha Christie stories made great plays." Kit lifted her clumsy glass with the toothpaste spatters on it and clicked rims with Temple's. "You found her dead, poor thing. Drink up, then tell me all about it."

"I don't know if I should," Temple said after a slow sweet swallow. "I'm here on police business myself."

"Listen. I am one nervous Nellie, niece. A coach was killed. They've got us judges and coaches cooped up in one wing, easy pickings. Who's next? Apparently, someone doesn't much like being made over."

"Maybe it's someone who doesn't like women reinventing themselves," Temple said.

"Like who? The Taliban?"

And that remark of her aunt's put Temple in mind of the lone Middle-Eastern man on the premises: Rafi Nadir. But hadn't he made over Carmen Molina, to hear tell? It didn't compute.

"Any controlling man," Temple said. "The kind who can't stand women getting out from under their thumbs and becoming themselves. Maybe it's a cliché, but there's truth under the truism. I'll never forget this case I covered when I was a TV journalist in Minnesota. A woman. A wife. A mother. A nurse. Just lost some weight. Just trying to enhance her self-esteem. Soon clear why. The husband—he had to have been abusive—attacked her in the family garage with an electric drill. And she lived. And stood. And he set her on fire. And she burned. And she lived. And she stood. And he ran. And they found her, burned over ninety percent of her body. And she spoke. Save her kids from him. They took her away. And she died. And, you know what, nobody would report what happened to him. Maybe a mental hospital. Maybe he's out there. I tried to trace where he went, but my station wouldn't support me. Everything about her was public. Nothing about him was. Reminds me of the vanishing Arthur Dickson."

"Arthur who?"

"There are too many men who don't want women to remake themselves. And apparently Arthur Dickson, the man who built this place, was one of them."

"Ghastly! I had no idea you dealt with such things." Kit the former actress and current novelist, a creature of empathy, was devastated.

Temple shook off the past and its eternal losses. "Marjory Klein was the most unlikely murder victim in the place. Do you know anything about her?"

"We had meetings together, ate together, compared notes on candidates. Yeah, I knew her, Horatio."

"Wait!" Temple waved the hand the glass happened to be in. "Is that Horatio as in *Hamlet* and the skull of Yorick, or Horatio as in *CSI: Miami?* Given your theatrical background, it's hard to tell."

"It doesn't matter anyway. I tell you the woman was

harmless. Good-natured. A widow. Um, two, I think, grown children. Utterly committed to her field of work. Been in eating disorder consultation for years. Thought this stupid show was an opportunity to set an example for teenagers with bad, even dangerous, eating habits across the country. She was a much better person than I was, and now she's dead."

"That's a very good point. If one of the coaches or judges was going to be killed, why not Dexter Manship, say?"

"He's insufferable, yes. And it just isn't an act. It's all the time. So tiresome. Egotistic. Elitist. Everything well-balanced people love to hate. But . . . it's also his shtick. He's an entertainer. Killing him for being irritating would be like . . . offing Jerry Lewis. He's a whipping boy for the rest of us, which is very healthy. And the French would be devastated."

"The feelings of the French are not a national priority right now."

"Oh, pooh. They're supposed to be that way, as Dexter Manship is supposed to be the way he is. I just don't understand why poor Marjory was killed. Strangled, I heard."

Temple considered and decided to keep the suspected manner of death to herself. Not that Kit would tell but she might not be able to down another legume in her life, and that would be a sad betrayal of Marjory's mission. Temple knew she was taking a very dim view of lima beans right now, as if she wasn't already skittish about them. Who knew?

"What should I do?" Kit asked.

"Keep an eye open. Does anybody here strike you as suspicious?"

Kit sipped and considered, considered and sipped. "That dark dangerous-looking guy that Savannah Ashleigh calls a bodyguard."

Temple frowned. "I know him. He's not Mr. Good Citizen but—"

But. Rafi was taking questionable jobs around Vegas, and she'd met him doing muscle at strip clubs. He'd been a strong suspect for the Stripper Killer. Just because he was Molina's loathed ex was no reason to become his champion. What if this time he really was up to something . . . ugly?

Molina would have her scalp. And neck. And rear end if she underestimated Nadir's reasons for being here when Mariah was on the premises and involved. Molina would have her skin for not mentioning that Nadir was here, period. Maybe she'd better tell her . . . and have Molina on-site, in everybody's face? Not productive.

"What are you scheming, niece? I see whole Elizabethan tragedies running through your mind."

"You have a theatrical imagination, Aunt Kit. It's fun but off base. Some of the dramatis personae in this thing are a little dicey, is all. It's the strangers I wonder about. We don't know enough about anybody to figure out who might want to kill them. Are any of the judges and coaches previously acquainted?"

"Sorry. Not a one. To hear them tell it. From my point of view, they act like strangers."

"Then . . . what about the people who put us all together?"

"Who? Oh. You mean the producers."

"Yeah, why are they so shadowy?"

Kit shrugged. "They always are, whether it's a Broadway play or a TV show. Only a very few producers develop a high public profile. I'm thinking of Don Hewitt of *Sixty Minutes,* and, my God, that show's been on since God made Eden. So sheer longevity gets his name out. Stephen Cannell, a lot of people know him, fans of *The Rockford Files* and a few dozen other TV hits."

"I've been calling our absent producers Goodson Toddman."

"Oh, yeah! A play on the names of the old game-show kings, Goodman-Todson. But you're in publicity. You know the people behind the people. The public doesn't."

"Wouldn't that be a great way to set up a sting, a revenge plot, a murder, then? Produce a show as an excuse and pop off your enemy. Or enemies."

"Oh, great. Now I have to worry what producers I might have ticked off during my distant acting career. I'm just a paperback writer now. Please, sir, no more. Don't kill me."

But Kit's touching theatrics didn't touch Temple. She was standing up, then pacing in the bathroom's limited space. She liked that idea very much. Don't look at the Teen Queen show as what it purported to be but as someone's elaborate revenge plot. And it had to be revenge. You don't kill someone the way Marjory Klein was killed for any other reason.

So. Reality TV as a setup for murder. Maybe . . . for multiple murders.

"Kit! You're a genius. I've got a whole new take on this thing. Pick up thy bottle and toddle on home."

"But, Temple, if it is indeed a setup and some of us, maybe all of us, aren't here by accident, I was invited. Out of the blue. For no discernible reason."

"Some people were invited as cover, like maybe all the contestants."

"Cover. I'm cover. That's good. I can live with that. I wouldn't know anybody in common with a dietitian, would I?"

"Of course not. Where was Marjory from?"

"Ah, Los Angeles, I think she said."

"See. Wrong coast, Manhattan baby. You're safe. They say not, but I think the police must have someone undercover here."

"Besides you?"

"I'm told I'm only good for babysitting."

"Not your forte. I know. I'm your aunt."

"Keep that under your hat, if you have one with you. And we both better keep an eye out to see that none of the little girls get hurt."

"Sure. But, Temple, all of the girls had appointments with Marjory. Maybe she really ticked one off with her healthy eating crusade. Maybe she found one who was seriously anorexic and was determined to have her put into treatment."

"And therefore removed from the competition. I didn't want to reveal the total grossness of the death scene, but I suppose a girl who purged herself would consider stuffing food down someone's throat a suitable punishment."

"Stuffed down her throat?" Kit put a hand to her own neck. "God, what a way to go. I hope nobody ever hates me that much."

She pushed the cork back into her illegal bottle, as if she couldn't swallow anything more. The gesture reminded them both that no liquor was served in the Teen Queen Castle.

Imagine, Temple could turn in her own aunt for violating the dorm rules! Teenage angst, revisited, made for many motives for murder.

Kit saluted at the door, then scurried back down the hall to her own wing.

Temple turned back to the room. Mariah was still doing the turtle under the bedcovers. Temple wished she could be as dead to the world and the schemes that must be swirling around here as Mariah was at this moment.

Chapter 37

American Tragedy

"You want what?"

Molina looked up from the phone receiver pinched between her cheek and shoulder. She held up a hand to signal Alch and Su to hold on a minute.

"I have more to do right now than act as a glorified file clerk," she went on.

Under the desk her toe tapped an impatient drumbeat on the vinyl tile floor.

Alch and Su exchanged glances.

"All right. I'll find someone to do it, although God knows we're understaffed. Yes. ASAP. My messenger boy may have to be a bit unconventional. Fine. Good."

She hung up with an undisguised sigh.

"More paperwork, Lieutenant?" Alch asked sympathetically. Paperwork was the bane of accountants, schoolteachers, and law enforcement types.

"Nothing germane." Molina sat. "What's happening at that damn house?"

"Nothing more. We have some uniforms on the set, so to speak," Alch said.

"Meanwhile," Su added, "I've found a lot out about Marjory Klein."

"And—?"

"She was somebody, Lieutenant. She has several books about nutrition and eating disorders on Amazon.com and eBay."

"Second coming, obviously," Alch mocked. "Amazon and eBay. The new carnival hucksters."

"The point is," Su said, pointedly, eyeing Alch askance, "that she was something of an expert in the field."

"Credentials accepted. What about her personally?"

Su flipped pages, quoting. "Associate Professor at Great Western University in Michigan. Blue-collar school but well regarded. Assisted various nationally known psychiatrists in treating eating disorder cases. She had some professional chops."

"In other words," Alch summed up, "she was an expert of a sort."

"Amazing." Molina was truly surprised. "The show producers actually assembled some credible advisors, unlike our own *CSI*."

"It's a national hit, Lieutenant," Alch said, "no point in being a nit-picker."

"There's always a point in being a nit-picker, Morrie, or at least some pleasure." But Molina smiled.

"Okay," she went on. "This woman wasn't a quack. Could she have professional rivals jealous of her new public profile with the Teen Queen gig?"

"We're talking academia," Alch said. "Always rivals."

"I have the autopsy report."

"What'd Grizzly say?" Su asked.

Molina smiled again. Her nickname for the burly brusque coroner, last name Bahr, had stuck. It gave her a certain cachet with him. Coroners were always a trifle vain, like Sherlock Holmes's older brother. They loved the tribute of a nom de guerre.

"Peanut oil. Peanut allergy. Deadly. Victims of this condition usually advertise it widely to avoid any contact with such a common food element."

"So the lima beans . . ." Su began.

"Were both a medium and a message, I think."

"Wow." Su was speechless for two seconds. "Any one of those girls could have had enough of Klein's 'beans and legumes' philosophy. And peanut oil . . . it's everywhere."

"What about the kitchen?" she asked Alch.

He nodded, consulting his notebook. "Bottles of the stuff, raw peanuts. 'Natural' peanut butter floating in oil. Anyone could have accessed it."

"Wasn't the kitchen normally off-limits?"

"Yes, but the show reveled in rebels." Alch looked up at Molina. Pause. "One Mariah Molina made an unauthorized midnight raid on the kitchen Tuesday night. And Xoe Chloe caught her with a hand in the Chips Ahoy."

A silence held in the small, narrow office.

"I suppose no one is exempt from suspicion," Molina said finally. "I am at a loss for a motive."

"According to witnesses, Klein was particularly hard on your daughter," Su said. "She was on the most stringent diet."

"Nobody else got bad news from the nutritionist?"

"Everybody had to consume more soy protein, low-fat dairy, and milk."

"None of that is a motive for murder," Molina objected.

"Agreed." Alch sat forward on the damned uncomfortable plastic shell chair. "We need to dig deeper into the victim's personal life."

"Hah!" Su crossed her arms over her size zero Donna Karan jacket. "Nutritionists don't have personal lives. Klein was a divorcée for twenty years, an academic drudge, a nobody outside a very narrow arena of expertise."

"She was somebody enough to get drafted for the Teen Queen Castle show." Molina sat back. "Find out more. Find out more relevant facts. Find me a motive."

Alch and Su stood. "Right," he said.

"Wrong," Su murmured as they shouldered out the narrow door together.

Molina leaned back in her chair's cheesy tilt setting. She couldn't agree with Su more. This murder was all wrong. The vic was all wrong. They were all wrong, or they would see the connections that were now invisible. But, like a magician's hidden mechanisms, those threads had to be there.

Magicians. At least Max Kinsella had nothing to do with this case, thank God and Harry Houdini.

Chapter 38

North into Nowhere

The Circle Ritz was a kitschy piece of fifties architecture clinging to the fringe of the exploding ultramodern Fantasia that the Las Vegas Strip had become.

It was round, faced with black marble, and sported triangular balconies at the "corner" units.

Max drove his latest dispensable vehicle, a black Toyota Rav4, into the familiar lot. He knew every dimple in the asphalt and every pothole the heat had burned into the surface.

Temple's new red Miata, caramel-colored canvas top up, sat under the shade of the venerable palm tree that overarched the lot.

He usually entered the unit he and Temple had shared—until his enforced disappearance eighteen months ago—like a second-story man: by the French doors on the balcony.

Part of that was self-preservation; there were those that

wanted him dead. Another part of it was the magician's need to surprise. Temple had always been a ready audience for the paper rose bouquet, the sudden flash of fire to light a candle, and especially the unannounced midnight assignation.

This time, though, Temple was gone and he'd have to enter by a more conventional route, the side door from the parking lot.

The Lovers Knot Wedding Chapel that landlady Electra Lark operated was in the building's street-facing front. Back here was only a long hallway, then the buzzer security system for the units.

Max had his own key but he buzzed his destination anyway. This mid-afternoon visit would be a surprise, and he wanted to ensure his quarry was in.

The answer was yes, so he pushed the button for the single elevator and waited for its slow descent. He felt like a visitor here at last, not just an errant resident who'd been AWOL too long. Not a good feeling. No wonder Temple was getting restive about their relationship. Ouch. That was the first time he'd thought of it that way.

The old elevator took him up at its usual charming cranky rate. When the door finally opened, his destination was just three strides away.

The forbidden penthouse.

Another button to push. Rewarded by the nostalgic chime of an old-fashioned doorbell.

"Max!" Electra Lark cast the door wide, her tropical-colored muumuu filling it like a flower-shop display. Beyond her came the chill and hum of air-conditioning. "Don't be a stranger. Come in."

"Are you sure? I've never been inside before. Most residents haven't."

"Tut-tut. You mean you never managed a clandestine exploration, like Temple's cat, Louie, that bad boy?"

"Magician's honor."

"Well, you're not really a resident anymore. Are you?"

"Not officially."

"Neither is Louie, but he's coming and going around here all the time."

Electra turned and Max followed her through an octagonal entry hall lined in vertical mirrored blinds that reflected his image in disconcerting slivered bits. He felt exactly that fragmented these days.

The rooms beyond were cool, almost cold, and dimly lit. The whole place smacked of an inner sanctum, quite different from Electra's bright, beachy appearance and personality.

"Have a seat," she suggested.

He wasn't sure which hunkering forties sofa or chair would accommodate his six-foot-four frame; they were all bulky, but the seating areas were oddly cramped. He settled gingerly on the maroon mohair sofa.

"May I offer you some sun tea?"

"No."

Electra sat on a rattan chair by the blond television set that must be fifty years old. "Well, you're an easy guest."

She herself was eternally sixty-something. Her white hair, normally a canvas for a variety of spray-on colors, like indigo or purple or magenta, was a tumble of golden blonde, giving her the look of an aging Shirley Temple doll on Hawaiian holiday.

"I just stopped by to ask after Temple."

"What about her?"

"She mentioned she was leaving town."

"Oh, yes. She asked me to watch her place, and Louie, for a week or so. I have seen about as much of Louie since then as I've seen of you in the past several months."

"That bad?"

"Oh, you bachelor boys have your rounds to make, no doubt, deserting us faithful girls at home."

Max let that go. "I wondered if you'd heard how Temple's father was."

"Father?"

"That's why she went home. Isn't it?"

"Goodness, Max! I don't know. She didn't mention why she was leaving and I'm not one to pry, not right out anyway. She was in a tearing hurry to leave. I hope it isn't anything too serious, although at his age . . . and mine, it could be."

"She said it was a minor heart problem. A stent."

"Listen, at our age, heart problems are not minor. Poor little thing. She must have been worried to distraction to forget to mention it to me. Or she didn't want me to worry. Oh . . . Max! Wait! Don't move."

Of course he froze at Electra's sudden command. Her eyes had widened like windows and she was staring directly behind him.

Max's muscles tensed to jump any which way necessary.

"What is it?"

"This is unheard of. She's . . . come out and is perching on the sofa back. Just behind your left shoulder."

"She. You're not referring to a poisonous serpent or a scorpion, I assume."

"Lord, no. *Shhh!* If you move very slowly you might see her."

Max could move as slowly as a living statue in the Venice hotel's central courtyard, in other words, almost beyond camera detection. In a minute, he had turned enough to stare into the most celestial sky blue eyes he'd ever seen.

He was facing a cat whose longish silky cream hair was accented with brown and white.

"Karma," Electra pronounced.

"You mean it was karma that she's shown herself to me."

"Maybe so, but that's also her name. Karma. She's a supersensitive cat, a Birman. They were sacred to the dalai lamas."

"Much was." Max rose, very slowly.

The cat remained in place, staring at him.

"This is so unusual. Karma doesn't take to strangers."

"I'm not a complete stranger."

"Not until the last few months. If Temple calls, is there someplace I can reach you?"

He jotted his cell phone number on a blank card from his pocket.

Electra rose to see him to the door. "It's good to see you Max. I'll walk out with you."

"Not necessary."

"No, but I want to see what you're driving these days. I've never seen anyone with such a habit of changing cars."

"Leases allow me to change cars as often as you change hair colors."

"Touché." She took his arm once they were back in the foyer and waiting for the elevator. "I'm upset that Temple didn't tell me about her father. You'll keep me informed if you find out anything, won't you?"

"I don't have her mother's phone number. I wasn't exactly a Barr family favorite."

"Why ever not, Max? I'd want you in my family album any day."

He shrugged as they rode down in the elevator. "Temple was the youngest child and the only girl. They didn't want her running off to Las Vegas with an itinerant magician."

"But you were headlining at the Goliath!"

"I'm not anymore. Maybe they were right. And families are funny." He couldn't help thinking of his own very unfunny family situation.

By then they were in the lobby. Electra took a firm maternal grip on his arm. "You're part of the Circle Ritz family, dear Max, whether you're in residence or not. So feel free to come visit me and Karma anytime."

Max smiled at her innate warmth. He'd been pretty insulated from family feeling most of his life. Surprising how good her encouragement felt.

On the back step, Electra halted them. "Wait. Let me guess which one is yours."

"Not much of a challenge. There are only seven vehicles out here."

"You are always a challenge, Max. *Hmmm.* The black Toyota SUV."

"Not the silver Crossfire?"

"Maybe, except I know who drives that."

Something guarded in her tone made Max ask, "And who is that?"

"Matt. Just got it."

"Devine? What happened to churchly frugality?"

Electra shrugged, her arm still linked through his. "Maybe it was time he broke out a little."

"You were letting him ride the Hesketh Vampire." Max referred to his vintage Brit classic motorcycle, also silver, which he'd given Electra way back when as a down payment on the Circle Ritz condo. For Temple and him.

"Right. Then he bought my old Probe."

"Now that he has the Crossfire, I don't suppose he gives the Vampire much exercise these days then?"

"Not much. I could ride it. Still have my Speed Queen helmet, but I haven't for some reason."

Matt stared at the low sleek silver car and the small red convertible and his own high-riding SUV, which looked ultra-conservative and dull alongside those two.

"I feel like taking a nostalgic spin on the Vampire. Did you know that there are only three left, outside museums? Come on; I'll give you a ride that will curl your blonde hair even more."

"I don't know, Max. You sound pretty reckless right now."

"Speed Queen isn't up for that?"

"Darn wrong!" She reached into her muumuu pocket. "Just let me unlock the shed and we'll be ready to rock and roll."

In minutes, Max had grabbed the no-name black helmet Matt had used. Electra had mounted behind him, her chubby hands locked around his waist. They cruised out of the parking lot through a few city blocks before hitting Highway 15 paralleling the Strip, then veering onto 93, heading north into nowhere.

He let the Vampire have its head, like a horse. After all, it was named for the unearthly scream its engine produced as it reached higher speeds.

Far past the city, he let the motorcycle run as straight as a banshee scream, due north. Electra whooped behind him and held on tighter. Wind lashed them both into a mute, moving altered state of speed and nerve and nirvana.

And finally, miles down Highway 93 en route to Ash Springs, the Vampire's triumphant screech drowned out the ugly, unwelcome questions in Max Kinsella's head.

Chapter 39

Awful Unlawful

The atmosphere around the Teen Queen Castle was rapidly turning into English country house boredom.

All the frenetic activity ground to a halt. Each faction clung to their "wings," lolling about the common rooms watching CNN (the coaches and judges), MTV and *E.T.* (the 'Tween Queen candidates), *Ambush Makeovers* and Home Shopping Network and QVC (the Teen Queen lions' mane den), and ESPN (the technical crew).

Xoe Chloe, the nonconformist, found reason to ricochet between all of them, as if on invisible Rollerblades.

And, of course, she kept bouncing off Alch and Su as they made their rounds interviewing the entire cast and crew.

There were two other people on board as unattached as Xoe Chloe, both unanchored and both unsavory. Temple wondered what that meant.

"Hey there!" The words were banal; the deep baritone that intoned them sent hacksaw blades up Temple's back.

She turned to find Crawford Buchanan attired in a banana-yellow jogging suit (which made him look like a tropical fruit with a shaggy, rotting end, i.e., his always too-trendy coiffure), trying to catch up with her in the artsy breezeway between the coaches' and candidates' areas.

"Yeah?" She turned and stopped only because it occurred to her he might be worth pumping.

"You sure do get around."

"Beach Boys. 1964. 'I Get Around.'"

"An MTV girl. If I were a judge you'd make my cut."

"You're a real Nowhere Man. Beatles. 1966."

"Okay. Cute. I'd still like to interview you."

"With no mike, Spike?"

He tapped his forehead. "I still have this. And maybe some paper somewhere."

While he patted his jogging suit pockets for the absent notebook, Temple snatched an *InStyle* magazine abandoned by a passing blonde on a nearby table.

"Write on this."

"Well, I guess I can. In the white spaces."

"You always been a radio guy?" she asked.

"Off and on. Used to have my own show. They called me the Provo, Utah, Kid."

"Real catchy."

He bought it. "What do you think about this murder thing?"

"I think it's ruining the reality TV show world. I mean, jawing with maggots, eating live lizards, winning a million for snagging some dork on live TV . . . or not, singing so bad you're an un-American Idol, that's all righteous stuff. Cool. But murder. Way too intense. Bad form. You know what I mean?"

"Uh, yeah. So . . . why'd you do this?"

"Thought it'd be a kick. Why'd you do this?"

"I have a chance to get syndicated and you could be part of it, Xoe. It's the pits that we're off camera. I need a telegenic personality like you. When we're recording again, I'd get you Rollerblading all through the house. You'd be our guide to the whole show, see? Great exposure. A shower scene maybe. Then jogging around the pool. Show 'em all sweating and primping. The public will love it."

"Whoa! Crawford, you devil, you. That's all visual material."

"Right. Radio sucks. I'm being recorded here too. I wanna go TV."

"Sure. You've got the chops for it. Say, if you solved this murder thing—"

He blinked, flashing his long, ladylike lashes. A supermodel would kill for those things.

"I've been thinking this police stuff is a hitch," he said.

"No, dude. It's an opportunity. *CSI Central.* Who d'you think done it? You've been all over this place. Unless . . . it's you-uuu."

He spat out a yoooh sound. "Right. I want to ruin a chance to change media. No way. But you're right, if I could find a way to capitalize on this murder . . ."

"So, what'd yah think of this Klein babe?"

"Nothing. I mean, she wasn't good-looking or even interesting."

"Interesting enough for someone to murder."

"That's true." The Crawf frowned, lost in the implications. "I interviewed her on tape. Had to. She was a coach. All she did was spout stuff about how girls eat bad just to look good but end up looking worse. I mean, I don't care how they get there, as long as they get there, and you got there, if you know what I mean?"

"I know exactly what you mean." Temple restrained herself from rolling up her *InStyle* magazine and stuffing it down his throat.

Then she took her own mental temperature. She felt, right now, just like the murderer must have felt confronting Marjory Klein. Only Crawford was a disgusting toad who deserved to eat his own words.

What could, would Marjory Klein have deserved? Mariah saw her as a diet Nazi, a nag, but Klein had just wanted young women to be healthy, hadn't she? Since when was that a sin?

Temple owed the Crawf big time for stirring an emotion in her that gave her a few seconds' insight into the murderer.

Crassford Buchanan ought to be a de rigueur fixture on every crime scene to inspire the detective to think like someone in a murderous rage.

The killing may have been sheer rage at the end but at the beginning, during the setup, it had to have been pure cold calculation. That gave her an interesting insight into the killer.

Temple wandered out to the pool area, still trying to put the pieces together. Whoever did it had to know something about Marjory. Her philosophy and habits. What she was allergic to. That meant the roots of the murder lay far away from this Teen Queen Castle on the Mojave. And therefore the motives were harder to find.

How could Temple contribute anything? She didn't have the access the police did to the victim's past. Or maybe she did. Molina.

The pool was deserted right now except for one lounge chair on which lay a bronzed body in a lime green bikini.

A big black cat lay under the lounger, basking in the shade of that B-movie body.

Louie blinked at Temple, his eyes the same lime green shade as Savannah Ashleigh's latest thong.

Savannah wore a silver foil collar around her neck like a high-tech Elizabethan collar. It focused the sun's lethal tanning rays at her neck and under her chin. No ugly untanned white streaks allowed just where they might make her look a trifle old and crepe-skinned.

Temple stopped to stare at this flagrant example of self-abuse. Even Hollywood George Hamilton had used self-tanning lotions for years.

"Reminds me of bacon," a voice behind Temple noted.

She turned to find Rafi Nadir standing at attention in the shade of the portico, sunglasses as dark as those on any South American dictator hiding his eyes. Nothing disguised the contempt in his voice as he regarded the object of his protection.

Savannah was courting melanoma while paying to avoid an unlikely personal physical attack.

"Yo," Xoe Chloe said.

"Yo, yourself, whoever you think you are. I know you," he added.

"Me?"

"You . . . now that the KISS wig is history. First, you're a thong-girl at a strip club, then you're a PR flack at a furniture store, and now you're a juvenile delinquent Valley Goth Girl."

"You made me! How?"

"Once that lame wig was gone."

"I didn't have much time to get an act together."

"So, now you're gonna tell me what you really are, a PI."

It was as good a secondary cover as anything.

"Maybe," Temple said, "and now the murder to go with me has happened at last."

"So. You want something."

"Not much."

"They always say that." He nodded at Savannah.

"I really don't want much."

"I must admit that you get around."

"You too."

"Yeah, well, I gotta take these freelance gigs."

"I'd think guarding a dedicated babe like Savannah would be a cushy job."

"She hasn't even got the integrity of a stripper," he said. "Look at that old alley cat sitting under her shadow. He knows what she's good for. Occupying space in this world, and not much else."

"She may have struggles we don't know anything about."

"Most people do. It still doesn't entitle them. So. What is a PR girl doing here playing a Bad Barbie PI?"

"I'm someone's bodyguard too. One of the 'Tween Queen candidates. Her mother hired me."

He nodded. "Her mother had the right idea, it turns out, now that murder's been done. Hey! You're rooming with the poor kid who found the body. What's her name? Marnie?"

"Mariah." Temple felt weirder than she could say introducing Rafi Nadir to the name of his unsuspected daughter.

"Mariah. Odd name. Mama musta been a big fan of Mariah Carey. The pop diva, you know."

"I do know. Actually, the name reminds me of the song."

"Song?"

"From *Paint Your Wagon.*"

Rafi's body language remained as blank as his sunglasses. "Paint your what?"

"A musical comedy about the California Gold Rush. The name of the western wind is Mariah. In the song."

"Well, this is the West." Rafi shrugged. "As if Las Vegas was anywhere real."

"What keeps you here?"

"I don't know. L.A. was a bust. I drifted. There are lots of temporary jobs here for a guy like me. If I don't get competition from know-it-all PR gals. You're quite a chameleon, you know that?"

"I don't want to be. I just keep getting drawn into these situations."

"So how's the kid?"

"Mariah?"

"Yeah. I've worked the death scene and interviewed citizens who found the corpse, but a kid? And this one was rough. You handle it okay?"

"Yeah. Except the victim was so harmless."

"Those are the worst. She seemed like a nice lady."

Temple eyed Savannah, who wiggled on the lounge chair, forcing Louie to move to keep his shady spot. Rafi was oddly unaffected by Savannah's vampish moves. Maybe he wasn't as knee-jerk a jerk as she—and Molina—thought. Was that possible?

"What a spotlight hog," Rafi said. "A little talent would help a lot."

"Maybe not. Look at this competition."

"Looks like a murder competition."

"You expect more?"

"There are so many more deserving victims." His blocked gaze clearly focused on Savannah.

"Don't worry. Louie is on the case."

"Louie?"

"The cat. My cat."

This kept him silent for a few seconds. "You and the cat are a team? I spotted him around Maylords."

"A girl can always count on a cat."

"Does this Mariah girl have a cat?"

"Two. Striped. And Louie by proxy."

Rafi's continually scanning sunglasses lowered to regard Louie, then lifted to Savannah with her foil collar, ear-plugging radio and the bikini a lime dressing on an oiled, silicone-stuffed breast of turkey prime.

"These cops on the scene," he said. "They haven't a clue. But I think you do. Keep me in the loop."

"Mr. Nadir, if it's loopy you want, it's loopy you'll get."

"Right. I liked the expression on that homicide lieutenant's face when you had me snag the Maylords killer. That do-able again?"

"Maybe. But I don't get your issues." Of course she knew more than he could guess.

"Nobody could."

Then Savannah called for a misting with distilled water and a green apple martini, and Rafi moved to oblige her.

Was that a motive for murder? Oh, yeah.

Chapter 40

American Idle

There is not much to be learned underneath the dripping shower of tanning creams.

Granted, my Miss Temple has made excellent use of the shower option in the bathroom for consultations and speculations. However, Miss Savannah Ashleigh proves to be a disappointment in this area, and I am sorry I am too far away to eavesdrop on my esteemed associate's parley with Mr. Rafi Nadir.

He keeps turning up in this town like the proverbial bad penny, but any human dude who can remain unimpressed by the too obvious attributes of Miss Savannah Ashleigh gets a free grade C in my book.

So, once Miss Temple, aka Xoe Chloe, leaves the scene to Mr. Nadir and his charge, I ankle across the hot concrete at a sprightly pace and head for the far door to the kitchens, which is often an open and shut case of folks coming and going.

And who do I end up nose-to-nose with but my own not-so-darling daughter. So-called.

"Louise! You nearly gave me a heart attack."

"No doubt from all those hours lolling with bimbos on the back forty," she retorts.

(Louise does not converse so much as retort. And riposte. And countercharge. And other annoying communication habits.)

"Information gathering," I report. (If she can retort, I can report.) "As you can see, my Miss Temple is on an important undercover assignment."

"She is a PR flack! How important can this assignment be? If you ask me, she is in her second teenhood. That is what happens to humans who have odd ideas about relationships with the opposite sex. She is bewitched, bothered, and bewildered by the choices available to the modern female. She should chill out and sample the buffet before she commits herself to 'until death do them part,' whoever 'them' may be. Or just get fixed and forget it."

"Easy enough for you to say."

"I am proudly neuter. Look at all the angst and time it saves. I would save even more time if my decidedly not-neuter Dad deigned to tell me what case he was working on."

"It is not a case. It is a personal matter. My roommate took on this nutso assignment and I have been dragged along like a Hello Kitty purse," I say, referring to line of feline-themed frivolities for the grade-school set.

"'Hello Kitty!' This is exactly what I say when I am visiting the executive suite at the Crystal Phoenix and happen to spy your puss on the nightly news. If Miss Temple is undercover here, you are way overcover: 'a passing alley cat who took one look at the lovelies in residence and stayed on to become an unofficial mascot.' One week it is masquerading as a domestic accessory in Fine Furnishings, and the next week it is scarfing up 'a lean fish and veggie' diet on a reality TV show set. You are getting downright decadent in your old age, Pop."

"Shhhh," I hiss, checking for any Persian girls who might be within hearing range. Overhearing such nonsense might give them the wrong idea about my age and carefree lack of encumbrances. "I am not your pop. Murder has been done here. I need discretion more than ever."

"Why do you think I am here? That nasty killing is all over local TV."

"What? The producers of this shoddy but hot show do not have the juice to squelch bad publicity?"

"Get with it. Nowadays bad publicity is good publicity. This the era of really cheesy reality, on TV or off of TV. Look at Paris Hilton and Victoria Gotti. Bad is good."

"Call me old-fashioned, but I like to think certain standards prevail. Why are the police not shutting this show down?"

"Why shut it down? The place is already wired from one end to the other, all kosher and everybody signed up to agree to it. They could not legally get a wire tap on a murder scene, but all they have to do here is review the daily footage and stalk the suspects. We should have it so good in our business. At least Midnight Inc. Investigations should have a full complement of staff on the premises. Especially since our prime client is here and in danger."

"And that would be?"

"'Your Miss Temple,' as you are always putting it. You know that she relies upon us for footwork."

"Um, me maybe. I do not believe she is aware of your occasional participation."

"All the better." Miss Louise makes my heart sink by nudging me under a shaded bench against the house and sitting down for a long consultation.

From this vantage point, we watch the humans come and go while I give a running commentary on who is who and who hates whom.

I learn that Miss Louise is one hundred percent in agreement with my Miss Temple on the vapidity of blondes of either gender. I then twit her on her fondness for Mr. Matt. She swishes her long fluffy train in my face and says that the rare exception always proves the rule, and I had better watch out because her Fancy Feast coupons are on him in the Miss Temple sweepstakes.

I then defend the suave man of the world, black of hair but pure of heart, and she concedes that she would not kick Mr. Max out of bed if she happened to be in residence there.

She predicts that my "honeymoon" with Miss Temple cannot last forever, and I should stick to working in the family business because soon that may be all that I have to keep me warm.

Before I can get my whiskers in a wad at this scenario, a glimpse of Mr. Rafi Nadir's motorcycle boots passing through on some demeaning errand for Miss Savannah Ashleigh interrupts us.

Louise recognizes him with just one whiff of leather sole. "Ah. The freelance muscle-about-town. I know you have a soft spot for him because he helped Miss Temple out during a dangerous moment once, but I find him turning up at criminous scenes all too often."

"'Criminous?' What have you been reading at the Crystal Phoenix while waiting for Chef Song to wave some effete delicacy of Chinese cuisine under your nose? Agatha Christie? Talk about decadent! 'Criminous.' That is not PI talk. Are you a house detective or a housecat?"

"Back off! The lone dude with the lone gun went out with the forty-five. Face it, Pops, it is the age of *CSI*. You want long words like 'criminous,' you should hear what the forensics folks toss around. This dead lady here was killed by something chemical, not a gun or a knife."

"Still plenty of that out there," I grumble, for the chit is right. It is science not horse sense (though I have never known an equine with much of it) that rules modern crime-solving circles.

While I am hunkering down, contemplating the demise of the lobo detective (as witness my own cravenly alliance with Midnight Louise herself), I cast an eye to see what Mr. Rafi has brought to the side of Miss Savannah.

I stiffen with surprise, all over.

He has brought two canvas bags, one pink and one purple, both with mesh sides, each containing an Ashleigh sister.

I cannot contain myself, although I try to not let Miss Louise see that.

"Must go interrogate a couple of witnesses," I mutter under my breath.

"Witnesses! Daddy-O! What would these two floozies ever witness except their mistress's indiscretions?"

"Exactly, Louise. A starlet of Miss Savannah Ashleigh's stature—"

She snorts but I step aside before my coat is sprayed.

"—of her stature is sure to hear all the latest gossip. Of course, the Persian girls overhear it all. Stay here. Two of us might look suspicious."

At this, I make an end-around approach to the Ashleigh lounge chair, for the woman is highly prejudiced against me, even though she knows I am a totally sexually responsible dude since my enforced operation at her hands. Well, at the hands of her plastic surgeon.

Now the V-word is my byword. Not Viagra, Bast forbid, but for V as in . . . vasectomy. I am a thoroughly modern male, even if by mistake.

Soon I am huddled under the lounge chair again, picking up tidbits of information from the girls.

"Our mistress is so unheeding," Yvette complains. "She likes to swelter in the UVs, so she assumes we would like it. With our luxuriant fur coats, of course, we prefer cool dark places."

"Me too," I say.

The paired purrs from the carriers nearly drive me crazy. "So what is happening with your mistress? She must surely be uneasy that a contest advisor has been offed."

"Mais oui." Only it sounds like "meow" to the uninitiated, i.e., humans. Solange presses her piquant face to the mesh so that several of her long curled vibrissae protrude and tickle my own whiskers. "She has been uneasy for some time. Someone has been lurking around, and it has gotten worse now that we are here at the Teen Queen Castle."

"Hmmm," I purr. I would normally think Miss Savannah was imagining this stalker or making it up for publicity purposes. Yet I glimpsed a dark figure in her room with my own night-vigilant eyes. "What will the death of one of the advisors mean to the show, once the police free the murder scene and shooting can begin again?"

"Shooting?" The Divine Yvette bats her black mascaraed lashes as a prelude to a swoon. "You think there will be shooting?"

"I meant cameras." But of course shooting is not impossible with a murderer among us.

And I recall Miss Temple telling her Aunt Kit about a notorious shooting death in this very house many years ago. I have not led Miss Louise astray. Eavesdropping is the low-key operative's biggest asset, and you cannot get a lower operative than me.

I glance back to where I left the young sourpuss, my partner. The spot is vacant. I cannot understand why she did not wait around like a good girl for me to return and make my report, but frankly, I am glad not to have her cramping my style with the sisters Ashleigh, now that I have them to myself.

She might blow my cover and refer to me by some demeaning nickname like "Snoozer" or "Geezer" or, heaven forbid, "Daddy-O."

Chapter 41

Wolfram and Heart

Matt wore a Carl Sandburg T-shirt, baggy khakis, loafers without socks, and a Chicago Cubs cap on backwards.

He'd arrived at eight A.M. and spent the day lurking in the halls and emergency stairwells of the building that housed Brandon, Oakes, and McCall. Just an ordinary guy, staking out who came and went through the doors of the prestigious law office.

He'd wanted to look like a guy who'd gotten lost in the lobby and was still trying to find his way out. Nobody questioned him.

Around two P.M., after he'd watched the noontime exodus return to the law firm, he bought lunch at the lobby coffee shop and pumped the waitress.

Even in his instant scruffies, his looks won smiles and chitchat and information. The coffee shop provided latte, yeah, they had a machine for every variety of espresso.

Lots of very big people went up there. So what was he doing here?

Waiting to connect with a contact. He was in the record business.

Reallly! Her cousin Stevie had a fab basement band. Radical but not too, you know? Ready for a big-time commercial break. He didn't look like a DJ. They were usually such losers in the looks department. He should be on MTV.

Yeah.

Matt finished the dregs of his caramel–whipped cream latte, just a dozen calorie counts shy of a hot fudge sundae, and went back up to the forty-fifth floor.

To lurk.

Krys, who had okayed his outfit this morning, would be amazed to know how dull subterfuge was. He was amazed to know how dull it was. He thought about Carmen Molina, back in Vegas. Had she ever done this detail? Maybe. Maybe not.

What were the chances? The law office staff seemed to recognize him. So how likely was it that some relative of his lost father would breeze up in the elevator and into Brandon, Oakes, and McCall? Today or any other day.

Infinitesimal. Matt bet that DJs didn't often use that word.

Ex-priests did, though, having been conditioned to think in terms of infinity.

In terms of infinity, what were the chances that he would find any trace or trail that led to the man who'd fathered him?

Almost zero. He didn't care. He'd learned long ago not to care. He'd tried to tell his mother that. Trouble was, she did.

What had been the high point in her life had been the nadir in his.

Nadir. Speak of the Devil. Rafi Nadir. Another unwanted father. Carmen Molina had made it clear that
Nadir hadn't deserved to know he was the father of a
child she would bear and rear without him.

The usual rap was men were unreliable. Men skated
out from under fatherhood and its obligations. They were
louts. Rats. Immature. They seduced and abandoned.
They made Matt sorry he was one.

Except . . .

He didn't believe it. He'd seen it during the Sacrament
of Reconciliation, formerly known as Confession. Men
were scared. They thought they had to be the whole en-
chilada, 24/7: strong, sole supporting, macho men. It was
too much.

He considered his mother at nineteen—her critical
condition. Pregnant, with him. Catholic. Young. Damned.
Despised. No support of any kind. Hard not to hate the
guy who put her there. Except that she hadn't. And he'd
gone off to a foreign war and died. No chance to prove
his mettle on the domestic front.

The elevator made all the grunts and groans of being
about to open again. Matt peeked through the stairway
door like a kid playing hide and seek.

Another "briefcase" walking into Brandon, Oakes, and
McCall.

Except . . . this guy didn't carry a briefcase. He wore
an expensively pale suit. His ash-blond hair was silver at
the temples. Same height, same build, thickened a little
around the middle.

Matt gaped, as if he'd seen a ghost walking through a
wall, as the form vanished into the dark wood door of
Brandon, Oaks, and McCall.

The proof of the pudding was what this man would
look like from the front, when he walked out.

Matt stuck the toe of his new sports tennies against the

heavy metal door. This he had to see, no matter how long it took.

It took forty-eight minutes by his stainless-steel watch.

Several people came and went. Matt began to worry about a discreet exit door farther down the hall . . . but, still, the elevator had to be taken, unless someone wanted to walk down forty-some flights. And then that someone would come face-to-face with Matt lurking in the hidden echoing concrete spine that ran up the length of every skyscraper.

The lawyers' office door didn't so much squeak as rumble a little when it opened and shut.

It was opening now, spitting out the front view of the man Matt had glimpsed from behind. He managed to eel out of the stairway to meet the man at the bank of elevators.

To meet himself.

Related, no doubt.

How to mention it?

The guy did the usual big-city elevator shuffle: push the DOWN button, stare at the computerized numbers of floors and cars above. Pace. Glance at his watch. Glance askance at the guy who'd joined him in waiting, trying not to stare at strangers, of course.

Matt's throat was so dry he couldn't have received Communion to save his soul.

Alex Haley'd had Kunta Kinte. Now Matt had his own *Roots*. Someone who looked like him. Someone he looked like besides his mother. It didn't matter, he'd always said. It mattered.

The man slipped a look at him again. He seemed nervous.

Matt took off the stupid baseball cap, stuffing it in the

pocket of his baggy Dockers. He regretted the carefully casual clothes, regretted not looking like himself. Not looking like this impeccably dressed man three elevator doors down the hall.

The man, maybe—forty-five. A cousin? Not a brother, his real father had been too young. Matt had to be an only child. The mystery man cleared his throat. Looked away.

The elevator indicator tinged.

They both froze.

Watched the door open between them, neither wanting to meet the other as they rushed to claim it.

The man glanced at the EXIT sign over the stairwell where Matt had lived most of today.

He knew. Or suspected. He wanted to run.

The elevator doors opened. Closed. A couple inside watched them with puzzled, and finally contemptuous, stares. Why call for an elevator if you weren't going to take it. Why indeed?

And then they were gone.

Alone again.

"I think," Matt said, "that your last name might be the same as mine should be."

The guy stared at him. His eyes were gray. So was his skin color. Matt saw he was older than he'd looked at first glance, and began to fear he might be having a heart attack.

He began to have one too. This guy was actually old enough . . . to be his father.

Chapter 42

Feline Shepherd

I am shocked. Shocked, I tell you!

With my own concealed ears, I hear my Miss Temple consign young Miss Molina to the questionable oversight of Mr. Rafi Nadir, who may be her unacknowledged sire.

Being an unacknowledged sire myself, I feel a deep sense of obligation to keep an eye on this extremely unlikely pairing.

If my Miss Temple has set the wolf to watch the lamb, I will be the mountain lion set to watch the wolf.

And when it comes to major matches, felinus versus caninus always wins.

So, when Miss Savannah Ashleigh betakes herself inside, I pad after Rafi who pads after her.

Once she is fully attired, if you can ever call the belly button–exposing, cleavage-baring clothing of MSA that, we follow her to her office quarters for the day and stand guard in the hall.

He is in the standard feet apart, hands crossed in front posture of security guys since my forebears stood guard duty in the palaces and temples of ancient Egypt.

I assume the deceptive stance of a sleeping feline. It works every time.

Sure enough, along comes Miss Temple, escorting Miss Mariah to her first appointment of the day.

"Mariah, this is Mr. Nadir. He will help you if anything goes wrong."

Mariah is having none of it. "You mean if Savannah Ashleigh is strangled in her own monokini by the time I go in for my appointment?"

"Hey," Mr. Rafi Nadir says in a cajoling tone. "Nobody buys it on my watch. What say I accompany you on your rounds and make sure?"

"What about your client?" Mariah asks, savvy kid that she is.

"Oh, I suppose your friend Xoe Chloe will be responsible for her."

Miss Mariah consults Miss Temple, who shrugs in typical, deplorable Xoe Chloe fashion.

And so the deal is struck. My Miss Temple will watch Miss Savannah Ashleigh, a personage we both wish would be boiled in canola oil and put on the South Beach Diet until death did them part. And Mr. Rafi Nadir, the bane of Miss Lieutenant C. R. Molina's life, past and present, will be watching over his own daughter, unawares. If Miss Savannah gets restive and calls for male reinforcements, instead of Mr. Rafi, I myself will rush to the scene to distract her and the Persian babes. It is the least I can do, and I have been known to drive Miss Savannah to distraction in the past.

It is amazing the things an observant feline can know, and not say.

I decide where to invest my time and energy, and decide it is the unlikely partnership of Nadir and Molina.

Miss Temple watches me ankle off down the hall after them, looking worried.

So we all three end up waiting outside various offices for Miss Mariah's daily consultations.

"You pull bodyguard duty often?" Mariah asks.

I am about to answer but Rafi Nadir beats me to it.

"Nah. Most people who hire bodyguards need the publicity more than the muscle."

"This is a weird place."

"You got that right."

"I mean, it is supposed to be a contest but it seems like someone is pulling the strings."

"How so?" He leans down like a gentleman to hear her answer.

I lean up.

"I mean, it is supposed to be a fair contest but everything so far is rigged. All the Teen Queen candidates are tall, thin, and blonde. They all look alike. Maybe it was a mistake that I was made a finalist."

This gives him pause.

"Hey, kid, you got it the wrong way around. Looking all alike is not the way to go. You look like yourself, then you'll know you're not a fraud."

"Girls change their looks all the time."

"Right. Because they have not found the way they really want to be."

"Like a singer?"

"That what you want?"

"Yeah."

"Okay." You can tell that Rafi Nadir knows a little about advising girl singers. He leans against the wall. "Sure you want to find a look to perform in but it should be what you like, not what everybody else looks like. You got lots of time—"

"No, I do not! The finals are just days away. I gotta polish my song and find out what they do to me and—"

"No, you do not. You do not wait to find out what they do to you, ever. You decide and you tell them, get it?"

"But, if I am not sure . . ."

"Then make sure before you let them at you. Me, if I was you, I would nix the blonde. They always do blonde. At least half the country is not-blonde. Look at that big old alley cat there. He could be any one of thousands. I bet there are more black cats than any other kind in the country."

"Maybe not."

"Why not?"

"I heard Tem . . . someone say once that they put black cats to sleep more than any other kind."

While I shudder to hear the truth so baldly stated, Mr. Rafi Nadir stops to reconsider.

"There are still a lot of them around, so I guess that does not work."

"So what are you?" Mariah asks.

"Not-popular."

"Why? What are you?"

"Me? This is not about me," Rafi says.

"You're not-blonde."

"I am worse than that. Arab American."

"Oh. I see what you mean about popular. I am just Latina. But even all the girls on the Hispanic stations are going blonde."

"You kids. Always gotta do what everybody else does. Grow up. Get past that."

Mariah nods to the door behind which Miss Savannah Ashleigh awaits her.

"She is blonde."

Mr. Rafi Nadir straightens and makes a funny face at the door. "Right. Case closed."

Mariah giggles, then knocks.

Point made.

In Old Cold Type

Newspapers sent out copies of old articles on white paper so heavy it had a chalky feel.

Temple lay an Atlas's worth of such pages over the bathroom twin-sink counter. They'd been delivered to the house in a king-size pillow wearing a flannel case in a frolicking kitten design.

A wretched note accompanied this innocuous delivery: "Please deliver to my little Xoe, who doesn't sleep well without her kitty pillow. She must have forgotten to take it. Her Mom."

Apparently this maternal plea had moved the powers that be, for they had sent the sleekest professional blonde in Temple's category to deliver it to her bedroom door just before dinner, with the hulking cameraman shooting tape over her bony shoulder. Apparently, now that the crime scene work was done and the detectives were gone for now, the filming ban had been lifted.

"Here you are, Xoe," Ashlee announced. "Something special from home for our resident tough girl. Oooh, the coot 'iddle kitty-wittys. Maybe now you can go beddie-bye."

Temple/Xoe snatched the ungainly gift away.

She must have blushed because Ashlee tittered for the camera.

Temple was embarrassed all right. Not because of the kiddie pillow but because the note had probably been penned by mother Molina.

"Thanks lots," she told the door she had slammed in Ashlee's face.

Temple had turned to drop the pillow on the bed while Mariah snagged the note that dropped off it.

"Hey, this looks like—" She glimpsed Temple's hasty shushing pantomime and came near. "—like a really soft pillow." She leaned down (how humiliating!) to whisper in Temple's ear. "Looks like my mom's writing."

Then they had adjourned to the bathroom. Although Temple was pretty sure bathrooms were a no-film zone, she was paranoid enough about their current task to hang washcloths and hand towels from any possible fixture that might hide a camera.

The copier hadn't captured every line. Many were blurred.

Mariah hunched over the assemblage, scanning the blurry type.

"Wow. This is ancient stuff."

"The mid-eighties."

"Right. Ancient stuff. My mom sent this?"

Mariah looked up and Temple nodded. "At my request."

"You tell my mom what to do? Awesome."

"I asked her."

"Oh. That doesn't usually work for me. Just asking."

"Mothers are like that. Luckily, your mom is not my mom."

"You sound like you mean that way too much."

"Guilty."

They settled down to read various pages, Temple perching on the tub rim, Mariah sitting on the closed throne. Then they exchanged sheets and read some more.

"What do you think?" Temple asked finally, turning on the bathtub faucet again. The Teen Queen Castle's water bill for this period would be humongous from resident spy work alone.

"This stuff is Tabloid City. The kind of thing you'd see on *CBS Investigates* today. With that Dan Rather-not guy with the so dingy buzz cut. Why do old guys do that?"

"Maybe so there's less gray showing."

"Oh. Anyway, this case is so clear."

"Yeah?"

"It's like a movie. Old-guy husband is major upset that his young bimbo blowup doll wife"—Mariah looked up to make sure that Temple had noticed she was drawing on her brand-new info on blowup dolls—"is divorcing him and getting half of his money, along with a new boyfriend. She even gets the house while the judge is considering everything. This house. And she invites the new young boyfriend over. Think Ashton Kutcher and Demi Moore."

"And Bruce Willis is the Die-Hard husband?"

"Right. So Bruce goes bonkers and puts on this ninja outfit with the Spider-Man hood—he was big on martial arts, remember, and Elvis and also Zen stuff, which you'd think wouldn't be, like, getting him into murder. So he shows up and shoots away at everybody and paralyzes the wife's daughter from her first marriage, wings the wife, kills the boyfriend, and disappears down the hidden passages and they never catch him."

"That left a lot of loose ends," Temple said.

"Yeah, but they're all, like, so old now. What could they do?"

"As you get older, Mariah, and you will, even old enough to drive a car, you'll be struck by how young all the old people who used to be around you actually were."

"Huh?"

"Age is relative. And bad blood has no expiration date."

This Mariah considered, biting on a painted nail that Temple grabbed away from her mouth before it became a serrated edge and ruined her 'Tween Queen score.

Mariah was still mulling over the implications. "You're saying what's happening now could go back to this stuff way back when?"

"Just add twenty years to everybody's ages."

"Well, the husband would be sixty-something. Too old to totter around here, I'd think."

"And the wife?"

"She was a lot younger. Forty?"

"Forty. Only ten years older than I am."

"No!" Mariah regarded Temple with true horror. "You're only ten years away from *that!* I'd be . . . twenty-three, and old enough to drink."

"And vote."

"That too."

Temple felt oddly deflated by the notion that she was only ten years away from forty. She'd always thought of herself as only ten years away from twenty. It was the same thing but much more depressing looked at from the other end of the telescope.

Mariah speared a blurred photocopy image. "She'd be thirty-five, the girl who was shot."

"Too old to compete here."

"Yeah. Not to mention crippled. None of it makes sense. They're all too old."

That was Mariah's callous teenybopper judgment. Temple shuffled the copies around. No matter how she juggled the dates and the dramatis personae, these murderous sinners and sinned against were indeed "too old" to be part of the Teen Queen reality show.

Unless . . . she was looking at the wrong parts of the Teen Queen show. And the wrong reality.

Chapter 44

Old Tyme Revival

If Molina prided herself on anything, it was on being a thorough supervisor. The minute Temple Barr asked for copies of the Dickson mansion murders, she'd ordered extra copies for Alch and Su.

"Savannah Ashleigh's bodyguard," Su said, looking up from the documents.

Unfortunately, Molina knew exactly who Savannah Ashleigh was: washed up cinemactress; neuterer of Temple Barr's cat, Midnight Louie; judge at the Teen Queen contest.

"Bodyguard?" Molina bit.

"This guy is forty. Too young to be the ex-Mrs. Dickson's boyfriend and no way her ex-husband. Still. A bodyguard. That puts him on the premises with the wherewithal to commit murder."

Molina was not pleased to see a contemporary photo

of Rafi Nadir spun across the table right in front of her nose. Her blood ran cold. Cliché, yes. Fact, you bet!

She kept all her physical reactions dampened as she frowned at the photograph in her custody, knowing she was being watched carefully by her troops. Seeing Rafi Nadir again a couple weeks ago had been easy. No one would believe he'd been a former lover and was even Mariah's father. He was a loser. She was a winner. She'd frozen, ignored, brushed by, brushed off, rushed out of there. Maylords Fine Furniture was just a crime scene and Rafi Nadir was just an innocent bystander in that instance. Or not so innocent. He'd found her again and now knew about her, who she was, what she was. Homicide lieutenant. He had reveled in delivering the murderer to her, bound over. And Temple Barr had reveled in helping him to do it.

Maybe she thought turnabout was fair play. Molina had pursued Temple's significant other; now Molina's ex-SO was in a position to embarrass, if not pursue, her.

But what about Mariah? Temple was supposed to be protecting her. Instead the poor kid had already had the rare life experience of finding a dead body. Now she was in danger of finding out her father wasn't a dead-hero cop but the disgraced private cop currently on the reality show premises. Molina's hands started trembling with fury. Alch was watching her curiously. He knew. Too many people knew. Just not Mariah yet, thank God. She spun the photo back to Su as if returning a tennis serve.

"We'll put him on the possibles list."

Molina put her mind as well as her emotions in cold storage. Nadir had been interred in the box of her past, which was locked up, like a gun in a cabinet. Safe behind steel doors.

Now . . . his orbit and her daughter Mariah's had intersected in this insanely trivial place, a reality TV show. His daughter Mariah, who he'd ensured had entered the world by foul means, not fair, but who's existence he had never suspected.

Not even the sleaziest producer could have scripted such an ironic, maddening moment. And Molina had to keep the peace, keep the secret, no matter what. What was Temple Barr trying to do? Destroy her before she destroyed Max Kinsella? They had a deal.

Everyone but Alch was watching her under the mistaken assumption that she was brilliantly analyzing the case at hand. She needed to distract them from watching her chewing on the conundrum of her personal and professional life and onto something else. . . .

"What about the cat?" she asked.

"Louie?" Alch smiled at a closeup shot of the feline in question. "The usual suspect. Big, black, and known to the police."

"Cut the humor, Alch."

"You're the one who sent the kitty pillow."

"My daughter shares the room."

"Oh, I see. The pillow was a two-fer: Trojan horse for the roommate and motherly gesture for the kid."

"Trojan kitty," Su said, snickering.

"The reality show may be a joke. What's going on there isn't. Who else on the grounds is suspect, just because?"

Su frowned, which drew her creatively plucked eyebrows into the kind of fretwork you'd find on an Asian table. Molina had never dared inquire into the inspiration for those brush-stroke eyebrows plucked into lines beginning thick and ending as fine as a mouse-hair brush. She didn't know if the motive was cultural or simply creative. But they made Su memorable. She'd never seen the like, and nobody else had dared to inquire either, not even sticklers for uniformity at high rank. It would be one mystery this homicide lieutenant would never solve.

"Everybody who's on the premises was 'picked,' in one way or another, except the producers."

"But they're all supposedly strangers," Alch added. "Back at the time of the murder, everybody was related, one way or another."

"Could the fallout from that violent episode be haunting this show? The suspected perp is at large."

"Disappeared," Alch objected. "There's a difference. Everybody's given up looking for him."

"Not me," Molina said grimly. She tapped the crackling white oversize sheets of paper with their blurred fine lines of newsprint. "Check out what happened to all these people."

"You think one of them might have come back somehow?" Su sounded unconvinced.

"I think something's going on that has nothing to do with Teen Queens or TV."

Chapter 45

Past Tense

The man who looked too much like Matt, or vice versa, shifted his weight from foot to foot. He glanced back over his shoulder, down the corridor leading to the law offices.

But Brandon, Oakes, and McCall were too far away to call on for help.

He cleared his throat. "They said . . . someone had attempted to find out information on me. It was some sort of a scam."

Matt just stared into the man's face. "Someone. Some sort of con man maybe?"

The man's expression hardened. "Exactly. 'Extortion' was the word. I guess you know I have lawyers."

"I guess you don't know you have a son."

"That's impossible."

"Why? The virgin birth isn't, to a good Catholic."

"How'd you know I was Catholic?"

"Guessed."

"Listen, this building has security cameras, and guards. Whatever you want—"

"Isn't what you'd think, or what they'd have you think."

The gray eyes flicked over Matt's casual clothes, avoiding his face. Matt had dressed like the nobody Brandon, Oakes, and McCall said he was.

"They stiffed me yesterday," Matt said. Explained. "So I came back undercover."

"You—what are you? You can't be a policeman."

"Actually, I could be. As it happens, I'm not. I'm a professional advisor."

"Oh, I see. And you want me to pay for your advice. I take the 'advice' of my attorneys first and foremost, and I don't need any outside opinion."

Matt took a deep breath. "Thirty-four years ago. You were, what—? All of twenty maybe?"

"None of your business."

"It is my business. I'm about my father's business."

The first frown of doubt. "Why do you keep quoting religious stuff to me?" He backed away.

Matt could read the man's mind: religious nut. He almost laughed, except that this was not a proper occasion for mirth.

"I'm surprised. Back then, you'd light a candle to a saint, down in the Polish district, where they still had statues of saints on the side aisles of those old churches, where belief smelled like incense and hot beeswax candles."

"You *are* some kind of religious nut." He was backing away, toward the corridor and the safety of his lawyers' offices.

Matt laughed gently. "I guess you could call priests that."

"You're a priest?" That stopped him. Still a practicing Catholic then.

"Ex."

That had him ready to bolt again: demented ex-priest, out for . . . what? Blood? Yes, blood, Matt thought.

"I have a regular advice stint on *The Amanda Show*, that's why I'm in town."

"You're a TV personality?"

"So they tell me."

"I don't get this. Stop being mysterious and cut to the chase."

"I wanted to spare you the shock."

"Shock? What shock?"

"You're not supposed to be alive. You're supposed to have died 'over there,' thirty-four years ago. At least that's what my mother was told."

"Your mother?"

"You might remember her. Pretty young Polish girl. Must have looked great in the candlelight from a bank of vigil lights before the white plaster statue of St. Stanislaus. It's still there and so is she, sort of. Mira."

"Mira."

The man actually staggered. Away from Matt. He glanced wildly down the hall, suddenly realizing that whatever was down there was too far and too late for retreating to.

Matt put out a hand. "I tried to warn you."

The man settled for leaning against the wall opposite the bank of elevators and staring up at the ceiling fixtures.

Finally he spoke. "You look like me."

"I thought you looked like me first." Matt allowed some weary humor to touch his voice.

"They said she'd disappeared. Girls her age did then. All the time. I knew nothing about her. Nothing about you. There was nothing left to pursue."

"Yes, there was." Matt heard his own voice like a stranger's, hard and unforgiving. "Only the lawyers handled it. They signed a two-flat over to her to keep us, silence being the price."

"She took it?"

"Her family had disowned her. Your family was willing to give her something to stay away. And . . . they told her you were dead."

He slumped against the wall that supported him. "I can't believe my family would do that."

"They're still telling you nothing. The moment I walked in the lawyers' offices yesterday, I got weird vibes from people, like I was a ghost. That's when I realized there must be . . . relatives around. I thought a cousin, an uncle. I didn't want to be there. I wanted to drop it."

"Then why'd you come?"

"My mother. She's never forgotten. She's had a rotten life, as you can imagine. It was the one thing she asked of me that I couldn't refuse. She would have made a great Godfather."

"And Mira. Now I see it. You look like Mira."

Matt kept silent.

"Not the Mira I knew."

"Once," Matt bit out. One night. One-night stand. "From what I understand," he added, watching carefully, "I was the product of a virgin birth, so to speak."

The man shook his head. "What's your name?"

"Matt, short for Matthias, the apostle who replaced Judas the betrayer." He let that sink in. "My last name is Devine."

"She married?"

"Yes, but to a loser. Who else would have her after that? She named me something different. After her favorite Christmas hymn. Can you guess?"

"Divine? Oh." He grew even paler, if that was possible. "'O Holy Night'?"

"'O Holy Night, O Night Divine.' Bingo. I'm named for a mortal sin."

The man pushed off the wall. "It's not your fault. Listen." He glanced down the hall again, then shook his head. "We need to talk. Privately."

"Agreed."

"I have a club . . ."

"You would."

"Then you suggest—?"

"I have a hotel. The Drake."

The man's pale eyebrows—almost dead white, though his hair was still steel blond—rose.

"*The Amanda Show* puts up its regular guests in style," Matt explained.

"We'll go there then."

"Yes, a hotel's so impersonal. Like a church." Matt was pleased to see him wince.

"You must be famous." The man came as close as he'd avoided doing before.

They stood shoulder to shoulder, awaiting the elevator Matt's finger had summoned. Father and son. God's finger to Adam.

Damn! They were almost the same height. No denying.

The man seemed to notice this. "How is . . . Mira?"

"She's pretty good. No longer a single parent with a kid at home. Has a job. Is widowed."

"My name is Winslow. Jonathan Winslow. And . . ."—he reported this dutifully—"I'm married. I have a family. Three almost-adult kids."

Matt noticed that he hadn't said "happily."

"I wish I'd had a son who'd do for me what you did for your mother."

"You have kids. No son?"

"Yeah. I have a son."

No more comment. Matt read bitter estrangement.

316 • Carole Nelson Douglas

"I'm sorry."

"That's the family mantra here, I guess. Keep in touch. Let me know when you're in Chicago. We should . . . learn to know each other."

Matt, surprised, hesitated. Then nodded. Maybe. Maybe not.

"Meanwhile, let's hit your hotel. I could use a drink or three."

How many bars in how many hotels the world over hosted lost relatives who sat and stared at each other over drinks they were reluctant to touch?

Matt supposed there must be at least eight.

He ran his fingers through his hair that the unaccustomed baseball cap had tamped down, like the wire ring of a kindergarten-play halo.

"You're blonder than I remember your mother being."

It was Matt's turn to feel put on the spot. "You remember right. The . . . my radio station had some stylist do my hair for the latest publicity photos. I'm told it'll wash out. Can't be too soon for me."

"Media." Winslow laughed a little, for the first time. "Image. Reality is never enough, is it?"

"No. Not in this day and age."

"So, you've been a priest."

"Until eighteen months ago."

"Why'd you leave?"

"Better question would be 'Why'd you enter?' I was looking to become the perfect father I'd never had."

"I'm sorry. I didn't know. I did not know. I looked for your mother after I got back from my tour of duty and couldn't find her. We only knew first names. I didn't dare probe further. My family would have had my head if they'd known about . . . what happened. I had no idea they already knew and had resorted to lawyers. I suppose they thought they were protecting me."

"They were. From unwanted consequences. Me."

"I'm sorry. I could say it a thousand times and it'd never change the past. You look . . . like you turned out fine."

"It could have been worse," Matt conceded, "although I could have done without the abusive stepfather."

Winslow's contrite expression was startled into shock. "My God! How did that happen?"

"She had no options. She was a pariah, an unwed mother in a deeply Catholic community. Oh, they 'supported' her but not without instilling this bone-deep sense of shame. She helped hurt herself, her upbringing helped. So strict. She took such a chance on you."

"It didn't feel like that. If felt like a miracle, like the inside of a snow globe when you shake it up and all the magical snow comes floating down on everything, making it . . . beautiful. What does she want now?"

"Not money. The two-flat kept us afloat. It was worth that much. But she's figured out someone had a stake in buying us off. She's gotten to be a lot tougher lady." Matt smiled. "It's been good for her, actually. She just wants to know who and why."

"That's a lot."

"She has no idea you didn't die. Neither did I, until today."

"Big day for us both," he noted, sipping from his scotch on the rocks, then setting the drink aside as if he was rejecting far more than an easy glow at a moment of truth. "I wouldn't have abandoned either of you if they'd have let me know. I'm not a naive kid anymore. I promise you, there will be hell to pay."

"I . . . we don't want to hurt anyone else. Just tell me what to tell her now that I know the truth. The kind lie? I didn't want to know this. I didn't need to know you. I wanted to find some crooked lawyers protecting an insulated, snobby family. Maybe I wanted to see someone sweat if I'm deep-down honest about it. But I didn't want to find you. I don't need you now. She doesn't need you now. You're irrelevant. Maybe you can make whoever in your family did this pay a little. Maybe that'll make me feel better for seeing my mother lied to and let down a second time."

Winslow folded his cocktail napkin into accordion pleats. "The Winslows do go back to the *Mayflower*," he noted wryly. "Not the Washington hotel, the ship." His face sobered again. "It would have been my father. He's dead now. No one can make him suffer. My mother's in a nursing home. She probably was an accessory. She has Alzheimer's."

"Your father. Your mother."

"Your grandparents."

"They're gone, then, both of them. What were they thinking?"

"What all parents do: don't let my kids make any foolish life-altering choices."

"I guess you didn't, really, then."

"I did. Because I've never forgotten her."

"Is that what I tell her?"

He pulled the drink back over and took a long hard swallow.

"No. That's what I tell her."

Chapter 46

Closet Encounter
of the Third Kind

Since this place is crawling with camera operators and just plain operators, I sic Midnight Louise on tailing Crawford Buchanan. (They deserve each other, in my opinion.)

I leave my Miss Temple poring over old newspaper clippings and preparing to take her rest on a pussycat pillowcase.

I decide to do what I do best: prowl by night. I have resolved to find and explore all the secret passages in the house.

One would assume that after my namesake hour, the house would quiet down. One can assume nothing when it comes to crime or hordes of teenage girls.

My midnight ramble will need some unwitting accessory work from someone human, and I am betting that enough humans are sneaking around unauthorized here to populate a small city.

Naturally, I am forced to head first to Miss Savannah Ashleigh's chamber. Some crass folk, including Miss Midnight Louise, were she here to know my plans, might imply that I am more interested in brushing whiskers with the Ashleigh sisters than in exploring secret passages. Quite the contrary. The one entrance to a secret passage I know of at this point is in the Ashleigh suite.

A dude must start somewhere.

So I amble down the deserted hall, rehearsing my speech to induce the Ashleigh sisters to let me in, when my first unlawfully wandering human comes shuffling down the same corridor.

I flatten myself against a baseboard and hope the shadows will hide me.

Not to worry. The sleepwalker is a blonde in pink pajamas, closely followed by a . . . a blonde in pink pajamas.

The first blonde, Miss Silver by name, carries a sinister canister. It resembles a harmless can of shaving cream but those have been suspect since the foamy-graffiti-on-the-exercise-mats incident.

"*Shhh!*" Second Blonde urges First Blonde.

"*Shhh,* yourself. All we have to do is leave this in her bathroom and her hair will be history."

"Are you sure that phony label will stick on?"

"I printed it out on my laptop on glossy adhesive paper. Looks like the real thing."

Sure enough. I crane my neck up and can read the name of a popular brand of hairspray. Makes one wonder what is really in it. Of course I have to follow them, and that involves backtracking to . . . Miss Temple and Miss Mariah's room!

The pair of evil blondes turn the knob about as slowly as they can think, which is very slowly indeed and quite impressive for sneak thieves. Only they are leaving something rather than taking it.

I tail them past the sleeping innocents. The kitty pillow is cast away on the floor, I am happy to say, both for my Miss Temple's taste's sake and because I will come in and squash it with my own body after my nightly rounds are made.

They sneak into the bathroom and leave the can on the sink ledge, among a skyline of similar products. It is called "Hair Today."

Right. As soon as they sneak out again I drag in the massive pillow from the bedroom (no easy task, even for a muscular chap like myself), then position it under the sink.

Then I leap atop the sink rim, balancing precariously, and bat the suspect can off its perch.

What a stunt director dudo I would have made! It lands, soft and soundless, on a particularly cloying image of a striped kitten dead center on the pillow.

I roll the can to the floor under the sink, where I can direct Miss Temple's attention to it in the morning.

Then I take the pillowcase in my mouth again (wet flannel, ugh!) and wrestle it back to its original position beside the bed.

Now I can begin my true task of the night. I retrace my steps to the Ashleigh bedroom but draw back when I hear voices inside.

It must be one A.M. Who would be yammering at this hour?

I press an ear to the door.

"Can you believe it?" Miss Savannah Ashleigh is wailing into her cell phone. "We are cooped up in here all the time with nothing but Teen Queens and a bunch of middle-aged judges and consultants and camera people. I am dying for a Rodeo Drive South Beach latte. Also a decent lay."

And the Persian sisters have to hear this sort of talk!

"Indecent would do," she agrees with the friend on the receiving end of her conversation.

Luckily, Miss Savannah is as careless with her door locking as her conversation, so I am able to ankle through the slightly ajar door.

The Persian sisters are languidly polishing their nails with their tongues when I arrive, and both perk up immediately.

"Want to go exploring down those dark and mean streets?" I inquire with a couple struts past their empty canvas carriers.

"Oh, no, Louie," Yvette replies. "We are ready for our beauty sleep. But we will distract our mistress for you, if you wish."

This was not quite the scenario I had in mind. Since their mistress is not in Dreamland but lusting after latte, I shrug and go to the mirrored wall panel.

The girls loft themselves onto the bed like the plumes de ma tante, which must have been pretty soft stuff, and start rubbing back and forth on Miss Savannah's phone-holding hand, waving their full-furred tails in her face and generally blinding her to anything that is going on in the room. Long fur can be useful as well as beautiful.

I leap up, hitting the secret panel right where it bows to pressure. I am through the slight opening before I can say, "Hey, there is no light in here!"

There is no light back there, either, as an obliging Persian girl, perhaps the over-thoughtful Solange, has run over to cast her weight at the door and shut it. Tight. It does not give to my exploratory nudge.

Not that I wish to return to light and softness and Persian girls when dark and hardness and danger call.

So I look from left to right, which is equally and utterly dark, and plunge ahead until my whiskers hit wall and I can follow the tunnel.

I soon also follow the hard narrow curl of electrical cable along the seam of floor and wall. A high pinpoint of red light freezes me for a moment. I think of the reflective eyes of a cougar on a rock, ready to leap down on me.

But further reflection convinces me the light only indicates the electric eye of a recording camera.

And then one wonders, why set up a camera to record the action in a secret passageway? Someone on the crew must have made a unilateral decision to film the crew itself, who are the only persons who would have a reason to lurk back here.

Hmmm.

Like all nocturnal sorts, from vampires to skunks, I find the dark only enhances my other senses. I sniff the mixed scents of the grounds . . . bark chips, leaves, sandy soil. Not unexpected. The technicians who wired this place for 24/7 snooping would be the same crew ranging from grounds to house, back and forth.

There is one odd scent: a sweet, fruity one. Could it be a trace of the Razor's Edge shaving spray that clung unnoticed to a shoe sole? They put some awful fragrances in human toiletries, possibly because most people do not take daily sponge baths as we hipper cats do.

I seem to be alone in these passages now but I sniff the presence of plenty of people coming and going. In fact, as I turn a corner I spot a faint light.

I am not pleased to see it because that means that someone might see me in this oversize air-conditioning vent.

When a faint sound comes from around the next bend I freeze like an ostrich. There is no hiding place in this purely functional conduit, not even the huge veiling spider webs beloved of horror films. I unlatch my shivs and practice snapping them in and out, in case I need to resort to a kamikaze attack.

As I hunch there, ready for epic battle, the sound that I hear begins to take on an air of familiarity. In fact, it is a song half-sung under the breath. "Suspicious Minds."

Well, that fits this place to a T.

The mutterer in motion rounds the half-lit bend and I view a human figure all in white, glowing like a ghost.

I am not a superstitious fellow, despite my breed and color. It takes but three seconds for me to recognize the Elvis impersonator judge who has been drilling the singing candidates for their big debut. (Miss Kit Carlson is handling the acting coaching and I am all atwitter over what my Miss Temple will come up with in the persona of Xoe Chloe.)

Anyway, the faux Elvis spots me and stops cold.

"Well, hello there, little fellow. Anything I can do for you? Need a new Cadillac?"

Only for sharpening my shivs on genuine leather.

This is not the first time I have encountered the likeness of Elvis Presley in this town. On some occasions, I was even convinced I was seeing the real thing.

So I amble over and rub my nose on the brass studs decorating the bell-bottoms on his jumpsuit. This is better than a sisal rope scratching post, let me tell you.

The costume, and the leg beneath it, are completely solid, by the way.

"You better git while the gittin' is good," the ersatz Elvis advises. "This joint will be jumpin' with bad mojo pretty soon."

I manage to meow plaintively. I hate to meow plaintively! It is the resort of cowards and kept cats! However, at times I must play dumb.

Elvis bends down and scratches me behind the

ears, as if I were a hound dog. Red-neck dudes are always more dog people than cat people. Their loss.

"I am tellin' you, cat. You better whiplash your ass outa here. Things are gonna get ugly."

Now what does Elvis know about it?

I pause to stretch low and long, doing a floor-dusting belly touch. Then yawn wide enough to swallow a Chihuahua.

Then I amble along past the dude and around the corner he rode in on.

It is suddenly darker there. I have to wonder why the light was following Elvis. Was that the real unreal thing? The ghost of rock 'n' roll? Or was it a pale imitation?

Either way, I do not like my recent dance in the dark with an ambulatory Elvis one little bit. The moment my vibrissae sense a stir of fresh air, I take a sharp running right in that direction . . . and fall three feet down onto a hard surface.

That does not give even a ninja a lot of time to do a double axel and land on his feet, spraying wood shavings like Tara Lipinski sprays ice splinters. Float like a butterfly, land like a lummox.

I barely manage to turn myself upright before I must dig my shivs into a wooden roof.

Which then plummets below at a speed fast enough to give my ears a Bing Crosby pin-back.

Landing is the bone-crunching shock I had anticipated.

I cripple my way over the edge and flip upside down again, hanging by a half-torn nail sheath.

Even upside down I can see Miss Midnight Louise in the night-lit glow of the kitchen where she is one with the black marble floor except for the cynical gleam of her old-gold eyes.

"Could not resist a midnight raid on the icebox, eh,

Dad? Do not bother apologizing. There is some very nice kipper a passing guest was kind enough to dig out of the Sub-Zero for me. And did I manage to dig up some dirt on the murder vic. Lose the death grip on the silent butler, come on down, and we will chew the fat. Yours, I hope."

What can I say? Nothing. So I do not.

And thus I learn what my Miss Temple and her roommate Mariah were up to in the Teen Queen Castle while I was communing with Elvis in the attic.

Chapter 47

Filing Their Nails

Temple and Mariah had played possum until the blondes' lightning raid on their bathroom was well over. Temple quickly found the added can of purported hairspray and tried it on a hand towel, which immediately turned as shiny and shellacked as a decoupage project.

"Liquid plastic spray," Temple diagnosed. "Those witches wanted my new blonde hair turned into an impossible mess. Too bad we have serious work to do tonight, or X. C. would sneak in and adhere a few sleepy blonde heads to their pillowcases. They're all feather-heads anyway. But I have something else in mind tonight."

They darted like dragonflies down the stairs to the first-floor hall, knowing where the cameras were positioned and trying to dodge them like bullets.

Mariah had insisted on coming along on this clue-fishing expedition and Temple, frankly, needed a lookout.

Now they stood outside the door to Marjory Klein's former office and Mariah was facing the first challenge of her crime-solving life: crossing yellow crime scene tape.

You'd have thought she was Matt Devine being asked to commit a little mortal sin.

"I don't know, Xoe. We're not supposed to."

"'We're not supposed to.' Where would that have gotten Lewis and Clark? *Lois and Clark* for that matter. TV characters you're probably too young to remember."

"Am not. Reruns. They were almost hot."

"Okay. 'We're not supposed to.' Where would that have gotten—?"

"Ah . . . um . . . Reese Witherspoon in *Legally Blonde?*"

"Right. Well, I'm legally blonde now, and I say we crash this party."

"Huh?"

Temple ducked under the tape and donned the thin latex gloves that came with her hair-dye product. The pros had ignored them to use their own professional-quality pairs, so Temple had appropriated them against a future need. She pushed against and opened an unlocked door.

Surprise! The cops were really lax. Or someone else had been here.

Mariah followed her inside, acting like Dorothy in the haunted wood: scared. As if she thought Mama Molina had some crystal-gazing globe that could follow her every move. Probably did.

Temple flicked on the mascara wand–size flashlight she always traveled with. A bright needle of light played over surfaces familiar to both her and Mariah.

"Too much to revisit?" Temple asked.

Mariah had insisted on accompanying her. Now the dark empty room made the reality of sudden death a more obvious deterrent than a thirteen-year-old might realize.

"No. And yeah. I guess. That poor lady! She just wanted me to do well."

"We will do well. By her. She was the only consultant who imported her own file cabinets. I wondered why when I had my sessions with her. Let's take a look."

First Temple scanned the room for hidden cameras and mikes. She was getting good at spotting them. They'd stockpiled cloth napkins at meals and now distributed them around the room like demented waitresses. Over the lamps, the power outlets, lighting fixtures.

Besides, they kept the room's lights off. Even if any cameras picked up intruders, they would be shadow puppets on a highly manipulated stage.

The file cabinets had always struck Temple because they were the Steel Case sort: heavy metal, with locks. This office's decor was more wicker basket style. They were the two-drawer variety on wheels that's easily overlooked as mobile work surfaces. There were three of them, all lockable.

That was the problem. Temple tried each one. Surprise. These drawers were locked.

"We need the keys," she whispered to Mariah. "And they'll probably be hidden."

Twenty minutes later, Temple had explored every drawer and Mariah had finished her more imaginative search, usually up above or under something.

No keys.

"Why didn't the police try the files?" Mariah wondered.

"Probably thought they came with the office and had nothing to do with Marjory. But we've seen all the other offices and no one else has these industrial-strength things."

"Still, missing them is shabby police work."

"Maybe the police checked them out and relocked them, then."

"If my mom had been on the scene, they'd have been shaken upside down. Why hasn't she shown up?"

"Probably to keep from ruining your big chance, remember? You made it pretty plain she wasn't to interfere."

"Yeah."

This kept Mariah silent for a whole minute. "Mrs. Klein was a food freak," she said suddenly. "Maybe it was for good and all but she was still freaked about it. She used to play with that fake fruit on her desk until I was ready to scream, or grab one and eat it. I bet—"

Mariah ambled to the basket of fruit on the desk and pulled out a plum (wax). From beneath it she pulled out a snake. "Hey, look!" A slim leather cord that ended with a trio of thin tiny keys.

"Brilliant thinking," Temple said. "Where would a food freak hide something but under fake fruit."

Temple grabbed the flimsy keys and tried them in sequence until all three file cabinets were unlocked. The open drawers revealed colored hanging file folders stuffed with a variety of colored file folders, each bearing a clear crystal tab indicating its contents.

"Reading rainbow," Mariah commented.

"Seriously neat freak."

Every food group, vitamin, study, and food additive had a file folder. So did every Teen Queen candidate.

Temple collapsed on the floor to read about her alter ego, Xoe Chloe, line by flashlit line. This wasn't just a food plan (more fruit and fiber, less empty calories like soda pop), it was a psych sketch.

"Am I glad I'm not really me!" she told Mariah. "I show 'clear antisocial tendencies magnified to chronic instability.' Hey. I'm better at being bad than I thought."

Mariah snatched the flashlight to study her file. "I'm the 'typical only child' who's 'hidden behind baby fat.' I'm 'desperately seeking a father figure!' Coulda fooled me."

"Listen, if Marjory Klein was so off about a fake personality like Xoe, she's certainly off about a real person like you. Makes you wonder how off she was about everybody."

"She did have a beans and legumes fixation."

"To the point of mania. No wonder someone crammed some down her throat."

"Look! Golly. Here under 'Miscellaneous' are some court orders."

"About what?"

"Kids ordered into therapy with her."

"Sad but true. Take a lesson from this, Mariah. You act like Xoe Chloe once too often and you're sentenced to psychobabble."

"I like Xoe. She's way more fun than you are."

"So are a lot of things that are bad for you." Temple sighed. "Working with the dysfunctional stirs up ugly emotions, especially if you're inept. I can see someone having a motive for murdering this woman now, I just don't see who or exactly why."

Temple ran her flashlight over another merry rainbow of folders. The light paused on a subject tab labeled "Indigestible."

It was a weird category, so naturally she pulled it.

"Mariah! Look at this."

"Do I have to? It's on that long legal-size paper that's so boring."

"Right. Boring but important. This is a lawsuit." Temple flipped back the pale blue pasteboard cover to skim the legalese inside. "Wrongful death. Someone sued her for malpractice! For . . . failing to prevent a fatal eating disorder, for creating it, actually. This is serious stuff."

"You mean, someone hated her enough to bring a suit against her?"

"Exactly. Someone's child died under her care."

"We hear about anorexia and bulimia and stuff at school. It's gross, and also nuts."

"And a heartbreaking, relentless condition. If someone thought Marjory Klein had contributed to his or her child's death by starvation, they might just stuff a bunch of food down her throat until she choked on it."

"I thought an allergy killed her."

"Her own food peculiarities must have been known. Or the killer mixed some poison in. We won't know the cause of death unless your mother shares it with us, and I can't see why she would. You'd think this suit was still ongoing, or she wouldn't have brought it along. But look at the date."

"Nineteen ninety-one. I wasn't born yet."

"This doesn't make sense." Temple ran her thin line of light over endless legal phrases, then paged back to the beginning. "The dead girl's name has got to be in here somewhere. Maybe it'll mean something."

Mariah hung over her shoulder, reading along with her.

"There!"

"Where?"

"Two lines below where you're reading. 'Chastity Cummings.' Man, I'd like to die if my first name was Chastity! That's worse than Mariah. I mean, think what the other kids would say the minute you got out of kindergarten."

"Kids are teasing kids over words like 'chastity' in the early grades?"

"In Catholic schools they are. The thing about going to a religious school is you get all those nasty words like 'lust' and 'adultery' and 'O-Nanism' and stuff early. It's all in the Bible."

"Right. Being reared a Unitarian, I was cheated of all that early lurid class content. Rats."

"What's a Unitarian?"

"Unitarian Universalist. We see God and the world as inclusive and tolerant."

"You mean you wouldn't stone or smite anybody?"

"Right. Ours not to judge."

"Somebody has to, or my mom wouldn't have a job."

"That's civil law. That's different. Anyway, I don't get why this old suit is still in her active files."

Mariah had pushed herself up to her knees to root in the file drawer again.

"Look! Here's a sheet of paper that caught in the fold-over part of the hanging file."

Piece was right. Just a torn-off triangle from one corner of a plain sheet of white paper. Not typed, written on. Just a date and a few scrawled words, the ends of three lines.

Maybe somebody had removed a folder in a hurry and a page had caught in the cardboard seam and pulled off. Recently, or ages ago.

Oops. Very recently.

"Ah." Temple sat back on her heels while her moving flashlight told a fascinating if somewhat staccato story. The date read February 14, 2005.

This scrap was as timely as today. Only months old. Valentine's Day. A favorite one for expression of sentiments sweet, and perhaps bittersweet, maybe even sour. Maybe even poisonous.

"Is it a valentine?" Mariah sounded hopeful. "Lots of people keep them. We do valentines at school but everybody's chicken and girls send friendship ones to girls and that's all. Boys would rather die than send a valentine."

"Just wait." Temple advised her. She frowned at the penmanship. Maybe her fake green contacts were coloring the ink, making it harder to read. She deciphered the few words ending each line:

> I'll never forget
> . . . murderous bitch like you
> . . . incompetent on national TV.

"That's it," Temple said after murmuring the words to Mariah. "That's the motive. We better get this to your mother."

Temple held up the scrap by her plastic gloves. "Thank God neither of our fingerprints are on it. Can you find the equivalent of a plastic baggie in this office . . . without leaving fingerprints?"

"Easy." Mariah hopped up. "Mrs. Klein handed out 'healthful snacks' in plastic baggies from the little fridge behind her desk. Sliced rutabaga, can you imagine? It is to gag."

Mariah was soon back with a baggie of sliced . . . Temple peered at the browning contents. Looked like shredded turnip greens and sliced medulla oblongata, or possibly liver. She dumped the mess into Mariah's palms as she dried the inside of the baggie on her T-shirt hem and placed the paper remnant inside.

"My mom's going to wonder if you're passing on evidence of a threatening note or a salad."

"Both."

Mariah dumped her sticky handful into a second plastic bag of unknown nibblies. "We'd better throw this mess out upstairs."

"Right. Now let's hope we can make it back to headquarters without attracting any unwelcome attention."

Mariah giggled. "You're so funny. The way you talk. I don't get why my mom considers you such an awful pest."

"I haven't a clue, Mariah. Sometimes moms are like that. Behind the times. Let's blow this joint."

First, they collected all their napkins. Then Temple used the flashlight beam to lead their way out. She shut it off before she edged the door open. Silence greeted the motion. She pushed the door open farther and heard nothing. Prodding Mariah out, she followed and slowly,

slowly shut the door, turning to duck under the crime scene tape . . .

. . . and spied a black cat sitting right there in the hall, like a welcoming committee of one, feet primly paired, ears perked, eyes inscrutable.

For once it was not Louie. This cat was smaller, longer of coat, and gold of eye, not green.

But its face wore the same superior smirk! *I see you.*

"Oh." Mariah reached out to pet the lovely thing but it darted away like a feral.

"Forget the cat," Temple whispered. "We need to get home without anyone noticing us."

In a house full of cameras this was always a problem. Which was why they headed first for the kitchen, then up to the room.

If any camera did capture some part of their wanderings, they could always claim a raid on the refrigerator.

Chapter 48

Recipe for Murder

Temple called Mama Bear as soon as they returned to their room.

The cell phone didn't produce the strongest signal in the world in the bathroom with the water running, but secret agents had to get used to adverse conditions.

Mariah was in the outer room, reading the paper fragment through the plastic baggie and munching on a stash of julienned raw carrots she was allowed as snacks. Yum.

The hour was late and Temple felt some unkindly satisfaction at getting Mariah's mother up.

"Yes." The voice was so sudden and stern that Temple momentarily couldn't decide how to begin. She wasn't used to being barked at.

While she hesitated, Molina's voice came back on the line even more demanding. "Who is this?"

"Ah, Xoe."

"Xoe?" Apparently, her alter ego hadn't made an impression on Molina. So much for a chance with the judges.

"Right. I've found some fascinating papers in the dead dietitian's office. You should have them right away."

"You." Molina actually sounded glad about that. "What papers?"

"A lawsuit involving Mrs. Klein several years ago."

"We know about that. My detectives did a background check and it came up. So you woke me up for that?"

"And a scrap of paper dated last February fourteenth. It sounds threatening. It apparently was torn off the contents of a folder as it was being taken out. Someone didn't notice."

"Valentine's Day hate note, eh? That sounds more promising. No nice and neat signature, like 'Your Killer,' I suppose?"

Temple didn't bother answering that bit of sarcasm.

"What were you doing in the woman's office anyway? That's still a crime scene."

"I am, therefore, I snoop. I thought that's what I was here for."

"You're here to keep an eye on Mariah. Where was she while you were on this law-breaking expedition?"

"Um, in our room, studying some papers and snacking on carrot sticks."

"Carrot sticks! Commendable if out of character. I suppose your prints are all over that office now."

"No. I used a pair of latex gloves, just like the pros."

"Where'd you get—"

"They dyed my hair as part of the makeover but had their own gloves. And I never throw anything away, so . . ."

"They dyed your hair? All of it?"

"This *is* a makeover show."

"What have they done to Mariah?"

"Nothing. Yet. Except make her work out and eat veggies."

"Don't let them dye her hair."

"I'll do what I can."

"So you wore hair-dye gloves to search the office. Unbelievable."

"And the paper scrap is in a plastic baggie fresh from Mrs. Klein's office refrigerator. I had to throw out some guck to get an empty baggie."

"That's all right. Our crime scene people have already taken samples of everything in there for analysis."

"So how do we exchange the evidence."

"'We' do not. I'll send Alch over in the morning. You know him, Mariah knows him, and one of you two should be able to pass him a baggie without undue attention."

"We've got a window of opportunity between 8:15 and 8:30."

"That early? I'll have to call Morrie tonight yet."

"This is beauty boot camp, you know. No laggards here."

"Except the dead."

Speaking of which, the line went dead.

Temple was slow in folding away her cell phone. Molina had sounded really growly when she'd first answered the phone, before she even knew it was Temple. Suspicious and growly. And something else. Temple called upon her theatrical background to conjure just the right word to describe the other note in the lieutenant's usual gruff and businesslike tone. Anxious, maybe? No. Scared.

Temple shut off the water and pulled down the washcloths. She was hanging so many napkins and towels around suspected camera sites she felt like a laundress.

In the bedroom, all the lights were blazing but Mariah had tunneled completely under the covers and was lost in sudden, absolute adolescent sleep, her rear end humped up to make an island in the pink silk sea of coverlet.

Temple went over to the table to inspect the papers that had put Mariah to sleep. The only sexy one was the torn scrap of threat. And something about that bothered Temple.

She sat down at Mariah's abandoned chair and read the

terse words. "Murderous bitch" was pretty damning. And "incompetent." But the last words were strange . . . "on national TV." Thing is, Kit hadn't been selected for the show until a month ago. Reality TV shows moved fast. They had very little budget, just a quick casting call to the public at large, assembling a panel of experts, scouting a ready-made site.

From what Kit had said, why would Marjory Klein have known about the show over three months ago? Because the note-writer was taunting her about appearing on it, was maybe stirred up by it. Was trying to scare her. And who took the folder out that had contained that letter? Someone who knew Marjory and her anal-retentive ways.

Someone who was announcing that he or she was aware of Marjory's every move scarily soon. A stalker. Maybe that's why Marjory brought the lawsuit papers with her. She didn't trust them left at home. Or she wanted to leave a clue in case anything had happened. Like the threatening note. Only the killer had taken the note. Or most of it. So the note had to be incriminating.

Temple read it again. Looked over the suit document. The case had been filed in Salt Lake City. In the wrongful death of the late Chastity Cummings. The name seemed familiar, but Temple had heard so many new names here at the Teen Queen Castle. Including her own pseudonym.

She pulled out the large white papers Mariah had been reading like a fractured fairytale. Newspaper clippings never presented the cleanest timeline. News reporting was staccato, it hit the highlights of action, not thought. Arrested. Makes bond. Autopsy results announced. Vanished. Anniversary of murder story. Wacky detective takes up case eight years later. Vanishes like the suspect, Arthur Dickson. House on the market. Doesn't sell. Becomes private casino. Another anniversary story speculating on who actually did it. Noting how long the dead have been that way.

Finally, it's a twenty-year anniversary. MURDER STILL

PUZZLES OFFICIALS. Arthur Dickson is still at large and missing. His bimbo ex-wife can't be found. Her younger ex-boyfriend is a Hollywood stuntman who worked on *Waterworld* before his career sank. The wounded daughter? Died in an Oregon nursing home years before.

Temple paged through the copies of the twenty-year-old photos.

It was like a Greek tragedy: rich, older man; young wife with young daughter. Wedding. Spending. Publicity. That was the public part. The private? Drinking. Fighting. Divorcing. Money. Rage. Murder going ballistic one night. A mysterious masked intruder with a gun. Innocents wounded. The wife wounded but alive. The husband with an alibi just possible enough to ensure reasonable doubt. Still, he breaks bail and runs. Never to be found again. Everybody else left behind to start new lives or cope with what remained of the old.

Temple stared at the old photos under the weak overhead lights they put in every bedroom, except maybe in expensive whorehouses.

What if the house was not a reality show set because it was grand and vacant and notorious? What if the chicken came before the egg?

She studied the photos again. Hey, this ploy had worked for Xoe Chloe, the undercover Teen Queen candidate with an agenda. Why wouldn't it have worked for someone else? A murderer?

Her forefinger speared one face in one photo, subtracting the negative, accentuating the positive past connection.

Yes. Clever and chilling.

She quickly grabbed a hot pink folder, either hers or Mariah's, and doublechecked the morning schedule.

If she worked it right, she should be able to hand Marjory Klein's killer over to Detective Alch along with the borrowed baggie Molina had openly discounted.

How sweet it is . . .

Chapter 49

Conscentual Adults

Miss Midnight Louise and I rendezvous in the kitchen at twelve o'clock high, a very appropriate time.

Miss Louise is rude enough to suggest that the kitchen has become our favored rendezvous point because I have an eating disorder.

I point out that it offers the advantages of being periodically deserted and that the black marble floor and black granite countertops afford us a degree of camouflage we can obtain nowhere else in this huge house.

She sniffs.

Which is exactly what we are here to discuss.

When she showed up on the scene so unexpectedly (probably just to complicate my life), I was forced to come up with a task for her that would occupy her over-busy brain and yet keep her out of my way. (You can imagine how she would interfere with my necessary interrogations of the Persian girls!) I do believe there is a reason for the great detectives having a right-hand gal in the office, not on the mean streets with them. Dames do like to ride herd on a dude!

So I had to share with her, by proxy, the one precious clue in this case that I have held close to the chest hairs from the beginning.

Had I not followed my protective instincts in following my Miss Temple to the shopping mall, where she made herself so obnoxious in her brilliant way, I would never have picked up the trace of a killer.

We are not dogs, but do we not have noses? Do we not lay our own scent of ownership hither and yon? Are we not better equipped than humans for following the trail of murder? Or, as in this case, murders?

So I had conveyed to Louise as best I could the strange, sickly sweet odor of the puddle outside the mall.

"You are sure it was not diluted blood?" she had demanded.

"I know blood in any state, my dear Louise. No, it was the sort of thing humans eat but should not."

"That is legion. Can you be a tad more specific?"

"Something cloying, and it was pink."

"Everything pink is cloying when it comes to humans."

"I hope you except the cat world Swiss Army knife from that judgment, that marvelous instrument of myriad uses, the feline tongue."

"Speak for yourself, Romeo. So what is the scent I should search for?"

"Strawberry."

Louise makes a delicate gagging sound, a prehairball sortie.

"Or perhaps cherry or raspberry. I am no connoisseur of fruit flavors. Then again, it could be that dreadful pink bubblegum flavor. Whatever it was, it was tacky enough in both senses of the words to cling to someone's shoes. I have been tracing it upstairs, downstairs, and everywhere but my lady's chamber."

"So why should I pollute my nose following disgusting Dumpster leavings?"

"Because I first sniffed it someplace else than here."

"Such as?"

"Such as the parking lot of the mall, where I tailed my Miss Temple when she made her debut as Miss Xoe Chloe by auditioning for this very madness."

"Parking lot?" Miss Louise is sounding properly intrigued now.

"Right. I found it next to a body that was the focus of a lot of police attention, including that of Miss Lieutenant C. R. Molina and her new squeeze."

"No."

Louise is sounding satisfactorily shocked at last.

"Miss Lieutenant C. R. Molina has a new squeeze? I thought she was beyond such things."

"Apparently not, but the point, Louise, is that a poor young girl had been struck dead on the spot. And there was this melting puddle of sticky pink stuff beside her. I have smelled the same stuff on some shoe that has been moving around the place, from the pool area where the mats were sprayed with shaving cream to these supposedly secret passages."

"Me-wow!" Louise has sat down in front of me in a dazed condition. I can finally see a bit in the dark and I do not like what I am seeing. "I never dreamed Miss Lieutenant Molina would be a traitor to the cause of female independence."

"Maybe he is not her boyfriend. Maybe he is just a new associate. I merely remarked that something more seemed to be going on, but forget it! The point is, whoever killed that girl is here and has killed again. We must follow the putrid pink trail."

So I had argued with Miss Louise until she felt her feminine sensibilities were on the line, i.e., anything I can smell she can smell better.

Passing on a scent, no matter how strong, by proxy, is not easy. But Miss Louise spent several diligent moments vacuuming my whiskers for any remaining traces and pronounced that she had the idea but the methodology of getting it was most repugnant.

Forensic evidence is often like that, I told her.

So we have been sniffing our way through the Teen Queen Castle ever since in search of likely candidates. For I had observed at the crime scene that the killer, with the usual insufficient human olfactory equipment, had trod unknowing in the melted ice cream.

Sickly sweet strawberry scent does not go gently into that dark night. Observe the car freshening products so beloved of patrol car and cab drivers. And most of them strawberry scented.

Miss Louise is indelicate enough to point out that this could confuse the issue.

I point out that we are inside a house, and a huge house, not a moving vehicle. (Although I do wish that Miss Louise was inside a moving vehicle at this moment, headed for the Valley of Fire.)

However, the trained professional does not allow personal druthers to affect his effectiveness in the field.

"So," she asks, "what is our total suspect list? Although I report the strange actions of your Miss Temple and Miss Lieutenant Molina's Mariah in the dietitian's office, I could detect no more cloying scent upon them than one usually encounters paging through certain fashion magazines. Strawberry is far too bourgeois for such venues."

Huh? Normally I am in command of French, for it is one of those languages that you are in command of or it is in command of you, but I am a little lost here.

So, when in doubt, hold forth. I pace back and forth on a floor so clean there is not any odor other than Pine-Sol to distract me.

"I have detected suspiciously sweet odors on the footwear of a cameraman who tried to kick me in the pool area."

"You have a pool area? I am impressed, Pops. Is it a front bay or a back bay pool area?"

"Most unamusing, Louise. You are right that I am ill-disposed to a kicker, but unfortunately the gorilla in question has no other counts against him than slinking through the technical corridors, and that is his job."

"I have traced a sickly sweet odor to the tacky Payless loafers so appropriate to the person of Crawford Buchanan," she says. "I would so like him to be a murderer. Say it is possibly so."

"It is. He is what humans call a 'lech,' which means he likes to chase young girls. Molesters are in big disfavor nowadays. Perhaps the murdered woman was trying to interfere in his pursuit. They could have destroyed his reputation just as he was trying to make the leap to TV media."

"Ah." Louise digests that idea happily. Like my Miss Temple, she cannot stand Crawford Buchanan.

"Sickly sweet odor?" she offers. "Did you ever check his cologne? *Me-eeeuw.*"

"Agreed. A guy knows these things. He uses Old Lice, I believe, which I understand is good for repelling mosquitoes as well as females. It could be possible he spilled some, from the amount he slaps on each morning, and stepped in it."

"Speaking of sickly sweet in the face of sickly sour,

Dexter Manship's suede Bass shoes have that odor about them. I fear it is that illegal weed people are so fond of smoking."

"Close but no cigar. I must confess, with regret, that my most recent Elvis visitation—"

Here she snorts her disbelief with a vehemence that would get her arrested were she not an innocent-looking feline.

"You and Elvis! That is a delusional mutual admiration society. As I recall, he was a dog and horse man. And I would not expect his ghost to be any different."

"That is just it, Louise. Not every Elvis apparition is the real thing."

"Not *every!* Like any one of them could be!"

"Your Mr. Matt had his suspicions."

"Elvis might look up Mr. Matt. I might look up Mr. Matt if I were returning for my tenth life. Neither of us would look you up."

What is a guy to say to such a blanket dismissal? A few choice expletives cross my mind but I am ever the gentleman. Especially on *Candid Camera.*

"So," I sum up. "We have three suspects, so far. I think tomorrow we shall have to arrange to trip them all up. Literally. And soon."

Chapter 50

A Hasty Hand

Temple hadn't really been able to sleep.

She'd set the bedside clock radio but it was like clock radios in hotels: so many hands had been on it that it was unlikely its current reading was correct.

Luckily, Mariah was out cold. Temple felt a twinge of guilt after she turned off the possibly unreliable alarm and unplugged the unit just to be safe.

Better Mariah should miss breakfast and her first consultation of the day than that she should be involved in a confrontation with a killer.

Actually, Temple only needed to confirm where the suspect was, then dash to the entry area and await the arrival of jolly old Detective Alch. He could do the takedown and Molina would be seething with . . . gratitude?

Well she should be, Temple thought. The clear and present danger would be over. Mariah would be safe,

along with everybody else, and still an innocent contestant with a chance of winning.

Xoe Chloe, alas, the incorrigible roommate now revealed as an overage fraud, would be outed and kicked
out of the Teen Queen Castle. Fair exchange: Temple
cherished no delusions of ever becoming a teen queen,
back then or here and now. She'd been lucky to go to her
high school prom, even with a dorky date, much less be
crowned queen of it. Or anything.

There is something strangely unreal about thinking
you've discovered a murderer. It gives you a sense of in-
vulnerability, oddly enough. After all, you know what's
what when nobody else does.

That's how Temple felt when she tiptoed out of the
bedroom, leaving it dim behind all the drawn miniblinds,
with Mariah's head still buried in the covers.

She checked Xoe Chloe's watch, a jingling band with a
cheery collection of skulls and Harley Davidson charms
mixed in with such girly icons as tiny spike heels she'd
found at the mall.

All Temple had to do now was ensure the perp was ensconced in the proper consulting room, then guide Alch
there.

He thought he was here as a mere delivery boy. She
hoped he still carried. Maybe she should have speed-
dialed the Fontana Brothers as backup. Her Aunt Kit
would adore meeting them.

She got down to the main floor, checked her watch, and
hovered at the front entry hall. No Alch yet but it was
only 8:25. Maybe she should pick up some muscle on the
way.

Time to skitter down the endless halls—where were
Xoe's Rollerblades when she needed them?

Temple's heart was pounding when she reached the

right door, and not from the run. What if she was wrong? She knocked. After ten seconds' silence, she pushed the door open.

The office seemed empty. Strange. The 8:30 slot was booked. Someone should be here.

Aware that her every move might be recorded, Temple played the curious arrivée, peering in, peeking around, moving around on silent little cat feet.

No bogeymen jumped out from behind furniture, so before she knew it, she had advanced to the empty desk.

Upon its admirably clear surface lay a note, scrawled in a hasty hand.

Temple cocked her head to read it sideways: "See me first thing tomorrow."

Hmmm. Sounded like the tail wagged the dog, although this dog had always been in charge of the manger.

Either way, she needed to hit another office fast. Her watch said Alch would be pushing open the Teen Queen Castle entry portcullis right about now. . . .

She dashed down another hall, around a corner, and into familiar territory.

Another door, another knock, another long silence.

Brash, bleached-blonde Xoe Chloe walked right in. Peered.

The high-backed leather chair behind the desk was spun away from the door to face the windows overlooking the pool area.

Temple had a very bad feeling. She should cut and run, whatever that meant.

She'd been here before. Empty office, sinister chair back. Cameras, anyone?

Why had Dexter Manship left that imperious note just sitting on his desk? Had he figured out what she had? She'd trespassed on his empty office before, but then there had been nothing sinister to find after all.

That was there and then. This was here and now.

Had he too tumbled to the bizarre truth? Where was he now?

Was she too late? Would Alch find yet another victim instead of a perp?

She didn't like Manship. Who did? Manship probably didn't even like Manship. But . . . he was a human being, sharp and observant. Maybe too much of both.

She approached the desk. Walked around it. Outside the Nevada sunshine was bouncing off the blazing white stone and blue water and basting bronzed blondes to French toast.

Inside, the office was dim. Silent. Still as death.

She grabbed the chair's high back and spun it around with all her might.

She needed all her might. The chair was heavy and only rotated forty-five degrees.

Enough to reveal a passenger.

An inert passenger.

The wrong one.

Xoe Chloe could have skated back down a quarter mile of hallway to the front door in about two minutes.

Temple was less athletic and way more practical.

She screamed. It was a wimpy thing to do but it would bring 'em all in about sixty seconds flat.

Chapter 51

Heartfelt
and Red-Handed

"They have you on tape," kindly Detective Alch said. Threatened. "We have you on tape, since their tapes are now our tapes. Slinking around Manship's empty office a few days ago."

"That wasn't me," Temple said. "That was Xoe Chloe. She's much nervier."

Temple wasn't nervy at all now, except in the wimpy meaning of the word. Her back was to the desk and Beth Marble's very dead body, but the grotesque image was branded on the movie screen behind her eyes: Beth's head tilted back, eyes open, the curled black hair slid back several inches . . . a wig like Xoe Chloe's ex-accessory, but the head beneath it . . . bald. It was bad enough the woman was dead; worse that the killer had scalped her in a sense. Temple wondered if gravity, or the murderer, had unmasked Beth after death.

"You say you were going to spring the murderer's

name on me when I got here. Then why the detour to Manship's office?"

"He'd left a note from my suspect on his desk, asking him to see her."

"'Your suspect?' Miss Barr, I personally think you're an okay person, and I get that my boss wanted you on this scene for reasons relating to her daughter. But you've been caught red-handed over a dead body. You see my position."

"Yup. You're probably sitting on the exact place the body was laid before it was propped up in the chair."

Alch eyed the large ottoman, then sprang up. "You think she was killed elsewhere and brought here? But how? This place is crawling with cameras and antsy contestants. You couldn't import a bedbug here without getting major notice."

"I don't know."

"So. Are we to suspect you, or Manship?"

"Good question. Since I'm a wild card here—"

Alch snorted.

"Probably Manship. He's the Big Meanie on board. The note signed by her was left in his office, so he probably was there."

"So how did he waltz a dead body three hundred feet through corridors that might be highly populated any second?"

"I don't know. He's Australian. They're used to wrestling crocodiles."

"Okay. Tell me about the vic."

"Well, I think the vic was actually the perp."

"You're kidding me, right?"

Amazing, Temple thought, how talking the talk cut through the fog. Vic. Perp. That made the so-intensely-personal act of murder strangely impersonal.

"Or one of them."

"Say you're kidding me."

"I can't. I do have a rationale for why I thought the perp who is now a vic became a perp."

"Rationale. Look, Miss Barr, the lieutenant told us about your pseudo-participation in this circus. We are inclined to overlook a great deal. But being found first on a murder scene is not one of the overlookable offenses."

"How many 'offenses' did Molina consider expected?"

His expression tightened. "A few. Like breaking and entering on the first death scene. And bringing her daughter along."

"You guys have taken over the show's secret recording duties."

"Darn right. Now. I'll take you downtown so the lieutenant can debrief you."

"Mariah—"

"Not to worry. Su's with her."

For some reason, Temple felt usurped.

"Why didn't Molina use Su in the first place? Why drag me into it and then punish me for getting ahead of the curve?"

"You're a head of something, all right," he said, gazing at her blindingly blond hair. Then he chuckled. "Don't sweat it. Somehow I don't see you as a candidate for stabbing someone through the heart."

"Was that the murder method?"

Alch put a finger to his lips and mustache. "Not for publication."

So she was escorted out of the death scene, a defiant Xoe Chloe to the last. Everyone gathered around: herd of tittering blondes, glad to have Xoe off the show; Crawford Buchanan, hissing a blow-by-blow commentary into his live mike; her own aunt, looking aghast but keeping her lips zipped like a good actress; a subdued Dexter Manship; and Rafi Nadir, bringing up the rear to give her a thumbs up, her only supporter.

Unless you counted Midnight Louie at the crowd's very edge, backed up by a trio of hip kits, one silver, one golden, and one as black as Xoe Chloe's hair used to be.

Louie did not give her a thumbs up.

But he did wink. Or blink. Whichever. He had a whisker's chance in hell of helping her.

"What did you think you were doing?"

Molina didn't waste words. Temple was in her office, which was a good sign. She doubted it was bugged but couldn't be sure. After living in the Teen Queen Castle, she was fairly paranoid. Police had a license to be tricky.

"I thought I'd lead Detective Alch to the person who'd killed Marjory Klein."

"Oh, you led Alch to something, all right. Another murder. And what the hell is going on with my daughter? You were supposed to protect her. Instead, your pet sleazebag is running loose on the premises and a pretty prime suspect for any and all of this."

"I didn't know Rafi would be there. Savannah Ashleigh hired him as a bodyguard. And Mariah's fine. Neither of them has a clue as to who is who. You really pulled the wool over Rafi's eyes. If he found out he had a kid, he'd probably stroke out and your problems would be over. In fact, that might be a nice sneaky way to get rid of him forever."

"I wouldn't count on convenient acts of God to get you out of this mess. Some amateur sleuth you are. You just led Alch to Beth Marble. This woman turned out to be a victim, not a criminal."

"Why does her killer have to be Mrs. Klein's killer?"

"We have a serial situation here. There was a young girl killed in the parking lot outside the shopping mall where you and your . . . peers auditioned two weeks ago. We've found defaced posters of the show flyer all over the place. Someone is targeting the competition and its entrants."

Temple absorbed this, even the additional details, with no surprise. "Those were the arguments you used to blackmail me into becoming Mariah's chaperon. You've always suspected an outside stalker."

Molina, her face sober to the point of grimness, nodded.

"Look. I don't for a minute believe that you'd stab any-one in the heart . . . unless they were going after your sainted Max Kinsella. You can bet I'd never turn my back on you in that regard. But you've put me in an impossible position. You were found where you were found. I had to abstract you."

"'Abstract?' Like I'm a hologram you erase?"

"Abstract like 'take out' before you're taken out. First, I'd like to know why you thought Beth Marble killed Marjory Klein. It's quite a leap of logic."

"Who do you think killed Beth Marble?"

"Haven't a clue yet. She apparently was not only the mastermind behind this piece of reality TV tripe but her personality was all grins and roses. A cloying personality type, I grant you, but why target her as a killer?"

"Why should I tell someone who ridicules my deduc-tions and jerks me around like a puppet?"

Molina leaned back in her skimpy executive chair, not even big enough to hide a dead body. She tapped a pen on her desktop.

"You build a good case, I'll buy it."

"And that's worth something?"

"It's worth our deal about Kinsella continuing."

"Okay. My reasons aren't entirely logical—"

"So I've been telling you about Kinsella. But go on."

"I just . . . felt from the first that the house's history had something to do with the sinister goings-on now."

"'Sinister goings-on.' Very good. Very Agatha. *Go on.*"

Molina was always a hard house to play. "I think, from

the old photos in your fairly lousy news-clipping copies, that Beth Marble was really that blonde trophy wife of yore, Crystal Cummings."

Molina neither moved nor spoke.

"After all, she didn't die in the attack years ago. She just went off the radar after all the court trials and hoopla and her estranged husband's disappearance. So did her seriously wounded teenage daughter. They became the forgotten victims."

"Have you any idea how many cold case files there are? How many suspects and almost victims drift off into the great anonymity of modern life? It's easier to lose people than to find them."

"Exactly. But I figure that this poor kid, Crystal's daughter, she would have had enormous emotional trauma. Maybe enough to create an eating disorder, which is a cry for control. Enter Marjory Klein, an inflexible, doctrinaire therapist. Believe me, I had to sit in her office swallowing her legume regimen, and poor Mariah—"

"What about 'poor' Mariah?"

"You know Mrs. Klein was hard on her weight issue."

"Hispanic girls often have baby fat but they get it off later."

"Right. A Weight Watcher would know, wouldn't she?"

Molina's face darkened but she didn't say anything. Kids will blab. Temple felt her ground hardening under her.

"And you're only her mother and Mariah was only in Mrs. Klein's hands for a few days and I did tell her to ignore the woman . . . and already the veins are standing out on your forehead."

"They are not."

"They would be if you allowed them to. So figure it's not just a few pounds and *your* daughter but Crystal Cummings's teenage daughter with a serious case of traumatic anorexia or bulimia brought on by the attack in the Dickson house.

"So she eventually dies, the daughter. Cummings would be her last name. Or maybe she'd have the last name of her actual, forgotten father. But maybe Crystal just used her mother's own last name. I hear that sort of thing happens all the time. Much cleaner, especially if the father has abandoned the child." Molina's face was getting grimmer by the second. "The point is, this young girl was only a stepdaughter to Dickson. That was the tragedy of her getting hit by one of the bullets. She was a truly innocent bystander."

Molina started shuffling papers on her desk like a madwoman.

Finally, she pulled one out and leaned back in her chair. "Tiffany Cummings."

"No, that wasn't the daughter's name. The articles said she was called Chastity."

"Tiffany Cummings was the name of the seventeen-year-old who was accosted in the mall parking lot during the Teen Queen tryouts and stabbed to death with a screwdriver."

"Ouch." Temple was stunned into silence. She kept quiet to think. For once, she and Molina were in perfect sync.

The notion of two young girls with their lives ruined and cut short so violently was appalling. Had Chastity survived just long enough to bear a daughter? Maybe postpartum depression had pushed her into anorexia. And maybe Tiffany was Crystal Cummings's granddaughter. A far fresher motive for a killing.

"We haven't traced any relatives to the parking lot vic. If she wasn't a runaway, she lived a gypsy life."

Finally Temple spoke. "If Tiffany Cummings was the first victim, Marjory Klein was the second victim, and Crystal Cummings masquerading as Beth Marble was the third—?" She fell silent. "I've got a headache."

"It's probably an allergic reaction to bleach. That dye job of yours is unreal."

"That was the idea, wasn't it? Just like the reality show was supposed to be unreal. Only it had ended up being a shadow of the Dickson house murders twenty years ago. If Crystal, aka 'Beth,' killed Marjory, who killed her? And why?"

"That's a very far-out theory of yours. We'll have to do a lot of checking to prove the entwined threads in this tangled web. Meanwhile—" Molina stood, towering like the Palms hotel. "You can go back."

"I'm disgraced. I was taken away by the police."

"That should only burnish Xoe Chloe's sorry reputation. Look. I don't want Mariah alone in that mess, and you do seem to have some sort of whacked-out handle on things. Finish out the assignment and Max Kinsella is all yours, off my usual suspects list forever."

"He already is all mine."

"Maybe." Molina's electric blue glance met and held Temple's a trifle too long.

"What do you mean?"

"I mean that nothing's certain in this world but death and taxes. Taxes I leave to accountants. Death is my beat. Magicians are one step behind the Grim Reaper when it comes to surprise appearances. I wouldn't count on them. Not a one of 'em. Especially that one. Deceiving the public can become an addiction that leaks over into a private life. That's all."

"Cops can't always be counted on either," Temple said.

Whether Molina got the reference to her ex, Rafi Nadir, or not, Temple left the office feeling she'd gotten a little of her own back.

But not nearly enough.

Chapter 52

Dress for Success

Temple finally understood Fonzie's appeal when she returned to the Teen Queen Castle.

The Fonz was the black-leather-jacketed "hood" on the *Happy Days* sitcom hit set in the fifties. The Bad Boy.

Xoe Chloe Ozone returned free and triumphant to the Castle.

Being taken away by the police, and released to return, made her a model of Teflon charisma.

Eyebrows may have raised but they'd been lifted by botox or Dr. Perricone formulations anyway. Xoe Chloe was cool. Nobody could tie her down.

Except maybe makeover madness.

"Where have you been?" Vanetta, who'd obviously had her head in her makeup case all day, asked frantically when Xoe appeared. "We're pulling wardrobe for the makeover debut and talent review. All the good stuff could be gone by now."

"That's all right. I'll take the bad stuff that's left over."

Temple could not believe that with two rooms taped off as crime scenes, the show would go on. But apparently it was good to go, for reasons best known to Molina and Co.

Somebody shrieked at seeing her. A fireball rushed down the corridor and embraced her like an upright lobster.

"Mariah?" Temple had to detangle from the hyper teen to see her.

Whoa! The makeover team had been busy during Temple's unhappy interview with the maternal unit.

Mariah's shiny brunette bob with bangs (so reminiscent of her mother's unfussy do) had been . . . well, further bobbed. And cut. And streaked. With—what else?— blonde.

It was still mostly brunette, though styled into one of those raggedly cheerful upflips so popular now. Oddly enough, the waifish cut emphasized Mariah's blackberry-dark eyes and even some surfacing cheekbones, thanks to a diet of beans and veggies.

"You look very cool," Temple told her.

Then she was yanked away into the adjoining library, which was filled with racks of clothing.

Kit Carlson came rushing to greet her, looking relieved. "I've saved some outfits for you."

"You shouldn't have," Temple began. But when she glimpsed the goulash of lime green ostrich feathers, sixties Op Art prints, and leopard skin draping Kit's arm, Temple knew Xoe Chloe had found her fashion muse.

Kit leaned close to whisper, "I wasn't wardrobe mistress for my high school production of *Hair* for nothing."

While Temple tried on various combinations of hip-huggers and chunky jewelry that would have made rock-star chicks look as staid as Laura Bush, Kit brought her up to date on the mood inside the Teen Queen Castle.

"The police are on us all like a cheap suit—that Detective Alch is sure kind of Columbo-cute—and the camera crew is eating it up. Our show has morphed into a combo of *Cops* and *Survivor.*

"Everyone said you were a murderer when the police took you away, so the producers have been madly assembling clips of every inch of footage on you for a special Xoe Chloe memorial montage. You are a *star,* kiddo! Clay Aiken has nothing on you.

"The Clairol horde were thrilled at your exit and are so terminally pissed at your triumphal return that I notice they're shedding brittle hairs like a miffed alpaca. Negative emotions are so bad for one's looks.

"Mariah is feeling supergirly about her transformation but she missed showing off for you, Big Sis.

"Savannah Ashleigh's glowery bodyguard, that Heathcliffy Rafi-guy, has been patrolling the halls and snooping around like a cop on the beat, way beyond his blonde bimbo duties.

"So has that black alley cat mascot that showed up. He looks a lot like your Louie, but surely he's safe at home and I suppose all black cats look alike. Does that old gigolo have a harem, or what? There are these white and yellow Persians with him."

Temple finally got a word in edgewise. "That is indeed Louie. He's doing some investigative legwork for me. And we say 'silver' and 'golden' in the Persian game."

"Well, la-di-dah. The fluffy black one must be an 'ebony,' then."

"She's not a Persian, just a long-haired American domestic. They call her Louise now, but I don't think she's Louie's girlfriend; she's way too independent."

"Well, call me a short-haired American domestic. Does madame find favor with her wardrobe selections?"

"They rock, Kit! And so do you. Thanks a gadzillion!"

"Only if I make it on *The Apprentice* with Donald 'Mr.

Comb-over' Trump next. With my luck, I'd have ended up on *The Benefactor* with that cheapo Mark Cuban sports nut."

"May the Force be with you." They slapped palms, then Temple gathered up her garish armful and fled.

Mariah ambushed her again in the hall. "I need you to check out my performance outfit."

"In the bathroom, no doubt."

"Where else?"

They returned to the room, and Temple found she'd been oddly homesick for it.

Steam heat was less welcome. Bleached blonde hair had a tendency to frizz, but Ken Adair had handed her an arsenal of moisturizers, softeners, and conditioners for its upkeep. Being a blonde was hard work, but Xoe Chloe remade (and still reasonably disguised) was worth it.

Mariah sat Temple down on the closed bathroom throne (Temple thought of Elvis's last hour) and grabbed her hands. "I was so worried."

"About me?" Foolish Temple. Teens were teens.

"No, about me! What do you think? Do I look hot? Will my mom kill me? Does this new haircut make my face look even more fat? What about these loser clothes they picked for me? What about my talent song? Is 'Defying Gravity' too obscure, too dweeby? Whaddayah think? Whaddayah think?"

"Chill, Baby-O. Xoe Chloe is on your case. *Wicked* is the hottest musical on Broadway, and 'Defying Gravity' is the current overcoming-teenage-angst anthem. Every girl feels like a misunderstood witch at your age. Plus the song's a showstopper for a darker voice, which you have in spades! As the song says, until you try, you'll never know. We'll run the wardrobe and the routine and we'll both come out smelling like, oh . . . Rose's green apple juice in a killer martini."

"Yeah. That's cool. Apple green. I saw those feathers. You'll knock 'em dead."

"Speaking of which—"

"The show's over, right? That's what my mom hauled you outa here to say. She always ruins it for me."

Temple grabbed Mariah's plump little shoulders and refrained from shaking.

"Mariah. She does not. She's putting her shield on the line to keep the lid on the murders here, just so you can get up there and be shallow like all the other little 'Tween Queen wannabes."

Mariah stared at Temple's sudden stern turn. Then her eyes teared over. "I don't know what happens. Sometimes it seems like everything's so endlessly awful."

"Sometimes it is. Not now. You're just feeling Wicked Witch of the Westly. The police aren't going to close the show down. They want everybody bottled up here while they do some very complicated background checks. And they've imported some undercover pros to prevent any more violence, so expect to see a couple new crew members. Your mom is following some very interesting leads, thanks to . . . us. We have to keep it together and let the show go on until the police have enough evidence to name and charge the person behind all this. We are . . . undercover distractions. We gotta be good at it, right? That's our real job. This stupid contest isn't the point. I'm not Xoe Chloe, and you're not Madonna, Jr. We're us, underneath it all, and we have more important jobs than winning this thing, right?"

"I guess."

"You guess right."

"But the talent show is tomorrow and then they judge and then it's all over."

"Right. Then *we* judge and then it's all over. Capische?"

"That is so *Sopranos*."

"And we are the contraltos, right? We are different."

"*You* sure are." Mariah grinned.

"Dare to be . . . you and me," Temple finished. "Defying gravity."

Chapter 53

Tailings

The hour is once again my namesake one and I am stationed outside the Ashleigh suite trying to figure out how to get in.

This is when Miss Midnight Louise happens along.

Yeah. Like she is following me.

"What ho, Romeo?" she inquires in the acid tones granted only to the female of the species, any species, and guaranteed to shrivel the cottontail off a bunny rabbit, not to mention other attachments of which I am unduly fond.

"Stalking the Ashleigh girls again, I suppose," she adds. "When are you going to get that those snooty purebreds are too good for you?"

"When I lose my self-esteem, which will be never. So. You are emulating the Crawfish and descending to domestic snooping."

"Just wondering why you were slacking off on the job."

"I am not slacking anything, Louise. I need to get through the looking glass again."

"You and little girls named Alice."

"You recall that one of ours started her on that famous adventure. Holy Havana Browns! How am I going to get in there without Miss Savannah Ashleigh seeing me?"

"I do not see why you cannot rely on your dubious inside connections. Of course, neither one of them would come if you came calling."

This gets my goat, and my llama too. I stick a mitt under the bottom of the door, shoot out my shivs, and make what pathetic scratching noises I can.

Sure enough. In thirty seconds flat, I am playing pattycake with a set of soft, moist pads from the other side.

Throwing Louise a superior gaze over my shoulder, I hunker down for a game of whisker teasing and whispering via the quarter-inch crack.

In a minute, I have convinced the Ashleigh girls to make a heck of a commotion in the service of getting me into the secret passage. They are quite aware of this area, especially Yvette, as she is wont to play with her own image in the mirror for hours, Solange informs me. But she thinks she can tear Yvette away from herself long enough to do what is needed.

Miss Louise and I retreat against the opposite wall and wait.

Not for long.

The shrieks, human and not-so, emanating from beyond the door result in an adjoining door slamming open against the hall wall, and Mr. Rafi Nadir, clad only in unzipped jeans and sneakers, charging down the hall and through the door like a cannonball.

Louise and I exchange a look, then shoot through on his sneaker heels. Well, sneakers do not have heels,

as such. Suffice it to say that we are in like dingleber-
ries dangling from a shih tzu's tail.

There is a lot of fluffy pale hair flying in the room, part
of it Persian and the other part of it Horst of Beverly
Hills, and most of it eiderdown from some terminally
clawed pillows.

Quick thinkers, these Persians. They have staged
the Mother of All Pillow Fights to upset their mistress
and bring the troops running.

While Mr. Rafi Nadir inserts himself into the pile of
flying fur, shrieks, and flailing claws both human and
feline—I admit that even I would quail at such a task—
I hurl myself at the pressure point that turns the mirror
into a revolving door, and Louise and I whisk into the
dark beyond, pausing to pull it shut behind us with paw
power times two.

"So this is what you wanted?" she asks in the absolute dark.

I wait for my eyes to acclimate. That probably takes a
little longer than for her, but I do not wish to make this
obvious.

"*Shhhh.* I am thinking."

"I can see you would need absolute quiet for that.
Why did you want to be here?"

"Is it not interesting that this house has been honey-
combed with hidden passages since the time it was
built?"

"I have heard that creepy Crawford dude prattling
about the big shootout here into his microphone. No
doubt these passages made the escape of the masked
killer easier twenty years ago. Everyone thought it was
Arthur Dickson himself, and no one could prove it. But
what does a long-dead scandal have to do with teen
queens today?"

I am about to tell her, which would be interesting as I

do not know yet myself, when there is a cracking sound
and a vertical bar of light appears behind us.

That is how I first saw Elvis, as a narrow bar of light
in the Action Jackson attraction tunnel under the Crystal Phoenix a few months ago.

I am eagerly awaiting a return engagement of the
King when the light vanishes with a click and another
click brings a swash of light into the tunnel.

Louise and I plaster ourselves to the dark walls,
avoiding detection but not avoiding the fact that it is
Rafi Nadir bearing a flashlight into our midst.

I also glimpse shadowy forms by the now-closed
mirror-door.

In sum, we are not alone, times three.

Louise has dashed across the aisle in the darkness
and now brushes against my shoulder. "Great. We are
here but so is the hired bodyguard. What do you suppose he wants?"

"Whatever he wants, it is worth tailing him. And keep
your nose alert for that noxious sweet scent I mentioned the other day."

"Shhh!"

Rafi turns and sweeps the flashlight over the unadorned wooden floor, missing us by that much.

We open our eyes once the searchlight has passed.
I hear slight scrabbling sounds behind us.

"Mice," Miss Louise dismisses them. "That is what
we are dealing with, not a murderer."

"A murderer is still in this house. We could, in fact, be
tailing him now."

This snaps her to literal attention.

"Rafi Nadir has the scent on his shoes?"

"Yes, but he could have picked it up out by the pool.
The hot sun had melted what traces of it I found that
day, so anyone could have accidentally stepped in it.

Except myself, of course. I have been certain to keep my toes well out of it."

Louise's tail is hitting the wood planking like a woodpecker's beak, hard and fast. That betrays her thinking. "So. This substance is a sure link to another murder scene . . . and to the mischief here, but like rabies it has spread to innocent carriers. Still, we might learn something by tracing every one who has spread it."

"Exactly."

"I admit that this Rafi Nadir has been showing up at every recent murder or crime scene for some weeks now."

"Agreed, yet I hate to suspect him. He treats my Miss Temple right, in his way."

"So he could not possibly be a killer," she concludes sarcastically. "Perhaps he is stalking your precious Miss Temple."

"I do not think so but I have detected the sticky substance on some others who might be."

"Such as—?"

"Do not forget the cameraman who tried to kick me when I first arrived."

"Right. I was not here then. I missed that. Pity."

"And Ken Adair, the Hair Guy."

"That could merely be some stinky hair gel that got on his shoe."

"True. Most of these girls would put recycled bubblegum on their locks if a beauty consultant told them to."

"Any other suspects?"

I hesitate.

"Spit it out, just not literally."

"Miss Sulah Savage, aka Miss Temple's aunt from Manhattan, whom I bunked with at Christmastime, Miss Kit Carlson."

"Whew! I did not guess the relationship. This place is a snarl of hidden relationships as well as secret tunnels. Miss Sulah Savage has been most generous to me with tidbits at mealtime. She could have innocently walked through a bit of it herself."

We hear a crack of something opening or shutting far down the corridor of darkness.

"Quick!" Miss Midnight Louise is all tracker now. "I do not want to lose Mr. Rafi."

We take off and there is a double echo of pad thumping wood behind us that only I hear, because I am listening for it.

We hit a hidden flight of stairs and go streaking down it too fast to stop. More dark hallway. Our whiskers ease us through, warning us before we slam our pusses into solid wall.

A far sliver of light tells us where Mr. Rafi Nadir has gone.

We race to that point, pause, and then Louise sticks her nose into the light. (She is very good at sticking her nose where it does not belong.) It widens to whisker width. The light comes from a lit lamp. In its intense circle, we spot Mr. Rafi bending over a desk and chair. I notice some fresh four-tracks on his upper arms, but he is too busy to pay much attention to a few wounds.

I realize where we are: on the wrong side of the crime scene tape, and so is he.

This does not seem to bother him as he moves around the room, examining this and that.

"This is Miss Marjory Klein's office," Louise hisses in my ear.

I flatten my offended appendage. Her hisses are sharper than a biker's switchblade.

We push against the wall as Mr. Rafi comes back into the passage, shuts the door disguised as a wall on the other side, and moves farther along it.

Last I had heard of the pursuing Persian girls was some muffled thumps on the surprise staircase and some choice curses in Farsi.

Amazing how one reverts to one's roots in times of stress, even natural blondes like the Divine Yvette.

Yet I dare not rush to her assistance and give away that we are not alone.

Rafi is sure giving the place the once-over. We follow him left and follow him right, and then follow him right into another office.

This is Ms. Beth Marble's office, and once again we are all on the wrong side of the crime scene tape.

Miss Louise is the first nose through the hidden door, of course, and she reports to me in short little pants.

"He is examining her drawers."

In other situations, this would not be rated family fare, but since Miss Beth Marble's mortal remains are long gone, I am sure that everything is above board.

Besides, it is clear to me that Mr. Rafi is tracing the passage's access to the crime scenes. Certainly it is clear how a body might be transported from Mr. Dexter Manship's office to this one without being observed.

In fact, I turn us around and, using my instinctive feline radar, lead Louise to a site that Mr. Rafi has not discovered yet.

There I instruct her to jump up at a certain spot until the apparent wall turns into a door.

I sit back on my haunches and enjoy the exercise, since it is not mine. Eventually she hits the sweet spot that opens the concealed entrance.

No light this time, as no one bearing a flashlight is in our party, but I bound inside, whisker my way to the desk, and leap up to punch the lamp's switch.

Light blinds me for a few seconds, but, sure enough, I am inside Mr. Dexter Manship's office. No doubt cameras are recording my presence. I recall too late the strange snipping noise that preceded Mr. Rafi into the offices he visited. He had cut the camera cords, which were no doubt placed too high for me to reach anyway.

Ah, well. I am very telegenic and will be dismissed as harmless vermin, as usual.

Miss Louise has skittered in at floor level and is sniffing deeply under the desk.

"Mr. Manship is indeed another bubblegum shoe suspect," she confirms my previous conclusion with satisfaction. "A pity everybody tiptoed through the exercise mats during the shaving cream graffiti episode. We need the film of that time to check who got close enough to infect their shoes."

"Yes, yes. Proof is fine, but right now I need suspects. Ours is not to make the case, ours is to point out the possibilities."

"How? We are hardly legitimate consultants."

"About your own suspected origins you may speak for yourself, Louise. I know my sire and dam."

"Braggart!"

I inhale deeply the atrocious tutti-frutti scent deposited under Mr. Dexter Manship's desk. It is particularly strong and there are even a few stringy remnants of the source. Let us hope his shoes are so endowed tomorrow, during the Teen Queen finals.

I have an urge to unmask a murderer, and cannot think of a more deserving candidate.

Miss Louise carps about our worthless expedition on our way back to the mirrored door.

I make no defense, and not only let her precede me back into Miss Savannah Ashleigh's domain, but show her the hall door with all due courtesy.

"I am going to inspect Miss Savannah's shoes," I tell

her. "No sense being sexist and omitting a female suspect. You may want to do the same with Miss Sulah Savage's closet. After all, she does use a pseudonym."

Off the little chit goes, dreaming of Manolos, as in Blahniks.

Personally, I do not think Miss Kit indulges in status symbols as blatant as Blahniks. So I wait by the mirror, checking the state of my best bib and tucker and licking it into submission.

On the room's king-size bed, Miss Savannah Ashleigh snores softly, no doubt the result of a Beverly Hills nose bob.

In a few moments, the unlatched door pushes open and girls silver and golden slide through. They are looking a bit mussed about the muzzle and decidedly annoyed.

"Louie!" Miss Yvette is in fine fettle, good mettle, and superb Ma Kettle mode. "You led us on zee wild goose chase. And aftair we had done zee hokey-pokey on the intruder's epidermis."

(When stressed, the Divine Yvette resorts to B-movie French.)

"Poor fellow," I say. "But I gathered lots of good intelligence."

"Somezing new *pour vous,* I tink."

Yvette is really, really mad. She is starting to sound like a voyageur. Wrong continent, wrong period.

"Those stairs were very sudden," her sister Solange rebukes.

And I am duly chastised. "But you both have the impeccable French nose for strong cheeses and rank fruit. Did you trace the raspberry/strawberry scent through the tunnels?"

"And banana," Solange adds.

"Banana?" I think she is making a value judgment. But *non.* I mean, no.

"There was a distinct undertone of banana. I ought to know. Our mistress uses a banana-scented sun screen."

Banana! Of course!

The scent that leads from the mall to here is not that of a mere ice cream treat; it is that of a healthful fruit smoothie!

Now I have nailed the full spectrum of ingredients that will lead to a murderer. Brought down by a high-protein health-food shake.

Somehow it is poetic justice.

I would boast of my breakthrough, but the Divine Yvette has lofted onto Miss Savannah Ashleigh's bed and wrapped herself around her percussive head.

Not only dogs are devoted.

Solange sees me to the door. "Was it something I said, Louie?"

I allow her to polish my sides with her softest, foxiest furs.

"Exactly. What a rare and subtle nose." (The French love these kind of compliments.) "Brilliant! Now I must prepare for the takedown tomorrow."

She wafts her fulsome plume under my own nose. "I am sorry Yvette is being such a pill. Perhaps you will come to tell me the outcome."

Perhaps I will. I chuck her under the chin with my most flexible member.

"Wish me luck, sweetheart."

"*Bonne chance,* Louie!"

Having restored international relations with our allies of old, I push out into the ordinary hall, walking on air and the inescapable scent of a spilled fruit smoothie that will trip up a murderer.

Chapter 54

No Glimpse
of Stocking

Max's watch read five past midnight when he climbed the Circle Ritz's conveniently stepped black marble facing up to the second-floor balcony of his and Temple's unit.

He was still officially half-owner. That's how he could make this clandestine expedition, knowing she was gone, with a semiclear conscience. No, nothing was clear about this intrusion except the night sky, spangled with stars.

He'd told enough necessary lies in his undercover work to recognize a story that was stapled together. Temple was gone, all right. Not to Minnesota though, and not to tend an ill father she hadn't even mentioned to Electra Lark. No, she'd just asked the landlady to look after the cat.

Speaking of Midnight Louie, Max had better be on the lookout for him. He wouldn't put it past the territorial old boy to trip him in the dark, since they both always wore black and were fairly invisible at night.

The French door lock gave to a few passes of Max's

tiny metal wand. He'd told Temple to secure these doors again and again, but she probably didn't want to interfere with Louie's comings and goings.

The main room was unlit. Faint night-light glows came from the office and kitchen, another concession to Louie probably.

He pulled out his slim high-intensity flashlight. The coffee table looked normal, including its clutter of scattered newspaper sections. Temple, an ex-newsie, was lost without newsprint nearby. None of the stories laid face up seemed relevant to anything: long security lines at McCarran Airport; one hotel mega-conglomerate offering billions for another; a reality TV show setting up shop in a deserted Vegas mansion. The usual nonsense that had made Las Vegas famous.

Max ran the light around the floorboards but no Louie lurked. Either crashing on the king-size bed or out to play while his mistress was away.

The bedroom would tell the tale of the trip. Max paused in the doorway, then shut the door and turned on the light.

Temple had definitely left in a hurry. Louie was not lounging on the bedspread because it was carpeted with clutter. Clothes, underclothes, and shoes were scattered everywhere. Everything but pantyhose. Temple hated hot, sticky hose. Never wore them. An admirable habit.

Empty thin plastic shopping bags also dotted the landscape, bearing names Max had never seen here before, like the Icing and Marvella's Marvelous Wigs.

Temple needed a wig to visit her sick father? Max started a serious search of the closet. Was she on some crazy undercover crusade again? All of her seriously dressy heels were still here. Her summer slides were scattered over the parquet floor, obviously tried on and stepped out of, but never put away.

She'd been in a hurry. She'd put a wardrobe together in

a flurry. At the dresser by the wall, a drawer had been plundered and left open, shutting askew and sticking, and then abandoned.

Max smiled to imagine Temple's hasty explosion of creative swearing. She never cursed with common expressions when a wacky euphemism was at hand.

The offending drawer was Temple's Sacrosanct Scarf Drawer, holder of every maternal Christmas present that had been found wanting, along with rosy purchases that soon proved completely wrong. All the things she didn't use but couldn't bear to throw out for one reason or another.

Max realized he missed the intriguing and amusing clutter of a female housemate. He missed Temple's clothes and sound and smell. He went over to set the drawer on its proper track, to stuff the colorful, gauzy scarves that refused to knot and tie properly for her back into their place of exile. As a magician, he had a far better way with scarves than she did. Maybe he'd make a bouquet of all her rejects and surprise her with it when she got back. From . . . wherever.

A tiny round box caught his eye, the cover off and something winking at him from inside it.

What winked was a ring, an inexpensive sterling gilt and cubic zirconia ring. The bottom of the box still had its adhesive price tag, thirty-eight dollars. One step above a Cracker Jack box trinket. Yet uncannily like the Tiffany opal and diamond ring he'd given Temple last Christmas when he'd come out of hiding and entered her life again. The ring that had been taken from her by a renegade magician named Shangri-La and had ended up in an evidence baggie in Lieutenant Molina's gloating custody.

Temple had spotted this cheap substitute somewhere and had bought it. Not worn it. Bought it. To remind her of the real one, and then tuck it away like something shameful.

Max could have strangled Molina if she'd been there. Could have kicked himself. He'd only learned what had happened to the ring recently. He should have gotten Temple another one ASAP, not left it to her to comfort herself with a substitute.

Not left it to her to comfort herself with a substitute. The echo of that phrase sounded suddenly sinister.

He sat on the bed and stared at the ring, then glanced at one of the abandoned shoes and picked it up. It lay on his large, strong hand like a curio. A curve of red silk-covered sole, a slender heel, a bejeweled band across the instep. Size five. Cinderella accessory, hands, and shoes, down. Made for a foot fit for a prince. One who actually showed up for balls.

Max put the shoe back down. He put the cover back on the box because he couldn't bear to look at the ring. Temple didn't wear her heart on her sleeve, or her disappointments on her finger. Obviously, his ring and its loss meant more to her than she'd allow to show. As had the promise he'd given with the ring that someday he'd be free to be a real boy, with a real girl for a wife and a public career again and a house somewhere full of the magic of her laughter, with a dragon of a scarf drawer he could tame into submission with the flick of one finger.

Another opened ring box caught his eye from across the room, this one plainer. He got up, put his hand out, then pulled it back as if contemplating touching white-hot metal. What the holy hell was this doing here? Gold metal. Real gold. A size big enough for a man's hand.

The ring was shaped like a huge snake coiled into a circle, its jaws closing on its own tail. The Worm Ouroboros. An ancient symbol of eternity. Given to Matt Devine by Max's own personal demon, Kathleen O'Connor, as a symbol of her undying hatred of them both.

Kathleen was gone. The ring had disappeared even before she had, to hear Devine tell it.

How the devil had it ended up here, in Temple's scarf drawer? Had Devine given it to her? Why? And when? And how could Max ask Temple without revealing that he'd come slinking around while she was gone, worried about her but even more worried about them, suspecting she'd lied to him? Now he was certain she had. About this trip, and about how much else?

How much had she had to comfort herself with a substitute?

He had to know. It couldn't be too late.

Chapter 55

Shoe Biz

To avoid an overstaged look, the madeover 'Tween and Teen Queen candidates would strut their stuff on a small stage near the pool at twilight time in Las Vegas.

Temple had thought the arrangement rather tacky until she saw the area that afternoon. Fresh lavender and yellow lotuses and lit candles floated in the pool. A semicircular array of clear Plexiglas folding chairs filled the large concrete expanse between pool and house. Banks of flowers turned the planting areas into mini gardens of Eden, with more candles burning on tall lily-shaped holders staked into the ground.

The raised stage was draped with pastel organza and seemed like a huge orchid cloud when viewed from the house.

Temple stared at the area's transformation into a kinder, gentler place, realizing that what would happen here tonight meant a lot to girls like Mariah. This was a kind of coming-out party, with the addition of killer media pressure.

"She may have seemed flakey," a voice behind her said, "but this event was really important to Beth Marble."

Temple turned to her Aunt Kit, who knew nothing of the woman's real identity, or her very dark history and issues.

"It reminds me of a garden wedding scene," Temple said. "I wonder—?"

"What?"

Temple only shook her head. She had wondered whether Crystal Cummings had married Arthur Dickson in this very spot. She'd have to look it up when this was over. If it ever would be over.

"Beth planned every detail of this setting," Kit went on. "It seemed to mean something special to her."

Temple nodded, glad that the police hadn't made the connection that the dead girl in the parking lot was Beth's granddaughter until after Beth herself was dead. Glad that she herself hadn't made that connection any sooner than now.

Even if Beth's hyper-happy exterior hid a vengeful heart, there must have been some healing energy there somewhere. The bald head under the wig screamed "cancer." Knowing you were likely to die might make the most stable person a bit crazy, maybe even for, or especially for, a long-delayed vengeance.

"You ready to wow them?"

Temple grinned at her aunt. "I'm ready to do the most unwinning act you ever saw. Get out your pencil and prepare to draw goose eggs."

"You should give it a real shot. I think Xoe Chloe could hit as one of those alter-ego personalities. Like Martin Short in the fat suit as Jimmy Glick on TV."

"Oh, Lord, no! There are enough closet performers in my circle."

"You mean Max?"

"Ah . . . yeah." She'd meant Carmen Molina but why confuse her aunt.

"Anyway," Kit said, squeezing her arm. "I think you underestimate Xoe's Midas touch. Break a leg."

On that contrary show biz good wish, Kit disappeared back inside like a fairy godmother off to minister to other Cinderellas.

Temple regarded the beautiful scene, not fussing about her little upcoming roller-rap routine, but about how to trick a killer into the open.

Beth Marble had dreamed up this entire event just to lure and kill a woman who had failed her daughter.

Who had penetrated Beth's carefully applied fake identity and used the hunter's trap to kill the hunter?

"Is she there?" Mariah tugged on Temple's ostrich-feather fringed sleeves, long enough for a medieval minstrel.

Temple pulled back from the crack in the side curtains.

"Yes. Your mother is about two-thirds of the way back, wearing 'our' outfit, with some guy."

"She's with some guy? That must just be Detective Alch."

"Alch is sitting elsewhere in the audience."

"Then it's some other girl's father or something."

"They were whispering with their heads together."

"Must be a cop." Mariah stuck her head through the curtain. "Must be . . . oh, gross. They're, like, laughing."

"Mariah. Audiences have a lot of time to kill. They do things like that."

"Where's Matt?"

"Out of town, I think. The guy does look like a cop, though. I wouldn't want to mess with him."

"That's not Xoe Chloe speak."

Temple pulled Mariah back to check out the open bar and the three bartenders. One of them was Su.

The videographers prowled the perimeter like hungry wolves, filming the audience, the scene, even the cat who dogged their footsteps, Midnight Louie.

In fact, he was doing more than dogging their footsteps, he was sniffing them, like a dog.

She spied Crawford Buchanan on the sidelines interviewing a Teen Queen candidate so tall he could look up her skirt by pretending to drop his notebook, which he was bending to pick up at the moment.

Creep.

Louie, perhaps drawn by the rolling pencil, had rushed over and was now sniffing his shoes.

Must be the muck that stuck.

"What's my mother doing now?" Mariah asked.

"She's, ah . . . pulling out one of those little mirrored lipstick holders and putting on lipstick."

"What? She never wears lipstick. It must be a secret signal." Mariah pushed past Temple to peek again.

"She is! And that guy is watching her. Ick! That is way too . . . too."

"I'm sure it's a signal," Temple said confidently. That was the truth. Public lipstick applying could be. But she looked again. Yup. The guy was watching Molina's every move. That kind of signal didn't usually bring on the tactical squad.

"Listen," she told Mariah, feathering her fingers through the new haircut for maximum "perk." "Just think about getting up on that stage without tripping and doing your talent routine. That's our job tonight. Let the police and your mom do their jobs."

"I wish Matt was here."

"I don't." Temple put a hand to her straight blonde hair, the lime green ostrich feathers on her long sleeves fluttering like wings in the corner of her eye. He'd have a bird!

"You look really . . . different."

"Higher praise I could not get. Now we better get into our lines and get ready to suffer through twenty-eight three-minute presentations. You know how long that is, counting applause, if we get any?"

That forced Mariah to think and get her mind off her mother's performance in the audience.

That's what it had to be, Temple decided. No way Molina was flirting. No way.

"Sixty," Mariah was saying, "an hour. And . . . twenty-four minutes."

"Add another forty minutes for the judges to score each act and for people to waste time getting on- and off-stage."

"We'll be here *forever!*"

"Certainly will feel like it." Temple pinched the curtain shut and prepared to be trapped backstage while all the action was going on out front.

Theater was like that. She just hoped the police found some likely suspect for the string of murders that had wiped out three generations of one family so far, a family already decimated by a miscarriage of justice that never ended.

Every blonde seemed to be ahead of Temple on the play list and every blonde seemed to do a Britney Spears song with every Britney Spears move ever patented.

The program alternated 'Tween and Teen Queen candidates, and Xoe Chloe was programmed dead last . . . wonder how that had happened, Temple thought, eyeing Dexter Manship at the judge's table. The peeping place she'd found was far stage left, behind a gargantuan array of gladioli spears. Nobody backstage or in the audience had spied her, so she was able to watch her competitors swivel and shake their way to true mediocrity.

When Mariah came through the curtain, it was like watching a tennis match. Snap her head to check her roomie's poise. Great. The judges. Positive. Mama. Stunned. The guy with her had to put a hand on her arm to keep her in her seat, or maybe to keep her from going for her semiautomatic.

Mariah looked, what? Girly grown up without seeming trashy. She looked all of nifty fifteen. She let the music precede her, as opposed to walking up to the mike and waiting like the other girls had, amateurs all. Make 'em wait. Then she began the strong yearning song of the lonely young Wicked Witch of the West from the Broadway hit, *Wicked*. Lyrics and melody showcased Mariah's girlish contralto. Even Molina was relaxing, tilting back in her chair. Shocked, awed, and smiling. "Defying Gravity" along with her daughter.

Way to go, roomie!

Temple joined the applause and watched the judges' pencils scratching high on their rating forms.

Somebody poked her in the back.

"Who is that?"

She turned. Rafi Nadir loomed over her and did not look happy.

"My roommate."

"Not the kid. She did okay. Who's that with—?"

He wasn't going to say but he was glowering at the unidentified man with Molina. Or maybe he was glowering at Molina.

Rafi did not know that Temple knew their personal history, so she just played dumb.

"Who?"

"Never mind. I'll go check the crowd."

He eyed Savannah Ashleigh, who had both cat carriers at her side. She'd take one or the other cat out from time to time and pretend the kitty was writing in the scores. Of course, she got lots of closeup camera attention every time she produced one of her gorgeous Persians.

Rafi vanished without another word, leaving Temple time to look around for Louie. Louie loved Persians, from her observation.

Yup. He was under the judges' table, the old dog! And snuffling at Dexter Manship's shoes. Maybe the old boy's sniffer was getting a little dull, to be diverted from nearby unfixed Persian pheromones to a neighboring guy's shoes!

Now he was nudging the Elvis impersonator's boots.

Louie must be losing it.

Oh, well, it happened to the best of them. Who knew how old he really was? Right now she herself felt about forty.

And nothing was happening.

The judges were watching. The audience was watching. And the police personnel were watching. Just watching.

Not only that, the evening event was almost over. Temple suddenly discovered a whole herd of butterflies in the pit of her stomach.

Xoe Chloe was up in two shakes of a blonde mane.

Time to stop fretting over hidden killers and start thinking about something serious, like sudden debilitating stage fright.

Why had she ever agreed to this debacle? Sure, it's fine for Xoe Chloe to make a fool of herself, but Temple had inherited some legitimate theater genes that demanded a decent performance.

Oh, well. Temple closed the curtain on her peephole and withdrew backstage to wrestle her contrary muse, Xoe Chloe, to the mat. Hopefully shaving foam free. . . .

The preprogrammed karaoke trio segued into the theme from James Bond.

Xoe Chloe burst through the side curtain, not the center one, on Rollerblades.

She spiked concrete on the space before center stage. Threw off her bicycle helmet, kicked off the blades. Tap danced up the three stairs to the mike.

She grabbed that sucker by the throat, tilted it almost horizontal like a rock star and strutted around it while rapping in rhythm, kick boxing, clapping, ostrich feathers flapping, on a beat in a counterpoint to the snare drum scratching and her high-heeled boots stamping and her blonde hair shaking and she said and she said, who knows, but the rhyme was the rhythm and rhythm was the reason and this was the Xoe Chloe season and . . . one . . . more . . . time, and then another . . . we speak to the sisters and we speak to the brothers and we walk around the world and watch it spin, and then we take it out for a walk and let the bows begin.

The applause was the climax to the routine. The judges were scratching furiously. Temple was blinking like the idiot she felt she was: standing center stage, the mike slowly swinging back to its proper upright position.

Louie was streaking out from under the judges' table—all their heads bent to the score sheets—and . . . apparently panicked by Temple's raucous routine, climbing up the judges with his claws.

Climbing up one judge's sturdy sleeve in particular, which resulted in a dark hairy object flying up, up, and away, toward the pool.

"Louie!" Temple wailed into the mike.

The audience started singing "Louie, Louie" as if cued.

But the dark flying object, or DFO, was not Midnight Louie. It was someone . . . some*thing* else.

A thing Temple knew well from personal experience. A black wig.

Elvis's sideburned headpiece.

Everyone eyed the bald man in the glittering jumpsuit, now flailing his arms at phantoms.

For Louie was gone.

Only the naked head was left.

The center of all regard.

The bull's eye that Alch and Su and a waiter and a man in the audience converged on.

Dexter Manship leaped up, snatched the score sheet from under the captive as he was rushed away, and leaped onstage to push Xoe Chloe away from the mike.

"Forget the fuss, dear hearts. We have our winners."

All the candidates rushed onstage to hear the verdict, pushing Temple to the back.

A hand was in hers, squeezing hard. Mariah's.

Manship's voice carried over everything, including the scuffle as Elvis was led away.

By the fringe of the pool, a rapt Crawford Buchanan was blabbing into his ever-present mike, unaware of a black stalking form closing in on him at foot level.

The black cat pounced, leaping, claws out.

Backpeddling, Crawford and his mike took a plunge into chlorinated water. No one even heard the splash. The night had an unhappy ending. He didn't drown.

Chapter 56

As Blind as Bast

Naturally, having masterminded the revelation of the criminal, I am thereafter ignored.

As soon as the police personnel present swarm the faux Elvis, they compare notes and conclude he bears a decided resemblance to a computer-aged image of . . . *ta-dah!* . . . Arthur Dickson.

The whole tawdry scheme is immediately clear to all and sundry, as it has been to me. (Naturally, I eavesdrop shamelessly, and unnoticed, as they gather to exchange notes.)

When ailing Crystal Cumming, aka Beth Marble, brought her scheme for the reality show to the producers, one of the silent partners was Arthur Dickson, forced underground by his narrow escape from prosecution for the first atrocity at his signature mansion.

Beth Marble, who no doubt took her false last name from the sad monument to the life and death of her shattered daughter and her own imminent fate, knew the mansion had passed through many hands. She envisioned it as a court of justice for the woman who had, perhaps inadvertently yet concretely, contributed to the final downward spiral of her unfortunate daughter.

In using the scene of the worst moment of her life for her revenge, poor Beth was unaware that her ex-husband had also been drawn back to the bloody battlefield. He had always known who she really was.

So he put himself into the TV show as a bizarre judge, and finally found Beth in his power again. Once she had stepped outside of the bounds of civility by killing her daughter's misguided therapist, he killed her, hoping to end forever the quest for vengeance that had forced him underground.

However—and this I heard direct from the lipsticked lips of Miss Lieutenant C. R. Molina as she explained it to a Mr. Paddock of her recent acquaintance, unaware of my collaboration at their foot level. Anyway, she told him (and thus me) that the body of the young girl in the mall parking lot was the suspect's step-granddaughter.

The police surmised that the poor girl had recognized "Beth Marble" on the TV previews as her grandmother, and had come to the mall to confront her and perhaps urge her to give up the quest for revenge.

Fate stepped in to demand a dance, as it so often does. A car nearly hit her in the parking lot. When the driver stepped out to see to her, young Tiffany recognized him from the old newspaper clippings she had been weaned on. Her surprise revealed her knowledge. Arthur Dickson, so long anonymous, grabbed a screwdriver from the back seat of his vehicle and ensured his continuing anonymity by killing his step-granddaughter, just as his violent actions twenty years before had wounded and ultimately destroyed his stepdaughter.

Whew. I am beginning to seriously re-examine my

relationships with my, er, esteemed long-lost maybe-daughter Midnight Louise. Like who wants a fang through the heart?

Before I can digest my ill-gotten information, I am surrounded by a congratulatory frill of Persians. Much thrumming and purring and swishing.

Miss Louise also shows up, returning from a successful expedition to scare Crawfish back into the pool a second time. It is certain he will never cross paths with a black cat again.

"Louie," cries Yvette in her sweet soft voice. "You have singlemittedly revealed a villain and also dunked the lowlife who was always after zee dirt on my mistress."

"Well, yes," I admit. Then I glance at Miss Midnight Louise, who is a trifle damp but no less triumphant. "However, my associate was on the Crawfish Puke-cannon case."

"Your associate?" The Divine Yvette lifts a perfectly groomed eyebrow.

"Actually," I say, "she is my partner. In business, that is. And my . . . possible offspring."

"Louie! You have admitted offspring?"

"Well, just one. One small insignificant one. Maybe."

"You are an admitted single father?"

"Maybe. These things happen to a guy. Like they have been known to happen to a girl. It could be worse. It could be a whole litter. Or a few dozen."

The Divine One shows me the underside of her tail, which is not too tacky, as she leaves. "I do not date secondhand goods."

I am left alone with Miss Midnight Louise, who is not looking any too happy at my recent description of her.

But she holds her tongue for once, and sniffs, as I have been doing much of lately.

"Good capture," she notes. "Small loss."

That is for her to say and me to gnash my fangs over.

The Past Is Prologue

Supposedly Matt had people skills.

Sixteen years as a parish priest and one as a hotline and radio counselor should qualify him for anything.

He sat at a table in the Drake Hotel bar, all wood paneling and leather. His hotel would be the neutral ground. He felt like an anxious diplomat arranging for a secret meeting between Bush and Osama bin Ladin. The situation was explosive. So much could go wrong.

His mother arrived first, as arranged. She was wearing the Virgin Mary blue blouse and blue topaz earrings he'd bought her for Christmas with a gauzy black and silver skirt that had the Krys influence all over it.

She was a knockout.

She scanned the room expertly. Confidently. Serving as hostess at a popular tourist restaurant had given her a new social poise. Dating again must have helped. Matt remembered the distinguished man in the camel-hair coat she'd seated so graciously when he'd dined alone in "her" restaurant last Christmas.

Finding him, her dark eyes sparkled with greeting. She rushed over on her low-heeled pumps. Another symptom of the hostess job. Easy Spirit shoes for tired feet: neat, attractive, but not showy. The phrase could describe his mother's overall impact.

He stood to seat her. Bars always had such heavy chairs that women found hard to sling around. Maybe to promote male chivalry. Maybe to anchor tipsy customers for another round or two.

"Matt." Her lips brushed his cheek before she sat.

No one would call this woman beaten down but that would have described her just months ago, before she moved out of the old two-flat filled with bad memories in the Polish section of Chicago and into a new apartment, job, and the strange cross-generational alliance with her punkish art student niece Krystyna.

Somehow, they were good for each other; so good they sometimes scared the heck out of him, between Krys's obvious interest in him and his mother's simultaneous emotional unthawing after years of repression and guilt.

She knew that she was to meet someone important to her quest to find out about the man who'd fathered him, the boy who'd gone off to combat after meeting her in the St. Stan's church the night before Christmas.

"I can't believe you've found something out," she told him, ignoring the waitress who hovered behind her. Matt had been out of the priesthood long enough to know that cocktail waitresses at your table side were a boon in most bars, a boon that might not be repeated for too long.

"Have something, Mom."

She glanced at the lowball glass in front of him. "A . . . scotch on the rocks."

"House brand okay?"

She expertly eyed the bottles behind the bar, another new talent. "No. Johnny Walker Black."

Go, Mom, go! You'll need it.

"Who is this? One of the lawyers who offered me the deal back then?"

"I met him at the lawyers' offices." Temporizing.

"Thank you for doing this. I know they just would have blown me off."

Blown me off? Krys again.

She sat back as the drink was wafted onto a napkin before her.

"I can't believe you got somewhere. Cheers." She lifted the glass. Their rims clicked. She seemed excited and happy.

"It wasn't easy. They blew me off too on the first visit. So I came back and hung around the floor, watched who came and went."

"Just like a detective. Like that young lady friend of yours you say isn't a serious girlfriend. Tamara, was it?"

"Temple."

"Odd name for a girl." She sipped again, and sighed. "But they're doing that these days."

"It suits her."

"That's just because you're used to it. Because you like her. A lot. Don't try to duck that. A mother knows. Maybe you can bring her up here for next Christmas."

"Maybe. Mother—"

"I thought we'd gotten past that formal stuff. Krys doesn't even call me 'aunt' anymore. In fact, we were out shopping and someone mistook us for sisters. Can you imagine?"

"Yeah. You look . . . really great, Mom. Someone would probably mistake us for siblings too."

"I'd be honored to have such a handsome brother. Your uncles have all let beer bellies have their way with them. Don't you do that."

"No chance. Uh, Mom, this person we're going to meet, he didn't know anything about what the lawyers arranged."

"You mean he was taken in the way I was?"

"Well, he was pretty young back then too. That's how I connected to him; he had no idea that they'd offered you the two-flat as a bribe to keep me and you out of the family. He was pretty shocked. And angry."

"Anyone decent would be. It's not that I would have wanted anything more than some legitimate child support. The two-flat did help but it wasn't a substitute for a simple acknowledgment. So how did you find this man with a conscience?"

"A paralegal dropped a name she shouldn't have."

"What would that have to do with it?"

"It was my father's name."

"Why would that mean anything to you?"

"Because I saw a man who had that name. And he looked like me."

"Oh, Matt." Her celebratory air crumbled. "That must have been so . . . shocking for you. I didn't think that might happen. That any relatives would still be associated with that law firm. What . . . was he? To you." She bit her lip, reached out a hand to his. "I'm so sorry, honey. I didn't think what sending you there might mean. I was so selfish."

The old apologizing-for-existing Mira was back. As much as her concern touched him, her regression chilled him. Maybe this was a very bad idea, even though it had been hers. He could still head this off.

"It was rough. I was way angrier than I thought I'd be. Then I found out that . . . members of the . . . other family had been duped too. It was the parents. Your parents. His parents. They took over and managed their errant kids, the hell with what the ones actually involved needed or wanted. Or what it would mean to me."

"You shouldn't swear," old Mira said primly, falling back on the party line.

"I should do a lot more than that. I should dig up all those dead grandparents who decided what was best for my parents and hit them."

She looked shocked, then smiled nervously. "Berating the dead is a waste of time. You know that. If they'd have known you, they'd have been proud of you. My parents couldn't quite get past your . . . manner of birth but they didn't dislike you."

"Not a positive relationship, Mom. I was tolerated but I don't remember them much."

She sighed and sipped her drink.

"So," he said, "given what a shock it was for me to meet a . . . relative, I'm thinking maybe you don't need to go back like this. Maybe it's enough to know not everybody in the family would have disowned us. That it was a Romeo and Juliet thing, where the older generation controlled the younger at a horrible cost."

"Romeo and Juliet." Her smile softened her features to a girl's dewy promise. "That's right. That was the way it was. Have you ever glimpsed that connection so right the whole world fades away?"

He wanted to temporize, as he always did on this one thorny subject but . . . his mother needed the truth, from everyone.

"Yes."

Her eyebrows lifted. "Someday you'll tell me more about that. Or maybe not. Someday maybe I'll meet her."

"Mom, I've met yours."

"My what."

"Your person who made the world fade."

"You can't have."

"I did."

"Someone close . . . a brother? Is that who we're meeting here? I don't know if I can stand to meet a brother."

"Mom." He stretched both his hands across the table to cover hers, which were fanning and fidgeting with panic. "I've met him."

"He's dead. Are you crazy?"

"He's not dead. That was a lie."

She stood, despite the heavy chair, pushing it back with her legs as if she didn't feel the effort.

"What are you saying?"

"You know what I said. But it doesn't have to go further. I have a cell phone number. He can go away and never see us again at all."

Her hand covered her mouth as if choking off a terrible cry.

"Not . . . dead? But—"

"He was . . . is from a wealthy family. Mistakes weren't welcome in it. That's all. He was told you were impossible to find."

"The lawyers found me fine! He believed them?"

"They were convincing. Private detectives reported that they could find no girl named Mira in St. Stanislaus's parish."

"There were three in my high school class!"

"No right girl named Mira."

"He believed them."

"He'd been wounded. He was tired, confused. I can't blame him, and, believe me, I wanted to more than I knew."

"So. You've sorted it out. You two. You men. And now it's up to me if I want to see him again."

"Yes."

"Does he want to see me?"

"Yes."

"Why?"

"Because he hates that he was deceived. He would have done the right thing."

"But he doesn't love me."

"He's married."

"With children?"

"Yes."

She folded her lips. "I'm sorry, Matt. You're the real victim of this. I'm sorry you had to learn what cold people you came from, partly. I'm sorry, sorry, sorry I asked you to look into this. You have a very stupid mother."

"I have a very stubborn mother and I'm not sorry."

"Why the hell not?"

"Swearing, Mom?"

Her lips twisted into an unwilling smile, despite the tears in her eyes. "Sometimes it's called for. Why aren't you sorry?"

"I'd rather know my father was lied to as well. That he wouldn't have turned his back on us."

"So he says now, seeing you face to face."

"I believe him."

"Well, fine. Can we go now?"

"Let me pay the tab first."

"Tab? You expected a long night of drinking and reminiscences maybe?"

"I don't know what I expected. You're the one. Whatever you want or need. We agreed on that."

"You and your . . . father. Why do I feel it's always a conspiracy of men?"

"There are so many of us? Really. Take your time. You can always change your mind."

"No, Matt. I can't. I haven't been able to act according to my own mind since that night that changed everything. Let's leave. Your cousin Krys gets moody when I monopolize you too much. That girl! All hormones. No shame. Wish I'd been like her. Nothing would have mattered as much."

"You underestimate Krys. Everything matters too much with her. And I like you just the way you are."

"You can't fool me. That's a Billy Joel song. 'Just the

Way You Are.' The Muzak at the restaurant plays it all the time."

He sighed, signed the credit card slip, and left a generous tip.

They walked out of the bar's calculated dimness into the glaring brightness of the hotel lobby, all slick marble floors and walls and glittering oversize chandeliers.

At the bank of house phones, he saw Winslow and nodded imperceptibly.

He thought.

His mother wrenched her neck in that direction, stared for a long moment, then took his arm and drew him toward the rank of glass doors leading to the hotel porte cochere.

He saw her into a cab and sent her to work at Polandski's Restaurant.

Then he turned and went back in to have a postmortem with his father.

"So how did it go?" Krys asked when he got back to his mother's apartment way too late.

"You didn't have to wait up for me."

"Mira won't be off her shift until midnight. How did it go?"

"It didn't."

"You look horrible."

"From you, that's a new one."

"I mean you look like you've been through it."

"Imagine brokering a truce between Israel and Palestine."

"That bad? I made some hot tea."

"Like I need caffeine."

"I've never seen you testy before."

"She didn't want to see him and I had to tell him afterward."

"Testy on you is not bad, mind you."

Matt wasn't too emotionally exhausted to smile, which she'd wanted to make him do. Among other things. He couldn't encourage her hopeless crush, but he knew a lot more about longing and forbidden love and all that sticky emotional stuff now than he'd known the first time they'd met last Christmas. He had to respect her feelings even as he had to discourage them. Had to clear the decks for the real guy who was waiting for her somewhere down the road to maturity.

"Krys. Mom's going to be coming home very soon and I don't want to go into anything deep now. I'd like to be safe in my room, totally out of it."

"That could be arranged."

"Krys. No. You're a sweet, funny girl but not my girl. This is way out of your league."

"No, it isn't. It looks like it's about them—him and her—but it's about you. You're in the middle. I don't care how smart you are, or how cool you act, or how . . . shrinky. It's gotta be awful."

He took the cup of tea she held out. "Herbal," she told him, sounding like a nurse. "Won't get on your nerves, like I do."

He had to smile. Again.

But he was glad to be leaving Chicago tomorrow.

Chapter 58

Showdown

Mariah searched the audience. The spotlights had panned earlier on Molina and escort in row five, beaming. Well, Molina was actually smiling. The guy with her had the quizzical expression of a classic observer.

"Mom!" Mariah ran to join her in the audience now that the swirl of excitement was over. Mariah had lost but so had Elvis. Not bad company.

A vapid blonde had won Temple's erstwhile division, and a younger vapid blonde had won Mariah's. They'd both applauded politely, and whispered "wicked" at each other, then giggled.

Temple glanced out of the corner of her eye at Rafi Nadir. He was watching the Molina family reunion with the slow-mo reaction of Tommy Smothers trying to come up with the right answer for his brother, Dick. Wheels turning, mired in alternatives, searching for the one, the right answer.

With the Smothers Brothers it was high comedy. With Rafi Nadir and Carmen and Mariah Molina it could be high tragedy.

Temple felt her neck and shoulder muscles clench. Nothing a knowledgeable PR ace could do about this kind of crisis.

Molina never acknowledged Nadir's presence, existence, anything about him.

Temple could read the pantomime in the impromptu family vignette arranged for the cameras: Larry, the new guy, scooted down so Mariah could sit by her mother, who was making all the proud and proper maternal motions. Larry was leaving the spotlight—and the television coverage, Temple noticed—to mother and daughter. Was that sensitivity . . . or a need to avoid being recognized?

She eyed Nadir again. Still mentally doing the math, trying to figure out when Mariah must have been born . . . impossible to calculate without her birth date.

Temple bet he would get it somehow, as soon as possible. Molina had ducked the inevitable tonight, partly through the strategy of her new male escort . . . was he hired muscle? Something about him read "professional" along with "don't tread on me."

Temple waited until the spotlight and camera lens had moved on to the next performer before skittering over to congratulate Mariah in a whisper.

". . . great," Molina was whispering to Mariah. "Listen. I think you're old enough now. There's something you should know."

Molina spied Temple and stopped talking, darn it!

Temple leaned down and hugged Mariah. "Great job on the song. Sorry you didn't win."

"Wow. I feel like I have. Mom, Temple has been just the best roomie in the whole world."

"Apparently, you're not the only one who thinks so," Molina responded. Mariah missed the sardonic tone, and the veiled reference to Max Kinsella. "She certainly delivered when it came to crisis control. Let's all go out and celebrate. No, don't slink away, Miss Barr. You too, 'roomie.' Larry can take you girls in his car and I'll run ahead and get things ready.

"First I have to settle the hash of the creep behind all the nasty pranks on the set."

"You've got him?" Temple asked.

"My excellent undercover officers." Molina looked a bit uneasy. "They found incriminating materials in his camera bag but it seems he hated cats as well as women."

"Often goes together," Temple said. "Both can be independent."

Molina sighed at her political comment.

"Whatever." She paused, then grimaced and plunged ahead with the apparently galling facts. "Seemed he tried to kick a couple of Persians out of his way during the mass exodus. My guys were already looking to grab him, but they found him pinned to the latticework wall beside the pool by a pair of rabid black cats and Savannah Ashleigh. I think she broke every artificial nail on her fingers clawing tread marks into his face. The arresting black cats, being shorter, went for tender parts lower down. We don't have to worry about getting a confession."

"Gross. But what's the big secret about tonight?" Mariah was finally coming down from her performance afterglow and tuning into her mother's strange comment.

"You'll find out soon," Molina said. "If Hollywood doesn't come calling right away, we can leave."

"Oh, Mom. I knew I wasn't gonna win. But who needs to?"

"That's a very mature attitude, Mariah."

"Who needs to be a stupid 'Tween Queen? I'm going for *American Idol* next."

Molina speechless was a sight to behold. "We'll see," was all she could come up with.

Temple tried to slip away. "Stay," Molina said. "Sit," Molina said next.

They were commands you gave to a dog, but Temple decided she would be magnanimous and not ruin Mariah's big night. Poor kid. She was about to learn the bodyguard at the competition was her daddy.

Molina had more guts than Temple gave her credit for.

Larry winked as he moved over to give Temple his seat, as if guessing every turn of her internal debate.

After the closing hoopla was over, Kit came running up to them.

"Fabulous job, girls! Of course you both earned my top honors and should have won your divisions but that cretin Dexter was fixated on boob size and that tipped the balance, excuse the expression. I am so disgusted. The other judges and I are making protests but frankly without Elvis—I mean just by the numbers—we're not likely to make anybody listen. The cameramen and producers are fixated on boob size too."

Her effusions stopped as she regarded Temple. "Ah, a limo service has arrived to convey me back to my hotel, but the vehicle seems rather crowded by individuals and accessories of purely Italian manufacture. Am I going to get 'taken for a ride' out into the desert, or what?"

Temple grinned. "I see the fabulous Fontana Brothers have arrived. You may recall my mentioning them to you."

"Yes, I do. And they are as collectively cute as a silencer on a Beretta, but is going with them safe?"

"I don't know, Aunt. Do you particularly care?"

"You're so right. I'll take two aspirin and call you in the morning." She was off on her high-heeled Blahnik slides. Off to see the Wizards of Las Vegas. *Wicked!*

"I don't get it," Mariah said. "They sent her multiple limousine drivers?"

"It's a very long stretch limo. Let's blow this crooked contest, kid."

Mariah and Temple/Xoe left in turn as the crowd shuffled out. No easy way for Rafi Nadir to fight the flow and reach them, though Temple knew he could if he wanted to.

But she never saw him again, not even when she and Mariah stood under the porte cochere and waited for Larry and whatever kind of car he was driving.

"Good job," she told Mariah again. "Your mother nearly flipped when you sang that song."

"She liked it? I couldn't see with all those lights."

"She loved it. And I did too."

"It didn't win me anything though."

"How about your mother's confidence? That's a hard thing to get when you're thirteen to nineteen. Trust me. Been there, haven't done that yet."

"Your mother doesn't have faith in you?"

"Yeah, sure, in a general way. But mothers have a hard time trusting that you'll hang with a decent crowd at school, or wear non-slutty makeup and clothes, or lock your car doors when you're driving alone at night."

"I don't have to worry about that driving thing for three years, remember. You're the one who harped on it."

"Right."

"So your mother still doesn't really trust you. And you're . . . ancient."

"That's true. My mother doesn't entirely trust my judgment and I'm ancient."

"It's not us then, it's our 'judgment.'"

"Right. They think any hunky guy can send it out the window."

"My mom thinks your hunky guy should go out the window. I know that."

"She's not my mom, thank goodness. The one I have already is enough."

"What do you think of that Larry guy?"

"Too soon to tell. What do you think of him?"

"I can't believe she's, like, dating him. I've never seen

her date anyone. Is that what she wants to tell me, the secret, do you suppose?"

"Too soon to tell." Temple felt like a skunk for ducking the issue, but this really was just between mother and daughter.

A black Jeep Cherokee pulled up. Larry's angular face caught the wall-mounted torch light as he leaned over to open the passenger door.

Mariah hopped into the back seat, leaving Temple to scramble up into the SUV passenger seat in her tight skirt and heels.

Larry gave her one of those quick assessing male looks that said he wasn't displeased but not personally interested. Maybe Molina had hit paydirt.

Temple looked around, hard, before they took off. Rafi Nadir was nowhere in sight.

Now why did that scare the living shih tzu out of her?

They ended up in the Blue Dahlia parking lot.

Temple gave Larry a warning look when he came around to help her and Mariah out of the Jeep.

He shrugged at Temple and gave Mariah a reassuring grin. "That was a world-class performance, kiddo. You've got a ripe set of pipes."

Temple scanned the parking lot for signs of Rafi Nadir. That was the trouble. If he was here, there would be some.

"You always this nervous?" Larry asked with a quick whisper.

"We did just come from a murderer-grabbing scene."

"History. I have a feeling you don't dwell on it. Neither do I. What else is bothering you?"

"Nothing."

He laughed. "Women are the best little stonewallers in the business. And we guys call you the weaker sex."

Temple eyed Mariah nervously. She'd been through a lot, plus the poor kid was half-starved.

"It's their business," Larry warned.

"True, but why do I feel you're butting into it?"

He laughed again. "You're one sharp cookie, aren't you?" His hand on her elbow was custodial as he steered her inside behind Mariah's happy jazz steps as she took in the artsy neon and the bluesy adult façade of the Blue Dahlia.

It was the kind of place Travis McGee would boogie into without a regret.

Temple hoped that more modern folk of the female persuasion wouldn't regard it as a hothouse of worse things than mere regret.

"This place is so cool!"

Mariah eyed the cocktails on the surrounding tables, the all-adult clientele.

She was feeling thirteen-going-on-thirty tonight, an emotion Temple remembered well.

So this was the secret Molina was going to unveil. A small, glamorous secret to start with, before the main course, which was large, hard to swallow, and indigestible.

Temple had become close enough to Mariah during their days as faux roommates to feel her stomach churning with anxiety. What if her own mother had revealed a hidden past as a . . . belly dancer! How would Temple, age thirteen, have reacted?

She couldn't be certain, but not with unbridled joy, for sure. Oh, Mother! The breed was so embarrassing to begin with. What if Mariah found Carmen laughable? Temple felt herself cringing for the risk Molina was taking, then thought of the bigger one she'd have to take later.

"How long have you known Molina?" Larry asked her

after ordering a Shirley Temple for Mariah and a half-bottle of pink zinfandel for them.

"Too long and not enough."

"My feelings exactly. She isn't easy."

"Why should she be?"

"Right. I'm not either."

"What are you, then?"

He glanced at Mariah to make sure that she was busy eavesdropping on the sophisticated blues lovers at the other tables, and the sophisticated lovers, period. The Blue Dahlia was a favorite trysting place. Carmen's torch songs were music to make semipublic love by.

"I carry a shield, like you didn't know," Larry said, way too laidback for a man in blue.

Temple didn't doubt him. This was a cop but an unconventional cop. The combination was intriguing and, she sensed, dangerous. She hoped Molina knew what she was doing.

The jazz trio ended a riff. There was a moment of transition. Were they going to take a break? Or not?

Not. Carmen merged with the narrow velvet curtains behind the instrumentalists, then passed through, blue velvet fog in motion.

She was at the lone stool, mike in hand, like smoke in a mirror. Not there, and then there, etched irrevocably.

Mariah's jaw dropped before the first low, minor notes of "The Man I Love" escaped her mother's lips.

Everything about Molina that was larger than life and downright intimidating in reality became cinematic and dramatic on a musical club set.

It was intimacy writ large. The microphone seemed an accessory after the fact to her true, husky voice, both bel canto and hip.

She wove a vocal spell. The dignified sheen of vintage forties blue velvet that made femininity into a sculpted, strong icon was part of that spell. Women had seemed both sturdy and sexy then, part of the war effort maybe. Rosie the Riveter as Venus de Milo.

It was hard for Temple to credit this view of womanhood, her being so small and so often underestimated because of it. But . . . hey, the goddess/Amazon type never died.

"That's my mom," Mariah breathed.

"Yup." Larry.

Boy, men were inarticulate about feelings!

"Yeah," Temple told Mariah. "Quite a set of pipes. I don't think anyone knows about this now, besides us."

Mariah sat back, a troubled expression on her face. "Why'd she keep it a secret?"

"Imagine what the guys at work would say? What would the boys at school say about you? Miss 'Tween Queen singer/hip-hop heroine/beauty queen?"

"Oh. Not good. I don't get it. We're supposed to be pretty and talented and we're supposed to be . . . no competition."

"You got it. That's right. Doesn't make sense. Guys often don't."

"Then why do we bother with them?"

"You gotta answer that one for yourself."

Mariah regarded Larry.

"What?" He sounded defensive.

"You don't look worth much."

"Appearances are deceiving. Look. I'm your mother's biggest fan. She's good, isn't she?"

"Yeah. She is. Is that why you like her?"

"Right." He high-fived her.

Temple watched Mariah ratchet another puzzle piece of life into place. This had been a busy week for her.

Something was disturbing here though. Molina had left the real secret, Mariah's father, securely closeted. Temple had assumed that was the thing Mariah was "old enough to know" now. Apparently not. Apparently Molina could be as much of a coward as the next woman, if the right stakes were involved.

And then, at the mike, Molina/Carmen sat back on the stool. She nodded at the instrumentalists and segued, a capella, into "Mariah."

She sang it low and slow. It wasn't nightclub fodder. It was a musical-stage number, dramatic and mock Western. It wasn't urban, it wasn't hip but it was powerful and it was pure torch song in its dark, contralto melody, meant for a man to sing, with unexpected hints of tenor, or tender soprano in this case.

The song started "way out here." The frontier. The urban edge. The selvage of self. The rain had a name. Tess. It hissed. The fire had a name. Jo. It spat. The wind was something else. More than monosyllabic. The wind was a woman named Mariah. *Mah-rye-ah.* This woman turned the stars around and made the trees sigh and whine. This woman wind was an icon for "only" and "lonely."

Molina's voice made the wind mourn, made loss a sustained note, made the word "Mariah" into the most beautiful elongated three syllables in the English language.

Temple, caught up in the exquisite beauty of the styling, still managed to gauge the reactions around her. She was a PR woman; she always took a room's ambient temperature.

Mariah, herself, was enraptured by the poetry of her name, which she really understood for the first time.

Larry. Larry was no doubt enamored by the artistry of the woman he escorted, but was there more than that to his sudden pursuit of Molina?

Temple sat by herself, moved but measuring, sensing, understanding. A siren had sung, momentarily throwing off her human guise. Each person here had heard a different song.

Temple—cursed by the gift of Cassandra, the prophet

no one would believe—could see that some good, and a lot of bad, would probably come from this night, this siren song, this guarded family of two that was being inexorably circled by unpredictable outside forces.

Chapter 59

An Invitation She Can't Refuse

"Temple."

Matt stood speechless when she answered his knock. It wasn't just the longish straight blonde hair—

"Don't worry. I'll get rid of it."

"Your *eyes* will wash out? Temple, they're green. Is it some strange dietetic reaction?"

"Don't mention dietetic reactions! One of those was murder on my last case."

"Have I got the right unit?"

"I just forgot about the green contacts. Let me go change them. The hair will have to be redyed to my natural color, then grow out. Come in. Sit down. Hang on. I'll be right back."

Matt did as instructed, which left him confronting Midnight Louie and his thoroughly natural green eyes over the flimsy barrier of a throw pillow.

Other than Temple's radical change of appearance,

everything else around her place seemed the same. Seemed . . . normal.

She came clattering back over the hardwood floors on a pair of feminine and creative shoes. That was the same, thank goodness.

"So. How was Chicago?" she asked.

He was still speechless.

"Well?"

"I found my father."

"Matt! No. I can't believe it. You found out who he was, finally?"

"No. I found out who he *is*. Found him."

"Found his grave, you mean?"

"No. Him. The Jonathan my mother only knew by his first name. I had to stake out the Winslow family lawyer's office to do it. You'd have been proud of me, undercover detective."

"But, Matt, wasn't he supposed to be dead? My God! You're so calm."

"His family told my mother he was dead to get rid of her, and me. It's all over. We met and talked. It's pretty disconcerting to meet someone you resemble for the first time, but he's a stranger, after all. It wasn't his fault. His family was wealthy and controlling, which goes together all too often. They high-handedly rearranged his life too."

"I can't believe it."

"It's pretty amazing. My mother wanted to find out who he was. The family had told her, via their attorney, that he'd died overseas and they gave her a two-flat, a Chicago-style duplex, as a sort of settlement. So she never expected to see him again on this planet. When it happened, when I discovered him while badgering the attorney's office—"

"'Badgering'? You?"

"When some high-end attorney starts brushing you off with obvious evasions it makes you pretty darn mad. I thought I might find his parents. My grandparents. I wanted no more to do with them than they had wanted to do with me thirty-five years ago. I only did it because my mother wanted closure and I thought that would be healthy for her. She's never really tried for a real life of her own. So . . . I find him. And she wanted nothing more to do with it. Or him. Funny. I couldn't have cared less until it happened."

"So, what's the story?"

"Ancient history. His family kept them apart, kept him ignorant of her, and me. He's got a whole new family, and life. Seems like a decent guy. He feels pretty cheated too. My mother's . . . not happy. I'm okay with it. I'm here."

Temple plopped down next to him, forcing Louie to scramble for new high ground: the cushion tops behind them.

"Amazing. You're so calm."

"What does it change? It was Romeo and Juliet from two different classes instead of clans. Their families imposed their own priorities on their wayward kids. I feel for my mother but it's too late to change anything. Except," he added, "the present. So what kind of tangle have you been involved with while I was gone?"

She told him, including her reservations about the Molina/Nadir/ Larry/Mariah quadrangle.

"Wow. Carmen is ratcheting up the stakes on all fronts, isn't she?"

"Carmen? You call her that? Since when?"

"Occasionally. When I really want her attention. Her name is the key to her background. That's why she doesn't use it professionally. Carmen Regina. Regina means 'Queen of Heaven.' All very Hispanic and very Catholic."

"I'm not very Catholic."

"That's what I like about you."

"Why?"

"I get to keep the guilt concession all to myself when I'm with you."

She looked a little nervous. He discovered he loved being able to make her nervous.

"Guilt isn't a Unitarian thing," she said finally.

"Fine. Leave it up to me."

"Have you something guilty in mind?"

"Maybe. Let's go out."

"The Bellagio, you said."

"The new you deserves it."

"You won't be ashamed to be seen with my blatantly blonde hair?"

"I wouldn't be ashamed to be seen with you with chartreuse hair. I've still got a couple days left on my vacation from the radio station. They're running 'Mr. Midnight's Classic Moments' this week." Matt shrugged an apology at the corniness of his employer. "Okay if I pick you up tomorrow at eight? I'm thinking of that purple taffeta dress you wore once."

"You want me to wear it again?"

"It wasn't too shabby."

"You want me to dress a certain way?"

"Catholic guilt."

She hesitated before answering. "That's kinda . . . erotic."

"The best kind of guilt."

"Not the black with the buttons—?"

"Not this time."

She swallowed. She was right. This conversation was getting incredibly erotic. "'This time'?"

"I hope so."

"Matt—?"

"Temple."

"You are way too . . . confident."

"You like dithering?"

"Maybe."

"Tomorrow. Eight."

Her eyes were wide, blue-gray. Looked incredible with the blonde hair. The Teen Queen people had remade her into somebody beyond her current persona. For the first time, Matt felt that Max Kinsella could be a name in a history book. For the first time, he felt like he was writing his own life, and maybe Temple's life too.

"I think you're saying yes," he said.

"Yes."

He left, feeling something in his core that was deep and tender and strong, stronger than anything anyone had ever taken away from him. Strong beyond weakening. Love, surely.

Sex. Maybe.

Chapter 60

Caught in the Crossfire

Temple wasn't usually nervous before a dinner date. Dinner dates were the most formal form of coupling, easily written off as exploratory and way too public to offer anything more than mild flirtation.

She wasn't stepping out on Max. Just socializing, right? Besides, Max was pretty hard to step out on since he'd hardly been around lately. He'd never noticed she'd been away from the Circle Ritz. Had left her high and dry in the hot tub, his hot tub. This had nothing to do with Max and their long monogamous relationship. Right. The relationship that was turning into a monologue instead of a dialogue, with Temple asking the leading questions and Max ducking them like she was an obnoxious insurance agent. This was not about Max. No. It was about Matt, who had been ducking her for good and scary reasons but was definitely over that now.

Maybe digging out her old purple taffeta prom dress

and trying it on in the bedroom mirror was putting her on edge. At least the Teen Queen diet ensured she could easily pull up the back zipper.

Temple surveyed her past self in the full-length mirror, ignoring the bizarre hair color above the neck. This dress was so twelve years ago. Strapless, close-fitting ruched princess torso. Sheer chic then, today it felt like wearing curtain from an Austrian whorehouse. Belled skirt like an exotic blossom with her legs the stem. This dress had been selected after she'd been invited to the prom by a dorkish date. Temple, too soft-hearted to just say no, had chosen the full crackling skirt so she wouldn't be afflicted during slow dances by knowledge of the casual date in homo erectus state. It was icky to think of oneself as a blowup doll for the socially challenged set. Poor guys, hormones will . . . well, out. That didn't mean she had to be the scene of the crime.

Back to now and a definitely nondorky guy. Being a vintage-everything lover, Temple wasn't bothered by the dress's dated look. But something bothered her. Maybe it was her unadorned chest and neck. She couldn't remember what she'd worn with the dress to her real prom back in Minnesota, which showed how unmemorable that had been. In fact, it had been the usual night of uneasy embarrassment, having been asked by someone she wouldn't have asked to the prom if girls could do the selecting.

So . . . she needed a fresh necklace anyway. Her three-tier costume jewelry chest didn't offer anything right. And then she remembered . . . Should she? It would be a nice gesture. Maybe it would be too nice a gesture. Take a look, she told herself. If it goes with the dress and the Garnier hair . . .

She pawed through her scarf drawer, a repository of all the gifts she'd never used because she couldn't tie an attractive knot to save her soul. A little round box. What was that? She opened it and found the old gold ring of a dragon biting its tail she had been mistakenly given at the women's exhibition. Way too big to wear and way too clunky and not-her.

Her fingers found the shape of another box. She opened the velvet case and pulled out the black cat necklace of crushed black opal Matt had given to her months and months ago. She had given it to her scarf drawer in turn because she was an almost-married woman. In her own mind. Then.

Now . . . if he wanted her to wear this dress, he'd want her to wear his present. She fought the tiny clasp to a TKO and went to the mirror to adjust the lay of the delicate centerpiece on her collarbones.

Maybe a bit subdued for the dress but not bad. She shook her head. The curl was creeping back into her colored hair but she still looked so radically different to herself. Max wouldn't believe it. Maybe she'd keep the color. It made what she'd always considered her lukewarm blue-gray eyes look startlingly strong. Why be a Lucille Ball redhead forever, even if hers was natural?

Temple scavenged among the shoe racks in her wall-long closet, rejecting several candidates before finding the pair of purple satin sandals she'd got on sale at Designer Shoe Warehouse.

Perfect, the mirror said. You look way too hot, the voice in Temple's head warned the blonde in the mirror. So? Her date had just faced a huge personal shock. Might as well take his mind off of it. He seemed to be in the mood. Besides, what could happen at the Bellagio that they couldn't backtrack from . . . which they'd gotten very good at . . . in a heartbeat?

"Wow. You look like a movie star," Temple greeted Matt at her door.

He was wearing a cream blazer over an open-necked cocoa silk shirt that showcased his unusual brown-eyed blond coloring.

"You took the words right out of my mouth."

"Then we'll really wow them at the Bellagio."

"Not that I want to obscure your glory but do you have some sort of wrap? Could get chilly later."

"Oh." She'd figured they'd use valet parking but maybe not. "Just a sec."

She darted back into the bedroom to raid her scarf drawer for an airy lavender and silver-thread stole-thing.

Midnight Louie, stretched out on the bed, opened one green eye to watch her swing the stole over her bare shoulders. He looked like he was winking approval.

"Back before midnight, boy," she reassured him, as if he cared.

When she returned to the foyer and grabbed her tiny silver evening purse again, Matt opened the door. Before she could glide through, his finger touched the necklace in recognition.

Temple stopped as if hitting an invisible wall.

"Looks even nicer on," he said.

"It's lovely. I . . . just needed the right occasion to wear it."

"This is the right occasion."

When his finger dropped away from her skin, she felt like someone who had been released from a spell and hurried out into the short hall leading to the elevator.

The one-floor elevator ride was a study in awkward silence.

When the door slid back, Electra Lark was waiting for them. Mega-awkward.

Actually, she'd been waiting for the elevator.

Electra stepped back in mock awe, clutching her hands over the terminally floral muumuu covering her buxom body in the region symbolizing her heart.

"I'm stunned. Don't you two look like escapees from the top of a wedding cake; good enough to eat! What's the occasion?"

There was nothing to do but step out into lobby and explain themselves.

"Dinner at the Bellagio," Temple said.

"That'll set you back! Must be a big celebration."

"I wrapped up a big account," Temple said, just as Matt said, "A family reunion."

"Well." Electra looked from one to the other, speculative, surprised, and pleased at the same time. "Temple, love the hair! Nice to have such snazzy tenants add class to my lobby. Enjoy yourselves."

"We will," Matt promised in farewell, ushering Temple down the side hall to the parking lot at the rear.

She giggled as they left the landlady behind. "Suppose that reaction means she's used to seeing us in our scruffies."

"And separately."

The parking lot was only half full.

Temple came to a full halt again as they emerged into the still-warm night air. "That's right! I get to ride in the Crossfire."

"The Hesketh Vampire would hardly do for that get-up."

"Guess not." Mention of the silver vintage motorcycle that had been Max's, then Electra's, and now was Matt's to borrow when he pleased drew a thin curtain of what Temple would from now on consider "Catholic guilt" over her mood.

Matt established her in the passenger seat of the low silver car. She oohed over the leather interior and futuristic dashboard until they were well underway.

"Regret not waiting to buy until the convertible model came out?" she asked.

"Not really, given both our needs to avoid too much exposure to the sun."

"I suppose my Miata ragtop was a dopey purchase but it's great to tool around town in, and I wear a vintage straw hat with a built-in scarf I can tie on. So forties."

"Risk taking is good for the soul," he said, while Temple decided to reparse his last comment about the Crossfire convertible being dangerous to their skin types.

It was true. Natural blondes and redheads were sun-sensitive. Skin cancer was an ugly reality in a sunshine state like Nevada. So why should Matt be thinking of the Crossfire in relation to her skin tones as well as his? *Hmmm.*

The Circle Ritz building, dating from the fifties, had been erected amazingly close to the Strip. Nowadays, it couldn't afford the location, had it not already snatched it. In moments, they were cruising the Strip's overheated neon length. The Paris Hotel's festive balloon floated above the traffic like a tattooed moon fallen to earth. The Mirage's volcano flashed fire and outroared the MGM-Grand lion. The Hilton's chorus line of neon flamingos pulsed their hot-pink plumage.

They were heading south.

"The Bellagio—" Temple was about to point out that the hotel was north from where they were now. They were heading away, toward the Crystal Phoenix Hotel's neon namesake looming large on the right. It vanished into their wake.

"I decided someplace off the beaten tourist path would be better," Matt said. "That all right?"

"Uh, sure. All the restaurants in the Bellagio cost an arm and a leg and a first-born child, anyway."

He just smiled at her. The dashboard lights made his features look, not eerie, as that kind of theatrical uplighting usually did, but gilded.

For some reason, Temple felt that the tiny metal purse on her lap required the tight custody of both hands.

In moments, the Strip was glittering history in the rearview mirror. Oceans of bedroom communities twinkled across the broad valley floor.

Max's place was somewhere out there.

And then the desert darkness swallowed even that, leaving only the Crossfire's headlight beams sweeping the deserted highway ahead. From the darkness all around came the intermittent rhythm of the one mysterious light glimpsed now and then. Who lived way out there alone, you wondered. What were they doing now?

What were they doing now?

Temple racked her brain for some new chichi restaurant out in the boonies but she could only think of Three O'Clock Louie's at Temple Bar on Lake Mead. That was definitely not chichi and not in the direction they were heading.

An antsy little spasm started in the pit of her stomach. This was ridiculous! She was with Matt. He wouldn't take her anywhere she didn't want to go.

He wouldn't take her anywhere she didn't want to go.

Oh.

When he reached a break in some barbed wire (all this land was owned, no matter how deserted looking), she glimpsed another of those cryptic highway mile markers. Fifty-one, it read.

Fifty-one! Area 51. But, no, that was farther north than this.

Temple cringed as the Crossfire jolted over a winding sandy road. Hard on the brand-new suspension.

"Where are we—?"

"The horses know the way," Matt said. "Don't worry."

"I'm not worried." Liar.

He'd had such a huge shock back in Chicago. Finding a father he'd never known and thought was dead. She remembered the Matt who'd been obsessed about tracking down his stepfather. He'd been relentless, angry, explosive sometimes. She hadn't glimpsed that side of him for a long time. Still . . .

The headlights finally revealed another sign.

Salt Cedar Springs.

For a moment, Temple had thought it read "Saltpeter Springs." She giggled to herself. Nervously. "I didn't know there was a restaurant way out here."

Matt turned off the engine. Turned to her. "It's Alice's restaurant. You can get anything you want."

Then he came around and opened the door. She stepped out onto sand.

The car's headlights revealed an expanse of water. The surface was so gently riffled by the wind that it resembled the tiny ridges of sand dunes in the uncertain light. Silk moiré.

Temple peered around for a source of light. There was none but the sickle moon and the shimmer of headlights on the water. And, if she turned around to look back, the distant ground-bound aurora that was Las Vegas.

"Matt—?"

"You remember. Isn't this familiar?"

"Yes and no."

"It's a natural spring in the desert. Been here for centuries. That salt cedar tree, the giant weeping willowlike one there, is maybe five hundred years old."

"It's spectacular, but—"

But . . . Matt was leaning back into the car. Music started pouring into the empty desert night. "Sometimes When We Touch."

He came around the open door, carrying a white box. "You still don't get it, do you?"

Temple nodded. "Call me incomprehensible."

He took something out of the box and slid it around her left wrist. Scent exploded on the dry desert air, intense, sweet as syrup, yet amazingly delicate.

A white moonflower blossomed on her arm. Three of them. Gardenias.

"Matt. We did that prom night thing, way back months ago."

"That was you taking me to my high school prom, the one I never went to. This is me taking you to yours, the one you went to but never liked."

Temple brought the gardenias to her nose. Did any scent in the world pack such an intense emotional punch?

"I had a prom night," she said. "You didn't."

"That's the single nicest thing anyone ever did for me. Thought I'd return the favor."

"You don't have to. I'm a veteran. Been there, done that."

"Not the right way. You asked why I bought the Crossfire. I bought it to take you to the prom."

"Me? Your car? Why?"

"Don't you remember? Curtis Dixstrom and his father's dweeby Volvo station wagon?"

"Oh, yeah. I told you that so long ago and you remember every detail? No, the most handsome popular guy in school didn't ask me to the prom. Yes, I was humiliated going with some fourth-tier guy who wanted an excuse to get a lot closer to me than I ever did to him. But . . . that's life. That's high school. I'm ashamed I was ever so stupid and shallow. If I ran into some Mr. Hot Stuff Who Didn't Ask Me today I'd be bored to tears in two minutes. I bet my actual date would be a lot more interesting. I grew up. He grew up. The guys and girls who had it all in high school never did. You don't have to make up one damn thing to me."

"But I want to."

He'd bought a thirty-five-thousand-dollar car just to take her back on a sentimental journey! Should she just say no? Hell, no!

"Oh. Well. The wrist corsage is—"

"I remembered that dress didn't allow for anything pinned onto it."

"So . . . gardenias. Thank you. I've always looked for a perfume that duplicated their scent but everything artificial overpowers reality."

"Overpowering reality. That's what this is about."

Matt brought out a crystal plate of hors d'oeuvres, an ice bucket with a bottle of champagne, and two crystal flutes.

Temple recognized the products of the best caterer in town.

"Um, this is a big cut above the prom buffet table of Ritz Crackers and Cheese Whiz and seriously nonalcoholic punch."

"The past can be improved upon; that's what this is all about. Have a seat."

Just as Temple was about to ask where, he picked her up by the purple taffeta waist and set her atop the Crossfire's warm hood.

"A rough road trip out into the deep desert," she observed. "Serving as an impromptu buffet table. That's a heck of a way to treat an expensive new car, Devine."

He sat on the other side of the hood, so they were facing in opposite directions, like on those old Victorian seating pieces. Courting sofas.

She held her flute up for a bubbly infusion. The music on the CD pulsed softly.

"Won't the battery die?"

"I put the headlights on parking. They'll last for hours. Long enough, I hope."

Long enough for what?

But the shrimp and salmon and cream cheese and all the chilled appetizers were a piquant contrast with the thick soupy warm desert air. And the dry champagne went down like very sophisticated Sprite.

Temple was swinging her feet against the front tire to

the rhythm of Rod Stewart's romantic anthem "The Rhythm of My Heart."

"Great soundtrack," she said when the edge was off her hunger and the champagne flute was on its third refill. "To whom do we owe the pleasure?"

"Ambrosia of WCOO-AM."

"Your boss? The Queen of Late Nite Music to Sigh By?"

"Yeah. I asked her for the appropriate background music. Some of it's thirteen years old and some of it's today."

"And all of it's classic." Temple set her flute on the Crossfire hood, mellow enough not to worry about maltreating a hot car.

"Shall we dance?" Matt asked.

She was ready to jump off to the ground herself but he was there to catch her, and before you could say "Canadian Sunset" they were slow dancing, swaying to the music.

No. That was on the radio. The car CD, rather.

Temple's corsage-bearing left hand (with Max's emerald ring on the middle, not the third, finger) was resting on Matt's shoulder. She and Max had danced around the marriage question a few times, but that was two years ago, when their romance was as fresh as a daisy and as hot as a hibiscus and anything seemed possible. Not lately. Max was married to the mob lately. The counterterrorism mob. Danger was his sole dancing partner. Temple had defended him to Molina and every other comer, excused his absences to herself, accepted his apologies, and understood and understood and understood until she took the word for her middle name.

Suddenly, she couldn't see or touch the past. Only the present. She could see only Matt. Feel only him. And nothing about that seemed wrong, only absolutely, infectiously, incontestably right.

The gardenia scent enveloped her, enveloped him. It swirled on the dry night air like a drug.

Something brushed her temple. An insect. No. Someone's lips.

Her cheek. Her chin. Her lips.

They were kissing. And kissing. Separating and touching. Tilted this way. That way. Again. Scent and sound. Feet stepping together. Apart. Lips together apart. Always new. Testing. Tasting. Slow dancing on the desert. Surprise and collusion. Collaboration in rhythm. No missteps. Perfect harmony.

Slow dancing.

Just me . . .

And my . . .

He lifted her up on top of the car hood again. Better.

Liquid gardenia moonlight. Radio at the midnight hour.

Temple knew better. But she couldn't think of a better way to be. Matt matched her. Motion for motion. Surrender for surrender. She thought of hovering humming birds darting at blossoms. So swift. so graceful in their elegant hunger.

Separation. Intermission. When it came, it seemed unnatural.

"I've thought about it," Matt whispered.

Whispering in a desert was ludicrous but it was the only appropriate response to this infinitely delicate, devastating situation.

"I want it to go fast. I want it to go slow."

Seconded. Jimmy Buffet was singing about a slow boat to China. He knew sailing ships.

"I decided slow."

"Slow," she repeated. Dutifully. Running a very slow tongue tip along his upper lip.

And she had to wear this balloon of a dress meant to keep her from feeling anything below the waist. That was then, this was now.

She pushed her upper teeth into his lower lip and felt his hands convulse on her waist.

A finger, or thumb, ran down the long zipper at the back. Desert air struck her spine with the shock of hot water. His hand was hotter.

"Slow," he said.

Oh, yes. Oh, no. Vive la différence!

"So," she said, remembering certain concerns, very remote. "What about your religious whatever?"

He let them pull apart.

"I am not going to mention you in confession."

"Charmed, I'm sure."

"No. I'm serious. I won't deny what happens with us. But—"

But. Always but. Temple opened her eyes. She was staring up at a lot more stars than she'd ever glimpsed in the overlit city she called home. Because Matt's hair was brushing her cheek, and his lips were on her throat, her shoulder, her small claim to cleavage.

"So I've figured it out," he said, lifting his face to hers.

She breathed softly onto his mouth. "How? You still can't sleep with anyone outside of marriage."

"We get married."

"Married?" That snapped her out of Foreplay 101.

"Yes. Civilly. Electra could do it. Would love to. I finally realized: this is Nevada. People marry instantly here. If you're not satisfied—"

"Shut your mouth. On me."

"We can divorce."

"Divorce?"

"Or . . . if not, we marry again. Church ceremony. Catholic. Unitarians are easy when it comes to ecumenical. In the Twin Cities or Chicago or Milwaukee halfway in between. White gown, ring bearer, relatives, everything."

"You'd marry me civilly first so I can have a test run?"

"Right. No strings, no obligation. You said modern women needed free samples. Of sexual compatibility, I assume. I can't blame them. I am something of a freak."

"Freaking nuts. In a very sweet way."

And having said the word sweet, Temple needed to taste it again.

"What about your Catholic conscience?" she asked finally.

"We'd be married in the eyes of the law. I think I can fudge a bit. I spent so many years not fudging."

"Matt." She pushed him away. That was against her religion, which was easy, he said, but she pushed him away with a surge of self-control.

"I'm on the pill. That's against your religion, right?"

"Right. But your religion isn't my religion. I suppose in the name of ecumenical tolerance . . . You're on the pill?"

This appeared to give him either pause or an infusion of fresh motivation.

"We have a lot of issues, Matt. Children. Like I may not be ready. Or . . . not."

"I may never be ready. People work that out. Forget the this or that. That's what had me all screwed up. You want to be my mother and father in thirty-some years? Afraid to face each other because they can't admit that what they had was lost? That it was really something?"

"You want to marry a bottle blonde?"

"I want to marry you, whatever shade you're wearing."

"Then this is a proposal."

He thought for a moment. "No, this is a free trial offer. A proposal would be much better than this."

"Can't believe it could be," she said, curling her fingers into the lapels of his jacket.

That ended discussions for a while.

Temple's heart was beating like the Rod Stewart–advertised drum but her mind was racing too, from the moon to the dizzying scent on her wrist that blended with the champagne and the music into an altered state.

To a low-profile emerald ring on her hand and a wrench of regret in her heart.

To a certain knowledge that there was no going back from here, no slipping away into separate Edens.

To a growing realization that she didn't want to go back from here. She wanted to go forward.

She so much wanted to go forward that it would have taken one finger pushing on the delicate necklace so near the pulse in her throat and she'd have been lying back on the Crossfire hood.

Maybe he knew that. Maybe that was what he meant by going slow (although it might be what she considered going crazy).

His parents had followed the moment and the magic and couldn't bear to face each other, and perhaps him, now.

Not for them.

They necked for another extremely overheated ten minutes, then packed up their salt-cedar picnic.

And left.

Chapter 61

The World His Oyster

I am waiting up for my Miss Temple, my tail thumping with impatience. It is not right for a roommate to announce a midnight return from a social engagement and then to be three hours late!

Normally, I am content to let others come and go at their pleasure and their leisure, since I do not want anyone dictating hours to me.

However, time and again I have proved to be my Miss Temple's muscle. Although I know Mr. Matt Devine to be such a straight arrow that he could aim his fancy new car at the town of Reno hundreds of miles to the north and hit it dead on, I have to wonder what he could be doing to keep my roomie up so late?

Could it be a breakdown of the Crossfire? Flat tire? Gas tank leak? An attempted hijacking? Kidnapping? Encounter with terrorists? UFOs?

Perhaps I have become a teensy bit too attached to my Miss Temple.

I should have hitchhiked a ride in the Crossfire. Then I would not be worrying now. I pace like a Big Cat. Hey! I am a Big Cat.

I chew my nails. I will certainly raise a ruckus when the truants come home safe and sound at—I eye the clock on the VCR. Three-thirty! What are they thinking of? Certainly not me!

But . . . now I hear voices. In the short hallway leading to our domicile.

Very low voices. Nice of them to worry about not keeping anyone up when I have been wearing out my pads with pacing!

A key in the door. I go to sit by it, assuming a stern, accusing posture. She could have left a note.

The door swings open a hair but no further.

I still hear murmurs.

I insert my head silently into the opening, assuming a put-upon look. I have not had a treat spooned over my Free-to-be-Feline since we left for the Teen Queen Castle. I am hungry!

My Miss Temple is leaning against the door frame with her hands braced behind her like she has all the time in the world. She looks half asleep. Correction: she looks like she is half dreaming.

Mr. Matt has leaned a hand on the doorjamb above her head. At least he is not neglecting her.

Miss Temple jams the toe of her purple silk sandal into the wooden hall floor, looking down. He is looking down on her shockingly blonde head.

"You could come in," she says, a strange slow, reluctant, warm, inviting tone in her voice, like she means it and is afraid she does mean it.

No! I am waiting impatiently for a long-delayed

spread of oysters and shrimp over my Free-to-be-Feline! Enough palaver!

Apparently, Mr. Matt agrees, for he drops his hand from the door frame and catches her hands tight behind her back and . . . well, his other hand lifts up her face and he does something totally unfeline and quite unfit for the youthful eyes of my species.

It is a good thing I have been around humans during mating season, for I shut my eyes in time to avoid witnessing something we would all prefer that I did not.

And then my Miss Temple is in the room at last, a silly sort of shawl trailing off of one shoulder, bringing with her a suffocating floral scent as well as the dreamy attitude.

The door is closed and we are alone at last! I howl my anxiety and indignation.

"Louie! So glad you made it home safe," she says.

So I could say.

"I will get you something," she adds.

But she doesn't. She turns back to the closed door and presses against it. Almost pulls it open again. Stops. Paces in the tiny hall. Goes to the living room and picks up her cell phone. Holds it to her mouth as if it were a flower.

Speaking of which, I wish she'd ditch the wrist corsage, which I have determined is the source of the noxiously sweet odor. I have had enough of them in this case.

She paces some more. Counts to fifty under her breath, then dials a number. And listens. And paces. And listens.

"What?" she demands of the room in general. "He has to be there by now!" Pacing.

And I thought my species had that down.

She kicks off the high heels. And paces some more. And then redials.

She stops suddenly to regard me as if seeing me for the first time. But not to proffer food or even a welcoming caress.

"Cold shower?" she asks me.

She hurls the cell phone to the sofa. Why is she mad? She is like, really angry.

She retrieves the phone and hits the redial button again.

People are so predictable with their toys. I suppose it is somewhat entertaining to watch them cavort with technology.

Then she stares at me again and bends down to swoop me up in her arms.

First of all, I do not "swoop."

Second of all, I weight almost twenty pounds so I am quite a bundle of bones for her to hoist.

Third of all, she is wearing this dress with only a halter top, so I have nothing but warm bare flesh to wrap my legs around. Ick! It takes all my considerable self-control to keep from latching on to her with my shiv tips.

Perhaps that is why she has goose bumps on her arms.

She carries me to the French doors leading to her petite balcony, opens one, and walks out into the finally cooling night.

Below us lies the scrone blue rectangle of the pool and, on the other side, the parking lot.

She gazes out, idly stroking my chin and throat.

All right. This is better. I think about rewarding her diligence with a slight purr.

Suddenly, she stiffens. All over. Her hand on my throat almost throttles me.

I look down to see that Mr. Matt has strolled out to the pool. He is far more clothed than usual in that area, and he too begins pacing!

My Miss Temple's grip tightens.

Mr. Matt sits on one of the lounge chairs and proceeds to remove his shoes and stockings! Well, I have always felt that humans were way overdressed. He looks like Tom Sawyer by the riverbank, I think, having lounged on a lot of library books in my time. (One does pick up things.)

Miss Temple edges, barefoot too, to the edge of the balcony.

I, of course, am carried along with her, unwilling. I have definitely revoked the purr.

He stands up, lays his jacket on the lounge chair, and starts unbuttoning his shirt.

My Miss Temple is as still as a stalking cat. I did not know she had such skills in her. She watches. I can practically feel her whiskers twitching, her pupils slitting. (These are figures of speech. She is not so elegantly accoutered as me and my kind, alas.)

But she is as alert as any alley cat, which is high praise from me.

Mr. Matt's instincts are nothing to spit at tonight either.

He suddenly looks up.

They see each other.

My Miss Temple does not move a muscle, except that her heart revs up.

He looks at her. She looks at him.

He keeps undoing buttons on his shirt. Then it is on the lounge chair.

He begins on the trousers—silly convention! He stops at the underwear, which is dark and understated, at least.

My Miss Temple's fingernails are starting to seriously impinge on my musculature, which is almost in as admirable a state as Mr. Matt's.

What is the big deal? She has seen him in his swim trunks before.

All I can say is the night is strangely charged until he

dives into the deep end of the lit aquamarine pool and begins swimming laps back and forth.

Some spell is broken. Miss Temple mutters under her breath, and incidentally into my ear, "Well, I suppose it's the equivalent of a cold shower. For *him*."

She sounds terminally angry with our esteemed neighbor and I chance a small *merow* in her ear.

"Poor Louie!" she says, back to normal and paying attention to me again. "Are you hungry? Was bad mommy away too long? Bad, bad mommy."

Well, I loathe the "mommy" stuff, which my Miss Temple has never resorted to before, but I cannot complain about the tins of sardines, shrimp, and oysters she piles over the ugly green, dry foundation of Free-to-be-Feline in my bowl.

I settle on my haunches to dispense with it bite by delicious bite.

Thank goodness things are back to normal around here and I can lie back, digest everything, and relax for a while.

Tailpiece

Midnight Louie, Paterfamilias

People! They are forever fixating on fatherhood. I suppose that is because of capitalistic materialism. They not only have territory to defend but property to inherit along with genetic traits.

Me, I find fatherhood incontinent, irrelevant, and immaterial.

I am like that Greek goddess who gave Zeus such a headache that she was born from his brain. She never had a mother and therefore gave Orestes his walking papers when he was up for Murder One for offing his mother. Mother offing is a big no-no even in the natural world but this Athena chick did not see it as any big deal, as she never had a mother, only a very powerful father with a headache.

Anyway, we street cats only know our mothers and they are pretty darn good to us until the hormones wear off and we are on our own. So fathers are no big deal. Even if we did run into one we would probably have to fight him anyway.

So I am mystified by all this brouhaha about Mr. Matt finding his father and little Miss Mariah's father finding out he is one. Miss Midnight Louise appears to have been infected by this human obsession also. She should understand that the way of our kind is serial fatherhood. It is not that lady cats are what humans would call promiscuous. They are just designed to enter the sublime state of heat, unable to say no. Naturally, there are all sorts of dudes out there with the same problem. So a single litter may have four different fathers. And who knows which kit is due to which father?

So why sweat it? In my case, Ma Barker made it clear to me that Three O'Clock Louie was my sire. And that is fine with both of us. We do not need to tread on each other's toenails but neither do we need to hang out and sing sentimental songs together once upon a midnight clear, or drear.

Humans are also ridiculous about the mating game. Here they have the option to have all the fun and pretty much ensure that no unforeseen consequences come along later causing them to look up innocent dudes as if they were criminals. Yet they keep subjecting their most basic instincts to intense negotiation, not to mention recrimination. Why bother!

I muse on these matters because it is clear to me that my Miss Temple is contemplating wandering in the congenial feline direction when it comes to matters of the heart and other organs.

I cannot say I am surprised. Mr. Matt was bound to outgrow his artificially extended adolescence one of these days and become a young tom with a lot of wasted time to make up for.

I cannot agree with those who do not much like Mr.

Max Kinsella. He is one cool cat in the street or between the sheets, from my observation, with obligations to protect the world at large that few can understand. Rather like myself. But he has other territory to guard at the moment and when the cat's away . . . the mice will play. And someone will pay. This is Las Vegas. Bet on it.

Very best fishes,

Midnight Louie, Esq.

P.S. For information about getting Midnight Louie's free newsletter and/or buying his T-shirt, contact him at Midnight Louie's *Scratching Post-Intelligencer,* PO Box 331555, Fort Worth, TX 76163-1555, or by e-mail at cdouglas@catwriter.com. Or visit Midnight Louie's Web pages at www.carolenelsondouglas.com or www.cat writer.com.

Tailpiece

Carole Nelson Douglas Makes Room for Daddy

You're a fine one to philosophize about fatherhood, Louie.

You've only just now barely acknowledged the delightful Midnight Louise as your daughter.

But you're right that the feline kingdom is a matriarchy when it comes to family life. A lot of human households are becoming more like that, since some human fathers are also likely to slip away from the confines of a domestic life.

Still, humans are hooked on relationships. They have a sense of history about where their forebears have been and where they and the whole human family might be going.

So when blood relations are missing, they find unrelated people to fill in for the absent father, or mother, or brother or sister, or child. Sometimes even your kind do the job, Louie.

As for your speculations on the uniquely human condition known as "romance," you are about as expert there as a lapdog would be at bloodhound work.

You're just lucky to have an alternate source of affection and support when your rambling and gambling days are over: all of those human females who don't mind a roguish ladies' man around the house . . . if he's of another species.

A preview of

Cat in a
Quicksilver Caper

By Carole Nelson Douglas

**Forthcoming
From Tom Doherty Associates**

A TOM DOHERTY ASSOCIATES BOOK
NEW YORK

Chapter 1

Swept Off Her Feet

Temple Barr woke up at 10:30 A.M. in the morning, in her own bed, which was hardly unusual, and supposed that there wasn't a woman in America who didn't ache for one of those Scarlet O'Hara moments.

Maybe it was Scarlet swearing to heaven that she'd never have to choke down another raw turnip (or broccoli or cauliflower floret . . . or diet book) again.

Maybe it was the spunky freshman Scarlet, telling that blind-stupid Ashley Wilkes right out that he ought to be dating her instead of some wimpy prom queen from the next plantation down along the Sewanee.

Maybe it was Scarlet cornered on the Tara stairs, shooting an attacking Yankee soldier dead.

Or Scarlet in any of the dazzling fashion-show gowns in which she schemed, fought, and flounced her way through the Civil War and its aftermath . . . especially the gutsy homemade green velvet-drape gown she wore to convince a jailed Rhett Butler that she wasn't down and out when she was.

But the most Scarlet moment of all involved the red velvet dressing gown she wore as Rhett carried her upstairs when he'd had it with her fickle, bewitching, bitching Scarlet ways.

Feminists long removed from the 1930s debut of Margaret Mitchell's *Gone With the Wind* choked on their turnips over that scene, which to modern sensibilities plays like date rape—in that case, wife rape.

But no matter how a woman might land on the swept-upstairs-scene issue, she couldn't fault the famous morning-after scene.

What a wake-up call! That was when Vivian Leigh's Scarlet awoke in contented camera close-up. When her eyes recalled the-night-before-the-morning-after with the recovering memory of a devilishly satisfied and distinctly un-downtrodden southern belle indeed. . . .

Temple awoke this day to one of those classic dawning moments. It made her world take an unexpected lurch toward a totally different axis than it had previously been twirling around like a ballerina in a well-known routine.

Oh. Right. Yes. Oh. My. Oh. Dear. Oh!

Because all morning-afters have their down as well as their up sides, and Temple was starting to see that. It didn't help that Midnight Louie, all fully furred twenty pounds of him, was sitting on her chest staring at her with unblinking feline green eyes like a guilty conscience.

His mesmerizing eyes and shiny black hair reminded her that she was betrothed (as much as you could be in a modern world) to Max Kinsella, a magician on hiatus. Louie's watchful presence also reminded her that Louie had been on patrol in the apartment early this morning when she'd returned from her supposedly bland dinner date with neighbor Matt Devine, during which certain overly neighborly things had occurred and mention had been made of the M word: marriage.

Louie knew. Somehow.

And that gloriously green stare said that he understood every miserable nuance of her now hopelessly complicated love life. And that he did not approve.

Neither, she knew, would Max.

Chapter 2

Louie Agonistes

What is a loyal bodyguard and bedmate to do? (And I am not asking you, Kevin Costner; I am no fan of anyone who dances with wolves.)

My charming roommate, Miss Temple Barr, is obviously undergoing a major life crisis. Now, were a serial killer breaking into our humble but homey unit at the Circle Ritz, I would not be at a loss for direction.

I would leap upon a pant-leg, ratchet my way up to his chest and shoulder area—making three-inch tracks a quarter-inch deep—lash out with my built-in switchblades and take out his eyes, then execute a thorough bit of plastic surgery on his mug for a bit of icing on the cake.

All of the above before the average bear could say "Hannibal Lector."

But nerve and brain, my two greatest assets, will not

work here. I am at a loss for once, waylaid by the tangled webs of human emotions when it comes to what are such simple matters to the rest of the animal world, i.e., what is called the Mating Game.

This is not a game, folks! It is the call of the jungle, the survival of the species, and the triumph of the Alpha Male. Of which I am, naturally, one. Although, not so naturally anymore, since I was relieved of the obligation of fatherhood by a villainous B-movie actress who had hoped to de-macho me. Whatever. Despite Miss Savannah Ashleigh doing her worst, I am still catnip for the dames and no back-alley offspring will ever come back to haunt me.

I am the 007 of the feline world, four-on-the-floor and one in the back seat, with an unlimited license to thrill. Even the animal protection people cannot fault my condition and habits.

And I face no messy consequences who might want to slash you across the whiskers and call you a philandering absentee father. I am thinking here of Miss Midnight Louise, my erstwhile daughter from the old pre-chichi cut days. According to her.

Anyway, this stuff among my own species I have aced.

Humans are a different plate of Meow Mix entirely.

I pace back and forth in front of the French doors that lead to our triangular mini-patio. By now my Miss Temple is out for the day, pretending that she is going about business as usual, but I saw her disarray the previous evening and am most . . . unsettled.

True, she lavished more than usual affection on me, even clutching me to her breast (which is not such a great treat for a dude such as I, if you wish to know; we do not like forced confinement, even in comfy places). Please, let us come to you. It works out much better.

Anyway, I put up with this mushy stuff because we go back a long way and have done some heads-up crime-solving together. A dude owes it to his partner, even when the going threatens to get slushy.

And it is not that I am such a big fan of Mr. Max Kinsella, who previously occupied pride of place here at this Circle Ritz unit, i.e., the bed. I mean, he is probably an okay magician and he does have undercover aims for the betterment of humankind—not that humankind much deserves it, from my observation—but there is only room for one black-haired, agile, and sexy Alpha Male in this unit, and it is I.

You will note that I am schooled in the nuances of human grammar as well as kung fu.

And I have nothing against Mr. Matt Devine, who once devoted himself to the service of humankind (boy, they do get a lot of devotion for such a sorry species) and actually gave up using what I almost lost during his priesthood days. Even Miss Midnight Louise has a soft spot for him, and she is one hard mama, let me tell you, speaking as her delinquent supposed-daddy. So I do sympathize with a well-meaning dude who is trying to get into the Alpha Male stakes so belatedly in life. Not everyone can have my advantage of being born to be bad.

But my first and foremost loyalty is to my Miss Temple. She is not only Recently Blonde, she is recently tempted by the New Dude on the Block.

Well, I am the grayer head here, by a single hair. I will not tell you where it is.

So I sense that I will have to seek advice outside my usual, normal guy-type venues.

Ick!